Praise for *The Heart of Bennet Hollow*

Joanne Bischof DeWitt's reimagining of Jane Austen's *Pride and Prejudice* is a clever blending of familiar story elements with a refreshing take on situations and settings peopled with characters who readily capture sympathy and interest. With plenty of nods to Austen's classic, this tenderhearted journey through the flaws of human frailty toward the grace of second chances is sure to please.

LORI BENTON, Christy Award–winning author of the Kindred series

Joanne Bischof DeWitt pens a sweet tale inspired by an enduring classic but adds her own lyrical prose to create an eloquent story of culture clashes, simple loves, and finding where one's heart belongs. In *The Heart of Bennet Hollow*, DeWitt beautifully recreates Austen's familiar and beloved characters.

PEPPER BASHAM, author of *Hope Like Wildflowers* and *Sense and Suitability*

Welcome to the world of Bennet Hollow where a memorable cast of characters opens the door to a turn-of-the-century *Pride and Prejudice* retelling in 1904 Virginia. Witty and pretty, *The Heart of Bennet Hollow* overflows with Appalachian heart in Joanne Bischof DeWitt's wholesome signature style.

LAURA FRANTZ, Christy Award–winning author of *The Indigo Heiress*

Set in beautiful Appalachia, Joanne Bischof DeWitt delivers another heartwarming tale with a classic twist! *The Heart of Bennet Hollow* is sure to delight readers of historical romance, especially fans of *Pride and Prejudice*, who will see some fun reflections in this new story.

CARRIE TURANSKY, award-winning author of *A Token of Love* and *The Legacy of Longdale Manor*

THE HEART OF BENNET HOLLOW

An Appalachian *Pride and Prejudice* Retelling

the heart of BENNET HOLLOW

JOANNE BISCHOF DeWITT

Tyndale House Publishers
Carol Stream, Illinois

Visit Tyndale online at tyndale.com.

Visit Joanne Bischof DeWitt online at joannebischofdewitt.com.

The Heart of Bennet Hollow

Cover design by Sarah Susan Richardson

Interior design by Brandi Davis

Edited by Sarah Mason Rische

Published in association with the literary agency of Books & Such Literary Management, www.booksandsuch.com.

Scripture quotations are taken from the *Holy Bible*, King James Version.

Library of Congress Cataloging-in-Publication Data

A catalog record for this book is available from the Library of Congress.

ISBN 979-8-4005-0223-1 (HC)
ISBN 979-8-4005-0224-8 (SC)

Printed in the United States of America

31 30 29 28 27 26 25
7 6 5 4 3 2 1

To my husband, Bryan

"If I loved you less, I might be able to talk about it more."

—JANE AUSTEN

autumn

1

October 1904

Lizbeth Bennet clutched the handle of the wicker basket with hope. The same hope with which she'd gathered each and every wildflower within. Slipping inside the farmhouse, she traded the brightness of day for the dim light of Ma's kitchen—the very heartbeat of Bennet Hollow.

"Did you spot the new train car, by chance?" Jayne asked from the table, her voice as soft and mountain grown as a wild birch grove. "They say it's called the Pemberley."

Lizbeth lowered the basket to the table and handed a sprig of lacy white yarrow to her older sister. "I didn't wander far enough. Have you seen it yourself? This Pemberley?" Having just come in from the sunny garden, she brushed her hands clean and sat. "Clearly I've missed the gossip."

"I saw it when I walked into town this mornin'." Jayne examined the contents of the basket. Her golden hair was bound up in rag curlers, and a single band of gray twine wrapped her pale wrist, holding a tiny nugget of violet amethyst that Pa, a geologist, had unearthed in a mine. "It's the prettiest sight, Lizzy. Brighter than a new penny perched there right on the track."

Lizbeth rolled back the sleeves of her striped work dress and tried to imagine such a view. A breeze blew cool against her bare neck from the open window, causing her homespun collar to flutter. Her sisters had been on the lookout ever since some weeks back, when the owner of the New River Coal Company had announced his coming guests—a slew of coal barons and investors, all eager to bid on the property that was now for sale.

And the best part of all among the Bennet sisters . . . the dance that would mark their arrivals.

"Do you know his name?" Lizbeth asked. "The man who owns this train car?"

"I can't recall. But . . ." Jayne's voice dropped to a whisper. "I hear he's the wealthiest of the investors. Maybe even more than all of them put together."

"There's no way folks could know that."

"Well, the rest of the investors arrived *on* the train. This other man owns a whole piece of it." Jayne's pretty eyebrows lifted.

From where she stood at the stove, Ma chimed in. "And I'm sure one of these fellas'll want to buy the coal company with Mr. Jorgensen so bent on retirement." She shook her head slowly as though unable to decide if that were a good or bad omen. "Change is comin' to New River and it's gonna affect more than just the coal mine. Mark my words, girls."

A slow shiver crept up Lizbeth's spine. No wonder murmurings were spreading from one end of town to the next.

How could only a few men spark such attention?

"Mr. Jorgensen's all but flung open the doors to the hoist barn." Ma stirred the fire with an iron rod. "Wants these investors to see the town at its best."

"How do you know this, Ma?" Lizbeth asked.

Ma winked. "It's my job to know these things. I saw his wife and the other ladies wipin' dust from the windows. Some boys tried to peek inside, but Mrs. Jorgensen shooed 'em off." The iron poker clattered as she coaxed the flames brighter. Sparks popped and sputtered. "The rest'll have to remain a mystery 'til tonight."

With a sigh, Jayne lifted a snip of wild roses from the basket and plucked petals from the stem. A tiny puddle of pink formed on the rough-hewn table.

Lizbeth did the same with a bundle of chamomile. She'd gleaned the green and white buds from the meadow behind the barn where blackbirds lined the fence, squawking for the scraps of table bread she sometimes brought them.

"Now whatever's this about?" Ma tilted the basket to peer inside.

Lizbeth lifted a scrap of linen from her embroidery stash. "Sachets. Jayne hatched the idea and I searched the farm." Now they could fashion scented secrets to tuck beneath their bodices for the dance this evening. An event mused to be the finest they had ever attended.

Or might ever hope to attend.

Ma nodded, looking pleased. "It'd do well to marry a few of you girls off sooner rather than later. And to think of such wealthy men here in town. I hope they stay a good long while."

"Ma!" Lizbeth gasped.

"Well, you two are of age, and your sisters are right behind. It doesn't seem like anyone 'round these parts has caught your eye. A mother can hope. Least give me that."

Jayne widened her eyes playfully and chose another flower. "I've been told the train car has a parlor *and* a dinin' room. All dressed up in velvet curtains as deep a blue as the midnight sky.

Just imagine being whisked away into the grand unknown aboard such a dream."

Lizbeth smiled softly. At twenty, she was two years younger than Jayne. Her other sisters—Maryanne, Kit, and Lacey—stairstepped after her. Though the younger three still walked to school each day, they were just grown enough to attend the coming barn dance. The very girls that bounded down from the second story now, brown braids flying. Like chicks on a stoop, they filled the crooked stairwell in a chorus of sun-faded skirts, mountain drawls, and tattered boots.

"I heard tell the owner's a sight to see as well!" Sixteen-year-old Lacey winked brazenly and twirled around the post. "A coal baron all the way from Vermont. They say he's rich enough to own all of New River if he fancies to. Oh, I hope he notices me." She gasped at the basket of flowers and climbed beneath the banister for a better look. "Whatever's this for?"

Lizbeth and Jayne exchanged knowing smiles.

"Just a little somethin' for tonight." Lizbeth nudged the basket aside.

But Jayne patted the bench beside her. "Have a seat and join us. There's larkspur and some wilted mint, but I reckon the herbs'll be the most fragrant." Squinting, she adjusted one of the rags in her hair, appearing eager that the curls would turn out.

Like two curious colts, Kit and Maryanne edged nearer.

Lizbeth loosened a length of thread from the spool. "Better get a move on and fetch the kettles, girls." She gauged the light through the window where a late afternoon wagged its finger at them for dawdling. "Time to hurry if each of us are to bathe before the dance."

"Water's steamin'." Ma flapped a rag at the white cloud billowing from the kettle's spout. "And the iron's hotter than the July sun. There won't be a wrinkle among my girls tonight."

The younger three grabbed kettles and basins, starting for the stairs.

Ma continued. "We may be poorer than the Jorgensens but we can make just as fine an entrance. Even if we *don't* own a coal mine. And we best find out this new man's name so your pa can introduce you girls proper tonight. Lizzy, I hope you've finished sewing your new blouse."

"Yes, ma'am." Eyes down, Lizbeth tried to focus on her task as she unraveled the same spool of thread. Her other sisters were more patient with the details, and her newest blouse had a flaw or two that she hoped would go unnoticed. She was better at embroidery than more practical sewing. The very reason Ma had her refocus on stitching up a sampler this year. One that was only partially finished.

With a two-story farmhouse, a well-tilled garden, and two loyal mules, Lizbeth knew her family was better off than the mining families on the other side of the river, but not by much. Now, just past sixty, Pa ran their home from the modest savings he'd tucked away before he slowed down his work as a geologist for several mining companies. Such circumstances had all of them considering who might marry first . . . and when.

Lizbeth knew some fine colliers, but something in her heart longed for more than sweeping the porch steps on one of the row houses where miners and their families dwelled in the shadow of the coal company. A place where grime and dust tried to coat anything in its sight.

Was that the life she was meant for? Who was she to think that there might ever be more?

Ma had fussed that she was *headstrong*. Pa dubbed her *noble*. And all the girls knew her as *well-read*. Those weren't particularly good qualifications for a bride. No. Men around here needed women who could diaper a baby and store coins beneath the mattress. Stretching provisions remained the order of the day, not reading books or caring for her mules or hoping she could have a purpose that she'd been uniquely made for.

Tilting the basket, Lizbeth searched for more chamomile, unable to believe that a man might love her *and* her purpose. That he could *need* her for such. Especially since she didn't yet know what that purpose might be. Best she remain alone and live out a quiet life right here, surrounded by her sisters and her beloved mules. Perhaps that was her calling all along. Otherwise, she'd need to nail her dreams to the floor and go the way that all young women in New River went. To be a miner's wife, owing every cent her husband made to the company store just for flour and salt.

Upstairs, the younger girls chattered over which reels and waltzes they thought the band might play and which men they hoped would ask them. By the sound of it, Lacey had her eyes on the lead spragger while Kit fancied a jig with his younger brother. As for Maryanne, the girl was as sensible as a mile marker, so she hushed their squeals, hoping this might be a night for conversation instead.

Threading a needle, Lizbeth reached for a scrap of linen. Should any fellow notice the earthy scent of chamomile, he would find Lizbeth in his arms. But should a man favor the fragrance of rose, he'd be charmed by a turn around the floor with Jayne tonight.

If Jayne made a promising match, the dear girl could fly from these crowded walls and narrow beds. Perhaps one of these fine men who'd come to town could be right for Jayne. Maybe it could even be the owner of the Pemberley. A man who could give Jayne a life as grand as she deserved. Not only was she the prettiest sight to behold, and more ready for marriage, she was worthy. A good heart and a sweet countenance. An ideal wife for any bachelor, especially one who could give her a safe and secure life. Had the opportunity just ridden in on the rails?

"Did you see him while you were in town?" Lizbeth asked. "The one with the train car?"

A twinkle lit Jayne's blue eyes. "No. But I overheard him speakin' to Pa about the mine and he sounded pleasant—"

Ma gasped. "Your pa didn't tell me he spoke to him! Mr. Bennet! Best get yourself in here." She tapped her spoon on the edge of a pot. "What does a wife have to do to get a man to talk about these things?"

Pa entered with his newspaper. "Just a hot cup of tea should do me." He winked as he settled into his armchair near the window, worn smooth from use. Just beyond, mature poplars blocked the Virginia sky, sending glittering shadows across the room.

"Tell us more, Pa," Jayne said. "About the newcomers."

"Five of 'em to be exact." His voice was as deep and aged as the hickory chair he sat in. "A handful of coal barons. All owners of other mines across the east."

"And the one that all the fuss is about?"

"He's a younger fella. Younger than all the others. Arrived here with his business associate. Fine-lookin' boys with steady manners."

Ma cracked open the oven door to a loaf of fragrant pumpkin bread. "I've never seen such a commotion as I saw at the company store this week. I watched two bolts of calico sell in less than ten minutes. And today, I saw a whole mess of hair ribbons fly out the door just as quick. You mark my words. Our girls won't be the only ones in New River dressed up in their finest tonight. To think of Mr. Jorgensen hosting such a fuss."

"Well, this is just the first step in convincin' folks 'round here that change doesn't always have to be bad," Pa mused.

"Does that mean one of these men would own the town of New River?" one of Lizbeth's sisters called from upstairs.

The others giggled.

"Not quite," Pa answered back. "But it does seem that way."

"I hear they've cleared the company's barn from stem to stern." Lizbeth snipped the end of her thread. "It sounds ever so pretty."

"I've been told there'll be over two dozen pies and punch sweetened with sugar." Jayne added another stitch to her fragrant sachet then moved Lizbeth's embroidery hoop aside lest it get buried in stray petals. Lizbeth had gotten so far as embroidering *The night is* on a square piece of linen. A sacred sentiment that lingered far from finished. Both on the cloth and in her understanding.

Ma wagged her head. "This'll be somethin' to remember!"

Pa examined the newspaper. Though he'd never been a miner by trade, he'd worked for mines in eight counties across the state before finally landing in New River to lead a quieter life when the girls were little. His gnarled hands were stained black at the creases from over forty years of scouring the earth for minerals and uncapping ink pens to create maps and ledgers that documented his findings. A gentle soul who taught Lizbeth how to recognize rocks and features on their walks through the woods.

Pa's bristly brows lifted to match the amusement in his tone. "We'll just have to wait and see, then, won't we?"

"How do you sit there, the picture of mischief?" Ma asked.

Pa finally lowered his paper to his lap. "Do tell a fella what you'd like to hear."

"For starters, we're all burstin' to hear more of this train car. I only saw it from a distance. Does it really have a glass observation dome?"

"I do believe I counted two."

"Oh, how grand. Imagine seeing the stars at night from inside a train." Jayne blew on a dandelion weed, scattering its delicate seeds.

Kit returned with empty kettles, her hair glistening and clean. With a sigh, she nestled a sprig of chamomile behind her ear. "Like a mansion. How could one man be so rich?"

Lizbeth tugged the stem loose, replacing it with a dainty rosebud. "You don't even know what a mansion looks like. And off with you. The others are waiting!"

Kit fetched the kettles for the next bath. "Well, I sure hope it has runnin' water!"

Pa chuckled.

Lizbeth pondered such luxuries as running water and blue velvet curtains. She knew only the frayed cotton of her apron and the sun-streaked quilt that graced her tiny bed in the second story room she shared with Jayne. A place where the floor was knobby but clean and the washbasin made of rusted tin, not porcelain. She'd hardly know how to peer inside the window of such richness, let alone grace its aisleway.

"Does he own the engine too?" Lizbeth asked.

"Just the car." Pa tucked his creased paper into the edge of his chair for the next time he re-read it. "Engines are owned by railroads. Wealthy folk pay to have their private cars hauled by an engine that's either comin' or goin'. It costs a pretty penny to do as much, mind you. Hundreds of dollars for the fare alone."

"Incredible," Jayne breathed.

Ma sighed. "To think of it."

Pa went on. "The depot has three tracks so there's plenty of space for it to linger."

"What a pity that such a shiny new train car'll soon be covered in coal dust like the rest of the depot," one of the younger girls called out.

Ma fanned a rag for them to hurry and fill the tub again.

Rising, Lizbeth used the edge of her apron to pull out the loaf of pumpkin bread. She felt the tin's heat through the cotton fabric as the air warmed with nutmeg and cinnamon.

Ma checked the loaf with a practiced touch. "And to think of it parked here." Ma often fussed and fretted that Pa had chosen to settle down in New River where the only thing separating their farm from the clatter of the mine was the glittering river from which the town gleaned its name.

"It's the blessings of the Lord that maketh a man rich," Maryanne called down from the stairwell.

Everyone looked up at her at once.

"So the Proverbs say," she added.

Lizbeth smiled at her sister's tender reminder. "Hear, hear." Then for Jayne's ears alone: "But you still must dance the first reel with the man."

Jayne blushed. "He'd have to ask me, Lizzy. And there'll be so many people there tonight. It seems the whole town is coming."

"Yes . . ." Lizbeth returned to her seat. "But you'll be the prettiest."

Jayne shook her head. Needing to wash up next, Lizbeth rose to fetch the kettles from upstairs. Already, she could imagine the duet of a mandolin and fiddle. How welcoming and warm it would sound as couples paired up on this autumn evening. Maybe the fiddler would play a waltz or two.

Ma's voice broke through the daydream. "I hear the young coal baron owns several mines already and other companies as well. A logging firm out west, and some sort of factory in New York."

Lizbeth paused at the top of the stairs to listen.

Pa nodded slowly. "That's what folks are sayin'."

"Have you found out his name? Does the boy have kin to speak of?"

"That's two questions at once, my dear. I don't know about kin—don't know the man's story."

"But we only need his name," Jayne chimed in. "The owner of the Pemberley."

Lizbeth seconded that, though she didn't want to admit it.

Pa's laughter danced across the room. The first note of music to be heard this evening, but certainly not the last. "From what I gather, someone as wealthy as that ought to be called by his proper title, which is Mr. Drake. But seein' as you girls must know . . ." He winked. "I believe his name is William."

2

Late afternoon light streamed through the train car window as William Drake tipped his chin up, knotting the necktie at his throat. This he could do—dress like a gentleman and be a gentleman. He'd attended dozens of high society events in Boston, New York, and Philadelphia, because it was easy to stand stiff-laced in a corner and talk finance or listen to business tycoons scheme to be as wealthy as he. But to enter a dance hall filled with miners and their families who understood a hard day's labor? Toiling with their hands as opposed to with other people's lives?

That terrified him.

He glanced in the narrow mirror of his private stateroom. His skin, freshly lathered and shaved, was an unusually pale contrast to his dark brown hair. "I think I might be coming down with something." Hopefully his voice sounded rough enough for a thermometer.

Callum Brydolf, his best friend and lawyer, appeared in the doorway with one untied shoe in hand. "Nonsense. You look the picture of health."

"No, really. It may be serious."

Struggling to balance in the train car's narrow hallway, Callum pulled the shoe on. "I've heard you talk like that before and you're not getting out of this. These people live in the middle of nowhere and have nearly nothing to their name, yet they're merging all their resources to host a bunch of bigwigs tonight including the sullen-faced William Drake." He straightened and sniffed his wrist, the source of the spiced cologne trailing him. "Besides, you're not the only knight on the board. You have to play the game. Otherwise what was the point in coming? Give the poor souls an hour of your time. Maybe two. Then you can cut out and read a boring book as usual." Callum strode to William's mirror and examined his own necktie. "You'd spend half your life cooped up if you could. But there's more to experience than lifeless pages on an empty Pullman car, my friend. Think of this as a night for unexpected opportunities."

"Right. But this is a dance. Not a board meeting."

"All the more reason to find a smile. I guarantee the other coal barons will. And guess who will be watching? Mr. Jorgensen and the men in his employment. This is not just a dance. It's an interview. Make no mistake about that. It's your job to be the man Mr. Jorgensen can entrust this town to. No one wants a revolt on their hands the moment the deed is signed. So twirl a nice girl or two around the floor, shake a few hands, and show them who their new leader could be."

William searched for a response but Callum snapped his fingers as though he'd forgotten something. He retreated down the hallway and William heard him digging through a cabinet against the shared wall.

Alone, William rolled his shirtsleeves up to his elbows. Then unrolled them. If only he could be as engaging as his friend. The man sparked a room to life simply by entering. Callum proved jovial, hardworking, and endlessly popular.

Meanwhile William felt as approachable as a marble statue, which he probably looked like half the time. His mind was a system of levers and pulleys. Files and calculations. There was a depth within him—a true and honest beating heart that he didn't know how to show.

He'd handled enough unknowns with the death of his parents and the care for his younger sister, not to mention the responsibility for the family name and fortune. Matters of the heart were much too complicated . . . and best left under lock and key.

No wonder he was twenty-eight and unmarried. The charming women in his circle admired him and indicated as much, but such beauty came at a cost. They were women who sought a future with his wealth, and their fathers often had ulterior motives for dangling their daughters under his nose. For William, that wasn't the best soil to form a relationship in, let alone a marriage. But society frowned on him engaging with women of any other status. And he felt bound by the same creed from his Aunt Catherine, who always stared down at him from the portrait hanging in the dining room with her silvery stare and decades of wealth.

Regardless, he had different dreams in mind. William wished for a woman who could match him step for step. Not in wealth or prestige, but in mind. In interests. In curiosity. A woman who brought beauty and intentionality to his world, as he meant to do for her. So far . . . no such woman had crossed his path. So here he was. A bachelor. Perhaps until the end of his days.

"Stop staring at the wall and fix your tie," Callum muttered as he returned. The man slid on a black satin waistcoat.

As for William, he'd opted for gray tweed, hoping to blend in better. Though he doubted any of these miners owned a waistcoat. "I did fix it." William turned his head to study his reflection.

"You look like a door-to-door salesman who got dressed in the dark."

Impossible. The suit he wore was of the finest wool, cut by a tailor in Chicago. But William's hands were unsteady, and his heart not exactly inspired, so perhaps those causes were to blame.

"You really should have a valet," Callum continued as the man knew how to fill any space with twice as many words. "You could afford ten."

"I don't need a valet. I can dress myself."

"Clearly." Callum tugged on William's necktie and adjusted the folds.

Here on the rails, William employed both a porter and a cook who boarded at the other end of the car in the servants' berths. The cook kept William and his company well-fed, while the porter attended to luggage, assisted with the Pemberley's travel itinerary, and kept each room in tip-top shape from William's private study to the fashionable dining parlor. While William often travelled alone, Callum occupied the guest stateroom on this excursion. A champion best friend who had a knack for lending sound advice whenever needed. Insights William already appreciated and they'd only been in New River for two days. Since this business trip could very well cost him a fortune, his friend's opinion was crucial.

William moved to the window and nudged the curtain aside. A humble dirt lane meandered past the depot, to the row houses where miners lived with their families. Chimneys spouted smoke, strings of gray laundry graced front porches, and doors angled open to the early-autumn air. Children ran around, playing with sticks while a cart meandered by, laden with lumber.

William closed the curtains, blocking the depot from view. "So, tell me something. What types of songs do you think will be played tonight? Will we know any?"

"If you're anticipating the foxtrot, you may want to refrain from filling in any dance cards."

William drew in a slow breath. Good thing he asked.

"I suspect this will be more the down-home type of event."

"What exactly would that mean?"

"Meaning that was a joke about the dance cards. Don't expect any. As for music . . ." Callum gave a half shrug. "I don't anticipate a twelve-piece orchestra. There may be a fiddle. Perhaps a harmonica—saw one in a fella's pocket earlier. Other than that, it's hard to say. I haven't exactly spent a lot of time in a town like this. My cousin once lived on an estate in Charleston and she used to sing 'In the Sweet By and By' to my sister and me whenever she visited. I expect that type of music tonight. Of some variation, maybe. And no"—Callum fastened one of his silver cufflinks—"I'm not going to sing it for you."

"Well, that was the next thing I planned to ask," William said dryly.

Callum's laugh was too big for the master stateroom but welcome all the same. William needed his friend's carefree outlook just now. He could use more lightheartedness himself. Easier said than done when one of his reasons for being here was to investigate a land dispute that the New River Coal Company had created with several of the local occupants. Four names were listed in the claim file in his desk drawer.

Webb. McMahon. Hatcher. And the last—*Bennet.*

Returning to the window, William nudged the curtains aside again. A group of young folks strolled down the road, all dressed up. Not in the fashions he often saw, but they'd made an effort. And here he stood, a guest of honor.

A bad idea perhaps. Especially with so much at stake.

While William was no lawyer, he knew the coal company owned several parcels of valuable land that local residents occupied for one reason or another. Each deal done on a handshake with little legal documentation. An issue that needed to be settled here. How the information regarding these arrangements had sat in a desk in Richmond the last two years gathering dust, he didn't know. Now it was up to him to ensure the issues were finally resolved. The result? Much of the surrounding farmland would eventually belong to the coal company.

And the company, Lord willing, would belong to him.

While renting land to local tenants was a nice idea, it also created awkward loose ends that needed tying up. For the company owner to accept William's purchase price, the finer details must be settled. Especially when they were attached to tens of thousands of dollars.

It had the owner, Mr. Jorgensen, all but rolling out a velvet carpet for him and the other coal barons. All in hopes of finally retiring. Should William make the most attractive offer, he could rightfully own the land surrounding the New River mine. A responsibility that weighed like a stone.

With his trunk open, William pulled two gold cufflinks from a polished box. He fastened the cufflinks into place and inspected his reflection again in the mirror. His thoughts were easier to focus on than his stiff appearance. Was this a town he could put down roots in—at least as a business owner, even if he never intended to reside here? Pierce his vision—and even his life—deeper into the soil? Were any of the other coal barons wrestling with such ideals? Or did they simply see this town as a blank check to cash?

Difficult to know since it remained unclear what lay untapped here. The fertile farmlands could be ripe with coal. While there was no guarantee of profit beneath the soil, the existing mine had a few decades in it still. Even if the investment failed to produce an ounce of coal, all that acreage would rise in value and he could, at the very least, profit from a real estate deal when he chose to retire. Still, he could not in good conscience take ownership of a company that he truly couldn't see through to a viable future.

Awkward, then, to think of tonight's festivities involving some of the very families who would have to relocate. Maybe that's why he was pallid.

"I suppose we're to walk over," Callum said.

At the sound of his friend's distant voice, William returned to the present. "I'm sorry?"

"I believe we're to walk over." Callum brushed aside a corner of the nearest window curtain. "It doesn't seem likely we'll have a way to call a carriage."

Another one of his jokes, clearly. There probably wasn't a carriage within a hundred miles. "No. We'll walk." The evening air would cool his head.

Callum eased open the door to the rear observation deck. The night air was cool and spiced as though even the distant cedars and balsams of the surrounding woodland were putting on a show for him.

As William followed his friend down the shallow stairs, a group of young women passed by, done up in ribbons and laden with giggles. Four—no, five of them, walking the road into town in touches of gingham and bows.

William took a steadying breath of the evening air and said a sincere prayer that this transaction would go smoothly and that he and the Pemberley could pull out of this town before the last autumn leaves fell.

3

"Would ya dance with me, Miss Lizzy?"

"Why certainly, Jeb." As the band struck up a reel, Lizbeth faced the miner who lifted a well-worn hat from combed hair.

His eyes glistened dark as slate, hands roughened by ax and shovel, and his demeanor was bright. Just like the lantern he'd taken down into the mine since he left school at age twelve. Now grown, he'd never once called her "miss," which made Lizbeth smile as she accepted his outstretched hand. Just beyond him, decorations of early-autumn apples and late-summer sunflowers draped the beams of the great barn. As they walked toward the dance floor she soaked in the sights, from slices of pie on mismatched plates and more sunflowers filling glass jars of every size. Even the air seemed to know it graced a special night, smelling of rain and fresh cider.

Pa had already pointed out the handful of coal barons who stood in their midst. Each wore a fancy suit, all looking out of place here in New River. Most were older, with crops of silver hair and wedding bands.

Lizbeth had managed to keep to the outskirts so far, awaiting sight of Mr. Drake so she could point him out to Jayne, but the most mysterious of the coal barons was yet to arrive. More than a few women had settled in near the barn entrance where two doors as sturdy as oak trees sat braced open to the evening air. The moment the famed man approached, the gaggle of women would sound the alarm.

With her hand in Jeb's, Lizbeth followed the young miner into the center of the barn. While she'd worked hard on the blouse she wore, the seam was a mite crooked so Lizbeth kept her elbow close to her side. Her calico skirt was scarcely a year old, so the hues of autumn gold and chestnut brown were as rich and bright as the polished rafters overhead. She'd even wrapped a sash of ivory muslin around her waist where Jeb's hand now rested.

Lizbeth felt the coarseness of his other hand from years shoveling coal. She braved a look at his face. He was a nice fellow and hardworking. Amiable qualities to be sure, but she'd never imagined she'd live in the row housing one day. There would be no place to pasture her mules there. No place to spread out in the grass at night and search the stars with Jayne.

For now, there remained rows of bush beans to hoe, cucumbers to pickle, and apples to preserve on a farm that she loved. Thanks to Pa's teaching, the pair of them alone knew the farm's secrets. Then there were her younger sisters to help raise. While Ma was capable and loving, she could sometimes go into a flutter, so Lizbeth helped all she could. Life proved full, and abundantly so.

Should a man take interest in her, he would have to call louder than the voice of her responsibilities. And that, she believed, was simply too much to ask. Especially from a young man like Jeb who had enough burdens to bear.

Lizbeth's loose bun, pulled up and fastened by two brass combs, caught a draft from the open doorway as Jeb turned her in time with the reel. Her feet tingled as their boots tapped the wide-plank floor beneath them. While neither she nor Jeb stayed true to the steps, it didn't matter with the banjo's extra notes twanging along with the lighthearted tune. Her breath quickened as Jeb turned her alongside other couples. She tried to spot her family, but the room spun until nothing made sense except her feet against the floorboards and the way laughter wove in harmony to the banjo. Jeb turned her once more and Lizbeth finally caught sight of Jayne near the wall along with Kit and Lacey.

When the dance ended, Jeb thanked her. "Perhaps another one soon?"

"Certainly." Cheeks warm, Lizbeth backed away.

The fiddler struck up the next song as she turned, trying to get her bearings, but just as the music swelled, it faded. In the doorway of the great barn stood two men in suits. One was fair-haired and grinning. The other, tall and shadowed. Could it be?

She slid behind a group of townspeople and cast another glance toward the doorway. Both men were a few years older than she, strapping and handsome yet as contrasted as night and day. One stood bright like sunrise, the other restrained like starlight. One of them had to be William Drake, but which?

Hurrying onward, Lizbeth reached Jayne alongside her other sisters who stayed silent as field mice. Even sensible Maryanne stood in awe as she balanced a plate of buttermilk pie. A baby fussed in the corner where a woman bounced it on her hip. The fiddler bumped a rogue string, sending a sour note into the room's silence. The other coal barons stopped as well, each sizing up the newcomers as though they could gauge one another's schemes in a single glance.

Mr. Jorgensen approached the two young men with open arms. "Welcome! Welcome!"

The fair-haired one shook his hand as though taking a quick shine to the mine's owner. The other did the same but his brown eyes filtered across the room, then he forced a stiff smile.

Lizbeth prayed the latter one wasn't the famed Mr. Drake. It had to be the more jovial fellow. Any man so rich as Mr. Drake would most certainly sport such a contagious grin.

The men's voices faded into conversation as Mr. Jorgensen led them around the room. The whole town began chattering at once.

Maryanne raised her eyebrows and took another bite of buttermilk pie. Kit elbowed her, insisting that wasn't ladylike. Meanwhile, Lizbeth strained to see as Mr. Jorgensen introduced the young men to a clutch of families. With such a brimming crowd, it would take ages. Jayne gave a wink that said there would be plenty of time for introductions later. Lizbeth smiled.

As conversation rose louder than ever, so did the band. The banjo and dulcimer twanged out a brand-new jig as Lizbeth whispered to Jayne, "I'll fetch us something to drink."

Jayne froze as Mr. Jorgensen approached them. Lizbeth stepped away so her sister could take center stage, hastening to a large kettle in the far corner next to the bowl of punch. A quick sip of the drink tasted too sweet, so she opted for cider and filled two tin cups. Would Mr. Jorgensen and the young men have reached Jayne by now? Lizbeth turned and to her surprise, it wasn't her sister she found first, but Hattie, her closest friend and Mr. Jorgensen's own daughter.

"Lizzy!" Hattie nabbed one of the cups and swallowed a gulp. "Come see! You gotta see Jayne!" She pulled Lizbeth through the press of people.

Lizbeth struggled to balance the cup. "Slower or I'll spill."

Hattie tugged her to the other side of the dance floor. There Jayne stood speaking to one of the wealthy young men.

The man's fair hair lay slicked neatly to the side and his blue eyes sparkled as they talked. Jayne moved her delicate hands in conversation, the gesture so lovely that the gentleman peering down on her didn't waver. Curiosity lit Lizbeth's heart, just as it seemed to light the stranger's face as he studied the young woman before him.

"Oh, do you think that could be Mr. Drake?" Lizbeth asked.

"That one? Lands no." Hattie polished off her cider and set the cup aside.

"No?" Lizbeth studied the figure in the lantern light.

"That's his business partner. A Callum Brydolf, who Pa says is a lawyer. Rather handsome, ain't he?"

Lizbeth nodded absently. The wrong man, then? Still, she couldn't help but notice how much Jayne admired the stranger, and he her, as they made small talk amidst the jostling crowd.

"I say she's caught his eye for a dance," Hattie called over the music. "I sure hope he asks her."

"I daresay he has." Lizbeth laughed as Callum Brydolf led Jayne onto the floor.

She and Hattie exchanged wide-eyed gazes then melted into giggles that they had to hide. How Lizbeth would look forward to hearing about Jayne's first dance come midnight when they climbed into their bunks and whispered about it until dawn.

Not wanting to stand and stare, Lizbeth glanced toward the open doorway and the wagons parked just beyond. "I best take a moment and go check on Sassafras."

"Nonsense. That old mule will be fine." Hattie tugged on her arm. "My pa's introducin' folk and I don't wanna be standin' here alone."

"Oh. But no—"

"Hattie, my girl!" a deep voice bellowed.

At the sound of Mr. Jorgensen's voice, both Lizbeth and Hattie spun around.

There neared the mine owner. And just behind him—the famed Mr. Drake.

The elegant gentleman stood nearly a head taller than Mr. Jorgensen and a far reach more handsome. But Mr. Drake's brown eyes were more intent on the floor than the merriment all around. So tense was his jaw that it would take a key to loosen the lock.

A key Lizbeth wouldn't begin to know how to search for.

Then his gaze lifted and, for one fleeting moment, met hers. At first glance, she found cool disinterest in his eyes, yet with a second blink, his gaze roved her face. The man shifted quickly, studying the room, the soaring ceiling, anything but her.

Mr. Jorgensen cleared his throat. "Mr. Drake. I'd like to introduce you to one of my daughters, Hattie. She's also the bookkeeper for the company. The girl computes sums faster than any man in my employment."

Mr. Drake nodded.

Hattie, never shy, continued the story. "If there's anythin' you need, Mr. Drake—any sums you need figured out about the mine—I'll be glad to help."

"Thank you," he said stiffly.

Hattie blushed. "Though now I recall Pa sayin' you went to Harvard with a degree in mathematics. Top of your class, was it? I doubt there's sums you'd need help with."

The man gave a thin smile.

Embarrassment deepened the flush in Hattie's cheeks and she glanced to Lizbeth as though needing to be rescued. "And oh, I'm sorry." Hattie inched Lizbeth forward. "This is Lizbeth Bennet. Her pa owns the Bennet farm. But most folks 'round here call it Bennet Hollow."

Mr. Drake's gaze filtered over Lizbeth's face as though he were startled by that last detail.

"Pleased to meet you." Lizbeth set aside her cup of cider and extended a hand.

His eyes found hers again. This time, they were filled with curiosity as he locked gazes with her. "Good evening." He took hold of her hand, formal and firm.

She envisioned the train car he owned. A stately presence. A rigid exterior. And soon to leave.

This man seemed one and the same.

Lizbeth lowered her hand as Mr. Jorgensen clapped Mr. Drake on the shoulder. A muted sound against his wool coat. Never had Lizbeth seen such finery. His jaw, cleanly shaven, bespoke an elegance far beyond her imagining.

"What do we need to do to get you out on that dance floor, William? Why not take a turn with one of these young ladies?" Mr. Jorgensen angled toward Hattie, but Hattie nudged Lizbeth nearer.

"Lovely idea," Hattie blurted, still pink cheeked and wide-eyed. "Lizbeth was just saying she wished to dance."

Lizbeth threw Hattie a glare before peering back to the men. "I—I—"

The last thing she wanted was to dance with William Drake herself but Hattie's silent beseeching all but begged her to bridge the gap. Made easier when the man held out his hand. His voice, though soft, somehow reached her ears over the ruckus of the room.

As though it was a voice she alone was meant to hear.

"I'd be honored, Miss Bennet."

4

The last time he'd danced, it had been with Harriet Rockford—heiress to more real estate in Manhattan than he'd even visited. Her hands had been silk, her red-lipped mouth sophisticated, and her scent like the open doors of Bloomingdale's on 59th Street.

But this woman was different.

Miss Bennet's hands, while scrubbed clean, spoke of work. They lay small and warm in his own. Her brown hair was as deep a chestnut as his gentle racehorse, and there lingered around her an herbal scent. He couldn't name it, but it harkened back to his childhood when Nurse would settle him into bed with a cup of steaming chamomile tea. Comforting and calming.

The smell of home.

And here she stood, one of the very Bennets he might uproot from their land, about to take a turn on the dance floor with him.

William stuffed down his discomfort as he angled the young woman to face him. He touched her lower back where the coarse fabric of her high-waisted skirt met her simple blouse. Both styles were a decade behind the latest fashions, but the cut and pale hues complemented this lass's willowy figure and soft coloring. As she wasn't as tall as him, her brown eyes lingered on the ridgeline of his shoulders—not meeting his face—and he didn't blame her. They didn't know one another.

Rarely had that affected him before but the unbalance of understanding in this moment was unnerving. No, unjust. He *knew* who he was and his goals here in New River. He sought land . . . maybe even her father's. This young woman remained none the wiser.

The cogs in his mind turning, William gulped as he led them in a small step to the right, hoping to find the slow rhythm with her quickly. "It's a fine song," he said in desperation.

"The music?"

He nodded, his chin dipping near to her forehead as he turned them to the right this time. Something felt off.

"I—I do not believe the song has begun." She followed him regardless.

Stilling, he listened more closely, finally recognizing the humble scales the ragtag band worked through. Oh, he was an idiot. No wonder their feet had been out of step. There was no melody.

He freed her hands and took a step back. "So it seems."

Lantern light swirled around them, as easy on its feet as the laughter and conversation that ebbed and flowed from the crowd of townspeople. Unlike him.

Miss Bennet clasped her fingers in front of her dress. "I s'pose it'll begin in just a moment." Finally her eyes met his. An ancient soul in a youthful face.

"Yes." And in the meantime? How was he to pass the moments? "Would you care for some refreshment? I believe there's punch."

"Oh, I just had some. Well, the cider that is. The punch was a mite sweet for my taste." She winced as though not meaning to admit all that.

"Would you mind? Showing me to the cider?" He needed something for his parched throat. For his guilt, really. Though a drink so wholesome would hardly do.

He followed her toward the refreshment table. Music swelled again. A waltz. Soft and slow. He kept walking and thankfully, she pretended not to notice as well.

At a table covered in a checked cloth, a young boy dipped two tin cups of cider. "Here ya are, Lizbeth. And for yer gentleman friend." The boy's drawl was as stamped into place as everyone else's.

Yet it was her name that lingered in his mind. *Lizbeth.* William would aim to think of her only as Miss Bennet. Formality created distance and that's what he needed in all circumstances here.

They turned to survey the dance floor. He a shoulder width apart from this young woman and none the wiser for what to say. In the awkwardness that lingered, she swiped her fingertip across the bottom of the cup, catching a droplet of rich cider. She tasted it and he diverted his gaze. Sipped his own cup. William swallowed the savory taste, trying not to think of her enjoying the same.

He'd come here on business. Nothing else. He couldn't afford to be sidetracked by a brown-haired local with a pretty face and curious gaze. Lizbeth. He'd do well to forget her name after this moment.

Tricky when a few more minutes of survival were at hand. William cleared his throat. "Tell me of this barn." It was all he could think of. Before them, couples turned in slow rhythm to the band. A dozen hues and textures moving as one.

"The barn?"

If he stalled longer, the song would end. They could part ways, and he'd be none the ruder for it. "Yes. Of its history."

She surveyed the ceiling with its soaring rafters and massive beams. Water marks ran dark talons down the western ridgeline, but the building was sound, and impressively grand.

"It's the hoist barn," she said. "For the coal company. Just beneath these floorboards, the mine sinks down five hundred feet."

Already the owner of two coal mines across the East, he knew the basics but feigned interest all the same. Especially when she pointed to the far end of the building where a series of mechanical cranks spoke of sound engineering. "Do you see that hatch there?"

William nodded.

"That's the hoist and the cage that takes the crews up and down. I've never seen inside of it. Girls aren't allowed to." She held her cup between pale, youthful fingers. Perhaps nineteen . . . maybe twenty, she had to be nearly a decade younger than he. Likely, she'd be as glad for this encounter to end as he. "Pa always told us to stay far away as children. Not that my sisters or I had much reason to come here. But when we were younger, whenever Pa forgot his lunch pail, we fetched it for him."

William nodded absently, not interested in learning more. The less they spoke of her pa the better. He needn't know anything else about her origins, nor she about his. "Fascinating."

"Have you ever been inside a mine?" She peeked up at him as though unsure what a coal baron did exactly.

He didn't blame her. Most men of his status bought their wealth, but he tried to earn his. "I've been down in mines a few dozen times."

Her eyes widened. "And the dark?"

"I can't say I fear the darkness, but I'm not too keen on the stillness."

She looked to be waiting for more.

"It just comes with the territory." His men wouldn't respect him if he didn't know how to crouch low beneath a jagged outcropping of ore. Or crawl on his belly in the blackness of the earth. He did both as often as needed but he didn't want to overexplain and wasn't usually one for many words. He didn't want to risk her thinking that his curiosity about the building had been in jest. She'd been kind enough to point out its features and that needn't be doused by his blabbering about mines.

Lizbeth lowered her cup, studying it now as she spoke. "Pa's told me of how canaries fall from their perches, hearty flames flicker out, and grown men cry for salvation. But I think that's sometimes to keep us girls far away from the hatch."

Wise man. William had seen enough of the world below to understand what the folks in these parts faced day in and day out, and he didn't need to know any more of the aged Mr. Bennet. The knowledge this young woman had just given him was unnerving enough and his senses needed to stay taut as steel cables if he were to make it out of New River unscathed in a few weeks' time.

With that reality clouding this moment, William struggled for what else to say. In the distance, Brydolf and another of the Miss Bennets were dancing. Her yellow curls were wound up in a romantic fashion—just lyrical enough to distract his best friend. The man was utterly beaming. William shook his head to gather his wits. He'd have a few choice words for his friend come dawn and the walk back to the train yard.

As for now, William tried to ignore the thread of jealousy that wove into his spirit. How was it so easy for Brydolf to engage with others? If only his friend would cease this merriment and join him here in the wings. William could use a dose of the man's energy and enthusiasm.

But no, it was just William and this young lady. So, he had to think of something.

Lizbeth fiddled with a strip of cloth wrapping her waist. While he meant not to admire the trim shape of her waistline, the crooked seam running up her side was strangely endearing. Then something akin to guilt struck him. He didn't know why. He had nothing to do with the origins of her dress or the fact that she was poor. She and he existed at opposite ends of industrialization. He the money. She the humanity.

She was also fidgeting nervously. Growing bored no doubt.

Words, man. "And you, Miss Bennet? What is it that occupies your time?" While he gathered this one too old for schooling now, she appeared just shy of matrimony and motherhood.

"I enjoy going for walks or finding a spot to read. I also spend time each afternoon stitching on a sampler. But first, I tend the gardens at home and keep the mules fed and watered."

"Do you have a lot of mules?"

"Just two now. Though we used to have a fair deal more before they were sold to the mine." Her eyes looked sad over that detail.

"I see."

"Yesterday, one of our mules, Eugene, toppled over the garden gate. Ma sounded the alarm and my sisters and I caught him before he threw the whole patch asunder."

William tried to imagine such a scene. Of this young woman going up against a mule and coming out victorious. "Sounds like quite the feat."

"It wasn't so hard. Just needed to open a jar of dried apples. They're his favorite. He doesn't hear very well, but he'll follow me just about anywhere with them."

These garden exploits explained why her hands felt as though they knew the earth better than the next woman's. More curiosities came to mind, but he stemmed them. Was that enough conversation? Perhaps it would have been safer to dance. The stringed instruments crested their refrain now. The song would end soon.

He was half tempted to state as much so that Miss Bennet would at least think him knowledgeable on music. Seeing as he'd gotten off on the wrong foot and all.

But conversation just wouldn't flow naturally for him. It rarely did with strangers. Especially with the way this young woman observed him. He sensed she was more intrigued by his soul than his wallet. What would she see there?

What did *he* see when he glanced her way? Eyes—copper brown and focused—seasoned by a hundred novels or as many stories around the fire, no doubt. She looked sharp as a whip, and he'd take care not to cross her lest he encounter the sting. If this mule of hers was so easily tamed, he didn't guess he'd be much of a match for her either.

"And what of your business, Mr. Drake?" she asked. "I've heard it said you own coal mines up north. Is there a favorite region you've visited?"

He didn't sense an ounce of greed in her tone. No prying into the wells of his wealth. Only a gentle curiosity—even more unsettling when the map of New River filled his mind. The blocks of land he'd carefully marked. Including her own. *Bennet Hollow.* A twenty-acre plot of forest and streams that he'd journeyed here to claim along with the other farms. Lines on the map that just yesterday had meant only fences, but now, looking down on her crown of braids and faint smattering of freckles, he saw a glimmer of the vistas and views she called home.

What had only been an equation in his mind now spanned into a portrait. One of beauty and life. The image—the vulnerability—stunned him.

Chest pounding now, William took a small step back, not meaning to sideline her question. He could scarcely recall it and that unsettled him more. He wasn't used to his mind being disrupted so. In the distance, he heard only a lone fiddle playing now. The other musicians were all reaching for mugs of drink.

"Well, it seems the song is nearly done, Miss Bennet. I'll leave you to your acquaintances." For surely he proved dismal company himself. Gulping, he backed away. "I hope you have . . . I hope you have a pleasant evening."

He nodded and gave an impossibly formal bow. Mortified, he turned and trudged off before she could see his lack of composure. Or worse—see him for who he truly was.

5

Lizbeth plunged a trowel into the earth and popped a radish loose like a button on a shirt. She repeated the motion as though the trowel were a seam ripper, and this row of radishes a mistake. *Snap. Pop.* Soil splattered the skirt of her apron.

Beside her, Jayne sighed. "Is it that man? The one from last night?"

"If you mean the proud one with scarcely a few words to his name, then yes." The one who had sidestepped a dance with her. How could she ever have thought that such a man might be a match for Jayne? Lizbeth blew out a breath. Best not to dwell on Mr. Drake. There weren't enough radishes in this garden to make sense of the man. Worse yet, she had the niggling sense that something was about to change for the town of New River. Perhaps not for the better. "Tell me of the fella you danced with instead. Three times, if I'm not mistaken." The idea alone cheered Lizbeth and she leaned back, resting soiled hands on her apron. Much easier to think on Jayne's evening than her own.

"Callum Brydolf. Oh, Lizzy." Jayne's blue eyes rivaled the sky overhead. "He was so refined. And friendly. The whole town knows him as Mr. Brydolf but he asked me to call him Callum." Jayne waved a hand at the notion. "Not that it means anythin', or that I would—"

"I say that means something."

Jayne's cheeks colored rosier than the crisp air accounted for. "Think so?"

How to strike the balance between encouraging the intrigue that Lizbeth saw blossom last night with the very real fact that Mr. Brydolf would only be in town for a short spell? "I think he saw a young woman who was so lovely and gracious and good that he had to make every moment count."

Jayne's smile widened as she fiddled with the amethyst tied to her wrist.

"And it seems like he's a wise man to have noticed those traits. Was he a good dancer?"

"We fumbled the steps since the dances were new to him, but he was so warm and kind that we laughed about it."

The row of radishes finished, Lizbeth wiped at her hands and stood. She fetched up her full basket and together, she and Jayne slipped out the crooked garden gate that Eugene the mule had made a mite more lopsided. One more reason Ma fussed that he should be sold. But Lizbeth couldn't. Never would she forget the day when she was just a girl who had walked with Pa to town, helping him lead two mules in harness. She'd stood at the entrance of the coal office as Pa exchanged money with Mr. Jorgensen. Money that put food on the table. All at the cost of sending the unsuspecting mules into the depths of the earth, never to surface again.

Lizbeth swallowed back the regret, still wishing there might have been a different way. For the animals and for her family. At least Pa had let her keep Eugene, on account of his only having one ear. Pa had suggested the mine might not want such an animal and that Lizbeth could raise him.

In the pasture, Eugene and Sassafras grazed contentedly, just far enough from the mine that they weren't as affected by coal dust as the rest of town. Overhead, the morning sky held puffs of clouds, as though the early-autumn weather matched the lightness of Jayne's spirits.

Lizbeth nudged the kitchen door open.

Lacey and Maryanne looked up from their baking—two bowls and several spoons coated in dough. "Tell her, Jayne! Tell Ma the way you danced three times with Mr. Brydolf."

"Tell me everythin'!" Ma sang from her spot at the stove. "I was all the way on the other side of the room and could scarcely see what was happening."

Lizbeth plopped the basket down and smiled, knowing better, because Ma never missed a lick.

Lacey twirled around them, the dough now abandoned. She turned in a circle, humming one of the tunes from the night before. The same waltz that Lizbeth herself would have danced had Mr. Drake not sidelined them.

"Mr. Brydolf was so polite." Jayne seemed to choose her words wisely in front of the younger girls who were prone to gossip and giggles. If Jayne stated too much, she'd never hear the end of it. "He asked good questions. I don't think we stopped talkin' the whole time."

"And what about you, Lizzy?" Lacey crooned. "I saw you on the arm of that other fella." She scrunched her nose. "The one in need of a good thaw."

Jayne brightened. "I want to hear more of this man too."

Lizbeth snuck Jayne a look that said she'd share more later. In secret. "Oh, there's little to say." In truth, she didn't want all her sisters to know she'd been passed over on the dance floor by him.

"Oh, Lizzy. At least a few tidbits!" Ma declared.

Just then, Lizbeth spotted Hattie through the window, strolling up the lane with an envelope in hand. She swiped again at her apron. "It looks like Hattie's brought us some mail and I promised I'd give her sash back before church on Sunday. Then I'll be back to help scrub the dishes." Lizbeth pulled the sash from a pile of shawls near the door.

"Promise you'll tell us when you get back!" Lacey cried.

Lizbeth flicked the end of her sister's braid playfully. "You'll hardly know I'm gone!" She hurried out the door, the sash trailing from her hand.

She met her friend on the lane where they linked arms.

"I've never seen you run so fast before." Hattie handed over the envelope.

"Thank you. I'll get this to Pa, and you just set me free from talkin' about last night."

"But that's just what I came to hear about!"

Lizbeth elbowed her. "Oh, don't you start. I don't even wanna remember it."

"Fiddlesticks. You danced with the wealthiest man any of us has ever seen. Or will ever see again. He owns more than we could even imagine and Pa said his farm in Vermont is an actual *estate*." Her eyes widened. "Says it's a sight to behold with dozens of servants and groomed gardens just like in some of the books we've read. And *you* danced with him, Lizbeth Bennet."

"I stood with him holdin' a cup of cider, that's what I did. I hardly think that'll make headlines."

"But you were the only woman he spoke to the whole night—cider or not."

She was?

"So, tell me more. Tell me *somethin'*. These are days that'll never come again 'round here."

Was that what their world whittled down to? That last night was the best to ever come?

Lizbeth stilled on the pathway. "Fine." Might as well draw this out in a way that satisfied. Leastways, she could put an end to it. "He was fine spoken. A real gentleman. Refined and sturdy."

"Sturdy? Oh, you can do better than that."

Lizbeth laughed. Then again, when she thought back on it, though stoic, he wasn't brash. It had made her feel comfortable. Even safe. Lizbeth shook off the thought. Now for details more thrilling. "He took my hand and then touched my waist just here." Brief as a lightning flash, it was, but it seemed to satisfy Hattie's curiosity.

Still arm in arm, she and Hattie continued up the path as leaves crunched underfoot.

"He stayed quiet, rather." Lizbeth twirled the sash around her finger. "Sort of like the sky after a storm. Or maybe before one." She was yet to know. "His eyes were brown, but the warm sort. The color of gingerbread."

"And was he a good dancer?"

"As stated . . . we did *not* dance." The memory prickled again. "More or less, he stood stiff as a fence post and stubborn as a thorn. Anything else?"

Hattie brushed a low oak branch aside as the path curved up the grassy knoll that led toward the New River mine. From here, Lizbeth could just envision the clatter of dozens of men and their mule teams. A place where young women her own age had already birthed a baby or two.

"Just one more thing. Somethin' else that's nice," Hattie said. "I think he might have fancied you."

"Nonsense."

"Well, you were the only one I saw him watchin'. He might have been the quiet type, but he didn't take his eyes off you for the rest of the night."

"Fiddle-faddle."

"Just statin' what I saw."

They walked farther down the lane—Pa's pasture to their right, wild woodland to their left. A robin fluttered past. Finally, Lizbeth drew in a slow breath. "If I give you one more thing, do you promise to put an end to it?"

"Promise."

She pressed the rolled-up sash into Hattie's hands. "I have to hurry back for my chores, but first . . ." She closed her eyes briefly then opened them. "He was tall. Taller up close than I thought he was from far away. It made him seem very present. Like you couldn't help but reckon with the fact that he was there, standin' beside you." She let that settle as Hattie breathed in deeply. "It was as though he was tryin' to understand me somehow but couldn't. As though we spoke the same language but began at different ends of a story." With it time to part ways, she released Hattie's arm. "A promise is a promise so that'll be the end of it?"

"Fair. But—"

Lizbeth held up a hand. "You just worry about having a good day." She shifted back. "And I'll focus on not worryin' about Mr. Drake ever again for as long as we both shall live. Mr. Brydolf can linger and marry Jayne if he likes—and I certainly hope he does. Mr. Drake can leave alone and the rest of us'll carry on with our lives."

Alone. Something told her he might be rather good at that.

Something else told her that her wounded pride spoke a little too loudly.

"How can you already dislike the man so?" Hattie shielded her eyes from the sun as it broke through the clouds.

"I—I didn't say I disliked him. It's simply that I don't trust him."

"Well, by the way you put it, Lizzy, it's startin' to sound like the same thing."

Though her friend's words chafed, Lizzy watched as Hattie gave a small wave and continued back up the path. She thought of the embroidery she worked on by candlelight whenever time allowed.

The night is far spent . . .

That was all she'd stitched so far. The lesson beneath the linen surface was still murky. She sighed. Hopefully in time, she would come to understand more of the full verse's depth and meaning as she continued working on the piece. Wasn't that what a sampler was for? Not only to showcase the handiwork of women and girls, but to unravel an important lesson with each word carefully stitched. Lizbeth could still recall the day she'd chosen the guiding sentiment. She'd been wrestling with impatience over what she would do in this life and how she would live a life of meaning, when Pa lovingly read the Scripture aloud by firelight and Lizbeth had marked the passage to remember.

In the distance, Lizbeth could just make out the roofline of the hoist barn where the night before, lanterns had glimmered and a fiddle had played sweet and low. Even now, she recalled the feel of her hand in Mr. Drake's. Lizbeth studied her fingertips trying to conjure up the sensation once more. She'd spoken boldly just now to conceal the fact that she'd been honored by his offer to dance. Once they'd approached the floor together, she'd hoped they might even talk longer. That she could learn more of what the world offered beyond these hills and hollows from his own unique perspective. Even if just for a few moments more.

That perhaps they might have been glad to be standing in one another's company.

But that hadn't been the case. Which was just fine with her. Instead of disliking him so, she'd simply leave him in peace. That seemed fair.

Turning, Lizbeth strolled back down the path, beneath golden oaks and rust-hued maples, then over the footbridge where the creek gurgled and bubbled along the edge of Bennet Hollow. There, she found Pa at the gate.

Lizbeth withdrew the envelope from her pocket as he turned. "This is from Mr. Jorgensen. Hattie just brought it by."

He took the envelope and she searched his face as he read its contents. Was it bad news of some kind? News from the mine? "Is everything all right, Pa?"

The lines beside his eyes softened as his gaze angled her way. "All things in their time." He folded the letter tight and inserted it into his pocket.

Best not to press him further. Not even when the heavy expression returned to his face.

They stood in silence beside the gate, just a stone's throw from the garden and land they toiled and tended together. With only daughters in the family there were no boys to help Pa with the farm. Instead, Lizbeth tried to be his helper, so this was a lane they walked together most days.

As a geologist, Pa worked hard and sacrificed much to see them cared for. His wages had always been humble, but they covered the cost of flour and sugar, and they grew whatever else they needed. Kit gathered the eggs and milked the cow each day. Lacey helped

Ma with the baking, though she often burnt crusts and hotcakes alike. Jayne oversaw the laundry and cleaning. When her hands weren't deep in suds, she helped Ma ensure all the girls were on their best behavior and well-loved. As for Maryanne, when she wasn't humming a tune and dreaming of a new piano, she knitted them each winter sweaters and shawls. The patterns and details just right for her pensive mind.

Then there was Lizbeth. She kept them all entertained with stories each evening, and come dawn, she helped mind their farmyard from the animals to the garden. Just last week, she'd helped Pa mend a row of fencing.

Pa spoke in a measured voice. The way he did when mulling over too much for many words. "Another letter came just yesterday but you weren't around to read it over my shoulder."

"I promise I didn't see a thing just now." She placed her hand over her heart.

His smile was shadowed. "The news from yesterday is that my cousin'll be comin' in from Pennsylvania soon. He's a fair deal younger than me and is looking forward to meetin' all you girls."

Lizbeth took Pa's wrinkled hand in her own as they walked.

"He's asked especially after you and Jayne. I've written him of how you've finished your studies, and what a blessing you are to your ma and me"

"Oh?" Lizbeth had heard Pa speak of his young cousin, a reverend, over the years, but never had the stranger visited. "That'll be nice? His comin'?"

"Perhaps." The response stayed guarded as Pa glanced back toward the mine. Toward the sky where just beneath, Jayne had danced a trio of songs with a wealthy bachelor and Lizbeth had discovered that she wasn't as cut out for high society as her sister might be.

With a meaty hand, Pa swiped clean the property sign that angled against the fence. *Bennet Hollow.* Land that didn't have his name on the deed, but was instead marked with a sign he'd crafted with care. A way to mark this farm as home as best he could.

"How many years ago was it that you struck the deal with Mr. Jorgensen?" Lizbeth asked.

Pa blinked as though the memories were also draped in cobwebs. "Oh, some twenty years ago. No." He blinked again. "Just shy of that."

"And now this farm is more home than any place could ever be." She hoped to spark some indication of what the letter held.

Instead, Pa smoothed more dried leaves from the weathered wood and fingered the *B*, so that it hung clean of dust. "I know how all of you girls have dreamt of more. Of more than this old town could ever hope to give you."

"Oh, Pa. We prattle on at times, but New River's home."

"And it's been lucky to have you."

"Good. 'Cause I have no plans to leave." This town *was* home. As was this farm. Whatever changed with the sale of the mine, surely that would not.

His smile was sad as he lowered his hand from the sign. From the reminder that they borrowed this land and no more. As they walked, she couldn't tell by his quiet sigh if he was grateful for that or worried.

6

Disorderly and unsystematic. The only way to describe Mr. Jorgensen's office. William glimpsed the mess of papers and ore samples as he sat in the chair across from the man's desk. He didn't even bother to fan the dust motes away as he took off his wool flatcap and balanced it on his knee.

"Well." Jorgensen fumbled a few corners of a paper stack. "I s'pose it's time for us to negotiate." Behind him, a scale of ore tipped in the mine's favor. "Thank you for being willing to be the last man I met with today."

William nodded, preferring it that way.

"And I apologize that the other meetings went longer than planned."

"It's not a problem." He wasn't intimidated by that or by how much money the other coal barons Mr. Jorgensen had invited might lay on the table.

Only one would walk away as the owner of the New River Coal Company.

Would it be him? It still depended.

While he kept on the lookout for new business endeavors, he never pitched an offer until he was absolutely certain the deal would benefit his personal holdings and the existing employees.

William rubbed at his freshly shaven jaw, and while his wool vest and coat were overstated for the surroundings, he squared his shoulders, meaning to present himself as the potential owner of this entire establishment. Just beyond the office, a hundred men worked and toiled, both above ground and beneath as they carved out a scant living. They would all be observing the newcomers, including him. Would William be able to improve their lives? He had to, or he had no right tossing his hat in the ring.

William glanced around again. To show weakness was catastrophic in his line of business. As it stood, Jorgensen's cup of pallid coffee and cluttered desk told a story of desperation. Exhaustion. A void William was here to fill.

"I've studied the ledgers you offered and they've been very helpful," William began.

"Good. Good." Jorgensen leaned back in a scuffed leather chair. "I'm here to answer any questions you might have."

"I appreciate it." William's wooden chair creaked as he leaned forward.

He'd read for hours and still hadn't found much advancement for the company's procedures. As for updates to the mine? Nothing in the last thirty years. Not even a mention of introducing electricity here in this office as he had back at his Chess Creek mine. Then again, it was hard to fathom electricity this far removed from any major city.

William had a growing sense of how to view Jorgensen. The man didn't seem negligent but rather out-of-date in his practices, here, far removed from modern society. Jorgensen seemed like a man doing his best but who lacked vision beyond what was right before his eyes. Common in businessmen looking to sell. William had seen it many times before and that's where he came in—always with a new vision of some kind.

"I'd like to begin with any recent improvements or systems that I should be aware of," William said. "I didn't find any in my reading."

"Oh, we get by."

"And the fifty-four mules in your stables? I read in the record books that you've obtained about six new mules a year and that quite a few passed away before old age." Lack of sunlight? Nutrition? He didn't know the reason, but the animals cost Jorgensen dearly, to say nothing of their quality of life.

"Sadly the way of this business."

He wasn't so sure about that. The day steadily neared when electric energy could replace mule power and electric bulbs make carbide lanterns obsolete. As such developments had happened elsewhere in the country, William had grown more and more intrigued by the possibilities. These cards he meant to hold close to his chest just now.

Jorgensen opened a tin of tobacco and stuffed pungent leaves into his pipe. "I'll tip you off and say the other businessmen have asked about the state of the underground timber and the like, which we can discuss." He slid forward a document. "These are the ways we've worked to minimize risk and danger over the last few years."

William accepted the document. "I've had some success with the bolt and timber method at my Pennsylvania operation thanks to the guidance and innovation of some engineers."

Jorgensen nodded, looking more tired than intrigued.

"I'd like to go down in the hoist soon, sir. Could we arrange that?"

"You don't reckon on joining the men down there? Donning a headlamp?"

"I do." Friends often chided him for being too quiet, so William threw more words into the pot. "I'm willing to roll up my shirtsleeves, sir."

"A fine boy like you?"

"I've done such regularly along the Chesapeake and in Osage and Crumpler, where I did some recent scouting. I see it as part of the industry, even as an owner."

"W—well then." Jorgensen fumbled in the desk drawer for a match. "We'll make preparations. Give me a few days, and I'll see that you get boots on the ground."

William knew the drill. Mine owners didn't like prospective buyers to see the trenches untidy. Like a housewife flitting from windowsill to curtain rod, men like Jorgensen preferred to keep the cobwebs under wraps. This owner no doubt intended to tidy up.

Which meant William ought to extend a warning. "Each level if possible." According to the map of the mine, operations plunged some five hundred feet down. That meant five levels to explore. A nearly endless number of tunnels branched from the shaft.

Mr. Jorgensen blanched. "Th—that we can do."

"Thank you, sir."

"I must say, none of the other coal barons intend to go down into the mine. In fact, two are already assembling offers."

Based on conversations alone? Perhaps some men didn't care about the details, but William had no interest in purchasing a mine he hadn't taken careful stock of from top to bottom. Not only had he pored over the latest figures of the company, but he'd delved into its history. As for the lives lost in New River—both man and beast—he took each into account. He didn't mean to have more lives on his hands without knowing he'd done all in his power toward safety. He might not be born of backwoods earth, but his soul was made from dust just as everyone else's. Shaped by God's hands and held to a measure of conscience that stretched into eternity. William valued the lives that toiled to keep this land alive. Lord help him, he would ensure that no one had cause to curse him come his own final breath.

William watched through the window as workers filed from the hoist barn with dinner pails. "I'm interested to learn of the adjacent land as well."

"As were the others." From a drawer, Jorgensen pulled out yet another map. "Which leads me to a slight complication with the arrangement. I confess, I originally planned to sell the mine alone. But most of you men have come here with lawyers in tow."

William nodded.

"Well, one of those lawyers has unearthed an issue that may complicate the ownership of several of the surrounding farms. More will come to light soon and I'll be sure and keep all the prospective buyers up-to-date."

"Of course." In the meantime, William would do some searching on his own. All the more reason he needed Callum's skill with law.

Mr. Jorgensen offered over another document.

This one William had in his care, but he considered its duplicate. Every detail placed before him—from the way a man moved his eyes, to the tone of his voice, to the scars on his hands—held information. Valuable information that William committed to memory. He did the same with women, though they were much harder to unravel. Like Miss Lizbeth Bennet who called this plot of land home.

An encounter William had completely muddled.

With the map spread out now, William leaned forward. He'd

long since memorized the borders of the adjacent farms, which planted more questions. Now to harvest the answers.

"Tell me of this plot here." William touched the edge of a fifteen-acre farm just west of company lines.

"Leased to a family by the name of Webb."

"And the reason?"

Jorgensen cast him a curious glance. As though he'd never encountered a man who had so many questions about a matter.

William saw such inquiries as windows into truth, and he knew just how far to push. There was a reason his coffers brimmed full and his capital spread across the nation. He'd never made a poor business deal in all of his twenty-eight years. No reason to begin now.

"Webb works as a sheep farmer. Going on twenty years now. Leases the land from the mine in exchange for easy access to the railway."

Interesting. "And this one? McMahon?"

"Owned the land outright since the war so it no longer needs to be part of the dispute. It's protected ground. Mass graves—soldiers and the like."

"Of course." May the poor souls rest in peace. William intended to inquire next about the Hatcher farm, but slid that inquiry aside, opting for one that he was most curious about. "And how about this one?"

Jorgensen squinted as he angled the map. "Ah, the Bennets. They're quite the conundrum. Bennet was the geologist who helped survey New River from the start. We'd been friends for years. In exchange for his work with establishing the mine, he claimed a twenty-acre plot that was out of the way."

"That was his payment?"

Jorgensen nodded.

"And what of coal?"

"He claimed there were no minerals of value there."

"And you believed him?"

"I believe an honest man."

"What of the deed?" William adjusted the flatcap still balanced on his knee.

Jorgensen hesitated. "That's the catch. It was done on a handshake."

"A handshake."

"This was years ago. His daughters were but babies. Some not even born. An under-the-table deal, if you will. One that we both benefited from, and fairly so. Bennet even supplied several mules to the mine's stables in years past when his horse and donkey were both alive. All business settled in good faith."

William's mind whirled with what this meant.

Jorgensen continued. "For these families—Webb, Hatcher, and Bennet, the land is all in question for different reasons. For us to arrange the sale of the mine, we'll need to resolve each of these cases. Ways to tidy up the deed before this company can be sold."

That meant time.

After Jorgensen explained more about each tenant, he finished with the last of all. "You may've already come to this conclusion, but the Bennets don't have a single boy to work the mine. Other families have sons that become breaker boys. But not Bennet, poor soul."

William had first encountered the lives of breaker boys when he'd visited the Pocahontas mine a few years prior. There he'd witnessed lads as young as twelve picking apart coal and rock with bare hands, skipping school and the chance of an education. A dismal trade. All for the pay of a few cents a day and calloused fingers. When they came of age, they'd become nippers, spraggers, and colliers.

"And the girls?" William knew he'd nearly danced with one the night before. It was hard to forget the combination of bright, perceptive eyes and a homemade dress.

"The Bennets get by. They run a farmstand and once sold the mules I mentioned. Only a few left now and the Bennets are holdin' on to them." Jorgensen turned a fountain pen in his fingertips. Dried ink stained his skin. "Should you wish to acquire the New River Coal Company, we could strike arrangements with Mr. Bennet and the other residents to settle the matter. As mentioned, some of the lawyers are already looking into it. Bennet's a good man, so I'm hopeful the arrangement will be settled well."

"And what if coal dwells on his land?"

"It would require a new survey. I doubt it, but if there was coal, the land's too far from the hoist house to tunnel. A new shaft would be needed. That means a new hoist house. Roads. Lodging for miners. The place would show no memory of its former life. Woods and brambles wiped clean."

Made over into a wasteland and Mr. Bennet made out to be a liar. William leaned back in his chair. It was a responsibility that didn't sit well with him, but he'd come here on business, not to forge friendships. He could always bring in another geologist but the arrangements would take time as well. He'd need to think on all of this.

Jorgensen hesitated as though expecting a coal baron to disregard one lowly geologist. Not wanting to rush the discussion or begin bartering with such questions unanswered, William stood and shook the man's hand. "How does a week sound? Will you be ready for me to visit the tunnels by then?"

"That would suffice."

Then they could discuss how much this mine was worth.

As well as the issue with the local residents, including the geologist that William intended to better understand. To make out his character and intentions. That alone could tip the scales in this process.

With one more handshake, William exited into the sunlight, spotting Callum striding his way. William ran his thumb over his mouth, recalling the few words he'd shared with Lizbeth Bennet. In particular—any information it might give him to this case. The lass had alluded to her home life, and while he'd filed the details carefully away as with any conversation, the file wasn't so easily retrieved. Had it been distraction?

Had he felt something more for her than idle curiosity?

Impossible.

William blinked, sidelining the thought.

"Where are we going in such a hurry?" Callum asked as they fell into step.

"I need to wire Pennsylvania to bring in recruits. Borrow some of the employees from my Chess Creek mine." William wouldn't know for sure what state this mine's construction was in until he ventured into its reaches. Sense said to bring in the regiment: engineers and laborers that operated under state-of-the-art methods. His men were crucial in moments like these. Worry circled his mind, so he boxed it in with logic. He wouldn't allow any of his future investments to be a penny on a train track. Reckless and wasteful.

William would send the wire today and summon a crew.

"What did you think of her? Jayne Bennet?" Callum blurted as they walked.

Yet another conversation that included the name Bennet. "The fair-haired one?"

"Yes. She danced two rounds with me, and then yet another. Was she not one of the loveliest creatures you've ever seen?"

William considered the memory. It would do his friend no good if he fueled this infatuation. "She was pretty," he said glumly. "But she smiled too much."

Callum rolled his eyes and droned on, most of which William ignored. It would only lead his friend further into danger if this flame of romance were fanned. The man came from a family with both name and fortune. To consider compromising that on affections rooted in a place that no one had ever heard of was unthinkable.

"My advice?" William clipped. "When our business is settled, put thought of New River—and its inhabitants—far behind you."

"And that's coming from you. Didn't we come here for you to purchase real estate?"

"Which is a business deal. I have no plans of moving in." That's even if he won the bid.

When it came to the Bennets' land and the wealth that might dwell beneath the surface, if the mine were purchased by anyone but him, it would likely all have to go. The fields, the gardens, the house. William was still undecided as to what he would do if the mine and land became his. There were hard decisions to be made in the coming days. Though everything he'd just said had been directed at his comrade, William had some work to do of his own. Stamped in his mind were several sentiments that he needed to dispose of surrounding a young woman. The sooner he cut ties with a certain smile and the scent of chamomile, the better.

7

"I still can't believe he's comin' for a visit. In all our years, why come now?" Kneeling on the top bunk in her nightgown, Lizbeth shook open a blanket. It billowed back to the mattress. A softened sun glittered through the window, catching the twirl of dust and the memory of girlish laughter that this bedroom had always held. But there was no laughter today with the news that Pa's cousin, Reverend Coburn, planned to descend on their home.

Jayne tidied her own bed. "I've a hunch he may be comin' in search of a wife. He's not married and Pa said Reverend Coburn's written several times in the last year asking after us girls. Our ages, how we've been gettin' on." She fluffed a down pillow, flashing bare ankles beneath her nightgown as she turned. "Somethin's stirrin' but I don't know what. Pa's unsettled. As though there's business with this farm that he can't seem to reckon with."

"He's been so quiet lately. Hardly finishes his supper now." Lizbeth smoothed a wrinkle in her quilt. "As for this Reverend Coburn, I only know he's a preacher. What else did the letter say?"

"I didn't get a good glimpse but he wrote about the church he oversees in Pennsylvania and his cottage there."

"Nothing else?"

"That's all I could see."

Lizbeth scrunched up her nose. "I think you're right. He's a single man with a good living so he must be lookin' for a wife."

"I'd say the odds are pretty good."

"Even though none of us have ever met the man?"

Jayne sat on the edge of her bed. "I don't know if we can afford to be so romantic. Especially if change is coming."

Lizbeth perched on a ladder rung between the two bunks. Another room next door held three more bunks for the younger girls. By the sound of it, just starting to stir.

A chill seeped through the closed window. "So, Pa must be getting worried." Lizbeth rubbed the sleeves of her nightgown.

Things were about to change. It was just a matter of how.

From below, Ma called up to them. "Coal bin's empty, girls. Jayne, Lizzy!"

Lizbeth and Jayne exchanged glances.

"We've got wood aplenty," Ma called again. "But it makes me feel better when the coal's on hand and I'd like you older girls to do it this time."

"Yes, ma'am," Jayne called back.

"I'll speak to Pa." Lizbeth climbed down the ladder and tossed the final pillow into place.

"We both can." Jayne pulled dried flowers from a Mason jar on the windowsill. Pressing open the window, she tossed the spent blooms away. A fresh breeze drifted in. "Come along. Ma needs us." Opening the bottom dresser drawer where they kept their dingiest work dresses, she handed one to Lizbeth, along with a handkerchief for her hair.

Was it true? That they couldn't afford to be romantic?

The days ahead looked cloudier than the sky outside. As unclear as the sampler she stitched on each evening. Softly colored threads beginning to form the shapes of trees, birds, and flowers, yet a view that remained incomplete.

"There ought to be a man in New River who's caught your eye." Lizbeth pulled the old work dress over her shift, hoping to get the truth out of her sister. Even if it took a little bait. "There's hardworking miners and colliers around that would make good family men."

Jayne's cheeks, pale as the dawn, colored with a telling sunrise as she fastened her buttons. "Well, there might be one."

"Is it Mr. Brydolf? The man you danced with?" Lizbeth pushed her own buttons into place.

Her sister began to speak then started for the door. "There's no sense in us goin' on about this. Come on. We've got coal to pick." She tipped her head for Lizbeth to follow.

Sighing, Lizbeth trailed her from the bedroom and out to the barn, where she pulled the wheelbarrow from its side and kicked cobwebs loose. She pushed it along until she met Jayne in the middle of the dirt lane.

Jayne lowered tin buckets into place. "Off we go."

To their left, a ruckus of birdsong rang from the woods and a chipmunk scampered across dried leaves. To their right spread the farm's pastureland. Lizbeth tried to keep her feet and heart light on the familiar walk over the footbridge, which spanned the narrowest part of the river, and into town. In front of the line of row houses, women milled about in their tiny yards, scrubbing laundry or tending to children. Toddlers babbled through the picket fences and young mothers looked weary and worn. Some of the very young women that Lizbeth had once gone to school with.

"This way," Jayne called, veering them both away from the hustle and bustle toward the back yardage of the mine.

Shielding her eyes, Lizbeth spotted the culm banks in the distance, and soon, they reached the sprawling banks, all spread along the horizon like sand piles on the seashore. Except these banks rose dozens of feet in the air to block the sun and were made of crushed rock as far as the eye could see. Not to mention the fact that Lizbeth had never actually seen a seashore. Instead, this was a graveyard of rock that glittered with faint traces of coal. Ore that the miners had missed, or that was too small to be bothered with. While gleaning from the banks violated mine policy, residents were rarely turned away by the watchmen who themselves knew what it was to do without. For while there was coal aplenty for the rest of the world, those who lived in New River were too poor to afford it.

Rocks clattered underfoot and Lizbeth slowed the wheelbarrow. "Let's go up this way, to give the other women space." She pointed to a group of neighbors filling gunnysacks. Stumbling higher up the bank, Lizbeth knelt and picked through the fragments of rock for coal.

Bucket in hand, Jayne knelt a few paces away.

Lizbeth gathered her findings into a pail. Culling the banks was slow, tedious work that stained her hands as black as her boots. Jayne stayed no cleaner, but since she hummed as they worked, it helped to pass the time, and soon, Lizbeth had tipped two bucketfuls into the wheelbarrow.

Jayne wound her way through a series of hymns until the wheelbarrow brimmed full and the dinner bell rang at the mine. Lizbeth's stomach tightened with the same strain as the rain clouds brooding over the road toward home.

A rising wind stirred her hair and with thought of tea and bread beckoning, she brushed her hands free of dust, if not blackness. "Ready?"

"Just a few more here." Jayne culled more nubs of black ore from the bank then sat back on her heels. The front of her apron was blackened and anyone would think it ruined had Ma not taught them the best way to scrub coal from clothing.

Rocks clattered beneath their boots as they carefully picked their way back down.

"I'll take the first stretch." Jayne gripped the wheelbarrow handles and teetered it into motion.

The pathway stretched just wide enough for them to walk side by side, so Lizbeth helped balance the burden as it creaked forward. A long, laughing trek as they worked to keep their load righted and their hearts light back down the lane. Soon, it was just them and the woods. Quiet and familiar. Yet at the sound of voices in the distance, Lizbeth listened, finally spotting movement up the road. Two men strode around the corner, dressed in suits. Tall, handsome, and out of place on the country lane.

"Oh, heavens," Lizbeth muttered.

Jayne blanched at the sight of Mr. Drake and Mr. Brydolf. "Oh, Lizzy." Plunking down the wheelbarrow, she swiped at the front of her dress. "The mortification. We look like mice from the dustbin."

Had they whiskers, those would surely be dirty too. Lizbeth pressed the back of her hand to her forehead, trying to brush away any loose tendrils that didn't want to stay snug under her kerchief. "Nonsense. Who are they to judge us? We're hardworking women and have had a *very* fruitful morning."

Jayne swiped again at her blackened hands. "A little too fruitful." She glanced around as though to disappear into the shrubs lining the roadside. A smudge of black dusted the tip of her nose. Lizbeth swiped it clean, then braced the wheelbarrow handles and pressed forward with all the dignity she could muster.

Jayne trailed a step behind, scrubbing gritty palms on her apron. She looked about to cry and Lizbeth regretted her earlier attempt to draw the words from Jayne earlier. That this man—Mr. Brydolf—was the one Jayne had been too shy to speak of. Mr. Brydolf was the man who had caught Jayne's eye. The pair of them *had* danced most of the night in the hoist barn. But now, Jayne's gown was far from her finest, no fiddle struck a sweetened tune, and the air wasn't softened by a dozen lanterns. This was real life—in broad daylight—and they were two girls from coal country.

When the men slowed, Mr. Brydolf's blue-eyed gaze took in Jayne's appearance from the blonde curls that peeked out from beneath her own handkerchief to her dusty boots.

His smile was kind. "Afternoon, ladies. Where are you off to? I do believe rain may be coming."

Mr. Drake pulled off his flatcap.

Lizbeth and Jayne exchanged glances. "Homeward," Lizbeth answered for them both.

Was Mr. Brydolf really trying to make small talk with them? And with such jolly manners? There wasn't a soul in twenty miles who didn't know what they were doing, but these men surveyed the scene before them with marked curiosity.

Well, Mr. Brydolf seemed curious. His friend looked hassled.

"I suppose rain might be on the way." Jayne noted the sky, her expression easing some.

Mr. Brydolf's attention dropped to their load. "Coal. Have you ladies pushed this all the way from the mine?"

Lizbeth glimpsed Mr. Drake's stony face. If he were the owner of the mine one day, this would be cause for trouble. Gleaning coal from the banks was illegal in most mining towns, and while Mr. Jorgensen turned a blind eye about the castoffs being taken home, this man might not be as generous. Nor any of the other coal barons who'd come here to strike a fortune on Mr. Jorgensen's urge to retire.

"Oh, we—we don't mind," Jayne stammered.

Lizbeth forced her voice to stay bright. "Not at all. The walk does us good."

Mr. Brydolf surveyed the way they'd come, to where they were going, then skyward where clouds darkened. "About how far do you have left to go?"

"A mile," Mr. Drake said stiffly, his voice so guarded it seemed intended only for his friend as he slid his wool cap back on.

Lizbeth's brow furrowed. How did he know the location of their farm?

Perhaps the other coal barons did as well. Was that what had Pa worried? That they were all under scrutiny?

"Yes, about a mile." Wind stirred Jayne's hair.

Mr. Brydolf was already pulling off his fawn-colored coat. "Might we—might we walk with you a ways?"

Mr. Drake gave a slight shake of his head, which his friend ignored.

Before Lizbeth could question further, Mr. Brydolf shoved back crisp white shirtsleeves. He offered Jayne his coat then gripped the blackened handles of the barrow with clean but able-looking hands.

Gulping, Jayne silently beseeched Lizbeth, who nodded an assurance.

"Just over the ridge." Jayne wiped her hands on the cleanest corner of her apron before draping his coat over her arm.

"Then lead the way." Mr. Brydolf smiled and together, he and Jayne fell in step.

Lizbeth hung back. While she couldn't be sure of Mr. Brydolf's purpose, she wouldn't let this moment go to waste. Could this be Jayne's chance at an all-new life? It was risky to hope, but even if these men would be gone soon to their world of riches, these encounters with Mr. Brydolf would at least be a bright memory for Jayne to carry with her. Lizbeth would hope for more—but secret-like for now.

Mr. Drake walked in silence at Lizbeth's side, his shoes clean beside her own. He took off his own coat and draped it over his arm. "I'll carry it myself."

"That's very kind of you," she said, a little too dryly.

As Mr. Drake rolled his eyes, the reaction seemed directed at himself. "I'm sorry. Callum has such happy manners and I can't seem to match them."

At the display of vulnerability, Lizbeth replied in kind. "I feel the same about Jayne. She's a true angel."

Mr. Drake's focus didn't drift to Jayne as happened with most men who soaked in the sight of her beauty. Instead, it lingered only on Lizbeth. "You are close in age?"

"She's older by two years. She's always been a big help to Ma."

"And you?"

"I do my best to help them both and then somehow the day always finds me outdoors." Realizing she'd already told him about that, she tried to think of something new. "Anything in the beauty of the day. New River has some lovely land by way of the forest for walks as well." She waved a hand at the trees around them. Perhaps this stroll might be her favorite part of the day.

That's if Mr. Drake didn't ruin it.

He made a silent study of her as though to find out what stories her blackened hem and streaked apron might tell. He was a curious fellow, this man who seemed to seek answers to unspoken questions. Divulging little, absorbing much.

"What else is it that interests you?" he asked. The question much like the one he'd asked her the night of the dance. She blushed at the memory of how she'd told Hattie that his hand had gripped her waist then and how his eyes were the color of gingerbread.

Unable to look at his face now, Lizbeth caught an early raindrop in her hand. "Well, I'd like to figure out a way to help my Pa. Our farm."

He nodded thoughtfully. "And your stitching?"

He remembered? "I'm trying to put more focus on my sampler. This week I finished the word *therefore*."

To her surprise, he smiled a little at her candor. "That *is* noteworthy."

Her cheeks warmed. "I should have made more progress but I got caught up in some reading," she added.

"Have you a library here?"

"There's a place to borrow books but it costs two pennies each time, so we only read the books we have at home. A few that Pa keeps on hand. I've already read them a dozen times. Jayne as well."

"You have to pay to borrow books here?"

"It's a coal town, Mr. Drake. Folks 'round here have to pay for everything."

"*Except* to gather coal."

Her feet slowed, but she wouldn't be intimidated. "That's free so long as you don't get caught." She cast him a sideways glance.

"Which you seem to have a knack for."

"Comes with years of practice." She fought the urge to prickle at his candor and instead turned the tables on him. "How do you like to fill the day, Mr. Drake?"

"Well, apart from business, I keep horses. I also enjoy reading, Miss Bennet. I have a small library on the Pemberley."

"You do?" She couldn't imagine a library on a train.

"It's just a few bookshelves, really. But it holds all the ones I like to keep with me."

The wonder of it. How she longed to see such a sight, though she'd never admit it. "Sounds very nice."

Where most people might extend an invitation, Mr. Drake remained silent. He adjusted his snug collar and his arm ever so slightly brushed hers.

They each took a step apart.

"And how long do you plan on staying here in New River?" she asked.

"At least a few weeks more."

Then this was her chance to unravel more of the unknowns. The mysteries that rose up from the ground beneath them. "The other businessmen who arrived, they all own coal mines?" She recalled the sight of them at the dance, all done up in suits and fancy hats and looking dreadfully out of place just as this man beside her had.

He nodded. "Most from up north."

"And one will try to buy the mine."

Another nod. "That's the way of it."

"All so Mr. Jorgensen can retire."

"Correct."

"Will it get . . . Will it be . . ." She struggled to put her worries into words. Especially now that they'd stopped walking and the eyes she'd been so bent on describing to Hattie suddenly searched her own.

Had they been standing this close all the while?

She blinked to center her thoughts back on the land and stepped on again. "It would seem right if one of the residents could own the company instead. Someone who knows the lay of the land. Its history. Its people." Someone even like her pa. "But no one in New River could afford it."

His gaze—pensive and somehow gentle—stayed focused on her face. "I understand what you're saying. In all fairness, I'm a little puzzled myself about the details of the matter. There are a few questions of my own to sort out still. From what I understand, the other bidders in the running are doing the same."

Bidders in the running. All for the only place she and so many others had ever called home. She thought of the young women she'd seen at the row housing. The children and babies. This decision would affect so many. Even for the boys in the mine who worked the same hours as a man. What hope might there also be for them in this?

Lizbeth found her voice again. "Which is why these proceedings will take several weeks?"

"That's the way I'm seeing it."

She peered up at him. Was it wise to try and better understand this man? Could doing so help her family? "May I ask how many coal companies you own already?"

"Two. If I purchase New River, it would be three." His eyes tightened a little as though regretting how calculating that sounded.

Before she could piece together more questions, the farm came into view from its low little valley surrounded by trees of birch and ash. Their haven and home.

Did these men understand what that was like?

Ahead, Jayne and Mr. Brydolf slowed, their exchange warm and lively. Mr. Brydolf laughed and Jayne's eyes were bright as fireflies. He took his coat from her, and held it open for her to wear. When she tried to refuse, he insisted.

Time yet to beat the storm if they hurried. Ma would no doubt be watching the road for them and want Lizbeth and Jayne to help take in the laundry on the line. They'd likely get soaked in the process, but no sense delaying these men any further from their return.

Lizbeth turned to Mr. Drake. "Good afternoon."

"And to you as well," he said quietly. He tipped his head and before his friend could even join him, he took a few strides back up the lane and waited.

Lizbeth couldn't tell if it was frustration or the gravity of the world on his shoulders, but she rationed all her curiosity for Jayne. As for Mr. Drake's hopes and fears? Lizbeth cared only in regard to what it meant for New River and her home. Beyond that? She had absolutely no need to understand more of the man behind the suit.

8

"You did *what*?" The wedge of hickory rattled against the grate as William added it to the fireplace.

"I suggested to Jayne that she and her sisters might borrow a few books from your library." Callum finished hanging up another sock in front of the fireplace. It dripped onto the brick hearth.

Just outside the Pemberley's windows, a cargo train lumbered by, clattering and swaying with dozens of boxcars. "I don't think that's a good idea," William said over the ruckus.

"Nonsense. You own more than enough books here, and it seemed like a nice gesture. Besides, I'd be glad for the chance to see Jayne again."

William stared at his friend as broken light from the moving boxcars shifted over his face. "So that's why you gave away your coat."

"She looked cold and it felt . . . right. I don't have as much time here as you do. I've got business back in Vermont and clients sending me telegrams nearly every other day. I have to return home before too long, and there's something about her. It's hard to describe, William."

"I just don't think getting too friendly will help anyone."

"You say that like it's a bad thing."

"Because I'm thinking more clearly than you are."

"I'm not so sure about that." Callum ran a hand through damp hair. He wore a dry set of clothes now. His wet shirt hung near the fireplace along with everything else they'd been wearing when the downpour hit an hour ago. "I saw the way you were captivated by Jayne's sister. I've never seen you so engrossed in a conversation with a woman before. Her name is Lizbeth, right?"

"That hardly matters."

"She's quite pretty, wouldn't you say?"

William was not about to be baited. "I've seen plenty of pretty women."

"So, you're admitting that she is."

"Her face was merely brightened by the exercise. Besides, didn't you see what they were doing?"

"Bringing home coal for their family."

"That they didn't pay for. Which is against the law."

"That's up to the mine owner."

"And the state they were in?"

Callum smiled. "A sight to behold."

Outside the window, boxcars still rolled past with the roar of steel wheels on tracks, adding fuel to William's agitation as he rose. "Are you honestly entertaining the idea of continuing a connection with Jayne Bennet?"

Finally, the last boxcar went by, and the rattle faded into the distance.

Callum sank into a chair. His gaze lingered on the flames that crackled brighter now. "Possibly. Your Aunt Catherine might be breathing down your neck to marry well, but I don't have to answer to anyone as you do."

William sank into the other chair, seated now beneath the very woman's stony portrait—the gilt frame reflecting Aunt Catherine's wealth and the stiff facade only a hint at the sternness with which she had helped raise him.

With silence settled, he searched for a fresh argument, noting the black streaks on Callum's dripping shirt. "Your clothes are ruined."

"My clothes are perfect. Did you see how lovely she was?"

"Lizbeth?"

"Jayne. And I thought you hadn't noticed."

William rolled his eyes. This was madness. On his own desk sat maps of the Bennets' beloved farm. A farm that William might soon own. His friend was losing his mind. William meant to avoid doing the same. Yes, Lizbeth was pretty. She was considerate and quick-witted and while he was occasionally struck by both, what tempered it—what *sobered* him—were the names on the map of the New River Coal Company. He knew better than to mix business with pleasure. The name Bennet would never be written on his heart. Not if it were to be written in his pocketbook.

Callum stared out to the distant countryside, the view open and wild again. All wet now beneath the autumn rain. "She's the most beautiful creature I've ever beheld."

William wouldn't argue with that. Even covered in coal dust Jayne was lovely.

Both sisters were.

Callum continued. "When I speak, she's sincerely listening. She's gentle and grounded. She doesn't lean into me or flutter her lashes. There's a genuineness about her that is indescribable."

William understood more than he wanted to admit. There was something about these sisters from New River that made for a stark contrast from the women they'd encountered in high society. But this could never be. Attraction—no matter how fleeting—could not be cultivated and fed. They were worlds apart. Two women who would become a distant memory and no more.

Time to dissuade his friend before this ended in disaster. "What you interpret as gentle may in fact be disinterest."

Callum squinted. "How do you mean?"

"Jayne Bennet says so little that I've heard. Perhaps she's merely being polite. Maybe she has different ideas for her life . . . or is already spoken for. Could it be that her modesty is due to her own uncertainty? It could be her way of not wanting to encourage affection."

Callum stared into the flames. When he finally spoke, William couldn't help but note the sound of pain in his voice. "Maybe I have been reading too much into it. When have we *ever* encountered an eligible and willing female who didn't make her interest remarkably obvious?"

"Correct." William recalled many encounters when both he and his friend had to practically pry loose from a woman's gloved grip. Rarely had they been in polite society without every eligible woman in the room casting them a sideways glance. It seemed women made it quite plain when they were interested. But Jayne was different. Likely thought differently about it too. He didn't see how a woman could hold the kind of interest that might lead to matrimony, if it weren't obvious. The sooner Callum understood that, the better off he would be. The last thing they needed to add to this trip to Virginia was heartache.

"Ma, can you warm the kettle?" Lizbeth called down the stairs. "I'm worried Jayne's caught cold from the rain."

"Oh dear." The kettle clattered into place. "I'll fetch your pa's canteen and we can fill it to warm her feet."

Lizbeth knelt beside the lower bunk where Jayne had fallen asleep shortly after their return. "I'll fetch her an extra blanket." Once the thunderclouds opened, she and Jayne had sent the men back on their way, insisting the weather would only worsen and that they were nearly home. Callum Brydolf had agreed to turn back only when Jayne accepted his coat which now lay folded in the washbasin, wet and wilted.

Lizbeth and Jayne had pushed the wheelbarrow the final stretch and been soaked by the time they finally parked it beneath the eaves. They'd changed into dry nightgowns right away, despite it only being the afternoon. Jayne was shivering while she crawled beneath her quilt, promising to only close her eyes for a moment.

Lizbeth touched the back of her hand to Jayne's rosy cheek then grabbed her needlepoint. She slipped downstairs to find her family gathered around the glow of the fire. Pa read from his paper.

Lizbeth kissed the top of his head. "Any news from the day, Pa?" She settled into a cushioned chair that had seen better days. "Anything new at the mine?" Still waiting for the kettle to steam, she plunged her needle into the linen, curious to learn more about what William Drake had alluded to.

"*New* at the mine?" Kit's brows furrowed. Her plaid nightgown fit a size too small, allowing her ankles to peek out as she sat on the hearth beside Lacey. A tin of paper dolls sat between them, dressed in fine gowns that the girls fashioned from scraps of paper as though to relive the glories of the dance from the week before.

"I mean about its sale," Lizbeth clarified.

"My . . ." Lacey's teasing voice spliced the room. "Someone's curious about these new coal barons in town."

Lizbeth ignored her.

"I've heard that one of the businessmen has already made an offer," Pa began.

"So soon?"

"I imagine some are anxious to get home. Not every man feels at ease here in New River. It's a different territory than they're used to."

"But not Mr. Drake," Maryanne said. "Not after what you told us."

"Right." Pa glanced to Lizbeth again. "I was just telling the girls that William Drake intends to head down into the mine himself and examine every level."

"Every level?" Ma cried. "A man like him?"

Kit and Lacey danced their paper dolls in a waltz.

"At least one of them ain't so eager to leave." Lacey winked.

Ignoring her sister's prodding, Lizbeth angled her needle back into the linen of her sampler, placing the final stitch into the letter *n*. Next would be a *d* . . . fitting considering the subject of conversation.

"Time'll tell." Pa bent to add another piece of wood to the hearth. "We've got our work cut out for us. I've had most of the bidders askin' for samples of ore, and Mr. Jorgensen has arranged for me to make sure they're properly weighed and stamped. Work I'm glad for, mind you." The fire popped and crackled, casting light on Pa's hands—marked and lined from years of scouring the earth. "It won't be long now until it's all decided. I've heard that Mr. Drake has miners coming from Pennsylvania who work for him. He set up enough space in the row housing for six men."

"Six more men!" Maryanne swiveled around in her chair.

Lacey squealed in glee.

"That's all I know, but we'll soon find out more when they arrive," Pa said.

"I heard a rumor at school today that there's gonna be a bidding war. Just think." Lacey squinted as she held a paper doll up to the light. "All these rich fellas tryin' to outbid each other! I wonder how much the mine'll sell for." She sighed. "If only we could see that much money."

Ma sat down with her knitting. "That's all none of your nevermind."

"We saw Mr. Drake walkin' today on the road." Lizbeth pulled her thread tight and reached for the tiny pair of scissors she kept in her stitching tin.

"Is that what took you so long?" Kit folded the hem on a paper gown with her fingertips.

"I thought we made rather good time. Mr. Brydolf even pushed the wheelbarrow."

"And Mr. Drake?" Kit scrunched up her nose.

"Never mind about that. I think Mr. Brydolf's taken a shine to Jayne. He talked and talked with her the whole way home."

"That so?" Ma's face brightened quicker than her needles could knit. "Tell us more, Lizzy."

Lizbeth threaded her needle with another shade of hand-dyed thread. This one a cheery green that she'd boiled with carrot tops to borrow the pretty color. "We met them on the road as we were walkin' back from the culm banks. Oh, we looked a sight." She slid the first stitch into the letter *d*. The sampler would soon read, *The night is far spent, the day is at hand.* Still only halfway finished. "Wait—" Lizbeth lowered her work. "Is that why you sent us to fetch coal today?"

Ma pursed her lips together.

"You knew Mr. Brydolf would be on the road!"

"I might've heard that they'd meet with Mr. Jorgensen in the morning and would be off to walk the length of the road to see more of the land. I was in the post office visitin' with the postmaster's wife. So, I hurried on home, thinkin' that if Jayne passed by, he might see her again and she him."

Lizbeth gaped. "But Jayne might've caught cold!"

"She'll fare just fine. Your water's boilin'."

Lizbeth rose.

"Take a hot canteen up to her to warm her feet, and she'll be as good as new in a few days." Ma nodded, looking pleased.

"Well," Pa teased, "if Jayne does die, it'll be a comfort to know that it was in pursuit of such a favorable match."

"Now, now, the lot of you!" Ma chided. "People do not *die of colds*. Least of all Jayne. She's a proper mountain girl. And so very beautiful. Mark my words, Mr. Brydolf'll be in love with her by the end of the week. That's if I have anythin' to say about it."

9

Lizbeth marched up the steps of the company store. Kit and Lacey trailed her like leaves on the breeze, as vibrant as the ones she shook from her cotton hem in the doorway. As the younger girls brushed their own hems clean, they chattered about the new miners coming into town, summoned by Mr. Drake himself.

"Don't you suppose it's time to talk about somethin' else?" Lizbeth opened the door to the building that was spiced with molasses and shaving soap.

"They're comin' all the way from Pennsylvania! To think!" Lacey threaded her arm through Kit's. "Those men'll have seen an awful lot of the world."

"Could you imagine?" Kit skirted around an orange pumpkin on the porch, all speckled in warts. "The stories they must have to tell."

"I hope they come before Pa's cousin, Reverend Coburn. If I'm gonna set my sights on a stranger, I'd rather he be a miner than a minister." Lacey flounced the ends of her rag curls as she entered the store.

Lizbeth shook her head.

"Can we look at the ribbons, Lizzy?" Kit asked.

"Look, but Ma's made us promise not to touch. I've only got the two nickels for Jayne's medicine." The coins were nestled against the small book of poems she'd brought along for the walk home.

Lacey and Kit flitted to a corner where spools of ribbons stood out among the more sensible notions of miners' uniforms and bolts of plain denim. The ribbons were priced well beyond their reach so like most of the young women in town, the Bennet girls made do by dyeing strips of cloth with black walnut and goldenrod.

Lizbeth's boots echoed hollow across the wooden floor as she approached the counter where the shopkeeper stood in his striped apron, cleaning out a metal scale beside jars of red and white candy.

"Good day, Lizzy. How can I help you?"

"I've come for some cough syrup. For my sister."

"We have two kinds." At a glass cabinet, he pulled out a pair of small bottles. "One from the Montgomery Ward catalog—their own brand. The other is Cook's Cough Cure."

"Is there a difference in price?"

He held up the cheapest bottle. "This one is twenty cents. The other, thirty."

Ma hadn't given her enough. "I'll take the lesser. Please put it on our account."

Warily, the shop owner opened the ledger to the name of Bennet and angled it Lizbeth's way. *Overdue.* She gulped. "Pa has had extra work this week. And I can give you this to help." She slid the nickels over and looked at the shop owner.

Compassion filled the man's eyes and after a soft nod, he noted the price of the medicine then deducted the ten cents. An expense they couldn't afford but with Jayne sleeping restlessly back home, it needed to be done.

"All yours." The shopkeeper wrapped the bottle in brown paper, tied it with a string, and handed it over. "Anythin' else that I can help you with?"

She had to ignore the way the glass jars of candy caught her eye and the dress patterns in the open catalog begged for new yards of pretty calico. Lizbeth smoothed the front of her skirt, as reliable and plain as the wool sweater she wore. "That will be all, thank you." She turned to gather her sisters. "Come along or the pair of you'll be late for school."

"Why do we still have to go to school?" Kit pouted as they pushed their way back outside into the autumn chill.

"Because you're scarcely seventeen and you've got a few things yet to learn. Be glad for it. Soon enough, you'll have laundry and babies to keep you busy all the day long."

"You say it so horribly, Lizzy. Do you think so ill of marriage?" Lacey flounced down the steps, swinging her schoolbooks.

"Not at all. In fact, I hope to marry one day, when the right man comes along."

Lacey waved the idea away. "I'll marry as soon as I'm able." Lacey skipped across the road with Kit then spun the pair of them around.

Lizbeth nearly called out to her when a voice stopped her in her tracks.

"Oh, a word with you, Miss Lizzy!"

She turned on the shop porch to see the postmaster waving from his open window near the depot. Lizbeth clutched her small package and aimed that way.

At the post office window, the man leaned an arm on the ledge. "A letter just came in for your pa. Mind bringin' it to him?"

"Of course." She accepted the ivory envelope, which, by the feel of it, held a single sheet of paper. "Thank you, sir."

It wasn't until she turned away that she let herself glimpse the return address.

Rev. Coburn, Stroudsburg, Pennsylvania.

Lizbeth angled the letter from Pa's young cousin up to the light. She squinted but it was no use. Instead, she nestled the envelope safely in her skirt pocket and, with the medicine snug in the other, started for home.

The schoolhouse bell clanged. Girls ran that way. Most of the boys were already at the mine, working in the breaker. Lizbeth glanced that direction with a heavy heart. In part because the boys went to work so young, and in part because neither she nor her sisters had such a chance to lighten their father's load.

Lizbeth skirted around a puddle as she crossed the road away from town. She aimed for the lane that led toward the bridge of the New River. She stepped over the first set of train tracks as she often did. Never had she given the depot and its winding thread of rails much notice except for the noise that steamed into town each afternoon as trains came and went, hauling supplies to the mine or coal to distant lands. But today, her focus lifted to the shiny train car parked just beyond a row of cargo freight.

Mr. Drake's living quarters stood shiny and proud beneath the morning sun, nearly whispering of the wonders the car had seen as it rested on the third track. The side nearest her boasted glittering windows. Even the observation dome glinted in the light as though it, too, were polished and buffed with care. How she longed to reach out and touch it. Or to know what sights lingered aboard. Lizbeth nibbled her bottom lip as she continued to pass by. Bright yellow filigree trimmed the car like the delicate borders of a fancy postcard. At its very top, *THE PEMBERLEY* shimmered in gold paint as ornate as a king's crown.

At the car's tail end the word *Private* was emblazoned beside the door. A declaration that this was no ordinary residence and that few belonged within.

Lizbeth turned away. "No need to linger," she whispered to herself.

None whatsoever. For at her back stood a railway car that spoke of the kind of life she wouldn't ever understand and in her pocket dwelled a letter from Pa's young cousin whose visit, if Jayne's suspicions were true and this man were on the lookout for a wife, could stamp their futures forever.

10

"Do you think there's a way to separate the local land from the sale of the mine?" Leaning back in his chair, William loosened his tie.

Eyebrows lifting in surprise, Callum pushed his breakfast plate away. "Did I just hear you right?"

"You disagree?"

Callum's mouth quirked up in a smile. "Not in the least. I'm just pleased that you think the same."

"I've given this land dispute a great deal of thought. It just doesn't sit right with me to go about it any other way." There was other land to be had and his coffers were full. He wouldn't be able to sleep at night if he knowingly took land from tenants who desperately needed it. And it was time to acknowledge that to his closest friend and the lawyer who might be able to fix this mess.

"I've been thinking a lot about it as well and I believe I should return to Vermont," Callum added. "Once I pull together my findings, I need to run them past several colleagues to see if there are any missing loopholes and to seek their advice on next steps. There are also some law books back home that will be of help. For now,

I've visited the county clerk and will keep digging as far as possible into land laws for the state of Virginia. My goal is to find a way to separate the Bennets' farm from the mine deed. Of course, the others as well. I'm gathering this is what you're suggesting."

"Yes." It had been the right thing all along.

"It's complicated. The properties don't fall under the Homestead Act since they weren't government land, which would have served the tenants well. Same with Mr. Bennet. So now I'm focusing on tax laws. But I need to verify some facts for the state specifically. There may be a loophole yet."

"At what point in this process did you want my opinion?"

Callum chuckled. "I already knew your opinion. That you'd do the right thing. You're too moral not to."

William lifted the coffeepot and filled his cup. "Then tell me what you're thinking."

"More importantly, here's what I believe Jorgensen is thinking: that of all the investors who've descended on this place, you're the only one who isn't going to swipe land right out from beneath the innocent bystanders. You have a conscience—he can see that—which is why you haven't made an offer yet. And why he's allowed you the time needed to decide what that will be. I think Jorgensen cares enough about this town and its people to stall on this land matter if *you* give him the right reason to."

"You honestly think he can see all that?"

"I do. You have a soul. And a growing soft spot for this community, if I'm not mistaken. You won't be able to live with yourself if you approach this business deal as callously as the others will. Or as detached as your aunt would expect. As for me, in order to help, I'll need to leave soon."

"You'd be willing to leave this young woman behind who's captured your attention?"

Eyes down, Callum fingered the edge of his cup. "If it could help her situation in the long run? Yes. Would you be agreed to that?"

"That's very noble of you." William didn't want to see the Bennets evicted either.

He never wanted to make a profit at the cost of another person's livelihood. But his own growing sentiments for a different young woman were harder to express. Instead, he'd keep them under lock and key as usual. William let his focus land on the mail that rested on the edge of the table, which the porter had just retrieved earlier that morning.

"Good news or bad?" Callum asked.

William moved the top correspondence marked from Pennsylvania, which he'd already slit open and read. "It's a response from the Chess Creek mine. The engineers and miners I've summoned are ready to travel." William examined the letter again, confirming that they'd be here by week's end.

"The timing couldn't be better. Now you'll be ready to explore the mine's secrets with the help of the experts. Decide if this company is worth its weight in gold."

"Or coal." William noted Callum's own stack of mail. "What word from Vermont?"

Callum fingered the letters. "A few messages from clients along with a rather detailed list of woes and worries from my sister."

William couldn't read through the sheet of paper but saw enough black ink to promise that the delicate Miss Brydolf had plenty to say.

Callum offered over the letter. "She's intrigued by a number of things that I wrote to her about these hills. She's also reminding me of my duties back home. And your own."

William expected nothing less from Callum's sister, who had

an air of correctness about her. One who upheld her opinion over those of others, William included. She often gravitated toward him or found cause to take his arm. Despite their years of running in the same social circles, he had no interest in pursuing his best friend's sister. Year after year, he tried to make that obvious, but Miss Brydolf was not easily dissuaded.

"I think she sounds jealous," Callum added.

"What would she have to be jealous of?" William dropped his gaze to penmanship that had taken nearly ten years at a prestigious finishing school to perfect. The very same finishing school that William's own sister now attended. But unlike sixteen-year-old Anna, Miss Brydolf was cunning and shrewd in a way that kept William wary. When Callum hesitated, William's unease grew. "What did you say to her?"

"I might have written about the dance last week." Callum took his fine time with serving himself more ham.

"I trust you said that the cider was flavorful and the music fine but nothing more."

Callum cleared his throat. "I relayed how pleasant the company was around here."

William rolled his eyes. "You shouldn't have done that. I didn't even engage."

"You *did* socialize though. Spoke in several complete sentences to one young woman in particular."

"You couldn't hear me."

"Yes, but I could see. And William Drake actually seemed *intrigued* by a pretty lady for the first time that I can ever recall."

"What do you mean by that?"

With a chuckle, Callum leaned forward. "That for once in your life, you didn't look at a woman with hooded indignation. Instead, you seemed . . . unnerved."

"Is that how you described it to your sister?"

Callum chuckled. "I thought it noteworthy. You know how she pines after you. I figured it was high time for her to catch on to the fact that she's wasting her time."

"I politely agree and thank you for the support. But now I'll never hear the end of it. And it's hardly worth the trouble since neither of us will be in New River for long." There were no ties worth making. At least not of the heart.

He could do right by the Bennets but that didn't mean he needed to become attached.

William set the letter aside, along with Miss Brydolf's wishes for them to return in *due haste* and her annoyance at how they could *possibly find a town in the middle of nowhere so entertaining.*

William cut into a thick slice of ham. That was enough talk about female forces. "A fine meal," he muttered.

"Excellent. And this place sure builds up the appetite." Callum added cream to his coffee.

"That it does."

"And I hear the pantry aboard is well stocked with enough delicacies to last weeks at a time."

"Correct." The head cook even travelled with him on business trips, lodging in the berth right next to the porter's at the servants' end of the car. "And what are you getting at?"

"I'm just saying that with a washroom and an icebox along with a galley outfitted with dinnerware for a five-course meal, you could entertain should you wish."

"I see." William considered Callum again and wondered if they should extend such an invitation to the Bennet daughter whom Callum was so taken with. It would give the man an opportunity to converse with her once more before leaving. Caution reared its head. Would that only bolster the growing infatuation that was more dangerous for his friend than anything else? William sidelined the unspoken offer, feeling guilty as he did.

He rose. "I'll be right back." Leaving the dining room with its polished tables, cushioned sofas, and glass observation dome, William retreated down the narrow hallway. He passed the door to his private room with its double bed and hickory wardrobe, and then the second stateroom with enough bunks for four guests, including Callum. At the end of the car, light from the train's second observation dome drew him forward as he entered his study. His favorite room.

Here beneath the glass dome, he stood surrounded by sky, books, and windows. A peaceful place to sit whenever rolling hills and foaming oceans passed by. Vistas that spoke to his soul more than any cityscape ever could.

His study offered views from three angles, including the end of the car where the rear balcony lent space for fresh air on a summer's night. Today, William paced the length of the room, stopping just shy of his bookcase. Maybe he could give Callum a book for Jayne Bennet to borrow. Even as the thought awoke, William caught sight of someone just beyond the windows. A young woman crossed the tracks, holding tight to a small package. Her hair was unbound, trailing down to the middle of her back. No bonnet or hat in sight. Just brown locks beneath sunlight.

William stilled.

Lizbeth. Sister to the young woman who was consuming all of Callum's focus. Lizbeth gripped a book in both hands, holding it close to her nose as though to see both the text and the road. She turned a page, walked several more paces and closed the cover. The end perhaps? She slipped the small text into a skirt pocket that may have cradled her beloved books many times by the way she'd described her reading habits. Her long skirt flounced around her laced-up boots, and the sweater she wore boasted as many autumn shades as the trees in the distance.

She was following the road that wound through town, away from the store and post office, when a wagon passed in the opposite direction. A man and woman shared the seat, along with a babe in arms who lifted a knitted blanket into the air. The blanket caught the wind and tumbled to the road.

As the wagon slowed, William stood watching.

Lizbeth reached for the blanket. Her skirt spun as she did, every fold and ripple catching the light along with her loose hair. Wind worked to pull the blanket farther down the road, but Lizbeth was quicker. A bright and willful determination. Despite himself, William felt his chest tighten at the sight of her. She shook off the dust with care then held up the offering to the babe. The child took it with flapping, happy hands. A quaint picture of family. Of kindness and generosity.

Of a thoughtful act between one neighbor and another.

That's what people did in these parts.

Ever studious of the world around him, William was more absorbed than he wanted to admit. More enchanted than his aunt would ever condone, William took the chance to gaze at Lizbeth. Any longer and he may as well kiss his inheritance goodbye. While he could handle the loss, it could cost him in other, unexpected ways.

Lizbeth turned back along her way. While William could never hear the sound over the din of the depot, he wondered if she wasn't humming as she walked, so light were her steps. What he could hear, though, was the memory of Lizbeth's voice in his mind as she described her love of reading. How the books in this mining town cost two pennies to borrow. Pennies she lacked.

As for him?

William stepped back and surveyed the shelves. They held over a hundred novels and nearly as many informational texts on every subject from botany to politics. Books he'd collected on his travels, many bought in New York and Boston. From prestigious to entertaining. Titles these young women would never hold for they weren't the type to be sold in any Montgomery Ward catalog. He even had an entire collection of poetry that offered sunlight to the soul. The type of sunlight that he sensed the lass on the lane would be enchanted with.

William caught his reflection in the window. His face was stony, but his heart was coming to life. Cracks formed around the edges of his resolve and for the first time, he didn't know how to patch over the vulnerability.

Breaking his stance at the window, he returned to the dining room, tugged his napkin from the chair, and sat before dropping it on his knee. Callum's glance seemed more puzzled than pointed. He said nothing as William poured all his focus onto the meal.

"Go ahead and invite them again," William finally mumbled. A kindness as seemed right. "We might as well be neighborly like those around us."

Callum looked surprised. "The Bennets?"

Aunt Catherine somehow glared down from her portrait now. William angled his shoulder to ignore the stare. "To see the library. I know I put a damper on your earlier offer and I apologize. They'd be welcome to come and borrow any books they like."

"Name the day!"

"Next Saturday? If you'll still be here."

"I'll leave just after." Vulnerability ran rampant in Callum's gaze. God spare the poor chap, but William didn't know how to hinder his comrade anymore. In fact, he was starting to understand Callum's lapse in judgement. "Make the offer as warm as you like."

He gave what he knew was a rare smile. "I'll have Cook set out a pot of tea. To be polite."

Callum rose, nearly tipping his chair back. "Wonderful! Shall I go tell them now?"

"Perhaps not exactly now." William waited as Callum sat again. "You'll see them soon at church." He placed the suggestion gently to guide his friend. When it came to matters of the heart, Callum wore every hope on his sleeve, displayed for the world to see.

As for William's heart, it remained buried so deep that even *he* didn't understand its contents.

The invitation was simply for a few amiable neighbors and an afternoon of books. That's if they even chose to linger. There could be no harm in that. The Bennets might very well wish to leave shortly after pleasantries and a sip or two of Earl Grey with a few novels in hand. An outcome that would serve them all for the best.

Neighborly, he reminded himself. As was polite.

There'd be time enough to sort out any other notions that flitted through his mind—and worse, his heart. Time enough to sort through those sensations when the residents of Bennet Hollow were a forgotten memory and William could set his world in order once again. For today, he meant to offer his friend a chance. At happiness? William didn't know, but only a fool could discount the appreciation in the man's countenance.

Sitting again, Callum gulped. "Right. Church. I'll have to think of what to say."

"Yes, you do that." Reaching around the side of the table, William gave a firm pat to his shoulder. "For the both of us."

11

"Hold on tight, girls. Steepest part's comin' up," Pa called over his shoulder.

Lizbeth held tight to the shuddering sideboard. Wooden wheels rattled over the bridge then wound upward. The wagon ambled past a whitewashed gate and into the churchyard. *The church on the hill*, it was fondly called. Curious since the quaint white chapel with its peaked roof and small bell tower was the only one to be found in New River.

Lizbeth watched as the wagon jostled and bumped over the familiar road, rattling her sisters' bonnets and the laces on their freshly polished shoes. Just ahead, the church building stood out bright and cheerful against the foggy dawn. Beside her, Lacey yawned, Maryanne perused the pages of the hymnal she always borrowed, and Jayne's cheeks flushed healthy again. Callum Brydolf's fine coat—as smooth and golden as a fawn's hide—sat folded in her lap, all clean and pressed with care.

Their loyal mule, Sassafras, pulled the wagon into the churchyard. Lizbeth might have helped Pa hitch her beloved Eugene to the wagon each Sunday, but the poor fellow got skittish when in town, so back at the farm he stayed. A peaceful way to pass a Sunday morning with his affinity for watching the big, clear sky.

Pa parked beside other wagons and climbed down, then helped Ma down from the wagon seat. "Here, girls." One by one, he helped each of them climb over the sideboard.

"I don't mind hoppin' out on my own." Kit eased one foot onto the wagon wheel.

"Nonsense." Ma smoothed her silver-speckled bun. "With Reverend Coburn scheduled to arrive this week, you may as well practice behaving ladylike."

Lizbeth allowed her pa to help her down. Just beyond, the churchyard stirred with miners and their families—each soul knowing all the others by name and all the tombstones by heart. Folks who had celebrated weddings and funerals and everything in between together in this very churchyard. Today, instead of pick-axes and dynamite, men held the hands of their wives, age-old Bibles, and infants on strong arms.

"Are my curls wiltin'?" Lacey fretted as she scuttled ahead of Lizbeth and Jayne.

Jayne set Mr. Brydolf's coat on the pew beside her. "Your hair looks perfect."

Lacey straightened the cloth ribbon that held her rag-made curls over one shoulder. With her own hair bound up in a ribbon, Lizbeth tidied a loose tendril as she trailed her sisters up the front steps. They each shook the minister's hand then squeezed into the same pew they always shared. Here, she could keep sight of the pulpit along with a generous view of rolling hills through the window as both were good for the soul.

"How I loathe a two-hour sermon." Lacey smoothed her skirt.

"Try to think of it as a time to be grounded amid life's uncertainties," Maryanne said.

Lizbeth settled back between Lacey and Jayne. "Well said." She tilted her face toward the sun's glow where it brightened the windows.

Lacey rolled her eyes.

From her end of the pew, Ma's sideways glance silenced them all. Lizbeth closed her eyes, scarcely noticing the creak of a door opening. Nor the hushed wave of murmurs building once it closed. Little whispers filtered through the surrounding pews followed by the quiet thud of two pairs of boots down the center aisle. The footsteps halted beside them.

A soft, heady cologne made her think of the woods on a sunny day. Lizbeth dared a peek ahead and met with the sight of Mr. Drake's back as he entered the pew in front of her.

He squared his stance, adjusted his black coat, and sat. After tugging off a woolen cap, he righted his cropped brown hair then bowed his head along with the rest of the congregation. Startled, Lizbeth closed her eyes and listened to the minister beseech the Lord for guidance and grace.

She braved one more peek, this time at Jayne who, with flushed cheeks, may have also spared a glance to Mr. Brydolf, sitting at Mr. Drake's side. Lizbeth squeezed her sister's fingertips. Jayne squeezed back. Perhaps they shared the prayer between them for Jayne's guidance. A beseeching that Lizbeth trusted the minister would add an *amen* to. A blessing to guide Jayne and her heart.

Lizbeth stood for the first hymn and with Mr. Drake in front of her, she had to strain to see the pulpit now.

Jayne lifted a tattered hymnal from the seat and after she fumbled several times to find hymn 119, Lizbeth offered to take the book from her. The song was "Abide with Me," which they knew well, so often had they sung it within these walls. Lizbeth clutched the hymnal to her simple blouse and sang. Jayne followed suit. Around them, half the town struggled to read, so most men sang by heart, along with their wives beside them.

In front of them, Mr. Drake's shoulders were still as the landscape, but Mr. Brydolf belted out the words in a curious pitch. He sang happily and Lizbeth, among others, cast him a quizzical glance. Folks around seemed pleased to have such noble gentlemen in their numbers. Not because it signified any meaning in status, but because the newcomers felt comfortable enough to join them on this glad morning.

Through song and Scripture, the service swept on and Lizbeth savored the rest and refreshment, surprised when her gaze kept returning to the steely posture of Mr. Drake in front of her. She cleared her throat. Too many times, perhaps, based on the knowing smile Jayne slid her. Lizbeth ignored it. When the service came to an end, people rose and spilled down the aisle, and Mr. Brydolf turned toward Jayne.

"Good day, Miss Bennet."

Jayne dipped her head. "And to you, Mr. Brydolf. I wanted to thank you again for sharing your coat the other day." She offered it back to him. "It was awfully kind."

He smiled. "You're welcome to borrow it again anytime you feel the least bit chilled."

Lizbeth bit back her own smile.

Mr. Drake angled their way and offered a polite nod to them both, his gaze scarcely crossing Lizbeth's in passing. "Good morning."

"And to you as well," Lizbeth answered stiffly.

Mr. Brydolf chatted easily with Jayne, inquiring about the age of the building and what the weather was often like this time of year. As he spoke, the warmth in his countenance said more than his humble queries did. It was as though he hoped Jayne might see as well and understand that he spoke to her not out of necessity but out of desire.

Lizbeth's cheeks warmed at the thought.

Nearby, Mr. Drake dropped his gaze to the floor, raised it to the pointed ceiling, then returned it to Mr. Brydolf, who chatted on. He didn't look as annoyed as usual which was a curiosity in itself. Suddenly, his attention landed on Lizbeth's hands, then rose to her face where he focused on her for several steady seconds. He finally blinked away.

Perhaps she shouldn't tarry. Lizbeth rose. "If you'll excuse me. A good day to you gentlemen. Jayne, take your time. I'll be in the churchyard."

Once outside, Lizbeth wove through the crowd, finally reaching the aged fence where a soft breeze hit her face. The mine dwelled so far in the distance that its shape could scarcely be seen. Instead, miles upon miles of open pasture and rolling woodlands stretched far and wide. Lizbeth breathed in deeply.

Hattie scurried over, wool shoulder cape stirring in the breeze. "Lizzy! I rushed over soon as I could get away from the neighbor women's questions. *Why Hattie Jorgensen, how have you not settled down with a man of your own yet?* and the like." Hattie placed a hand to her narrow cheek. "But none of that now. I hear you got all kinds of news."

"If you count Pa's cousin comin' soon, then yes."

"Well, don't let those ladies know or they'll be pesterin' you from dawn 'til dusk." Hattie put extra vinegar in her voice to match that of a busybody. *"Now Lizbeth Bennet, when do you plan on settlin' down?"*

Lizbeth had no time to respond.

"And oh!" Hattie touched her sleeve. "Tell me about Jayne and this new fella. How long do you think he'll be stayin'? I can't help but notice how taken he is with her. Ma mentioned how long he's been talkin' with her. They're both still inside and they'll soon be the last ones left!"

Lizbeth glanced that way again.

"But what of this Reverend Coburn? Ma made mention of him as well."

"The minister? He's comin' to stay for a few weeks. Pa hasn't told me much else. I don't know where he's gonna sleep—we have no spare rooms, and Pa wants to make him feel welcome. The younger girls might bunk with Jayne and me to free up a room."

"That's what I want to tell you." Hattie led Lizbeth to walk the length of the churchyard with her. "Your folks spoke with mine and your fancy minister is gonna stay in our spare bedroom while he's here. My folks don't mind a smidge. The man ain't yet married, I hear."

Lizbeth propped hands to hips. "How do you know so much?"

"You know how much our mas talk." Hattie winked. "And as for Jayne, she's so pretty, it's no wonder she's caught Mr. Brydolf's eye. I've hardly travelled in my life, but it's hard to imagine a young woman as fine as your sister."

"It's more than that." Lizbeth cast a glance over her shoulder. "Jayne's graceful and good. I think that's what's caught the man's attention as well."

"I daresay you're right." Hattie's own face, narrow and angled, didn't speak of beauty, but her heart was kind and her mind sharp. "But oh, that other man, Mr. Drake." Hattie pulled her cape snugger. "I've never seen such a glum man—"

Kit and Lacey raced over to them in a flurry of skirts and trailing bonnets.

"Lizzy! Have you heard?" Lacey panted. Despite the chill of the morning, her cheeks blossomed pink. "Mr. Brydolf's invited us all to see the private train car and its library. Shelves and shelves of books I hear. They've asked us to tea as well! This coming Saturday!"

Lizbeth's brow furrowed. "Are you sure you heard right?"

"It was just Jayne who told us. Mr. Brydolf invited her himself, along with us as well. It sounds like even Mr. Drake'll be there which'll be rather dismal but we won't complain about that. He is terribly handsome. And so very rich! Did you see his fine posture? Like a brick tower." Lacey fanned her face. "Though I reckon he's like that all the time."

"And here I thought you were bored," Lizbeth countered.

Rising onto the toes of her boots, Lacey searched the crowded churchyard. "Jayne's somewhere 'round here lookin' for you to explain it all."

"Well, I'll be." Hattie's close-set eyes looked as stunned as Lizbeth felt.

"I don't even know what to say," Lizbeth admitted. To think of it. They were invited to Mr. Drake's beautiful train in less than a week's time? "The library?"

"Oh, Lizzy, how can you care that much about books?" Lacey threw up both hands. "It's that big old train that you oughta be pinin' after. How splendid it'll be inside. We'll have to wear our best dresses." Lacey fussed with the limp folds of her plain brown skirt. "How I wish I had somethin' nicer than this old Sunday dress."

Hattie touched Lacey's arm. "Your dress is perfect."

Lacey smirked, easily swayed by vanity. "Well, I s'pose it don't matter all that much. What a time it'll be!" She skipped off, pulling Kit with her.

"And what of you, Lizzy?" Hattie's question lay gently placed. "Will you join them?"

"I suppose I will. It'd be a rare chance to see so many books.

And I do think that Mr. Brydolf sat in front of Jayne on purpose." She smiled.

Even as she said the words, Mr. Drake and Mr. Brydolf passed by, deep in conversation. For the briefest of moments, Mr. Drake's focus caught hold of Lizbeth's own. Just as quick, he made a study of his boots as he walked.

Lizbeth shrugged, never quite sure what to make of the quiet man.

The air once again held the scent of woodlands and spice from his skin. A reminder of wealth so grand, she couldn't begin to fathom it.

"Yes, books." Hattie smirked. "Which I hear belong to *Mr. Drake*. That sure is awful generous of him."

Lizbeth shooed the implications away. "None of that now."

Hattie chuckled as they faced the view of the distant pastures again. "To think, Lizzy. You're gonna get to see all the books he's collected over the years."

"Indeed. I'll look forward to it," she said sternly.

Which only made Hattie smile more. "Oh, Lizzy. Just make peace with the notion."

"What notion?"

"That Mr. Brydolf might not be the only man who chose his seat on purpose."

Lizbeth rolled her eyes.

"See it this way now. The pair of you nearly danced, have strolled together twice already, and enjoy a number of the same things."

Heat warmed her cheeks. "What does that mean?"

Hattie grinned. "It means that one of these days, you might actually have to like William Drake."

12

William descended the train car steps at the same pulse as the engine whistle's blasts. He turned up his coat collar, stuffed both hands in his pockets, and crossed from his own stretch of track in the rail yard to the platform of the depot. In the distance, the whistle pierced the afternoon again with its melancholy cry. The four o'clock train approached right on time.

Mon. Oct. 27 1904

William,

It's hard to imagine a coal town this engaging.

Do tell of its wonders.

Your Aunt Catherine grows impatient as we both await word. Write soon.

Caroline B.

William bent the missive in half. Confounded woman. How mortifying that every stationmaster between here and home had been obligated to translate that. Letter by *blessed* letter via Morse code at the cost of a man's daily wage. All because a wealthy heiress was bored and not keen on the local color. William pocketed the slips of folded paper. He'd deliver the third to his comrade, though if it was also from Miss Brydolf, he doubted its importance.

Needing to clear his head, William retreated to the edge of the platform. Puffs of smoke billowed above the distant tree line, then with a final cry skyward, a black steam engine lumbered into view. The engine chugged, belching smoke. A sight he saw daily, but on this sunny Monday, this train's arrival held the power to advance his own business endeavors.

William anticipated at least three of his finest engineers and just as many miners. A small regiment of men as intelligent as they were capable. He'd already secured lodging for them in the row housing where they'd settle until the assessments were finished.

The train ground to a stop.

As steam cleared, the first man disembarked, tall and wiry and wearing a clergyman's hat and collar. William shifted his focus past the stranger, but the minister approached. He consulted a sheet of paper and examined their surroundings.

"Excuse me, sir. Are you familiar with New River?" the minister asked.

"Only somewhat."

"Do you know of a family by the name of Bennet? Distant relations that I've come to visit. I'm in need of the way."

William sized up the gentleman from his bent hat to his shoes, which looked cinched painfully tight. The minister gripped a suitcase that had seen better days but appeared sturdy enough to hold more than a week's worth of clothing.

William shook the man's hand and kept his response short. "That way. Up the lane about a mile." He tried to recall what he'd seen of the property the day he and Callum had ventured that direction with its fair inhabitants. "The farm slopes to the west. It's hard to miss."

"Wonderful. In truth, my lodgings are stationed here in town, but it seems polite to go there first for proper introductions." The stranger pressed his heels together like a tin soldier. "And are you . . . are you acquainted personally with the Bennets? I understand they're quite established in the community. We are long since connected though I've never journeyed here." The minister sized up the town that spread before them. From a pot of flowers nearby, he plucked a single bloom and, fumbling it, finally crammed the wilting stem into the lapel of his black coat. "I've been working on memorizing the names of all of the Miss Bennets, which was a rather satisfying way to pass the journey."

Strangely agitated, William shifted his stance. "Only recently acquainted and I cannot account for many of their names myself." Hopefully that would put an end to the discussion. What was the man getting at? William didn't like being questioned about the family that occupied his own attention more and more. All for reasons he didn't know how to admit.

"Hmm." The minister seemed pleased by William's indifference. He touched the brim of his hat. "Much obliged. I suppose I'll go on foot."

William nodded, still unsettled by the notion of a gentleman caller shadowing Lizbeth and Jayne's doorstep. William decided he wouldn't mention it to Callum just yet. No need to worry his friend. William forced his attention back to the passenger car where a group of men in suits disembarked. The engineers. Their briefcases may well have been packed with degrees from Harvard, Salem, and the like. If there was so much as a piece of timber missing in the mine, they'd spot it. William paid them handsomely in return.

Just behind the engineers came three miners, the sharpest men in his employment. With humbler origins, they weren't learned men. Not in books at least. Instead they understood how to navigate tunnels in near blackness and crawl through even the narrowest passageways. They were roughened men from birth and while William thought no less of them for it, there was one in particular he disliked seeing. A miner he'd known for far too long.

Still, he needed each man he'd summoned, so he would have to ensure this whole venture turned out well. While William meant to remain beside this crew every step of the way, he was grateful for the experts on hand.

Trying to employ the warmth Callum had taught him, William greeted each man with a handshake. "Welcome to New River. And thank you for coming. Allow me to show you to your quarters for the next few weeks."

They all doffed their hats and thanked him but before William could take two steps, the stationmaster waved a striped arm out the window. "Another message for you, Mr. Drake! This'un's marked *urgent*." Though the statement itself should have filled William with intensity, the stationmaster's expression was so lackluster that William took his time retrieving the telegram.

"Thank you." He slid a coin across the counter for the man's efforts. "And I apologize."

The man pulled off his cap and ran a hand over sweat-dampened hair. "Not to worry, sir. Just doin' my job, as I can see you are."

William considered the message from Brydolf's sister and crammed it in his pocket.

"So many in an hour," the stationmaster declared. "I ain't ever seen anythin' like it." He slid his cap on again.

"Nor have I." William's neck heated as he thanked the man again then turned back to the head engineer, ignoring Miss Brydolf's costly message to *overcome your fascination with nowheresville and hurry home to civilized living.*

As they walked, William lifted his gaze to the hills where close to a hundred men and boys toiled within their depths. All carving out a life that stemmed from survival, family, and determination. Growing inside him was that same purpose and integrity. To live a life he could truly be proud of.

As they crossed in front of the depot, the lead engineer walked at his side. “We’re eager to see the insides of this mine of yours.”

William considered that statement. Would this mine truly be his? Would he soon hold the keys to the lives of this town? A notion more sobering than enticing. “As am I, my good man. As am I.”

13

Surrounded by their humble orchard, Lizbeth dropped another wilted apple into the bucket. All around, wind stirred apple leaves and dried stems rattled in the breeze. As the last of the harvest, the fruit was sound enough for cider but today held a different purpose. While her younger sisters sold produce to the mining families each week, helping those who needed it most as Pa and Ma always instructed, Lizbeth's own calling felt closer to home somehow. This earth.

On winter nights, she would help her sisters knit socks and fingerless mittens for the boys who worked the mine, but right now, something more was calling to her.

She closed her eyes, imagining the dozens of mules who dwelled deep in the mine. Some that had been born on their farm, that she had helped raise. Animals who would never again know the clearness of day or taste the sweetness of a harvest. Her skin prickled with sorrow as there was so little to be done for them. So little in the way of hope.

Once again fresh to mind was the day she'd walked side by side with Pa, helping him lead a young pair of mules to the mine, not knowing that the money Pa needed for their family came at the cost of the mules' livelihood. That in exchange for dollars, the animals would be sent hundreds of feet down into a working grave.

Lizbeth swallowed hard. Blinking back into the daylight, she searched for another apple.

She never would have known differently as a child, but now, could there be another way for them to get through the leanness of the years? She understood only a fraction of what weight rested on Pa's shoulders then and now. She had only a small understanding of the burden he had to raise five daughters in these hills and not a single son who could bring home a day's wage by picking coal. Pa had to wrestle with the constant urge—the desperation—to make ends meet. He had done what he'd needed to do, then and now.

While Pa assured her that the underground stables stayed lit and the mules never wanted for company, Lizbeth could only imagine the dismal conditions since the livestock never got to leave the mine at the end of the day like the workers did. She wished there was more she could do, so for now, whenever they had apples or carrots to spare, she grated them into a bowl of oats, mixed up a batter with golden molasses, and baked sweet squares which Pa delivered to the mine stables on her behalf.

He always returned home to tell how the mules nibbled away the treats and how it put a new light in their eyes, so Lizbeth made a tray as often as possible without sending Ma into a state. Fall brought with it a chance to use a few unwanted apples so Lizbeth dropped another worm-holed fruit into the pail.

When it came to the yearning to look after this farm and all who called it home, she couldn't shake the memory of the mules that had once lived here alongside Eugene and Sassafras. They were pit ponies now. No longer Pa's and most certainly not hers. But thanks to the willingness of Mr. Jorgensen, she was still allowed to send them a little comfort now and again. A quest she only wished could be more.

Even as she bent for another apple, an idea struck. Lizbeth straightened and pushed the back of her hand against her cheek. Could she possibly?

Might Pa allow her to take the treats down to the mules herself?

That could be a way she might see their needs met more often without burdening Pa or the other miners. It could be a special task she managed. Each week even. And once down there, she could spend time with the mules. Brush their coats, bring them comfort, and the mine wouldn't see it as idle time since she wouldn't be on the payroll. The apple clattered softly into the pail. Doubt trickled coolly down her flushed cheeks. Entering the mine was unheard of for a girl. Only men were allowed into the shafts. Even the breaker boys stayed on the surface sorting ore until they were old enough to don a headlamp and a chestful of courage.

Courage she had. Permission . . . she needed to get.

The apples that grew on the edge of the woods here were theirs to keep so she and her sisters would soon be hard at work picking, pressing, and baking to preserve the year's harvest. Kit, Lacey, and Maryanne would sell the rest of the apples on the roadside for next to nothing. Just yesterday, the girls were there at the Bennet farmstand with the last of the summer squash, bush beans, and collards. Whatever hadn't been sold by suppertime was brought home for the root cellar. Since Lizbeth only took the fruit that would go to waste, Ma might allow her . . .

After freeing a stray leaf from her hair, which was capped with a kerchief, Lizbeth slid the tin pail with a scrape nearer to the tree. Kneeling, she added several more apples to the bucket, reaching the brim. The faint chill that stirred her unbound hair reminded her that winter approached at a brisk walk, if not a frosty trot.

"Lizzy!" A voice stretched across the glen.

Lizbeth braced a hand on her bucket for balance and turned.

Shielding her eyes from the brightness of day, she finally spotted Lacey dashing across the upper meadow toward the grove. "Lizzy, you gotta come!"

Lizbeth rose. "Whatever's the matter?"

Lacey slowed, panting. "Pa's cousin—the Reverend Coburn he's been tellin' us about—just came in on the four o'clock. He's here!"

"At the house?"

"We met him on the stoop just a moment ago. All of us were tryin' to bring the laundry in from the line and Ma was heatin' the irons. Why do you look so surprised? It's the day we expected him!"

She'd completely forgotten. "I thought he was set to stay with the Jorgensens. They have a spare room for him."

"Well, don't you suppose he meant to come over and say hello first? How is it that you're the only one who doesn't seem to care?"

"I care." Lizbeth picked up her pail.

"Then get a hustle on." Lacey shook out her plain brown skirt as though it would help a delicate pattern blossom where there were only garden-stained stripes. "Ma realized you were up here and she's frettin' somethin' awful. She sent me to come 'n' fetch you. She's all a fuss, Lizzy. Seems Reverend Coburn has asked after you twice already."

Lizbeth wrinkled her nose, not liking the feeling that she and her sisters were glass jars on the shelf and he a man searching for a drink of water.

Still, she couldn't very well linger on this hillside with a bucket of wormy apples. "I'm finished." Lizbeth led the way back, glad for the bucket's weight and how it slowed her pace.

Lacey dragged her feet dramatically. "Can't you walk any faster?"

"Only if you help me."

Lacey shrugged and skipped along, humming a silly tune.

Lizbeth rolled her eyes and followed the girl. Just beyond spread the farmyard where Sassafras and Eugene grazed in the pasture. Smoke trickled from the farmhouse chimney. The house appeared just as it always did, but as they came nearer, Lizbeth caught the chatter of conversation within and a haughty, formal voice that could belong only to the stranger.

Lacey pushed past the front door and Lizbeth lugged the bucket indoors. There in the front room sat her sisters, Ma and Pa, and a man in a dark hat. No one rose, save the man. His narrow leather shoes creaked on the floorboards as he shifted them.

Lizbeth straightened the kerchief on her hair.

"Miss Lizbeth Bennet, I presume." His mouth curved in a strained smile. His bony nose shadowed a thin mouth that was speckled with an uneven mustache.

Lizbeth nudged her bucket aside with the scrape of tin on wood. "Yes, sir. Pleased to meet you."

Pa rose. "Reverend Coburn, this is our second eldest, Lizbeth."

"Whatever are you up to, Lizzy?" Ma's eyes narrowed disapprovingly as she glimpsed the contents of the bucket from her chair.

"Oh, just a little somethin' for the mine stock." Lizbeth searched for support, relieved to catch Jayne's blue gaze and its quiet warmth.

Reverend Coburn swiped a long finger beneath his nose.

"I'll just wash up." She toted the bucket to the other side of the table and tucked it well out of the way lest Ma find another use for the badly bruised harvest. Lizbeth wet her hands at the basin and scrubbed them with soap.

"Lizzy, Reverend Coburn is a minister from Stroudsburg in Pennsylvania. He was just tellin' us of his train trip. Two days, was it?" Ma inquired.

After rinsing and drying her hands, Lizbeth found an empty chair beside Jayne. Inwardly, she sized up this newcomer. His clothes were clean and his posture straight.

He stared stiffly ahead, addressing no one in particular. "Oh yes. It was quite comfortable. The accommodations aboard were simple, but it isn't anything I'm not accustomed to. I've a modest living and consider myself a man of humble origins and desires."

Lacey peeked at Kit, who stifled a giggle. Jayne's hands fidgeted in her lap. Maryanne focused on Reverend Coburn's face with interest, no doubt grateful for fresh conversation that stretched the mind and imagination.

The man went on. "The weather stayed clear, allowing for easy travel. My berth aboard the train was of amiable size and the passengers didn't cause any disruption to my sleeping habits."

Pa arched an eyebrow.

Ma stared blankly at the man as though searching for what to say next.

Lizbeth tried to help. "And what'll your parish do without your presence, Reverend Coburn?"

His gaze found her own but nothing in his eyes sparked to life as he spoke. "Oh, they'll fare just fine with my replacement." The corner of his mouth twitched into a type of smile. She chalked it up to nerves. She herself would feel flustered meeting so many strangers at once.

The kettle whistled from the stove.

"Jayne, would you be so kind?" Ma asked.

Jayne rose. She moved the kettle to the table where empty tin cups waited beside the jar of black tea.

The reverend's focus sidestepped to Jayne and then to the stove itself. "I imagine you heat your house with coal, Mrs. Bennet."

"At times," Ma answered slowly, still sounding befuddled.

"With coal so costly, we burn wood as well. We're grateful for a full coal bin come winter when it's needed most. And do you—do you light your fire with coal?"

Kit released a giggle. Lacey elbowed her.

"I too gather wood from the surrounding forest near my parsonage. It's less costly for my parishioners to provide, as I do live off of their generosity."

"Ah," Ma said softly, then widened her eyes at Lizbeth as though hoping she might know what to say next.

To her relief, Pa spoke instead. "And how long do you plan to stay in the area?"

"Yes," Ma added. "I trust you'll find your room at the Jorgensens' very comfortable. And I hope you'll stay for supper with us as often as you can. My husband can hitch up the wagon whenever needed."

"How very attentive. I've made arrangements to board in New River for two weeks."

"Wonderful," Ma answered as though hearing wedding bells for someone in this room already.

The lines around Pa's eyes tightened.

Jayne carried over a tin cup of tea and served their guest first.

"I look forward to feasting and fellowshipping with all of you during that time." Reverend Coburn took the cup Jayne offered him, his focus on her face. "And I plan to attend the local church each Sunday to understand what day-to-day life is like for the Bennet family. I also believe that life must hold light diversions. I imagine New River has a number of sights to see. I'm an aficionado of architecture." His focus stayed on Jayne as she passed out two more cups. "Have you any favorite locations, Miss Bennet?"

Jayne froze with a cup partway held out. Ma took the offering politely. "Oh, Reverend Coburn," Ma began. "There isn't a whole lot to see around here as far as such things go. But I hope you'll enjoy the hymns on Sunday mornin's as well as the views New River has to offer." She gulped, seeming frazzled on Jayne's behalf.

If Reverend Coburn singled out Jayne, would that send the wrong message to Mr. Brydolf?

No. If the reverend intended to approach Jayne's heart, he would have to wait for Mr. Brydolf, who had bowed to her first.

Ma worked for words, finally answering with, "You'll find Jayne awful busy with her chores this comin' week. But Lizzy is amiable as well and so close in age. I'm sure she'd be glad to show you some of the sights. Perhaps a walk through town would be in order for tomorrow, Lizzy?" Anxiousness stood poised in Ma's gaze, all but insisting Lizbeth agree.

Gulping, Lizzy nodded faintly. "I—I don't see why not."

"Very good. Very good. That does sound agreeable." Reverend Coburn's attention shifted to Lizbeth, where it lingered.

If he was a man seeking that drink of water . . . she feared she knew which glass he'd just chosen.

14

Morning dew settled weighty upon William, much like the gazes of the miners who watched him approach the hoist barn with his men.

"I hear none of the other coal barons have done this," Callum muttered for William's ears alone. "Not a single one."

"I heard the same."

"And that all of them have already cut out of town. Several, I believe, are planning to make offers."

William kept his gaze straight ahead. "But what to make of that?"

Callum's voice dropped lower. "I think they see the bordering farms in question." He glanced around before tilting the worry William's way. "Land that could be ripe for the taking and make the prospect of buying the New River mine even more lucrative."

William forced himself not to gaze in that direction. Not toward the other properties . . . nor the Bennets'. He knew Callum was working on the issue night and day. Scouring documents. Ledgers. Laws. He kept mentioning a tax act from 1894 that could be problematic for the current land residents, but was still so unsure, he kept even William waiting.

All the more reason the man needed to return to Vermont where he had more resources available than what he had on hand.

As for this morning, the sun had yet to crest the mountaintops and the air snapped crisp through William's coat. He tried not to notice as shovels stilled in weathered, chapped hands. Carts creaked to a halt. Eyes hollowed with hard work watched their every step. A crunch of eight sets of boots crossed the yard, William at their helm and Callum taking up the rear. Even mules blinked slowly in their direction. William's chest tightened as the beasts held him and the newcomers in steady gazes. Untrusting. That was the truth of it.

Impossible to blame them.

Whoever purchased the New River mine had the power to change their lives forever. Be that for good or for ill.

These souls didn't know which. Did he? His conscience sagged with the notion of the farmland that remained in question. The four farms that were under so much scrutiny.

Webb. McMahon. Hatcher.

Bennet. This name amid all the others kept him up at night ever since he'd touched a fair woman's fingertips and heard the lilt of her mountain-grown voice speak of woodlands and books and her beloved animals.

A mule angled its weary head away from him and even as he swallowed hard, William dipped a nod to the nearest group of miners, respecting them despite their wariness. To them, he was a wealthy coal baron out to gain a profit from the sweat of their backs. But William intended for this to be an endeavor he could hang his hat on at the end of the day. One he could look upon with peace when he stood before God to give account for his life. That would take courage. For him to find a way to help this place thrive, the undertaking would require money, vision, and commitment.

Most of all, sincerity. He meant to prove that to the people of New River if he took up the position of owner.

He hoped to earn their trust and that would take time.

Today offered one step in that direction as he entered the massive doorway of the hoist barn. The room was sharp with the scent of grease and the familiar dusty, hollow air that wafted up from the depths of the earth. How different it looked now compared to the night of the dance. On strange instinct, he looked across the barn for sight of Lizbeth and where she'd been standing beside the window after they'd parted ways. She'd laughed and smiled with her friend and sisters and he'd simply stood there, struck by the warmth and joy in her face.

"This way." Mr. Jorgensen led William toward the hoist cage. "We'll take this down."

Callum walked in strained silence, his mind seeming a world away. William didn't blame him but he meant to keep his friend attentive and safe. Once the last of his men gathered around, William accepted a small brass head lantern from Mr. Jorgensen.

"You've assembled quite a team," Jorgensen said. If the man was intimidated by the size of the crew summoned today, it didn't show.

"Thank you, sir." William accepted the dented lantern and slid it over his flatcap. By the weight of it, the lantern already held water and carbide, ready to be lit.

To William's right stood three of the best engineers he'd ever commissioned and beyond them stood the trio of skilled miners from his Pennsylvania location. William noted the tallest of the men. Fair-haired and square shouldered, he carried an air of conceit around him—one William knew all too well after the years the man had been in his employment.

"And what of that one?" Jorgensen inquired while a foreman counted off the number of men allowed to enter the cage.

"A miner by name of Westgard." William adjusted his lantern. "He's been in my employment for several years, though I've nearly fired him twice now."

"An interesting business arrangement."

"You could say that, but this venture calls for composure and a willingness to explore in uncertain conditions. Engineers will only venture so far into the earth, sir."

Jorgensen nodded the truth of that. "So, you brought a scout." He studied Westgard's confident air.

"Yes, sir."

Westgard feared nothing. The young laborer knew no boundaries. A cockiness that occasionally stirred up trouble among his comrades back in Pennsylvania. Westgard proved himself brave, yes, but that confidence saddled up with trouble at times.

When it came to bravery, it was possible for a man to bear too much.

"Sounds like a wise decision." Jorgensen adjusted his lamp a final time.

William wished he could have gone about it differently. Have a rabble-rouser like Westgard off his payroll once and for all. Yet the truth of it today? Westgard had a knack for squirreling into places he didn't belong. That would prove an asset once they were below ground.

Jorgensen approached the hoist cage. "My men tell me we can fit ten, but it'll be tight."

"Ready when you are." William followed him into the open lift. Behind them, the dim light of morning brightened the hoist barn. A comfort they were about to lose.

The cage was dim as they entered, the depths below darker still. The platform they stood on creaked with the shifting weight, and a cool, dank draft wafted up from below. William could handle the closeness of the earth. Even the reality that it could come crushing down at any moment. He didn't fancy himself immortal but was content for his fate to be braced by the hand of God. He was prepared for his death when and how it came . . . but he rather liked the sky. Its absence sparked the struggle he reckoned with each and every time he entered a shaft.

"Last one in?" Jorgensen said over the shoulders all crushed together.

"That's the last." William turned to face the closing bar door.

Their carbide lamps were slowly being lit, emanating a pungent gas along with the yellow-white flame that reflected against a small round mirror on each. Mercifully bright but deceptively dangerous. William lit his own.

With the recent introduction of electricity in homes and businesses across the nation, perhaps the time would come when lanterns might harness the same resource. New River had a telegraph machine, but that was powered by an antique battery, he'd noticed. Barely enough to send a pulse of Morse code over the miles, let alone power a house or a coal mine. William had brought electricity to the offices of his Chess Creek mine by tapping into the city lines. But could such a current reach even farther? Achieve all that and beyond in a place as remote as this? He'd recently read of the Pacific Coast Company which employed the use of electricity in their mine tunnels below the ground, so there *were* ways. The ways of the future, but for today, he was in New River, Virginia, with a burning flame strapped to his cap and trusty engineers at his side.

"See y'all on the other side!" The hoist operator cranked the steam engine to life. With a grinding squeal, the hoist drum churned. A clatter followed and the cage lurched.

William braced a palm to the cage door as the slow descent began. Their lives hung in the grip of a single hoisting cable that unfurled at a cautious pace. The four-walled shaft spread just as wide and straight edged as the cage, not more than ten feet in any direction. William had ridden in hotel elevators larger than this. The hoist cage was a world away from those with their gilt trim and shimmering mirrors.

Beyond the cage's slotted sides, earth-and-timber walls crept up to the level of their boots . . . then nibbled at their shins as the ground braced its mouth open to swallow the cage whole. Darkness edged nearer and William squared his chin.

"Just the beginning," a miner muttered.

The engineers all shifted their stance, seeming uneasy.

William blew out a controlled breath. They'd soon be deep in the belly of the earth. A still and silent cavern that was being carved from the inside out, without any say in return. A risky endeavor and one that William didn't take lightly. As he understood it, Jorgensen didn't either.

Overhead, the steam engine hissed and chugged.

"Maybe one day, such a device will be replaced by electricity," William said to the engineer beside him.

The man nodded. "Could be the way of the future."

"Which is exactly why we're here." William tilted his head back to watch the cable unfurl. At first glance, it seemed impossible, but William saved each idea to mull over in the quiet hours of his study. His purpose today wasn't only to ascertain the New River mine's value, but to consider what improvements might lay ahead, and what the price tag would be.

For now, he tried to disregard the fact that daylight was but a memory.

It was just them and their lanterns and who knew how many tunnels below where crews of men were already hard at work.

Beside him, Callum endured the descent with a spine straighter than the wall just inches from their faces. Yet a shift between his feet indicated life. The man cursed tight spaces and while William had insisted he need not come today, Callum hadn't been deterred. William clapped Callum on the shoulder and let his hand fall away.

On William's other side, Westgard muttered under his breath, "This cage is a mite cramped for my liking."

Jaw tight, William kept his focus on the timbers that lined the shaft.

Silence settled. Now and again, beams of light swung as one of their group lifted a head or craned a neck. One man cleared his throat. Another shifted his boots. On the nearest wall, scrawled numbers marked the descent. Twenty feet . . . then forty . . . and then a painstaking sixty.

"Just about there," the foreman said, his cramped voice void of any echo. "We'll stop off at the hundred level. Let you fellas out to poke around. We might have time to make it down to the two-hundred level today as well."

"Appreciate it." William tried to sound natural.

But there was nothing natural about this moment. Tilting back his head, he saw the world above as a mere pinhole of light. The number *90* passed them next and voices sounded from below as they neared their stop. Finally, the wall read *100*.

The cage slowed with an eerie rocking sensation. Callum sucked in through his teeth. William wasn't too keen to be hovering either. Relief spread wider than the cage door as it opened. He made space for Callum to exit first, along with the others.

Only a moment like this could make a dank tunnel inviting, but compared to the openness of the shaft and the chance of plummeting a few more hundred feet, William savored the feel of solid earth beneath his boots again. The tunnel bloomed with a chorus of metal against rock. Cart wheels, pickaxes, and shovels all worked in heavy rhythm. Men labored without slowing as their boss, Mr. Jorgensen, entered their ranks.

The air smelled of earth and sweat. All clotted by the stench of the manure lining the narrow cart tracks. Mules pulled loads of coal ore to be hauled above the surface, sorted by the breaker boys, and sold at a premium to distant towns.

"Would you like us to begin?" one of the engineers asked William.

"Please."

The plan was for them to survey every aspect from the state of the timbers to their age and gauge not only every detail of the mine's construction, but its health. As for the three miners from his Pennsylvania holdings, they picked their way along, greeting workers who labored under a different payroll but the same legacy. William listened as best he could as they traversed the hundred level, taking in every rut and coal vein.

A mule trudged by, straining to pull a cart laden with ore. Its hide lay matted and pockmarked. So different from the carefully carded sheen of his racehorse, Lady Light. The two beasts lived a world apart and it had little to do with breeding. A tunnel loomed a lonely place for even the lowliest of mules who were meant to be above ground, not below. But that was life in coal country. Still, as he watched the mule tread by, led by a young man who should have been in school, he filed the noticing—even the *wondering*—away where he could revisit it again.

William absorbed his every surrounding. Did change cry out to be made here? What developments might he employ? An electric engine for the hoist was just one of them if he could figure out a way to bring in electricity. Methods that could get those who didn't belong here such as boys off the roster of employees. By automating certain practices, it allowed the work to be more amply distributed among grown men instead of bringing children into the mix. The possibilities were endless . . . but what was right? A wise man would consider where the moral call on his heart led. That question among all others circled William's mind as he touched a hand to a bare stretch of wall.

Were he an engineer or even a geologist, he'd evaluate the soundness of the cold earth beneath his fingertips, but instead, William studied the demeanor of the men he'd assembled. His lead engineers were surveying the height of the roof, the width of the tunnels. Crouching down, they noted the age of the track and what material it was made from. William walked each step with them over the course of an hour. And then two. Joining in the conversation as they worked to unravel New River's mysteries.

After discussing the findings of his head engineer at the two-hundred level, William worked his way to where Jorgensen trudged along to the left of the track. With a door blocking the passageway, a young doorman opened it for them. William nodded his thanks to the grimy lad who couldn't have been but fourteen.

"Your man Bennet. Does he still work for you?" William kept his focus on the tunnel lest he blind Jorgensen with his lantern.

"On occasion. He's slowed down some over the years."

Now Mr. Bennet was well set up with both his house and his acreage. Views that made a person want to linger. Or perhaps it was merely the surrounding company. William sidelined the rogue thought along with the unspoken question he wrestled with of late: whatever was he doing longing for another encounter with Lizbeth Bennet?

Even as he chided himself, he nearly tripped over a pile of ore in the dark. If he was so bent on his future right now, he might as well pay attention to pointing his lantern flame in the right direction.

He slowed and crouched as this tunnel narrowed to a halt. "Might we summon Mr. Bennet for our next venture?"

"I don't see why not. But if I may . . ." Jorgensen lowered the flame on his own lantern. "How many times are you thinking to enter the mine?"

"Will you allow me three?" Still crouched down, William braced fingertips to the cool earth to balance himself. Jorgensen didn't need to go along with his request but might be willing if he sensed that the largest offer was yet to be made. "In the meantime, my lawyer, Callum Brydolf, is assessing some of the final details about the property. Once we have everything squared away, I'm hopeful to be able to make an offer."

Jorgensen turned away from the tunnel's end. "That we can do. Three it is." Headlamp aiming in the opposite direction, he started toward the rest of their group.

William followed, adjusting his own light as he did. When it came to assessing his future here in New River, he had only two chances left. Time to use them wisely.

15

"But I want a *new* sash." Lacey framed her narrow hips with both hands as they passed over the bridge into town. "It'll be the death of me to visit that train car tomorrow wearin' my old things." The sixteen-year-old twirled in a circle, sending her mud-splattered hem and pinafore swirling as well.

"You've got a sash. A fine linen one that Ma dyed for you," Lizbeth countered. The sunny yellow was lovely—all thanks to a generous field of goldenrod last autumn. "It'll pair with your best dress nicely. Besides, you don't have any money for somethin' new."

"I've got ten cents still. Could've sworn I had more." Lacey clutched her slate to her chest, smearing last night's arithmetic work and too busy pouting to notice. "It seems to vanish in dribs and drabs. Won't one of ya lend me some money?"

Lizbeth nipped the slate lest the distracted girl need to begin again. Beside her, Jayne accepted the slate and its chalky sums for safekeeping.

"Will you lend me somethin', Maryanne?"

Maryanne tipped her nose skyward, nearly bumping into Kit. "No, ma'am."

"How is it that you've got nearly three dollars?" Lacey wailed.

Maryanne tugged at a wool sweater wrapped snug around her sensible dress. "'Cause I've saved everythin' I've ever gotten. Every Christmas penny. Every extra chore."

Behind them, children laughed as they skipped toward the schoolhouse.

"You'll just have to make do with what you have, Lacey." Lizbeth touched the waist of her own plain skirt. She too saved most coins that crossed her palm, preserving even a little more than Maryanne in an old jam jar beneath her bed. "I'm not about to part with any of my savings over your fancies, Lacey. And what does it matter about having something new? It's going to be a lovely day regardless." All Lizbeth cared about was the small library Mr. Brydolf would show them. Her heart puddled with a mixture of trepidation and excitement. All those books. Along with an afternoon in the company of Mr. Drake.

"It's going to be splendid." Jayne sighed.

"And so many books," Lizbeth added.

Jayne laughed. "Yes, books," she teased.

"Oh, who cares about that!" Lacey twirled in another circle then stilled at sight of a trio of men standing on the shop steps. Miners, by their clothing that was grayed with coal dust and countless washings. The most handsome of the men was watching Lacey.

The girl giggled and flounced over a puddle in the road. "And I still want a new sash. 'Sides, my old one is the same kind as yours, Jayne, and we can't go like that!" Lacey snagged her slate from Jayne then skipped ahead, catching up with Kit, who recited her own schoolwork for their coming exam. "Can we just stop in at the mercantile? It's right there." Lacey pointed across the street to the shop with its tall false front and household staples within. Her focus drifted across to the handsome man again. "Won't hardly be out of anyone's way. For just a moment? School doesn't start for a while yet seein' as we walked here so fast."

Lizbeth silently beseeched Jayne for help.

"Only for a few minutes." Jayne patted Lizbeth's shoulder. "Lizzy, maybe you can show me the new writing desk you saw last week. I'd like to see it too. We *are* early and Reverend Coburn said he'd come along to meet us and I don't see him yet. We might as well get warm as we wait."

"Fair." Lizbeth followed them toward the mercantile. While Ma insisted they make Reverend Coburn feel welcome, Lizbeth wouldn't for one moment lead the man on to think that she'd taken a shine to him. Not with his fragile constitution and stuttering words. It would be unfair. She felt no spark of affection for the man.

Instead, a different man's face flashed through her mind. The thought of a quiet coal baron who *had* sparked new sensations. "Not exactly pleasant ones," Lizbeth whispered to herself. She blinked quickly to settle her nerves, startled by a growing fear that the thoughts she harbored for Mr. Drake were more than just dislike. That something more akin to intrigue was churning inside her.

Impossible.

The worry was stomped into oblivion as Lacey dashed up the steps of the company store. The place where workers and their families purchased anything from salt to sewing needles, giving not only their lives to the company, but their meager wages as well. Light brightened the windows as Lizbeth trailed up the steps next, all too aware of the men who stood watching their approach.

Lizbeth slowed her pace. The tallest of the men on the porch, who had been watching Lacey, shoved a hand through thick blond hair. The man had both youth and attractiveness on his side with his face clean and handsomely carved. His blue eyes landed on Lacey before moving to Lizbeth where his gaze stayed.

Lizbeth ducked her head to ease past.

But the stranger moved to the door and, with a rattle of the brass bell, opened it for them. "Mornin', ladies."

Lacey giggled as she clutched Kit's arm. Maryanne went petrified as she scuttled past. Jayne lagged behind, distracted by a mewling kitten beneath the step. Lizbeth's heart beat quicker as she crossed the porch alone. She reached the door that the man held with his outstretched arm.

"Mornin'," she said softly and tried not to brush against him.

He offered her no smile, but his gaze held amusement. She tried to ignore the attention as she entered. The aroma of freshly ground coffee and beeswax candles greeted them today. Lacey and Kit made a beeline to the shelves with bolts of cloth. Maryanne tiptoed toward a display of pens beneath a glass case.

Abandoned by Jayne, Lizbeth worked her way to a crate filled with fresh writing tablets. She pretended to examine the lined ledgers as she noticed the man on the porch through the nearest shop window. He spoke to his comrades then punched one amiably on the shoulder and entered the shop himself. The whole space dimmed as he passed through the doorway.

The stranger wore dark pants and a shirt of the same hue, his waist cinched by a leather belt like the other miners in the region. His scuffed boots were coated in coal dust. The only difference from his uniform and those of the local miners was a three-digit number embroidered on his chest pocket in gold thread. Every employee had a number that marked his presence in and out of the mine, but those in New River simply had a brass token that they placed on a peg board to mark their descent below the earth. None of them had uniforms like this. A stranger indeed.

His footfalls crossed the store and within mere strides, he

reached Lacey's side. He spoke softly, garnering more giggles from the girl.

Lizbeth narrowed her gaze. Lacey was too young for male attention at just sixteen and the girl was too foolish to recognize true sincerity. While it was too soon to judge this stranger, Lizbeth knew to err on the side of caution. Yet like a squirrel on a branch that didn't know when to quiet, Lacey chattered away with him as though he were an old friend. The spirited girl had little to no sense so Lizbeth finally broke her pretend reverie with a writing tablet and worked her way to that end of the shop.

"Lacey, we should be on our way again." Lizbeth absently picked up a spool of her favorite lace, hoping to appear natural. "School bell's about to ring."

"Nonsense! Lizzy, this is Mr. Westgard." She giggled. "He said we should call him *West*. He was just askin' us about the town."

The miner squared his shoulders and angled to Lizbeth, as though Lacey were a mere shadow against the wall and not an enchanted girl peering up at him.

"A pleasure, Miss . . . ?"

"That's Lizzy." Lacey thrust a bolt of cloth onto the shelf for someone else to straighten. "She's my older sister. Not nearly as much fun, if I do say so myself."

"Interesting." The miner—Mr. Westgard—gave Lacey his full attention for a long enough breath that she lost her own.

Then he angled back to Lizbeth. "Are you here for some fabric as well?"

"We're just browsin'." Lizbeth returned the spool of lace to the shelf.

Amusement flashed in Mr. Westgard's eyes.

"Have you seen that shiny train car parked in the depot yard?"

Lacey pulled a length of velvet ribbon from a paper box. "It belongs to a Mr. what's-his-name and we've been invited to tea." She beamed at Mr. Westgard—a schoolgirl's efforts at making a fellow jealous. "So that's what the necessities are for."

"Ah." Mr. Westgard's gaze shifted between them both, and to Lizbeth's surprise, she sensed a note of envy in his voice. "I see."

Lacey tugged another bolt of fabric down and cast a look of longing at the stranger.

He was handsome, yes, but Lizbeth would speak to her sister about prudence. A comely face gave no reason to be overly familiar. Perhaps it was more cause *not* to, in case beauty and vanity went hand in hand.

"Come along, Lacey," she whispered.

"Have you known Mr. Drake for some time now?" The man fingered a paper price tag.

"Only recently." Lizbeth brushed Lacey's arm to get her attention. Where was Jayne?

Mr. Westgard moved to the other side of the display so Lizbeth's eyes were forced to meet his again. "I myself have known him for some years. I've just travelled down from Pennsylvania where he owns a mine known as Chess Creek. I've never seen a place such as this. A curious plot of land, your New River. Is it always this musty?"

"Always," Lacey groaned. "Though we live out a ways where the air's fresher. The haze is from the mine. Have you seen it?"

"The mine? Yes. I went down in the shaft just recently with your Mr. Drake."

"Oh, he ain't *our* Mr. Drake," Lacey spat. "He's just friends with some other fella who's taken a shine to my oldest sister."

"Lacey!" Lizbeth said sternly.

"It ain't exactly a secret." Lacey rolled her eyes. "Whole town can tell."

Mr. Westgard winked in Lizbeth's direction as though to commend her for being the more prudent one.

The school bell rang and poor Maryanne made a dash for the door.

Lacey pouted before pasting on a smile. "I really do have to go. Been awfully nice meetin' you, West!" The girl straightened her smudged slate.

As the bell rang again, Lizbeth caught sight of Reverend Coburn on the shop porch chatting with Jayne, who looked in need of rescuing.

"I'll leave you all to your browsing." Mr. Westgard gave a small bow of his head. "It was a pleasure to meet you. I expect we'll meet again."

"Will you be in town for long?" Lacey slipped through the door, her rapture now for the tall, dashing miner and not on sashes or lace.

As though tugging gently on a fishing line to ensure the bait had been taken, Mr. Westgard braced the door open for Lacey. "I certainly hope so. Good day, ladies." His gaze met Lizbeth's again as more shoppers entered along with the breeze. "Enjoy your tea on the train."

As he departed, Lizbeth blew out a breath and retreated to join Jayne, who still waited with Reverend Coburn outside.

He touched the brim of his hat when she neared. "Good day."

"Mornin'." When had this town ever held such a bustle of social activity?

It was even a struggle to decide where to place herself as Jayne and the man turned, starting back toward home. With Jayne looking miserable, Lizbeth spared her sister and walked nearest to Reverend Coburn. She would let nothing derail her sweet sister or encourage the town gossips to insinuate another gentleman had caught Jayne's eye.

As for Lizbeth, she could sacrifice a morning stroll. It would cost her nothing. She had no suitors. No man seeking her hand or heart. Her gaze lifted toward the beauty of the Pemberley and she quickly shook her head. Not likely. Mr. Drake was here for business alone. He'd made that perfectly clear. Besides, she was a poor girl from coal country who had her own future to worry about. A man like William Drake surely had his fair share of women to interest him back home. It made Callum Brydolf's attention to Jayne all the more precious.

Beside her, the Reverend cleared his throat with a grating sound. "A fine morning for a walk, wouldn't you say?"

Lizbeth nodded. "The sunrise was lovely."

Jayne slid her arm through Lizbeth's in solidarity.

The man beside them made small talk about the buildings he'd sighted in town, about Mrs. Jorgensen's fine display of breakfast items and the pleasing angle of his window where he lodged there. Lizbeth listened to all of it politely, responding as she could, until Reverend Coburn turned the conversation toward her.

He smoothed a hand against one of his matted sideburns. "Tell me, Lizbeth, what sort of future do you imagine for yourself?"

Her eyebrows rose. "Well, I—I—" Did she truly know? "Well, I hope for a life of purpose," Lizbeth finally blurted. "And I see that in helping my pa run the farm. In helping to provide a good life for my sisters and me. All those who call Bennet Hollow home."

"Purpose. Good, good. There is much purpose for the women of this world. So much to tend to with hearth and home. Offspring to rear."

She sensed that the Reverend sought a wife whom he could mold and shape into his own ideal. A woman who would follow him without question. Lizbeth blew out a soft breath. "You offer much to think on, Reverend."

She had no qualms about the polite gentleman, but he didn't spark her heart to a new awareness, let alone a building desire or respect. Instead, her skin prickled with this awkward and strained civility. That could never be the foundation of a life of love. Perhaps she would end up a spinster, but she would rather live out her days unwed than bind herself to a man she could not admire.

Did such a man exist? One who could inspire her both in mind and spirit? A man whose touch she longed for and whose face she ached to see each dawn? She thought of the eligible bachelors she knew—including the ones she had met of late—and still rust ate at the answer with the same fervor it riddled holes through Pa's old wheelbarrow. In the empty spaces bloomed doubt thicker than the cream that Ma churned each week. Had she already met her match? Or might she hold out prospect for it one day?

She longed to marry, yes, but her roots sank deep into the soil of Bennet Hollow and so this was the place where she needed to carve out a future. The place where she belonged. A place where she could help her family hold on to this farm and keep it afloat in the seasons to come. Not because of who she might marry—but for what she might *do*.

If she could find a way to help this farm prosper alongside Pa, then her future and her sisters' futures would be secure. Whether love came knocking or not.

16

Squaring his stance in front of the mirror, William pulled both suspenders up over his shoulders, stealing only a moment to inspect his appearance before Callum burst through the door of the stateroom.

"Does this tie look all wrong?" Callum fiddled with the plum-colored knot at his throat.

"Your guess is as good as mine." William tucked in the tail of his shirt. Finished, he tossed his third waistcoat onto the bed and stared at the options. "I don't know what the occasion requires." It was merely an autumn afternoon with a small party of guests. A neighborly gathering. Tea would be served and books would be the topic of discussion.

No real need to be intimidated. So why were William's hands unsteady and Callum somehow flushed and pale all at the same time? William swung his mind to matters that he could solve—a mental checklist of the day. His porter would act as butler just as the man always did whenever the Pemberley dressed itself out for entertainment. Cook had prepared tea along with treats and pastries. And then . . . ?

"I don't believe we're used to entertaining such small numbers," he said.

"Nonsense." Callum leaned toward the mirror over William's washbasin. "We've both entertained small parties before." His voice dropped lower. "Just never a group of five sisters."

Fair.

Especially since Callum had grown more and more intrigued by one in particular.

Was this what the heart did to a man? William had little experience with affection and had never fancied himself in love. Were the traits which Callum exhibited *love*? Could it be possible that William was in the same kind of danger?

Alarmed, he continued to study his friend as Callum struggled with the knot at his throat. When their guests entered William's private car, there would be no crowd to hide among. Conversation and entertainment would be left up to him. Especially if Callum didn't pull himself together.

"Cook!" William called down the hallway toward the galley. "We could use your help."

Cook, a burly, ruddy-haired woman of nearly sixty, appeared with a dripping spoon in hand. "I've got cream about to curdle on the stovetop and the pair of you need help deciding what to wear?"

"Just for a moment."

Cook pushed a plump fist to her hip. "Well, I highly doubt the sensible young ladies due here any minute will care whether your cravat is made from satin or silk. A breath of fresh air if you ask me."

William led Cook across his stateroom where she assessed the three waistcoats he'd laid out. Her own attire—a black dress with a white apron—was splattered with the makings of jams and custards.

"The striped shirt. It cuts a fine figure." She pointed to what William already wore, crisp and white with faint blue stripes.

"Hmmm . . ." She scrutinized the options. "With the tan waistcoat." She patted William on the cheek. "It flatters you, dear boy." She turned him as though to ensure the straps on his shoulders were only suspenders. "No gun, though."

"Wasn't going to." His gun rested in the safe, beside his billfold and the funds he kept with him to ensure they travelled successfully. He only wore the weapon when the train was in motion and hadn't been armed since coming here.

She tossed a thumb to Callum. "You either."

Callum held up his hands peaceably. "It's under the mattress."

"Good. And wear silver cufflinks instead of gold. They'll look more like steel, which these gals'll be used to. And I suggest a different tie otherwise you're gonna match the marmalade."

Gulping, Callum retreated to his berth next door, and judging by rattling of hangers from the wardrobe, hastily revised his approach.

"You're an angel," William called to Cook as she walked off, muttering her skepticism of how two men so wealthy travelled without a valet.

Judging by the smell of lemon scones and egg pastries, she had outdone herself. Already, William and Callum had cleared their clutter from the main dining room. Now the table sat draped with a lace cloth and the finest dishes the galley had to offer. William wanted this day to be just right for Callum and Jayne Bennet. As for William, his first thought upon waking had been that he would see and speak to Lizbeth again.

William loosened his shirt collar. Was it suddenly too tight?

"I believe you've gotten too good at avoiding human interaction," Callum quipped as he returned.

William chuckled. "Maybe a little too good."

Perhaps today he could do better. William checked his pocket watch. It was also solid gold so he'd take care to keep it out of sight. He wanted these young ladies to feel comfortable.

William glanced out the window, thinking once more of Lizbeth. What was happening to him? He'd enjoyed hearing her ideals during the two times they'd conversed and seeing her genuineness from afar whenever their paths crossed. It didn't hurt that he was rather taken by her expressive gaze, youthful face, and wealth of curiosity. All marked by bright eyes and clever conversation that didn't flaunt or cower in his presence but instead helped him see the world through an unexpected lens. Interacting with her was like studying a novel. Except more vividly and in a way that made his ears warm. The fact that she seemed to truly consider him, even when he lacked the words to explain what he was thinking, only expanded his curiosity.

Who was he kidding? He'd already breached the gates of curiosity and was now staring down a building hope.

William swallowed hard. Therein lay the problem, because as sincere intrigue for Lizbeth was blossoming into unsteadying emotion, he was in uncharted waters. If he proceeded further down this course, he would be a man with no map. No sure answers. And that was something he'd always been too afraid to risk.

Even in the spaces of his mind, admitting his growing intrigue for Lizbeth was so discomforting that he kept it well under lock and key. This was madness. His life and hers were worlds apart. Made worse by the fact that her father's land hung in the balance and William's aunt expected him to marry well. Factor in William's inability to appear human when it came to matters of the heart and this afternoon had the potential to completely curdle. People often assumed him a statue, carved from stone, but it was flesh and blood beating within his chest all the same. For some reason the woman in question had the ability to amplify that.

"This was a terrible idea," William muttered to himself. Retrieving his pocket watch he checked the time. "The ladies will be here within the hour," he called to Callum and was answered with, "I'm all thumbs now!"

For the first time in his life, William understood.

Rising to her tiptoes, Lizbeth reached over the corral and clicked her tongue. Eugene lumbered nearer, his long-lashed gaze fixed on the apple she held out. Sassafras followed in the distance. Eugene's one ear perked in her direction as he chomped the fruit with teeth too big for his head. When he finished, Lizbeth took care not to get too close lest he soil her dress with the wilted clover that clung to his coat from a roll in the meadow.

Already, Lizbeth stood polished and styled for the afternoon in town. She'd chosen the same skirt and blouse that she'd worn at the barn dance only two weeks ago, along with a sash made from an old shawl that had once been her grandmother's. Now the plaid fabric cinched her waist in a coppery bow. This morning, Ma had let them bathe with special soap that smelled of roses. Lizbeth sniffed her softly scented wrist. Her cheeks had been scrubbed to a soft sheen, and her hair, braided and coiled in a crown around her head, lay pinned into place by Jayne's expert hands.

Hardly feeling like herself, the company of her mules provided comfort. The scents and sounds of Eugene and Sassafras rooted her to reality, where she belonged, as she pulled a second apple from behind her back for Sassafras. Lizbeth imagined her sisters up at the farmhouse, fussing and fretting in these final moments. Lacey was probably still moaning about the state of her shoes, while Kit would gallantly offer to polish them and Maryanne would chide them both for not having prepared their things the night before.

"Lizzy!" Ma called from the house. "Your sisters are ready!"

"Comin'!" Lizbeth hurried back into the house to rewash her hands. Finished, she scooped up the basket of hand pies that she and Jayne had prepared. Filled with blackberry preserves, they'd brushed each moon-shaped pie with egg yolk and baked the small pastries to a golden sheen.

"Thatta girl." Ma nodded. "As I always say—never show up empty-handed."

Peering into the basket, Lizbeth checked that the sweetest delicacies she and Jayne knew how to make were safe and sound.

"Off you go now. I don't mind stayin' behind. No sense me goin' along with this cold." Ma dabbed at her nose with a hankie. "I'd rather you girls have this chance than anything else."

Calling out their thanks, the girls ambled down the stairs and out into the yard. Lizbeth draped the basket on her arm and followed.

She watched as her sisters strolled down the lane, resembling freshly dyed skeins of yarn. Jayne wore a skirt of butter yellow, Kit and Lacey different shades of green and brown in their Sunday dresses, and Maryanne a sensible gray dress. The younger three wore freshly starched pinafores. Never had Lizbeth seen the aprons so white. Ma had spent the week brining them in liquid bluing to chase away any stains, then pressed and mended every inch to appear new. As for Jayne, she wore a delicate leather belt at her waist, accentuating her feminine figure, and a ribbon of lace around her soft bun.

When they approached town, Lizbeth spotted the ornate train car. A twinge of guilt needled her that Ma would miss whatever splendor dwelled within. Lizbeth vowed to recount it to her this evening in vivid detail as she clutched the basket close.

Their excited chatter fell silent as they neared. Large metal steps led up into the car from both ends, and Jayne chose the nearest set. "I reckon this may be the entrance," she whispered.

Jayne climbed the front balcony steps, appearing calm despite the fact that none of them had ever boarded a train car in all their lives. After exchanging a glance with Lizbeth, who followed close behind, Jayne knocked softly on the door. Despite the timid announcement, footfalls sounded and all at once, it opened.

Lizbeth expected to see Mr. Drake, but instead, an elderly gentleman with a friendly face bowed. "Good afternoon, ladies. Welcome aboard."

"Thank you." Jayne curtsied slightly. "I'm Jayne Bennet and these are my sisters." She named each one, and with a sparkle in his eye, the gentleman nodded as though introductions on the balcony weren't necessary. Lizbeth could see in his expression that it endeared them to him in an instant.

"I'm the porter on board so please allow me to see you in, Miss Bennet and all of the Miss Bennets." He turned and they followed.

Lizbeth hung back a step so that they could fit through the narrow hallway that was now filled with five skirts and silent stares. Despite the snug space, wealth announced itself from every surface. The paneled walls were intricate and polished as were the electric bulbs that glowed from their brass sconces and glass globes. Lizbeth had heard of such miracles but never had she laid eyes on the thrumming of light that required neither wick nor flame.

Within mere steps a large room invited them forward with stately furniture and vases of fresh flowers that didn't grow in these parts. Blue velvet curtains graced the windows, all pulled back with gold cording, inviting in the light of day. Overhead, the ceiling was fashioned from glass, the intricately paneled dome offering a view of the clear sky. The glass was cut and etched with such craftsmanship that Lizbeth couldn't speak.

She peered skyward along with her sisters. Kit gasped. Maryanne and Jayne stood speechless. Lacey clutched her hands to her chest, turning in a slow circle as though conjuring a reason she too could live in such a palace.

Velvet chaises edged both ends of the room and a dining table filled the center. The sunlight overhead glinted upon porcelain dishes and more treats than Lizbeth could have ever imagined. A silver tower of trays balanced glazed scones, miniature sandwiches, and fresh fruits that she didn't know how to name. She clutched her basket awkwardly at the sight of dainty jars of curds and jams nestled around. Silken napkins and glittering cutlery marked each seat. There wasn't a single item on the table that wasn't dipped in silver, gold, or glistening sugar.

"I thought it was only *a pot of tea*," Lacey whispered. She touched fingertips to her mouth, as wrapped in quiet awe as her sisters.

Lizbeth longed to draw nearer and paint every intricate detail in her mind—a memory to save for all her life—but her feet wouldn't move.

The porter grinned. "Please make yourselves comfortable and I'll summon the gentlemen."

He vanished down the train's main corridor and at the murmur of male voices, Lizbeth steeled herself for the approach of Mr. Drake. He trailed Mr. Brydolf into the brightly lit room by a shoulder width. They were both neatly dressed, both equally handsome, but in different ways. While Mr. Brydolf's gaze went straight for Jayne, Mr. Drake's focus landed on the table, on the seating arrangements, on anything but a human. Lizbeth was trying to think of what to say when he gestured to the assembly of chairs around the tea service.

"Welcome to the Pemberley, ladies." He dipped a bow to each of the girls, last of all to Lizbeth where his gaze finally met her own. "I hope you'll make yourselves at home."

17

William owed Cook a kiss on the cheek for the wonder she'd woven in the galley. The woman helped throw grand parties and balls back home, but with staff beneath her command. How she pulled off such a spread, and alone at that, he didn't know, but she'd laid out a miraculous offering as though Marie Antoinette were among their numbers.

William gladly waited as the Bennet girls stood awestruck by the sight, his attention catching on Lizbeth.

He forced himself to divert his gaze from her awed face to where Cook had placed fluffy meringue rosettes, dyed a pale pink and baked to a delicate crisp. She'd unboxed the chocolates he'd ordered from New York and tucked truffles and colorful marzipan in between her own baked goods. To witness the splendor through the eyes of his company was a reward that William had never quite experienced before. He admired their faces—in particular, Lizbeth's.

That's when he noticed the basket she clutched in nervous-looking hands.

"May I help you find somewhere to set that?" He asked, unsure how to begin.

Lizbeth blushed. "We brought hand pies."

The span of his chest warmed at the endearing way she said that. As though it were a confession and not a gift.

"Allow us to add them to the table."

The color in her cheeks deepened as she handed over the willow basket. Cook entered and, seeing the predicament, made room at the edge of the table, but William stopped her.

"Perhaps here," he whispered, touching the center cake stand where a toffee layer cake brimmed with gold leaf and trimmings.

Cook nodded. "Of course." With deft hands, the dear woman swapped out the place of honor for Lizbeth's own pastries.

William watched Cook display each hand-cut pie with care. The rustic edges were shaped with the tongs of a fork and one or two had a drip of dried blackberry sauce oozing from the center. William admired the homey sight, already knowing which dessert he would enjoy first.

Finished, Cook placed her own cake at the table's edge with a wink and vanished. Now Lizbeth's cheeks were redder.

Had he done the wrong thing?

"I trust you've all brought an appetite," Callum blurted.

William closed his eyes.

One of the younger girls giggled and William looked up to see that all the sisters were smiling. Even Lizbeth's ease returned. Callum chuckled and William's brow loosened. The man knew how to ease the tension after all.

"Please, have a seat," Callum said. "We're so grateful you could join us today." He pulled out the chair nearest him for Jayne, who sat. The other girls followed suit along with William. Relieved—and needing something to do with his hands—he lifted a tray of finger sandwiches, which were each tied with a strand of chives like tiny presents.

He handed the tray to the girl beside him. "I'm afraid I don't know each of your names."

The giggling girl touched fingertips to her mouth. "I'm Lacey." She took the offering and, using her elbow, indicated the sister beside her. "This here's Kit."

"And I'm Maryanne," a girl declared from across the table. She appeared to be the most plain and practical of the group.

"And of course you've met Jayne." Lacey—the outspoken one—passed the tray to her sister who sat the closest to Callum. "And that's Lizzy." Lacey tossed a nod to the young woman whose name and face William had already memorized.

"Lizzy," he repeated softly. A nickname. Yet one more stanza in the poem of her upbringing. A poem he wanted to know more about.

Needing to busy his hands, he removed the lid on a small silver pot of clotted cream. "And I'm William." He noticed Callum straighten in surprise. Yes, it seemed high time they use their given names. The formality of Mr. Drake and Mr. Brydolf didn't fit the day.

"Right. I'm Callum." The man's attention landed on Jayne again. "I do hope you'll all call me that."

Jayne smiled softly. "Certainly."

Beside her, Lizbeth looked pleased at their exchange. But was Jayne intrigued by Callum to the same degree? Could it be shyness William saw in her slight glimpses to the man at her side? Or aloofness? Rather difficult to discern, but for his friend's sake, William meant to try.

From across the table, one of the younger sisters—Lacey, he recalled—stared up at his Aunt Catherine's ornate portrait.

"I assure you, she's quite harmless," William promised. "Especially at a distance."

The girl smiled.

The tray of sandwiches went around the table as each young woman politely took a single one. Cook had prepared a luncheon fit for a palace, so William forced himself to speak again. "Please don't be shy. We'd hate for any of this to go to waste." He reached for a ripe strawberry and piled several onto his plate to second the point.

Lizbeth exchanged a glance with Jayne, along with the others. All at once, their joy brightened the room and they perused the table with all the excitement he had hoped for. Feminine hands reached for tarts and pastries, cookies and candies. The porcelain plates centered in front of each cane chair were soon filled with delicacies, and William found it easier to settle in and relax.

He broke one of Lizbeth's hand pies in half. Indeed worthy of the first bite—it melted in his mouth. Sweet, buttery, and comforting. Like a walk through the woods in summer. He sensed Lizbeth's attention from the corner of his eye and didn't dare look her way.

Instead, he pondered yet another line of the poem that was taking shape.

Amid the chatter and delights, Callum launched a conversation about horses of all things. "Do any of you enjoy riding?" he asked.

"We don't have horses anymore," Lacey announced. "But we used to. Pa sold 'em along with some mules a few years back to make ends meet."

Jayne nervously brushed fingertips over her forehead, and judging by Lacey's sudden jolt, someone had poked her under the table.

"But we've got a couple of mules still," Lacey blurted, steering the conversation away from finances. "Well, just two now."

A shadow crossed over Lizbeth's face but before William could make sense of it, Kit piped in.

"Pa and Lizzy used to raise 'em and Pa sold most of 'em to the mine. Remember that, Lizzy?"

The very woman nodded somberly.

Kit pressed on. "All's left are Sassafras and Eugene. They're awful stubborn creatures and Eugene can't hear half the time, but Lizzy does most of the work."

"Does she?" William had to fight the urge to look at her again. Already, he'd memorized the thoughtful tilt of her face beneath the brilliance of the observation dome and the crown of braids that she must have spent some time on. Her dress was the same as the night they'd danced, except now it wasn't his hand to her waist, but instead, his hand to his knee where he fidgeted with his napkin.

She was no stranger now. While he didn't know her well, there lingered a familiarity about her that was working its way into his awareness. Burrowing in deep. He didn't know what to do about that.

"And what of your horses?" Lacey asked Callum.

"Sadly my stables sit too empty these days," Callum confessed. "It's my friend here who is the true aficionado. Tell them, William."

William shifted in his chair. "I've got around a dozen horses on my estate in Vermont. Lovely animals. Easy to work with and a pleasure to ride." He broke his determination and caught sight of Lizbeth's face just as it lifted in wonder. "And I have a thoroughbred. A racehorse," he continued. "Sired by a horse named Fortuitous. My aunt's prized stallion. My own horse is three years old. Rarely wins, but she's a sight to behold."

"Why doesn't she win?" Lacey asked.

"She's much too taken with napping on the lawn. The mare, that is . . . not my aunt."

The girls all giggled.

"And I employ a jockey with a soft heart."

"May we ask the filly's name?" Lizbeth reached for the teapot that her younger sister set aside.

William moved it nearer for her, and their fingers nearly touched. "Lady Light."

Lizbeth's expression stayed soft. "She sounds lovely."

"She is rather. But please don't make any bets on her." He pulled his hand back into his lap. "You'd do better with a straight bet on anyone else."

This sent laughter around the dining room and William's mouth tipped up in a slight smile. He didn't make jokes often, and probably wouldn't attempt any for the rest of the day, so the effect was pleasant.

Lizbeth's eyes were still laughing and her tone sweet as she said, "I'll remember that the next time I'm at the races."

William knew full well they'd never witness a derby race in these parts, and she, a loyal lover of such animals. "I hope one day you'll see her for yourself."

He didn't know why he said it. Nor had he reasoned with the implication.

Her surprised gaze lingered on his own. "I'd like that."

William cleared his throat as this strange and growing sentiment threatened to distract him further. He reached for the pot of tea himself and filled his cup.

Lacey plucked bright green fruit from a tray. "Are these what I think they are?" She popped one in her mouth.

"Grapes." Callum gleaned several as well. "We had them brought in from California."

"Truly?" Lizbeth whispered. She reached for one and this time, William didn't hide his gaze as he witnessed her enjoy the fruit, perhaps for the first time in all her life.

Lizbeth closed her eyes for the briefest of moments.

"Oh, they're splendid!" Lacey plucked several more from the vine.

"Everything is," Jayne seconded softly. "And the tiny cakes are so delicious."

William nodded his appreciation. "I'll pass your compliments on to Cook. She outdid herself."

"Please do." Jayne admired the spread that was still so abundant, they could each eat for days.

Callum leaned into the opportunity as he lowered his napkin to the table. "We'll send for another pot of tea. In the meantime, would you like to see the books now, Jayne? I can show you to the study."

Jayne hesitated.

Was that disinterest or caution in her delayed response?

"Certainly." She rose and while William had a sense that Callum meant for a private stroll to the other end of the car, he could do nothing about the younger girls who shot up from their seats, murmuring at once as they followed in a chorus of ribbons and gingham.

Only he and Lizbeth remained seated. Lizbeth folded her hands, glancing from the lingering treats to the artwork on the walls. Her thumbs fiddled together nervously.

Not wanting to hold her back here alone, William set his napkin aside. "Shall we?"

She rose.

He motioned to the undiscovered end of the car where a second hallway led from the dining room to his study. "After you." He followed behind her.

Together, they passed his private stateroom—his world, currently—hidden behind a solid door. She studied its grandeur in passing. What was it that she saw? Of this place . . . and of him?

He trailed her past his room and then the guest berth where Callum dwelled a number of weeks out of the year.

"This place is beautiful," Lizbeth said over her shoulder. "You must enjoy your time here very much."

"I do, thank you. It's different than home, but I enjoy seeing new places."

She touched the ornate wall molding, and he watched, enchanted, scarcely hearing her ask, "The kitchen? Is it at the other end?"

William cleared his throat. "Yes, it's back the other way. If you'd allow me, I'd like to ask Cook to box up some of the remaining fare for you to take."

"Oh, we couldn't possibly . . ."

Such manners, and from someone who would have grown up rationing sugar and flour to make ends meet. "Consider it a token for your mother since she was unable to come. I'd hate for any of it to go to waste."

Lizbeth's eyes widened and she gave a small nod. "She'd be honored, I'm sure."

It was settled then.

As they entered his study, her face tilted to the ceiling once more. Here, the second observation dome let in the warm glow of sunshine from above.

"Lady Light," Lizbeth breathed softly. The whisper so faint that he nearly missed it.

Somehow her pleasure amplified his own. William had met people impressed with his wealth before, but this was different. Lizbeth didn't seem in awe of his pocketbook, but instead, of the things that mattered most to him. The things that brought him joy. They seemed to bring her joy as well.

William slowed to a stop, trying to comprehend what to do with that. What *could* he do? He'd known women who matched him in status, even in property, but never in sincere interests. What did a man do when he encountered a woman who seemed to mirror him in such ways? Especially when she came from a vastly different world.

He forced himself to study the floor instead of her face. What was happening to him?

William was grateful when the chatter of the others shook him to his senses. Jayne and Callum sat in the reading chairs near the window while the others perused the study, admiring everything from the drapes to his desk where inside the center drawer lived a dozen telegrams from Miss Brydolf—urging him to remember his purpose back in Vermont. His life. She wrote of the parties calling his name. Employees and staff. Responsibility for him to make a sensible match with a good fortune. A woman like Miss Brydolf herself.

All missives that William regretted having not disposed of. He would soon.

Here at the very back of the car, he pulled the door open so the Bennets might venture out onto the balcony.

When Lizbeth glanced his way, William gestured to the bookshelf. "As promised."

She soaked in the sight of his vast collection. "These are all yours?"

"All that I have with me when I travel." He had hundreds more back home if he were honest. "I've collected them over the years. Some I inherited. Do you have a favorite genre?"

"Oh, just about anything." She approached the nearest bookcase.

He motioned to the lower shelves. "These are all novels. Some classics. A few mysteries. A romance or two but none that I've read myself."

She smirked. "I'd like to see one of those." Lizbeth crouched and gently perused the titles with the tips of her fingers. "You have a copy of *Jane Eyre*?" she asked in surprise.

"Do I?" When she chuckled again, he knelt to see what she saw. "I suppose I do." He tugged the updated volume from its resting spot. "I have the original three volumes back home. I'd forgotten about this version."

"You have the first editions?"

"Have you read the story?"

"No, but I've always wanted to."

"Then please. Please take this one with you."

"You're lendin' it to me?" There it was: more surprise.

Quite frankly, he wanted to *give* it to her, but feared shocking her further. "It's been left unopened for far too long. Please." He held it out.

With a slow breath, Lizbeth took the book and turned it in her hands. "I'd be honored. And I promise to take care of it." Her copper-brown eyes lifted to his. "How long do you plan on stayin' in New River?" She gulped. "Just so I know how quickly I ought to read."

"Oh, well . . ." And all at once, he saw the map of New River in his mind. The borders of the land dispute that he'd yet to resolve—including her farm. The place she called home. The place where her mules lived and where she'd been born and raised.

A place on the brink of change.

Suddenly, one of the girls rushed out onto the balcony. "Oh, why hello, West!" Lacey hollered.

"Lacey, it's not polite to shout," Jayne said.

"But it's West," Lacey countered. "The man we met at the company store. He was awful friendly. No harm bein' friendly in return."

William moved to the door of the balcony as the man crossed the tracks.

Westgard waved to the ladies. "Good afternoon. We meet again!" Then to William, he touched the brim of his hat coolly.

William made no response. Especially when Lizbeth moved to his side. Westgard halted and gave a chivalrous bow. Without acknowledging him, William turned away. He'd check on that second pot of tea. Perhaps Cook needed help clearing the table. At his back, he could hear the cheerful words of Westgard and the ladies. He searched the sounds for Lizbeth's voice but heard only the excited croons and giggles of her sister Lacey.

Then Westgard murmured something, and William glanced back just long enough to see. Long enough to watch the way Lizbeth's hand rested on the edge of the balcony as with deft movements, Westgard tied a piece of lace around her wrist.

Stomach tightening, William turned away and walked back down the hallway.

He'd just tucked the last of Lizbeth's hand pies safely away when she returned to the dining room.

"Thank you again for the loan," she said cautiously as though sensing his shifting mood. She worked to unravel the piece of lace from her wrist. Her cheeks were pink and he knew it was from more than just cold autumn air.

William fought the thunderclouds in his mind and forced a weak smile.

"And I'm sorry . . ." Lizbeth tucked the lace into her skirt pocket. "We didn't get a chance to finish our conversation. How long until you'll need the book back?"

Reality crashing down, William fought for the words. "A few more weeks, at most." What had he been doing entertaining romantic ideas? He needed to clear his senses.

He'd come here for business. Nothing more. He'd do well to remember that.

They crossed the room in unison as Lizbeth said, "I'll have it finished and returned to you by then. Thank you, Mr. Drake."

He couldn't tell if that was regret in her voice. Or if it was his own sensibilities protesting the knowledge that a continued interaction between him and this young woman wouldn't make sense for either of them. She would one day be a memory of his past. Men like Westgard understood the kind of life she led and would long to lead. One of home and hearth and more familiar things than his world of empty marble hallways and a dozen fireplaces needing to be lit each day.

William excused himself to find Cook. It was easier than being in a room alone with Lizbeth.

He sensed himself in for a sleepless night. Since he'd met this young woman, it would be one of many. All because of this riddle he couldn't seem to solve. One sparked by the growing longing that she would stop thinking of him as Mr. Drake . . . and begin seeing him as William.

18

Lizbeth stepped into the crisp autumn air of the churchyard as the final hymn faded into memory. In her hand lay the family Bible, and beneath that, *Jane Eyre* as a stowaway. Having read late into the night, she couldn't resist finishing a few more pages on the wagon ride over here. The crowd from the morning's service proved a tight squeeze as she aimed for the crooked fence hemming the yard like wooden stitches. Chin high, she sought out Hattie but in rounding an old oak tree, it was William Drake who she nearly bumped into.

The woodsy scent of him swept her up even as she turned to avoid bumping into his shoulder. He stepped aside, their timing off, and they collided regardless. The Bible tumbled from her grasp, along with the novel. Before she could catch either, he fumbled for them as well, nabbing only the ancient text before it hit dew-drenched grass. The novel tumbled downward with a squishy *thump*.

"Oh! I'm sorry." Her panicked fingers reclaimed the book, but not before a wet mark marred the cover. Using the hem of her dress, she swiped at it. Her cheeks burned hotter than hearth coals and her best stockings were now exposed to the cold.

Yet she realized it wasn't an apology he sought as instead, he touched the book, his fingers wrapping gently around her own. If it was to still them, he succeeded.

His earnest gaze showed no concern for the novel, nor any interest in the lace of her petticoats, only for her face and peace of mind.

"It's nothing. The fault was mine. And you'd feel worse if it were the Bible." A dash of humor reached his voice.

"I—I—" She couldn't speak. Not with her hands tucked beneath his—a covering that was warm and steady and shocking her senses.

"*Miiiister* Drake!"

They both turned at the nasally summons of Reverend Coburn who waved overhead.

"Mr. Drake! A word!"

Gulping, Lizbeth stepped back as Reverend Coburn formed a third. She smoothed her skirt and the hem grazed her shoes once more. With William's focus still slanted her way, Lizbeth's mind filled with the memory of mahogany wood and his voice beside her on the Pemberley. All softened by the way his skin had just touched her own.

She tried to think of a way to excuse herself only to be jolted by Hattie joining her side. Nerves colliding, Lizbeth pressed a hand to her chest.

Still ignoring Reverend Coburn's appearance, William dipped her a small bow and she wished she could read the story in the lingering look he gave her before she retreated with Hattie.

"What on earth was happenin' behind that tree?" Hattie teased. "By the look that man just gave you, I'd say you startled him and he didn't mind one bit."

Lizbeth's cheeks only flamed hotter. "I don't even want to explain."

Hattie steered her in a new direction. "Tell me instead about yesterday, then."

Hoping William didn't overhear, Lizbeth kept her voice low. "Why don't you come over this afternoon? There's so much to catch up on and we've got cakes to share." She brushed a hand to the side of her forehead as her heartbeat struggled to find its normal rhythm.

"Why, I'd love to. I wanna hear everythin'!" Hattie thumbed the dampened novel. "Is that where you got this?"

Lizbeth angled the spine toward the light. "I couldn't help but start the first chapter."

"Oh, and what a pretty piece of lace." Hattie fingered the page marker.

"That's the other thing I need to tell you." Lizbeth opened the book to the strip of lace that kept her place. "This is from Mr. Westgard. One of the new miners in town."

Hattie's jaw dropped. "Mercy! We do have a lot to catch up on."

"He was there at the depot as we were visiting Mr. Drake's train car," Lizbeth whispered. "Mr. Westgard walked right up to the balcony, tied it around my wrist, and strode away."

Hattie gasped.

"I don't even know the man."

"But you cared enough to keep this."

Did she? While the miner was certainly attractive, Lizbeth felt more wary of him than anything else. "I needed somethin' to mark the page and it's too pretty to toss aside."

Hattie wagged her eyebrows, clearly not convinced. "Come along. Let's see if we can find Mr. Westgard behind a tree too."

"Don't make me regret invitin' you over."

"I promise to behave," Hattie laughed. "I want to hear everythin' and we're gonna discuss all these fellas, you can be certain."

Lizbeth shushed her as they squeezed past the churchyard gate and onto the road where wagons sat parked alongside her pa's.

"I'm just gonna drop my things at home and tell Ma, then I'll be along," Hattie said.

Lizbeth spotted her younger sisters still dispersed and Jayne sharing a bench near the cemetery with Mr. Brydolf. "Perfect. I'll fetch a jar of cider from the cellar and you and I'll take a basket out to the meadow."

"I'll be along soon!" Turning for home, Hattie paused. "Oh, it looks like you've got company."

Lizbeth turned as Reverend Coburn hurried toward them. Whatever was this day coming to?

"Morning, ladies!"

"Heaven help me." Lizbeth froze, her hand still on the churchyard gate. All morning, he'd been at her side. At breakfast, on the drive over, and even during the service. Was she never to dodge the man? No wonder her nerves were off-kilter.

Hattie's thick brows knit in question. "He's a rather nice fella. I've enjoyed listening to him read aloud each evening when he returns from your farm. He's often in good spirits."

"Fair, but there's more to his reason of bein' here, and I've been fearin' that—" Lizbeth clipped off the last of her words as Reverend Coburn caught up to them, panting.

Sweat beaded along his clerical collar. "I had hoped to catch you on the walk home." He nudged past the gate, trying but failing to avoid a rosebush that snagged the edge of his black coat.

Reverend Coburn fumbled with the rogue branch, plucking it free. "Er—Your ma suggested I walk you home, Miss Lizbeth, as she said they'd be awhile. Perhaps we can discuss this morning's sermon. If you'd do me the honor."

Lizbeth glanced to the safety of her pa's wagon then back. Even as she tried to conjure an excuse, Hattie hurried off, promising to be along soon.

"Miss Bennet?" Reverend Coburn angled his elbow out for her.

After a steadying breath, she faced him again. "I suppose a walk would do well. It looks like Pa's still busy so we can start for home. I'm sure my sisters might even catch up." How she hoped so.

The minister took off his hat before sliding it back over his oily hair. "My apologies for rushing after you in such haste. I got caught in conversation with Mr. Drake. Fascinating fellow. It turns out I've met his aunt—a Mrs. Catherine de Bourgh." He paused as though the name might impress her.

Lizbeth shook her head.

Reverend Coburn pressed on. "Old blood from New England and a *generous* patroness of the church. Remarkable woman. I've been told she once dined with Queen Victoria on her travels through Europe." Reverend Coburn picked at the rose thorn still wedged in his wool coat. He flicked it to the roadside before examining his fingertip overly long. "When I explained that you and I were family, Mr. Drake asked after you. He inquired as to your age and a few other odds and ends."

Had he?

"I told him that you were the fairest of my cousin's daughters and how you and I have been meaning to find the time to walk together."

"And—and Mr. Drake?" Lizbeth stammered.

"He took his leave without so much as a word. Right as I was explaining how much I've been enjoying your company these afternoons of late. How much meaningful time and conversations we've shared." Reverend Coburn surveyed the spot where William had been standing only a minute ago. "His retreat was rather abrupt, but men don't always agree on matters of beauty, I'm sorry to say.

Especially men of the upper class. Their standards are remarkably high, as you might imagine. Please don't take that to heart."

Unnerved, Lizbeth clutched her hands in front of her. She turned and started on. If only the walk home wasn't so far. She longed for her quiet meadow, Hattie's company, and a chance to make sense of life, especially after the events of yesterday.

Lizbeth fiddled with the strip of lace poking out of William's novel.

By sheer will, she fell in rhythm with Reverend Coburn's steps on the lane. As the grade rose, so did his breathing. His chest heaved and he clamped his lips together, all but smothering his gasps for air. His shoes squished through a patch of mud and he shook his foot.

The panting intensified.

"We can slow," Lizbeth offered.

"No need. The fresh air is good for a body." *Flick, step-squish, flick.* "Back home in Stroudsburg, I have the use of my neighbor's spare carriage whenever needed." *Gasp. Wheeze. Sniffle.* "It makes the journey to worship and back a pleasant one. As well as enabling me to complete my rounds each week in a timely"—he sucked in air—"manner."

"Ah."

Overhead, birds danced in the branches of the trees that lined the lane. A squirrel scampered up a narrow-trunked oak, peering at them with an acorn in its mouth.

"Would such a thing interest you?" he asked.

"The carriage?"

"Well—er—I mean, taking a ride in it."

"Is it not . . . far away?" She skirted around a puddle.

"That it is." He chuckled nervously as the road rose again. "Which leads me to something I wish to speak with you about." He clasped his hands together, then dropped them at his sides, swinging each arm with all the force he needed to reach the top of the hill.

The same hill another man had walked in ease alongside her with conversation that had stirred her senses and quickened her awareness of something puzzling and new.

Clasping her skirt in one hand, Lizbeth longed for sight of home.

She might have let her mind wander ahead to the hour or two she would pass with Hattie, visiting and dreaming, had they not reached the summit in time for Reverend Coburn to clear his throat again.

"I've spoken to your mother and gained her permission to walk you home as a chance to talk about matters of life . . . and of the heart. I—I aim to do that now."

"Oh?" Lizbeth hastened their pace.

Reverend Coburn matched her.

When they crested the final hill, he pulled off his hat and fumbled it as they passed the gate that marked the farm's border. "You see, after much thought, and deep reflection, I've come to the decision that it would be wise for me to set the example among my parishioners back home and marry."

Lizbeth slid past the gate, wishing she could squeak it closed between them. "Well, I—"

"Meaning." He wet his lips and, in the span of a moment, reached for her hand.

His skin cloyed against her own.

"It has been on the forefront of my mind to secure a wife, and from your father's daughters have I decided to make my choice. Most of all, it is here that I must declare to you my affections."

While Lizbeth longed to raise the hem of her skirt and dash down the lane and out of sight, she stood frozen in place by shock.

"If you would permit me, of course. And I promise to make no remark about the difference in our living conditions once we are married. I do believe you'll like the town of Stroudsburg even more than New River."

Her eyebrows rose and she coaxed her hand free. "Reverend Coburn. I—I haven't given an answer," she stammered. "While I'm flattered by the generosity of your offer, I—" She closed her eyes. "I can't accept."

"Now, I—I'm going to go out on a limb and presume that you're only delaying my hopes so as to be—"

"No, sir." Lizbeth wiped her hand on her skirt. "Though it pains me to say, my answer is no. Please believe me to be flattered but I must be honest that I can't accept."

"But I anticipated—" He glanced past her as Pa's wagon clattered around the bend.

Blowing out a breath, Lizbeth took several steps onward, relieved when Reverend Coburn did the same. He walked in silence, as did she, which made for a miserable stretch of pathway until they reached the house. "I'm dreadfully sorry and I do appreciate you understandin'," she said weakly. "I wish you the best."

Pa drove the wagon into the yard and in the flutter of chatter from her ma and sisters, Lizbeth slipped inside. She tried to hurry up the stairs but Ma called out to her. "What just happened on the road with you and Reverend Coburn? Did he ask you an important question? Lizzy!"

"Oh, Ma." Lizbeth slowed. "I just couldn't say yes." At the sight of her mother's fallen face, tears burned Lizbeth's eyes. "I'm sorry. I just couldn't."

"But, Lizzy. Don't carry on so. Think of the opportunity!"

Reverend Coburn filled the doorway and Lizbeth hurried upward. She aimed for her bedroom and collapsed onto the lower mattress.

She heard Jayne enter and felt her hand on her braid. "Do you want to talk about it?"

Lizbeth shook her head, which was now burrowed into a pillow.

"No need then. I'll just sit with you a spell if you don't mind. Reverend Coburn'll be just fine." She brushed her hand down Lizbeth's braid. "He's speakin' with Pa and Ma now and he'll be right as rain. You answered from the heart. In honesty. That was the wisest thing you could do."

Lizbeth pulled a second pillow over her head. "Why did he ask me?" she whispered.

"Say that again?"

She nudged the pillow away. "I just don't know why he asked *me*."

"While I don't know his reasonin', I can only tell you what I think: I think he saw a young woman who was pretty and smart. And he wished to marry her."

Lizbeth sniffled and sat up. "Then why do I feel so awful?"

Jayne touched her cheek. "Because it took you by surprise. When a girl thinks of a fella askin' her to marry him, she hopes it's her sweetheart. That the moment will answer the hopes she's been savin'."

Slowly Lizbeth nodded.

"And because you care to not hurt someone else's feelings."

Footsteps sounded on the stairs. Ma burst in, followed by the girls. "Lizbeth Bennet. How could you be so quarrelsome with your pa's own cousin? A good man."

She sat up. "Ma, I was as polite as I could be."

"But you didn't accept!"

"I couldn't."

"My headstrong girl." Ma sank on the bed and clasped Lizbeth's hands in her trembling ones. "Think of the chance this is. Think of the life he can give you. A good, steady future. No more whilin' away your days fussin' over those animals. This farm."

"But Ma. This farm and those animals—they're not a burden. This is home."

"You gotta think differently."

"Ma, I can't. I can't marry that man. I just wouldn't be happy."

"How do you even know what happiness is?"

"Because it's what you and Pa and our family have given me. All my days."

"That's no reason to be overly romantic."

"I've always known that in order to marry, it would have to be to someone I loved. Someone who understood me, and I him."

"Oh, nonsense. We know enough of him to know it's a good match."

"For someone else, Ma, but not for me." She needed a love that was built on respect. Nothing less would do. She needed a man who, like her, had his heart wrapped up in the sunrise over the meadow and a conversation filled with wit and laughter. Who understood why she cherished a soft muzzle against her hand as she sat atop the pasture fence. None of which Reverend Coburn could offer, nor could she be the type of woman he sought.

Lizbeth squeezed her ma's hand. "Please believe me. When it comes to happiness, I've had more than a body should, and when it comes to the future and where I'm to give my heart, I promise you—I'll know it when I see it."

19

Leaning back in his desk chair, William closed his pocket watch and smoothed a thumb over the engraving in the gold—the profile of his racehorse, done by an artist's hand. He stared at it now, already forgetting the time of day he'd just glimpsed. Instead, he was struck by his wealth and the growing realization that it may not get Mr. Bennet—or the other tenants—out of the bind they were in. At least not easily.

"So, what does that mean?" William angled his desk chair toward Callum, who held up the document he'd been studying for hours now, lit by the dome of glass overhead.

"It means that there's concern as to whether or not Jorgensen has paid taxes on the land he's 'given away.' Since ownership is in question, the state of Virginia will require those taxes to be paid before any sale can be official."

"Why do you think Jorgensen didn't pay them?"

"Because he imagined the land belonging to the tenants. By passing the land off—even unofficially—it's saved him the expense for over a decade. Since Jorgensen makes more than four thousand dollars a year, he's required to pay two percent to the state. Men like Bennet and the other tenants are below the financial threshold."

"So, Jorgensen needs to pay these taxes."

Callum loosened his tie. "Possibly, but it's complicated. I don't even know if Bennet or the others are aware of the implications yet."

William accepted the wrinkled document.

"It's hard to say who will end up with the bill. Should it be Jorgensen? Or would those living on the land be required to pay if they wish to obtain ownership? Regardless, the state will require *someone* to atone for those taxes."

"Do you think the other bidders are aware of this?"

"I'm certain of it. I'm not the only lawyer looking into this side of things. If one of the other investors has something to hang over Jorgensen's head, Jorgensen may bow out at a lower selling price to compensate. It makes this a dangerous game. I'm certain that Jorgensen would like to avoid going to jail or paying additional fines. Not all the investors are in this situation to act honorably, and if they can inspire him to drop the price, they will."

Absently, William opened the pocket watch again. "So, what now?"

"First, we need to find out if these ledgers are accurate." Callum held up a stack of dusty books. "From what we've read, Jorgensen doesn't even have the profit this year to pay those taxes if he wanted to. Not if he wants to pay his employees, which he must, and he's already taken out two small loans over the last two years. Second, you need to decide if you're going to make an offer on the place. If it's sincerely worth it to you."

"And third?"

Callum clicked his tongue. "Well, if you decide you'd like to move forward, then paperwork will need to be made official. The county will get involved, which will stir up an awareness that these taxes have fallen through the cracks."

"Meaning?"

"The sale won't be able to be finalized, most likely, until they're paid."

"Which a buyer could do." William snapped the pocket watch closed.

Callum's eyes narrowed. "Correct. But do you imagine that these other buyers would be so generous as to do that kind of favor for any of these tenants?"

Not in the least.

"So while one of these buyers might be willing to pay the taxes in order to secure the land, we both know they would scarcely allow the families to also keep their farms. One way or another, Bennet and the other tenants will likely lose their land." Callum's expression was pained. "Unless someone was able to do something about it . . ."

William blew out a slow breath and with the maps of New River spread out before him, he switched one for another. But no matter how he turned the pages, Bennet Hollow was still in the way of his dreams.

His old dreams.

William leaned back in his chair. A newness had awoken inside him and he didn't know what to do about it. A month ago, that corner of the map was a mere plot of land that he could have purchased and sold or staked a claim on. Land that belonged to people with no faces to him.

And now?

Bowing his head, William ran fingertips over his forehead and imagined the very tenants. Most especially, Mr. Bennet's second eldest daughter with her bright eyes and quick wit. The way she protected everything in her care, including her home that he'd had the honor of walking the length of at her side. It was clear, the love she had for her farm. A love she'd learned from her father and would no doubt pass on to her children. The notion pushed heat up William's neck.

Because he was struggling to imagine a future that didn't include her.

Not if he were honest with himself. He stared at his hands now. The same hands that had wrapped around her own after church on Sunday. There by the oak tree, his only desire at first had been to steal a few minutes alone to clear his head. And then she'd come along . . .

Once again, changing everything—his entire course—and making him glad for company.

Nearly impossible for a man like him, and yet she was doing so daily.

He couldn't, with any shred of sanity, turn away from that.

Folding his arms, William leaned back against the chair. So, this was what it felt like to be a wrecked man. He breathed in deeply, finally letting go of any prospect of keeping his sanity. It was gone now, and so he would start again. From the ground up. Recraft his approach and this time, that approach would *include* the Bennets. Not dismantle them.

The ship that bore this captain quaked in the wake of change and yet it was a wholesome and healing change. Life-giving. A thumping in his chest that meant he was human. Alive. Most of all . . . that the future held a God-given hope. Not just in business, but in his very life.

Hope that maybe, just maybe, he might grow his family. That he might have someone to come home to. That the halls of his estate could be filled with more than just servants and the sound of his voice as he spoke through the telephone line.

"There has to be a way of securing the New River Coal Company, while leaving Bennet land and its tenants at peace. Of purchasing the company without disrupting the family." William turned an ink pen in his fingers, which were stained black in the creases from all the sums he'd been doing.

Callum nodded.

The maps still before him, William assessed them with a fresh outlook. The Bennets lived on over twenty acres of valuable earth. William had gathered enough about Mr. Bennet and his family to know that they could never afford the farm outright. "The buyer could gift it to them."

Callum's brows lifted. "But only if that man outbid everyone else. Only if the mine were worth it."

Which was still unclear.

"Then there's a matter of pride," Callum added. "Bennet's."

"Right."

"Few men of worth would take to a favor so big."

So what to do? And how would William do anything without admitting to madness? "It would be a terrible business move," he admitted.

Callum checked his own timepiece and rose. "Right. But I like the way your wheels are spinning." He drew in a slow sigh. "Believe me, I've thought of it myself."

"But?"

"I wouldn't want it to seem as though I were trying to purchase anyone's favor. But I certainly haven't ruled it out. It's a lot to think on." His voice was heavy as he spoke. "I—I better go finish packing. Train arrives at four."

William nodded. He didn't want these business dealings to appear like a conflict of interest either. He simply wanted to pursue the coal holdings of New River and leave Lizbeth's home in peace.

As much as he meant to focus on his own vexations, the aggravated *thunking* coming from Callum's room made it impossible. Rising, William strode down the hallway and nudged Callum's door open.

"Is there any way I can help?" he asked.

Kneeling beside an open trunk, Callum looked as lost as any man he'd ever seen.

"This is because of Jayne," William stated. Maybe understanding Callum's mind would help him comprehend his own.

"It's certainly not because of you," Callum quipped glumly.

William smiled, grateful for the spark of humor still alive in his friend. "You'll see her again, no?" Words he spoke to himself as well.

"I hope so. But how can we ever really know?"

Consulting his pocket watch, two gold hands pointed to the truth: Callum had less than an hour left. "Do you wish to speak to her?"

"I don't know what I would say. But yes, I do wish that. I wish to see her. To speak to her and . . ." His voice trailed off and the lost look only intensified.

"Do you wish to *marry her*?"

An obvious battle waged as Callum stared at his hands with an unfocused gaze. "Those are strong words."

A battle of mind. Of heart.

Of propriety and even fortune. The same wrestling William himself was thrashing against.

All that a man like Callum, and like William, had to acknowledge whenever considering whom he could tie his heart and life to. Whom he could place his trust in, his hopes, and his future. There was a reason they travelled armed. This rolling mansion was ever in danger of being robbed and while most bandits centered their focus on passenger cars, a place like the Pemberley was ripe for the picking and never would William allow such without putting up a fight should thieves storm the castle walls.

So, when it came to his future, he'd only ever thought the same. That all vulnerability needed to be guarded behind lock and key. Otherwise, his heart would be ripe for the picking. The destroying. *That* he couldn't make peace with. Which made seeking a bride nigh unto impossible. Even so, he didn't sense an ounce of greed among the women they'd shared both table and church pew with of late. Which had him sincerely wondering . . . if men and women from such different worlds could meld their lives into a good future, was the woman for Callum . . . Jayne Bennet?

Callum fidgeted with the lock on his travelling chest. A lock more easily unfastened than that of the heart. As a lawyer, Callum had both fortune and prestige at stake. A life he'd worked hard to build. "I don't know. But . . . yes." It was a bold gaze that acknowledged William now. "If I had my way right now, I would say those words to her." Callum's focus rose to the sunny window. "Maybe I should just walk over there."

Caution climbed William's backbone. "Are you certain . . . Are you certain she feels as strongly as you do?"

Callum's response came out weak. "It's hard to say." He looked at William. "Be honest with me. What have you observed? Maybe I've been so distracted by my own desires that I haven't properly discerned hers. Have you noticed any indication of feeling from her?"

William pulled a chair closer and sat. "I can see that she's reserved. She's a gentle-natured woman, one of substance, and I can see *why* you are drawn to her. Despite her financial outlook, Jayne Bennet is a fine match for a good man." And a good man Callum was.

"But what of her feelings? What have you witnessed?"

Already, Callum was beginning to crumble. Yes, the woman was beautiful. Stunningly so. But so was Helen of Troy. While William didn't often draw upon Greek mythology for how to direct a man's life, Callum seemed in grave danger of being a sinking ship in the Aegean Sea, and William feared the man might never rise again.

It pained him to speak honestly but it needed to be said. "Very little, I admit."

Callum was still as William pressed on.

"I haven't witnessed any clear indication that she's in love. I'm hardly an expert on the topic, though," he hedged. Blasted emotions. How to navigate them? If only the hearts of women could be as easy to decipher as the columns in his ledgers. "I don't sense Jayne would marry you for money, though were you to offer her a future with you, she may very well accept. You would offer a life unlike she's ever known. Solve her father's problems in the process. Would you be happy in that instance?"

Callum's expression looked riddled with pain until he slowly shook his head. "No."

It was pride in Callum's tense jaw. Good. Better pride than the alternative.

Unfettered adoration would only plummet him into that unyielding sea.

William didn't blame the man. He too wanted a match based on sincerity, not wealth, but what chance did they have of that? There wasn't a woman they encountered who couldn't tell that they had enough fortune for one happy life if not a dozen.

"Has she given you some reason to hope?" William asked. "Something she might have said in private?" Maybe Jayne had spoken more frankly in the moments Callum had shared alone with her. "How about the other day in the churchyard?"

Gaze to the floor, Callum's eyes shifted as though the answer were woven into the Persian rug. "Not directly."

William pressed his thumbs together, staring there to try and conjure the wisest words he could. "Then perhaps you might give it a little more time. You could write to her. And see if she writes back. Allow even a few more weeks for matters to unfold. And soon, you could be right back here again."

Callum placed several books into the trunk.

"You could try and be more forthright in letters as time goes by."

"I suppose." Callum rose and grabbed several coats from the wardrobe. Hangers rattled together. One fell. "I won't be able to return right away. But if I were able to write . . ."

William planned to be gone in mere days himself to oversee his other business endeavors. By week's end, there would be nothing left on this stretch of track save a few weeds that had grown between the rails. But William intended to return to New River soon to finish proceedings on the mine discussion, and there seemed no reason Callum couldn't do the same. "Much could develop in that time."

"You're right." Callum clattered a hanger back into place. "It would be unwise to rush the process."

Yet in truth, if William were basing this experience on the legend of war between Troy and Sparta, he understood more and more what it was like to have an Achilles' heel. A weak point. One that he meant to protect with armor—but would never truly be able to. Clearly Callum had the same weak spot.

The only difference was that his friend was being honest about it.

Unease rising about his own insecurities, along with the cost of giving Callum any proper advice, William tried to rally them both. "Exactly. And the future can hold good things."

Did he believe that himself? He was trying to.

In fact, he was starting to.

"Yes." With a sigh of acceptance, Callum dropped the coats into the trunk. "Could you do something for me?"

"Of course."

"Could you find me a large piece of paper to wrap a package in?" Callum searched through his belongings.

"Of course." William hurried to the storage closet since the train would be here soon and was rarely late. He found just the right piece, returning in time for Callum to fill it and tie the package with a piece of string.

"Will you see that Jayne gets this?" The paper bundle crinkled as Callum held it out.

In the distance, a train whistle blew. There was nothing left to do. No time to aid his friend in changing course to let the winds of possibility blow his sails straight to the Bennet farm.

Instead, William took the package, holding it with all the dignity his friend deserved. "Consider it done."

20

A gray evening haze draped the sky as Lizbeth trudged down the road toward town. Along with the sounds of the colliery came sight of the tall roof of the breaker as she hurried along, basket in hand, toward the coal office and its open door. Filled with the treats she'd baked for the mules all afternoon long, any sweet aroma her basket might have given off was drowned out by the smell of coal and grease. Train tracks curved along the right side of the mine, and smoke spewed from a pipe in the ground. A shrill whistle split the chaos in two and she fought the urge to cover her ears.

The day shift finished, men spilled from the hoist house and beyond. Lizbeth wove through them and out of habit, her eyes scanned a distant hill for sight of the Jorgensens' house, where Hattie lived, and where Reverend Coburn had been dwelling since his arrival. She hoped to avoid the man today.

Finally reaching the office, Lizbeth ducked within.

Mr. Jorgensen stood at his desk with his back to her. At his side stood a man who cut a much finer figure in his tailored shirt and waistcoat. A man she recognized even before he turned. William

Drake. Splayed-out maps and documents sat on the desk between them. They looked at her in unison.

Mr. Jorgensen's mustache tipped up in a friendly smile. William looked mortified. The younger of the pair turned a map upside down and braced his fingertips against the desk's surface, the tension beneath his shirtsleeves as taut as the room now.

Her courage tripping over itself, Lizbeth forced herself to speak. "Good evening."

"Evenin', Lizzy. I figured I might be seein' ya soon. I'd say I smell those apple treats you make."

She held up the basket. "Yes, sir." This time around, she'd perfected the recipe by stewing apples along with carrots. She'd flavored it all with cinnamon and baked the dough in pans before cutting the results into squares. "I hope I've counted right. I made fifty."

"On the dot. I've got forty-seven mules stabled in the mine."

Lizbeth breathed in the number more bittersweet than encouraging. All those lives . . . so far from the sun and clean air.

William's eyes followed her every move as she placed the heavy basket on the corner of the desk.

Lizbeth wet her lips again. "Sir—"

"You can leave that with me." Mr. Jorgensen waved toward her handiwork. "I'll see that one of the spraggers takes it down tomorrow morning. I'll nab a fella who can deliver it straight to a mule driver to distribute them."

"Thank you, sir." Lizbeth nudged the offering farther onto the desk, taking care not to muss the paperwork already in place. "I was wondering if . . ."

After laying aside the rest of his maps, William pulled off his flatcap. He cast a glance at her and she couldn't tell if it stemmed from interest or annoyance, so sound was his stare. It was a gaze stronger than a lantern flame, and she alone the air that kept it lit.

Words tripped on her tongue. "I—I was wonderin' if I might be able to give these to the mules myself." Lizbeth gulped. "It's been so many years since I've seen any of them. Since they've been on the farm and I could check on them. Even help with their care. I wouldn't ask for anything in return . . ." Her voice trailed off, muted to silence by the shock in both men's faces.

"Well, I . . . I don't know." Mr. Jorgensen stammered.

William straightened. The light in his eyes snuffing out.

"I understand that girls haven't been allowed in the mine but . . ." She straightened her spine even as her hands, still clutched in front of her, trembled. "You see, I was thinking that—"

"It's out of the question." William rolled up a map.

"I promise I'm not afraid." She brushed past the desk to face both men more easily. "I was just thinkin' that I could—"

"No." William used the rolled-up map to point at her basket, which appeared lowly and ridiculous sitting in this place now. "And I'm sorry, but Mr. Jorgensen will see the goods delivered as promised. Or I will myself. You've no need to trouble yourself."

Her heart raced. "It's no trouble. I was thinking that I could—"

He spoke without looking at her, flashing only his profile. "As Mr. Jorgensen just said, consider your goods delivered. And please . . ." He looked at her again. "Think no more on it." His voice held an edge that sliced the conversation to an end.

Flushed, Lizbeth stepped back. The nerve of the man to make such a decision. New River did not *belong* to him. And neither did she. Mr. Jorgensen's expression held regret but she sensed his decision was the same the longer he remained silent. Lizbeth backed farther away, nearly tripping over a cluttered hat rack. It thudded against the wall. She balanced the rack and turned away.

William's jaw tightened. Whether over her clumsy request or clumsy feet, she didn't know. And here she'd thought he meant to be friendly to her. Opening a piece of his world to her as though to expand her own. He, the same man who had gently laid a novel into her open hands only days ago. A way of broadening her view of the world. Expanding her heart and hope. Who had made her wonder if he was in fact good and kind and gentle.

The budding peace she'd had about him caved in. Nothing left but dust and rubble.

Throat stinging, Lizbeth turned away from the office, only to collide with a crew of miners. The men slammed to a halt the same instant that she did. But not quick enough for Lizbeth to avoid bumping into the miner at their helm. One who smiled at her.

"Oh! Mr. Westgard. My apologies."

His blue eyes sparked with surprise as he caught her by the arms. "Easy there. Apologies are mine." He released her carefully. "And please, just West."

After nodding, she ducked her head and hurried on. The friendly miner didn't deserve her withdrawal, but she was in no form to attempt conversation. Nor did she care that the coal dust staining Mr. Westgard's uniform was now on her dress front. She could scrub it out at home. Maybe she could be like William Drake and shut out the world. Right now, she needed to. Lizbeth swiped at her eyes before anyone could see emotions betraying her.

Mr. Westgard matched her with his long strides. "Is something the matter, Miss . . . Miss . . . ?"

She couldn't bring herself to answer. Needed to be free of the wiles of men.

This one followed anyway. "Please help me remember."

"It's Lizbeth," she stammered in a rush.

He grinned at her flustered tone. "Of course. I was just meaning to be polite." He doffed a blackened cap and coal dust creased the soft lines around his eyes. "Might I walk with you a ways,

Lizbeth? I'm off shift now." His attention shot back to the mine office before settling on her face once more. His stride continued to match hers. "Was that Drake's voice I overheard?"

She pressed on.

"I can see you're upset and for that, I'm sorry." He shook his head. "The man means well, but he can be a real brute when he wants to be."

Lizbeth spoke without slowing. "You know him well, do you?"

"Fairly well. We've worked together for years." Mr. Westgard switched to her other side as Lizbeth crossed the road toward the edge of town.

Nearby, women and children greeted husbands and fathers from the narrow yards and spindly porches of every row house. A miner picked up his little girl and tossed her into the air. She shrieked before landing back into coal-blackened hands.

"Look, I don't want to delay you," Mr. Westgard continued. "But would you give me just a moment of your time? I think there's something you need to know about Mr. Drake. And your father's farm."

Her feet slowed.

"It has to do with the land. A dispute that Drake has with your father's ownership."

"I'm sorry?" Finally, she stopped.

He circled around her. "It might not be my place to say, but I believe in the truth above all else." His masculine hand rested against his chest. "Word around these parts is that Mr. Drake is digging into legal matters about your pa's land. See, he didn't come only to purchase the mine, but to obtain several surrounding properties as well. Farms in danger of being confiscated should the sale go through."

"Confiscated?"

"It's complicated, but the men like me who were summoned from Pennsylvania were all brought here for that reason." Mr. Westgard waited at the edge of the footbridge. A few dozen paces and she'd be out of New River proper and on her way home. But what was this man saying of their property?

He crammed both hands in his pockets and leaned back with an air of confidence before taking one more step toward her. His voice softened to a near whisper. "You see, *our* job here is to discover whether or not the mine is worth purchasing. Drake's purpose here is to squash anything standing in his way. Including the local tenants."

Lizbeth shook her head. "No. Our farm belongs to my pa now. By agreement. He worked hard for it and even Mr. Jorgensen would say the same."

"That may be, but there's some gray area, so the boys say. If the mine transfers to Drake, then that ownership transfers to him as well. He has no requirement to honor the understanding already in place, and from the way I've heard him talk, he has absolutely no intention to."

The evening dimmed further.

"I don't mean to bore you with business, just for you to know the type of person Mr. Drake is. The type of person that this town is dealing with. And for you to know that his goal is to make your father's land his own. As soon as possible, I understand."

Lizbeth tried to speak but no sound came out.

"That's the reason Callum Brydolf is here as well. Man's a lawyer, does Drake's bidding in these endeavors. No mere mortal can stand up to them. No matter how hard people have tried. You'd do your older sister a favor to caution her as well."

Her head was growing light.

"I don't know if it's been made clear just how much land Mr. Drake owns. Hundreds of acres across the nation. More businesses and employees than people like you and I could ever stomach. And he's always looking for more." Mr. Westgard shook his head slowly. "His greed has no end. Have you not noticed how he and the other coal barons have been sinking their talons into this town? Especially the young women? One of the investors even indicated he might want to marry one of the local girls as a business strategy."

Lizbeth felt sick. She hadn't noticed these things but perhaps she'd been too blind to see.

"Has Drake or Brydolf shown you or your sisters any of that kind of behavior?" His puzzled expression held an air of innocence. "If so, I'd advise you to be wary. They're not the only ones looking to *endear* themselves to the people of New River. The mine might go to the highest bidder, but the respect will go to the one who is best able to throw the wool over people's eyes."

At the sound of someone calling out, his demeanor changed. "You've got company coming."

Lizbeth glanced back to see Hattie hurrying their way.

"I'll leave you now, but . . ." He touched a hand to his chest again. "Please consider me a friend if you ever need one in the matter."

Hattie called out again from behind them. "Lizzy!"

The man angled away. "Just be cautious with Drake. I'm sorry to be the one to share that bad news with you. I figured it best to explain his true colors before it was too late." He gave a polite smile.

Overwhelmed, Lizbeth turned for Hattie's approach, her thoughts more on William Drake than the young woman who reached her side.

If William had the power to evict them from their home, why endear himself to her and her sisters? Was he deceitful? Was that why he'd stood as tall and taut as mine timber upon their first meeting? And once again today?

"Lizzy?"

How easy to recount the sweet pastries and glistening fruits she'd admired just days ago along with his speech about the beautiful racehorse she might one day lay eyes on. She'd been caught up in the moment—as enchanted with his train car as she'd been with him, admittedly.

And all of it only a show, then? Her stomach clenched.

"Lizzy!" Hattie dropped her shawl as she nudged Lizbeth's shoulder. "You're a million miles away." She bent to retrieve the tumble of wool.

Lizbeth tried to brush aside rising panic. How foolish she'd been. "I—uh, I've got too much on my mind."

Hattie winced. "That's why I've come myself. There's somethin' I need to tell you."

"Of course." Lizbeth went to loop her arm through Hattie's for support, but Hattie pulled away, putting a step of distance between them.

"What's the matter? Is somethin' wrong?"

"Nothin's wrong." Hattie pulled her gray shawl tighter. "In fact, it's quite good. At least, I think so. I just need to see you to say this."

Lizbeth clasped her friend's chilled hand as more worries rose. "Tell me."

"Well . . ." Hattie fiddled nervously with the fringe of her shawl. "Reverend Coburn has asked me if he and I might marry. And I've said *yes*."

Hattie's eyes were a bright shade of brown. Like coffee with a splash of cream. The color was all that Lizbeth could compute as she retraced those words in her mind. "Come . . . come again?"

"We're to be married. Reverend Coburn and myself. We've set a date already. For before his return so that I'll be able to accompany him. I do hope you'll come."

Lizbeth shook her head to jar her hearing. "You're plannin' to marry Reverend Coburn?"

"Don't say it like that. He's a fine man. A minister." Hattie smoothed a hand over her straight hair, which angled back into a tight bun. "He's got a good and sensible occupation and a nice livin'. I'll have a chance to do more with my life than be a burden to my parents. Pa's about to retire. They still have me to look after. I'll have the chance to prosper in this life. To run a home all my own."

"But this way? You're a smart girl, Hattie! You've had schooling—a tutor even. You're wise and capable. *Any* man would be lucky to have you."

"And one wants me!"

"But Reverend Coburn?"

"What other choices do I have? I'm plain, Lizzy." With dismay, Hattie held out her hands. "Even for the men of New River. 'Sides, what miner would ever dare to court the boss's daughter? They were too afraid to even ask me to dance. Or did you not notice that at the gatherin'? Did you not notice that I was the only woman our age without a man who extended his arm?"

"No, I'm sorry." She'd been too preoccupied with her own thoughts. Her own offers to dance. Shame burned Lizbeth's cheeks.

"I'm already twenty-seven years old, and with no other prospects at hand. My dear friend—by acceptin' Reverend Coburn, I'll have the chance to be a mother."

A joy that Hattie deserved.

"Hattie, I'm sorry. I shouldn't have spoken as I did."

"I don't need you to be sorry, Lizzy. I only need you to be happy for me." She smoothed her plain dress front as her thick eyebrows bridged in yearning. "I've shared many evenings lately listenin' to Reverend Coburn read. We've gone for strolls and he even helped me trim Ma's roses yesterday. Oh, he's serious in ways. Perhaps clumsy in others. But he's a decent man and I've enjoyed the time I've shared with him. Pa and Ma like him as well. His stayin' with us helped them get to know him. It helped all of us."

A pair of miners strode past. Some of the very men who'd showed no interest in courting Hattie Jorgensen because of all that she described. Now Hattie had a chance with someone who wasn't connected to a life of coal in any way. She had a chance at an all-new future with a decent man. Did that mean Hattie was marrying for love? Lizbeth searched her friend's watery gaze. Could sincere affection bloom in only a few weeks' time? Was it possible?

"You're gonna marry Reverend Coburn," Lizbeth said weakly, needing it to sink in. Which meant Hattie would soon be leaving for Pennsylvania.

She would be leaving this place.

"Yes. And please be glad for me."

Swallowing all her uncertainty over her friend's choice, Lizbeth reached for Hattie's hand once more to warm it. Just because Mr. Westgard had implied that Lizbeth was a poor judge of men, it didn't mean that others were. "I'm glad for you, Hattie. Grateful you've found someone who is your match. May it be a wonderful life that you share."

21

The Bennets' front door sounded more fragile with each knock of William's knuckles. The same way his spirit had felt ever since his encounter with Lizbeth in the mine office yesterday. Now to find the words again. *Better* words. He hadn't meant to disregard her feelings when she'd entered the office, her eagerness shining through as she clutched a basket handle. Quite the contrary. He only meant to keep her safe. She didn't know the horrors beneath the earth or what she suggested by asking to venture down into the shaft herself.

To think of her donning a lantern, entering the creaking hoist cage, and descending to the lower levels curdled his blood. Worse would be when she saw the stables and the poor creatures they held. The darkness. The stench. The bleakness of animals that had no one to fight for them. Mules that didn't know the soft touch of grass or the glitter of the moon.

A woman like Lizbeth Bennet belonged above ground where her spirit was free to soar. Much like her cherished animals deserved. To see them in any other condition would be a sight she'd never shake from her memory. So he'd slammed her inquiry to a halt. Much too forcefully.

Willam knocked again.

He'd been too harsh with her. Too protective and reactionary. Desperate to apologize, the delivery of Callum's package got him down the road to this very stoop. Not to mention, it was high time he speak with Mr. Bennet and try to help solve this land matter before someone else with darker motives did. Every step here had been in protection of the Bennet family. Now to express that more graciously than he had the day before.

Moving back, William glimpsed the second story windows. The faces of the younger girls peeked down. One of them giggled. They dispersed and the ivory curtains swished close. Voices rang out from within, the sound of his name capping the excited chatter.

The door swung open. Mrs. Bennet filled the doorway with her graying bun and flour-dusted apron. "Well, a good day to you, Mr. Drake. To what do we owe this surprise?" She widened the slant of the door, beckoning him in.

"Thank you, ma'am."

Inside, the essence of baking bread mixed with laughter. Someone had strung a garland of dried apple slices and acorns along the banister. Pine cones topped the stone mantle. William noted the tin cups dotting the supper table and its checkered cloth. A piano lacking several keys sat in a corner where a trio of potted plants caught sun from a window. He soaked it all in, this picture of home.

William shifted his feet, eager to stay and just as much out of place. "I've brought a package for your eldest, Jayne. And I was hoping I might speak for a few minutes with your husband." It seemed safer to ask for Lizbeth's father. He'd face Lizbeth before leaving as that would surely be the hardest conversation of all.

"Pa's not home," one of the girls announced from the tight cluster of sisters now gathered near the stove. They were all smiles, braids, and swaying skirts. William nodded, uncertain of which one spoke. He searched for Lizbeth but didn't see her among them.

"Then I'll just leave the package and be off." Why was he panicking? William held the paper-wrapped bundle out to Mrs. Bennet, who instead scuttled over to the stairs and called up to the second floor. "Jayne, girl!" The stout woman's apron strings swung as she leaned over the rail. "A package for ya!"

Jayne's footsteps sounded on the stairs. "For me?"

Lizbeth appeared right behind. Now his heart was really hammering.

Her hair lay pulled over one shoulder with a ribbon, and her brow pinched in confusion. She wore a skirt of brick red and a wool sweater that spoke of the coming winter and the crisp white snow that would soon fall.

Lizbeth's eyes went wide at sight of him. "Mr. Drake?"

"William, please."

Lizbeth moved around her sister so that Jayne leaned nearer to the banister.

He held up the offering all wrapped in paper and string. "From Callum. He sends this along with his regrets that he was pulled away for business."

"He's gone then?" Jayne whispered.

Had William advised his friend wrong? "Yes. But it's very possible he may return soon."

Jayne bent over the railing and accepted the package. "Thank you, sir."

"Of course." He glanced around at the faces. He'd just have to find another moment to discuss the farm with their pa and his intentions to be of assistance in the land dispute. Now if he could only summon the courage to get Lizbeth alone, to speak with her in the yard perhaps. But the words that came out were "I'll bid you all a good day."

He backed away, bumping into the edge of the table. Briefly, William closed his eyes. He mined for any shred of courage that remained. Perhaps the same kind that had fueled Lizbeth yesterday when entering the office. She inspired him. If only she knew that. "Before I leave, might I have a word with Miss Lizbeth?" he asked.

The entire kitchen fell silent. Outside, a woodpecker knocked against a tree.

"Well certainly!" Mrs. Bennet gripped the hem of her apron. "Lizzy, why don't you see Mr. Drake out? Jayne can finish up your chore."

Lizbeth fiddled with a wooden button on her sweater, the pale wool now the same shade as her face.

"For only a moment." William squared his shoulders. "And only if it would suit you. I don't want to take up your time and I can see you're busy."

Finally, she drew in a steadying breath. "Now would be fine." She angled to Jayne, whispering, "I won't be long."

Head light, William stepped back. No sense prolonging what he needed to say. The sun greeted him as he retreated to the stoop where a late October breeze lingered crisp and cold. With Lizbeth close behind, he strode into the yard. Still within view of her family, but not within earshot. He searched for the right way to begin, but to his surprise, she began first.

"Mr. Drake."

He turned and again said, "William, please."

She ignored the request. "Mr. Drake, might I ask you somethin'?" Lizbeth walked onward. Her bootheels tread across the path, the sound muted and soft.

He followed. "Of course." Why did his chest hurt? It might have something to do with the way she wasn't looking at him. He pulled his hat off. His porter had cut his hair that morning. For this very encounter. Neat and trimmed along the sides, as short as it would go. The morning air was cool to his skin without the wool's warmth. Intensifying the way he felt like a stranger standing before her. A foreign object beside her earthen beauty, one that didn't seem to belong. Despite his growing wishes.

Except for his own sister, never could he recall a time when he'd spoken to a woman entirely alone. The breeze stirred her hair, and a lightning strike held less spark than her eyes just now.

"I owe you an apology," he began.

"Is what Mr. Westgard said true?" She gripped the cuffs of her sweater, drawing her arms around herself.

"What *Mr. Westgard* said?" The name snapped off his tongue.

She looked small as her grip tightened. "About the land. The dispute over our ownership. That somehow all you investors have more of a right to this farm than we do."

Westgard had told her that? The man knew next to nothing about these dealings but clearly imagined himself with a few aces in hand.

William's heart jerked in regret. Out of anger toward an employee who had no business meddling in the affairs of others. A rogue man who didn't grasp the pains William was going through to right this situation. "If you'll help me understand what's been said," he began, "I'll do my best to clear the air for you."

"Mr. Westgard said you're after our land."

"That I am not. I assure you."

"And that you're no different than the other investors. Trying to endear themselves to us only to gain an advantage."

"I mean only to be sincere."

When she scoffed, he braved more.

"What else did Westgard say?" William's shadow crossed over hers when he stepped aside.

"That our days here—on this land—could be near an end because of you."

William shook his head. "It isn't so. In fact, I've spent my time here trying to—"

A single step forward. "You've been spendin' these last weeks tryin' to get us all to trust you. Only to deceive us. Just like the others." Her accent, stronger now, tangled like a thistle bush in a rising storm. She marched onward into the nearby field as though needing to hold ground in familiar territory.

William matched her pace even as he tried not to walk too close to her side. "Please understand. There's much more to it than that." Already, he'd scrawled an *X* across *Bennet Hollow* on his map, along with all the other farms. The land wasn't for the taking. At least not by him. "If I could only describe to you how complicated this matter is. How many pieces I'm still trying to sort out and why." He was desperate for her to understand. "I only wish good things for your family. And for you. I do care."

"Care? What you've been doin' here ain't carin'." Her lashes dipped as she searched the ground, casting tiny shadows on her cheeks from the distant sun. A silken strand of brown hair fluttered against the side of her face and she pushed it away with the same determination that he saw in her expression as she raised her focus to him again.

"Please allow me to repair that. Your comfort matters to me a great deal." Skin heating, he pulled off his coat and tossed it aside. Standing there in his shirt and waistcoat, he shoved back the sleeves to his elbows. "I mean to be of service to your family in the ways that I can. And a service to you in the ways you'd permit me."

She recoiled, looking puzzled as she halted in the long grass.

"Lizbeth, I have no intention of claiming your father's land. One of my reasons for being here today was to explain that to him. To clear the air once and for all."

"And back there? At the mine office?" She flung a hand toward town. "I was made to look foolish. You don't understand the time and thought I put into going there. Askin' what I did. You don't understand what I was trying to do."

"I don't?" Quite the contrary. "I have come to see how much you love this land and those entrusted to your care."

She shook her head as though to prevent his words from landing.

"The way I behaved at the office was only in protection of you."

"Protection?"

He'd done it now. William closed the gap that had grown between them. He longed to reach out and touch her. To touch her hand. The same fingers that had brushed against his own before. His very heart had begun to beat for this woman, and this woman alone. He'd encouraged Callum to hold his tongue when it came to matters of affection. A recommendation William now regretted. If he could turn back time for his friend's sake, he would.

Gently, he touched Lizbeth's wrist. Just barely grazing her delicate skin between his fingertips.

She pulled away.

"I'm struggling to find the words. But I—I mean to explain that I value my time spent with you."

She squinted at him and he couldn't tell if she was puzzled or still angry.

William pressed a hand to his chest, and as he did, he spoke the very words his aunt would disown him over. But he no longer cared. "I've come to have a hope for your—your company." Lord help him, he'd never said anything like this to a woman before. "Your companionship even. If I might inquire if—if you could ever want my companionship in return." He squeezed his eyes closed lest that sound improper. And he was running out of time to speak vaguely. "In a righteous sense, that is. A devoted one." He looked at her again as the puzzle in her brow only deepened.

"Are you . . . are you . . . ?"

"Am I asking you something?"

Eyes wide, she slowly nodded.

He tugged at the hem of his waistcoat. "I believe I am." William shoved one of his shirtsleeves farther back. "Never have I encountered a woman who has so enriched my world as you. Who has so made me long to enrich the world of another."

She stared at him. The sun pooled down on her brown hair, pulled back soft and low. Here in this field, he imagined her in Vermont, surrounded by horses in the pasture of his estate. Her hand to the proud, glossy neck of Lady Light and a basket of apples at her feet. No more mines. No more darkness. No more fears. He thought of how the sunlight would touch her hair there. Of how it would touch his life if she were with him.

Would she be the one to wind a garland of acorns around the banister of his all-too-empty mansion? His estate back home had never known such humble offerings, but the marble halls cried out for them as did his soul.

"Please allow me to state that I do not wish to be parted from you. Not now and not ever."

Lizbeth gaped at him, seeming about to sink to the ground. He reached a hand out to steady her but she moved away.

"You *hope* for me?" she whispered.

"Indefinitely." He stepped toward her. Time to face the fact that he would never be the same since knowing her. "And indelibly."

Her brown eyes, wide now, searched the ground between them. "This can't be so." She turned away, muttering something about what Mr. Westgard had warned her about. Finally, Lizbeth spoke to him over her shoulder. "You—you've confused me. And you've been *most* arrogant."

He came around her so she faced him. "For that I must make amends."

"You've belittled me. Yesterday—"

"If I was rude to you at the colliery, I apologize. Your request to go down into the mine caught me by surprise. I—I hadn't expected to see you and it shocked me. Your presence." In truth he'd been unsettled. More so when he learned she meant to put her life on the line in a pit of miners. All for a crew of animals.

"You hadn't the right to deny me. You're *not* the owner."

"No, ma'am. But I know the horrors in those tunnels. It's no place for a lady."

"I wasn't afraid."

Which endeared her to him all the more. "The mules you speak of, they're poorly kept. They know only the closed-in world underground. They are weary. Disoriented. They're not as well as your own beloved creatures. Seeing them would dismay you."

"It's the very reason I'm tryin' to find a way to help."

"Of course. But maybe you're not the one to help them."

She winced and he saw the wound his statement inflicted.

He tried to explain. "The drivers do their best, but there are rats in the underground stables. A constant stench with little air coming in or out. You wouldn't be able to stomach it." He moved closer, softening his voice lest his passion startle her. "That's after you've endured the descent in the cage for hundreds of feet. A cage that is so dark and narrow, it's soul-crushing." He didn't even know how to describe it. "Please know that I denied your request for those reasons alone. Not due to your ability *or* courage. Neither of those do I doubt."

How could he? With her peering up at him so? This young woman who was filled with so much strength and dignity that it stirred greater things within him.

"As for yesterday, I meant only to keep you safe and well." He took another step forward. "Lizbeth. I have given you a poor impression of myself. Please allow me to remedy that."

A breeze stirred the ribbon that bound her hair. "There's little you could say to change my mind about anything."

Was it time to end this agony? "And what is it that you see of me?"

She tipped her chin up. "That you are proud and unfeeling."

William tugged again at the hem of his waistcoat. Touched the knot of his tie. It felt easier to address these things than the pain she shot through him. "That is how you see me?"

"I was a fool to have believed otherwise."

Slowly William nodded. "Then I understand." Now his boots moved away from her own. His hand, which longed to brush her cheek, remained instead at his side.

If he had the chance to dance with her again, he would. If he had the chance to make her smile, he would. He'd do those things again and again until she believed him. More than her belief, though, he needed her trust. The very thing that he'd just lost.

He lowered his head. "I'll bid you a good day, then. And I do apologize for disheartening you so. It was not my intention."

With that, William grabbed his coat and forced himself to step away. Away from the woman who brought light to his world in a way no person ever had. Away from the woman who—he was finally able to admit to himself—he loved.

winter

22

December 1904

Snow whispered against the window. Lizbeth listened to its soft murmur as beside her, Jayne hummed a Christmas carol along with Maryanne's pounding at the piano. The music marched up the stairwell and into their room. "Hark! The Herald Angels Sing" sounded rusty from the old piano, but the addition was merry. Lizbeth raised her embroidery hoop nearer to the window and slid a needle and thread through.

The rich purple strand was one she had simmered with blackberries the summer before, thanks to Ma's guiding hand, and now the cheery color somehow chased away the cold. Lizbeth's rocking chair creaked as she stitched the next petal in the sampler's ornate border . . . trying once again to think about something *other* than William. It had been two months since he and the Pemberley departed New River. A churning of steel wheels on tracks. Determined and absolute.

Lizbeth squinted at her stitches. Best to focus instead on the need to finish this sampler. By doing so, she might earn a little income for her family, which had become the cry of her heart—and Pa's—ever since they'd gotten the news of the tax issue with the land.

The same news William may have been alluding to. And Mr. Westgard.

Yet which caution was right?

Following William's departure, Pa had explained to the family that they owed taxes on the land, which he'd learned in the formal letter Mr. Jorgensen had sent him the day Lizbeth had watched the shadows cross his face. And now, if they had any hope of keeping the acreage that was Bennet Hollow, nearly two hundred dollars was owed to the state of Virginia. An insurmountable sum, so with every stitch, Lizbeth ached to find the right ways to help.

With Christmas just days away, this should be a time for warm hearts and joyous spirits. Instead, she awoke each morning to the memory of William's face. To the shadows of regret and confusion. All sharper than the icicles dangling from the eaves. William's words filled her mind again and she pinched the thought off before it could continue. Before the memory became clear as it often did. His face—his heart—before her in all the clarity a man could possibly give.

A man she had turned away. Who had left, as was right.

She feared the thorny stem of frustration within her was born from the seed of pride and misjudgment. How wrong she now felt. How she wished to step back in time and speak with grace instead of prejudice against William Drake. She wasn't so naive as to not have thought about how he could have helped her family financially. That he could have been the key to her family keeping this farm—but would it have been right to accept a man she hadn't loved all for the sake of survival? And now? What did she think of him?

Sighing, Lizbeth centered her mind on the linen pulled tight in her wooden hoop.

"The sampler looks nearly finished." Jayne admired it from beside her. "It's ever so pretty, Lizzy."

"Thank you." She read the forming verse, all wrapped in curling vines along with a moon and series of delicate stars.

The night is far spent,
the day is at hand:
let us therefore cast off the works of darkness,
and let us . . .

She'd pierced each doubt one by one into the needlepoint, hoping that the words forming would somehow guide her in grace and wisdom. "I figured that once it's finished, I might try and sell it to a shop in one of the nearby towns." She'd heard of samplers this detailed selling for nearly ten dollars at a shop in Raleigh. If she could focus, and not make mistakes, then she could give the earnings to Pa.

Scissors in hand, Jayne trimmed off the edge of an old tablecloth from the attic.

"Are your Christmas gifts nearly finished?" Lizbeth asked.

Jayne snipped a rogue thread. "Just about. This one's for Lacey." She held up what would soon be stuffed as a little pillow. "I'm hoping it will cheer her up."

Lizbeth couldn't deny that Lacey had been glum ever since Westgard's leaving, the same time as William's. "It'll be perfect under the tree."

"Right next to the socks you darned for Pa and the new candles that Maryanne dipped from beeswax."

Lizbeth smiled, wishing it would truly feel like Christmas. But it didn't. Not with some of the very people on her heart so far from here. Dare she admit that to Jayne?

"If only I could send a gift along for Hattie," Lizbeth mused to keep from thinking of a certain man again. "Especially now that the new Mrs. Coburn has moved on to Pennsylvania."

As for the sampler, she would have to part with it. For some reason, she didn't feel ready. Somehow it seemed meant for her. A guiding hope of sorts when the rest of her world felt muddled. Much by her own doing.

William's face came to mind again—quiet and pained—and Lizbeth peered out the window to try and shake the memory from view. To try and dislodge it from her very soul. She hadn't succeeded yet and was beginning to worry that she wasn't meant to.

With a *whoosh*, an envelope slid under the closed door, followed by Kit's voice. "Ma and I fetched the mail!"

Jayne rose from the floor and tiptoed across trimmings of paper and ribbon. Her reach for the letter was slow, just as it had been for two months now. Whenever mail arrived, Lizbeth held her breath.

"Is it from . . ." She couldn't bring herself to say *Callum Brydolf.*

Jayne shook her head regardless.

From downstairs, Maryanne hit a clumsy crescendo on the piano keys.

Jayne lifted the envelope, veiling any disappointment. "It's for you, Lizzy. From Hattie."

The song reached its end, and in the silence, Lizbeth rose from her rocking chair. The spool of blackberry-dyed thread tumbled to the floorboards.

"Thank you." She took the envelope and turned it over in her hand.

Mrs. Hattie Coburn, Stroudsburg, Pennsylvania.

This letter was one of many from Hattie, whereas Jayne had received nothing from Callum in the post.

"I'm sorry, Jayne."

"Please don't be. I haven't been expectin' mail."

The rocking chair creaked as Lizbeth sat again and pulled her knees up. Her skirt and woolen petticoat billowed around her ankles, where her own stockings were also in need of a few stitches.

Slowly and softly, Maryanne began "Auld Lang Syne." Music filled the spaces that words couldn't.

A soft touch broke the letter's seal. "Have you thought of writing to Callum once more?" Lizbeth asked.

Jayne's scissors spliced through more fabric. "I've no plans to."

"May I ask why?"

"Quite simple." *Snip. Snip.* "I've written to him three times and haven't received anythin' in return. It'd be foolish to try again."

"Somethin's amiss. He'd write to you. Could it be that the address was mismarked?"

"I checked it each time." From where she sat, Jayne's blue eyes made a silent reckoning with a basket beneath her bed that held the tokens Callum had left behind for her—wrapped in paper and tied with string. The same day that William had delivered the package, Lizbeth had stood in awe as Jayne opened each of Callum's offerings: sheets upon sheets of the finest writing paper, crisp linen envelopes, a silver pen and matching inkwell, as well as two dozen four-cent stamps with President Grant's likeness.

Jayne's face had flushed almost as dark as the rust-colored stamps when she'd finished opening the gift.

In the weeks that followed, Lizbeth had witnessed Jayne pen each letter with care beside the light of their bedroom window. Jayne's eyes drifting often to the horizon and her face full of optimism as she'd written to Callum of the weather that cooler months rustled up, the quiet happenings of New River, and to thank him for the kindness he'd shown. Jayne had even asked him about news from Vermont.

Not a single letter arrived in return.

Jayne set her scissors aside. "So, there's no cause to carry on about it. What's settled is settled and I'm content."

"Jayne."

"I mean it. Please don't fret. I'm perfectly happy and am certain Callum is as well. He's got an awful lot to do in Vermont, I'm sure."

"Then why'd he leave you the package? Why leave behind one of the most beautiful pens either of us has ever seen? Why nearly a dollar's worth of stamps?"

"The man has wealth. These are mere trifles to him. Inconsequentials that lived in his desk. He could purchase a hundred more pens at the snap of his finger. Two hundred—"

"I don't believe a word of it and you can't either." Lizbeth moved to the basket and fetched the pen, wrought in elegant silver and carved with filigree. She turned the pen so the engraving glinted in sunlight.

C. B. Callum Brydolf.

A man didn't part with his own name as easily as Jayne implied.

"*This* held value to him. As did you. *That's* the message he intended to send."

Jayne took the pen and returned it to the darkness of the basket beneath her bed. Without another word, she resumed her seat on the floor.

Lizbeth pressed on. "He left you those things to make it easy for you to write him. Maybe the cost isn't so great in light of his wealth, but it was a cost of *intention* . . . an unspoken declaration."

Tears pooled in Jayne's eyes.

"*That's* what was important to him. He wanted to hear from you. To hear your voice. Leastways, to know you held these things in your hands. Make no mistake."

"Then can you explain why he hasn't written back?"

No, she couldn't. "There's gotta be more to this than what it seems." The past two months had been teaching her this. A humbling she didn't know how to fully reckon with, but it began by realizing that she only knew part of the story and that there were better and more noble ways of discerning the rest.

"Then I'll take comfort in the gesture of his gift, as I have, and let's not be carryin' on about it." Jayne's words were edged with finality. "Let's forget about the whole encounter with Mr. Brydolf."

"It's not that easy," Lizbeth pressed. "I don't believe it could be."

If Jayne severed ties with Callum Brydolf, should she work harder to forget about William Drake?

Not that she meant to renew those ties, but an absence lingered about her that she couldn't describe. William had been arrogant, prideful, and selfish. Or had that instead been her? Truth be told, she'd never spoken so harshly with another human in all her days. Nor had she done such based on a secondhand account from a near stranger, as Westgard had been.

Now she couldn't shake the feeling of having been mistaken.

Lizbeth wriggled her needle into the fabric of her embroidery hoop again, gaining only a single stitch before peering back out the window. While she couldn't see all the way to town, she imagined the empty depot. It would be blanketed in snow until the four o'clock train cleared the tracks as it did each day. She hadn't seen William leave nor known of his plans to. But one day he had stood beside her, and the next, he and the beautiful train car were gone. As for the book he'd lent her, she was nearly finished. If only she could see it rightly returned to him.

"Please read the letter, Lizzy," Jayne said softly. She folded up what remained of the floral tablecloth, pressing the charred bits into her scrap pile. Sincerity mingled with lingering tears. "Let's hear some cheery news. What of Hattie and Reverend Coburn? Is she askin' you again to visit? It's hard to believe it's been two whole months. Maybe now the discomfort has passed? What with Reverend Coburn proposing to you first."

Lizbeth tore open the envelope flap. "If I see anything differently, Jayne, it's that I ought not to be the one to judge a man—or woman—who yearns to share their life with someone they can see themselves caring about." Not Reverend Coburn, nor Mr. Brydolf and now, especially not Mr. Drake. "I suppose this life is less about being right in my own eyes and more about bein' gracious to see that others have perspectives that matter."

All the more reason she would press Jayne no further on matters of the heart. Lizbeth knew now that she wasn't the end-all on what was right or just in the matters of love, but that she was just like everyone else—trying to find the way forward that was *right*.

It was Jayne herself who had helped Lizbeth see this in those teary days that followed William's leaving. In the wake of Lizbeth's distress, it was Jayne who helped her consider that the very man might have been more fair in his dealings than Mr. Westgard had implied. From all of that, Lizbeth had begun to see that the world didn't hinge upon her opinions after all. Perhaps she'd been blinded by her own pride in more ways than one.

She broke the seal on the letter.

Clearing a tightness in her throat, Lizbeth shared aloud. "Hattie writes about the weather in Stroudsburg, where they're settled in the parish there. She says their cottage is near the churchyard. She feeds the chickens daily and has a parlor that she enjoys sitting in, and once again . . ." Lizbeth lowered the letter. "She wishes for me to come."

"Will you? This time?"

Lizbeth skimmed the rest of the page. "She writes that her ma and pa are plannin' to visit soon and that they'd like me to join them." She handed the letter to Jayne.

"Oh my!" Jayne abandoned both scissors and paper now to skim the page. "You'd travel by train! How splendid."

"We could never afford the ticket. Not with the debt Pa's dealing with over this land." Nearly two hundred dollars owed to the state of Virginia if he wanted to establish his ownership. Money that even Mr. Jorgensen didn't have to loan him or the other tenants, not until the sale was finalized, and by then, it would be too late. The land would transfer. Lizbeth considered the sampler abandoned on the rocking chair. Even if she sold it, she'd hardly make a dent in the debt, but if she could finish it in time, this could be her chance to try and find a buyer in Stroudsburg for it and perhaps another, and then another. Yet the trip would come at a cost. "I—I don't know."

Jayne skimmed the letter again. "We always get a half dollar in our stockings at Christmastime. While we might not have one this year, all things considered, we both have a few saved away."

"Scarcely enough for a train ticket to Pennsylvania."

"More than enough if you ride coach."

She hadn't thought of that.

Jayne rose and moved to the dresser that they shared. "We could turn some of this cloth into a new skirt for you." From the top drawer, she dug beneath her stockings and petticoats, retrieving a small tin can.

"You're right. Riding coach would cost very little. Then I could sell the sampler to have something extra to bring home to Pa. And if I can commission another piece, maybe more than one, I could stitch and sell them by post. Turn a bigger profit." She braved more. "Beyond that, I just might learn more about Callum Brydolf from Mr. Jorgensen, who knows him well."

"Likely not. But if you're to travel to Pennsylvania, it could be near Mr. Drake's Chess Creek mine."

She hadn't thought of that either.

Jayne's eyes glistened as she searched Lizbeth's. "You need something to do about all this and sitting around waitin' will only be harder." Jayne laughed and swiped at her eyes and squeezed Lizbeth tight.

Pulling away, Lizbeth started for the door. "I'll go and talk to Pa." Before she could expect to face the great big world, she needed to face the first of her regrets.

Lizbeth climbed the attic stairs and knocked softly on the door. "Pa?"

"Is that my Lizzy-girl?"

As she entered, Pa pulled off his spectacles. He sat near to the stovepipe, which slanted up through the floorboards. The snug space brimmed with warmth. His desk, where he often worked, sat near a small window looking cozy despite the snow that blanketed the land beyond the four windowpanes.

Pa leaned back in his chair and reached for a half-empty cup of coffee. "To what do I owe this surprise?"

"I need to speak to you about somethin'. Well, two things." Lizbeth held over the letter from Hattie then pulled a footstool near. She sat as he read in silence.

"I see." His curiosity slanted her way. "And the second thing?"

"It's about the farm."

"Ah."

"Is it in danger, Pa? From William Drake?" She needed to know once and for all if she'd been wrong about him.

Pa rested a thick hand on his desk where layers of documents might disclose the truth. "It *is* in danger. Grave danger, to be frank, but not from Mr. Drake." Pa lifted two documents bound with a metal clip. "I know for a number of reasons, including this. It's a letter from William himself, explaining the situation and for me to be in contact if I'd like his help."

"When did this come?"

"A few weeks ago."

Her chest tightened as she touched the paper—his neat script strangely reassuring. She bent the first sheet forward to study the second. "And this?"

"It was attached in the envelope. It's from his lawyer, who you met as well. The one so enchanted with Jayne. It furthers the explanations and the advice. Of all the investors that came here to New River, these two seem bent on helping us."

Lizbeth folded her arms around her middle, still clutching the pages. "So what do you plan to do?"

"I've been working hard—earning some extra income. Not there yet, but I've made a dent in the tax debt."

"Will we ever make enough?"

"I'm sure gonna try to."

Lizbeth laid the letters on the desk. "Pa, if there's some way I might go to Stroudsburg with the Jorgensens, I'd like to try." She pressed on, explaining about the sampler and her hopes of how she might help him.

Pa gave her a sad smile even as his eyes twinkled with pride. "Well, now, Lizzy. That's terribly brave of you. And generous. You've been working a long time on that sampler."

"That's why I hope it might be something worth selling. As for the train ticket, I have a little money that should cover the seat. From there, I'd be staying with Hattie so there's little to no extra cost."

"Well, now . . ."

"Please, Pa."

"This isn't the first time you've been invited by Hattie, is it?"

"No, sir. She's asked already. I just haven't known what to do."

Pa considered the written words again, finally lowering the letter amid the rest of his papers. "I've known of the Jorgensens' trip to Pennsylvania. It's one of the reasons I've been workin' more hours. Partly due to our need to scrounge up these taxes. Jorgensen has passed more work—and pay—on to me. It's not much but he's doing all he can with what he has. He's asked me to survey a series of maps of the mine, and I'm nearly finished. I'll be sending them along with my findings. I've also been surveying several maps for Mr. Drake."

"For William?"

"He's added me to his payroll as well."

"Truly?"

"I should have mentioned it sooner, but was so grateful, I've poured all my focus into completing the work he's given me. His pay is generous, although I can tell he's trying not to wound my pride. I don't expect he'll let us or this farm fall if he can do anything about it, but a man like me is grateful for the chance to earn the victory."

Lizbeth's throat tightened even as her heart swelled. "Oh, Pa." So that was how they'd been able to pay off their tally at the company store. She'd been wondering.

"As you can see"—Pa indicated a slew of maps across his desk—"I've had my hands full."

Rising, Lizbeth examined the sketches of the mine. Levels that wove this way and that, all numbered with the feet of their depth.

Two hundred. Three hundred. All the way down to the very bottom of the main shaft. Beside the maps sat lists of minerals and ore varieties, along with percentages that Pa had calculated.

Last of all, she saw a sketch of their farm. Of home.

The very hollow that stood in the balance.

"What might this mean in regard to Mr. Drake?" she asked.

"You've asked me the same question twice now, Lizzy." Another soft chuckle. "I don't count the man an enemy. Instead, he's earned my growing respect. Especially now that another investor has travelled to New River to see the mine."

Her heart skidded at those words. "Someone else has come?"

"Another coal baron. A new one in the running. This one from Boston, and he's circling the mine like a vulture, I tell you. That's the way of it, Lizzy. If Mr. Drake were in the business of swindling us all out of house and home, I daresay he'd have done it by now. The man's wealthy enough."

"So, William has made no offer."

"Not yet. By the looks of things, time may be runnin' out with most of the other offers already in play. Jorgensen is stalling, for our sake and still waiting for an offer from Drake. Who I sense is stalling for our sake as well. It's as though he's put a wrench somehow in the whole operation, halting anything from moving forward too quickly. He's an intelligent man and for that, I'm grateful."

Lizbeth touched the hollow of her throat and sank back onto the padded footstool. William. All her anger—her passion—and he had been the one trying to keep them safe.

Pa tugged open the top drawer of his desk. "Which makes it a rather good time for the extra work." He pulled out a small metal box. "The Jorgensens, I suppose, will be travellin' in a sleeper car by way of his business connections."

"I expect so."

"And you'll be brave enough to travel coach?"

"I think I can sleep sitting up."

He chuckled. "I see." Raising the lid, Pa pulled out several more coins. He placed them on his desk. "Then take this as well. A little somethin' for your travels. If my girl is to see the sights, she'll need a few hot meals on the journey." He rolled up the top map with the words *New River* stamped in black ink. "Consider it your first payment as my trusty assistant. I need someone to deliver this to Mr. Jorgensen today. While there, you can let him know your news." Pa wrapped the map with twine.

"Oh, Pa." Lizbeth skirted around his desk and wrapped her arms around his neck. "Thank you," she whispered. "I promise I'll see it done."

23

Christmas Eve, 1904

Lady Light lowered her head and sniffed at the raspberry drop in William's hand. "I need to stop spoiling you with sweets," he whispered. "But it is Christmas after all."

The thoroughbred chomped the treat and sniffed for more.

William stood in the aisle of his stables with ten stalls looming on both sides, filled with his horses, save the two that were being hitched to the sleigh outside. Along with his sister, Anna, who'd come home on school holiday, William was scheduled to arrive at the Brydolfs' this evening. He needed to get back to the house and change, but first, a few more minutes here where the earthiness of the stables reminded him of a different farm entirely.

In the space of his mind—his heart—he imagined Lizbeth in a faraway barn, giving her own Christmas treats to her mules. Chest throbbing, William started for the house.

He tried not to think of what she might be doing this night as he climbed the stairs to his room and donned a tuxedo and bow tie. William slung a cashmere scarf around his shoulders, nabbed a glossy top hat, and headed into the hallway, where Anna met him.

"How handsome you look!" His sister wore a gold-colored skirt that shimmered like a glass ornament. Her high-collared blouse would have made her appear grown-up if it weren't for her hair, which she wore down and pulled back with a velvet ribbon.

"And you look magnificent."

She beamed a sunny smile at him and adjusted the new fur shrug he'd had tailored for her.

As was tradition, his servants lined up in the front foyer, uniforms neat and tidy. Maids wore black dresses and white caps, and the footmen wore liveries. Though everyone faced forward, William noticed a sparkle or two in the younger staff's eyes at what festivities the night would hold. The same sparkle that Anna shared. Another reason to visit the Brydolfs' estate since it would allow his staff the night off. He'd only requested his butler leave a fire going in the occupied bedrooms. William could add wood to the flames on his own. A notion the butler had scoffed at, but Anna had joined in insisting they were quite capable.

William gave the very butler a friendly nod as he lowered an envelope to his gloved palm. "Merry Christmas." William went down the line, offering such a gift to each of his staff members.

At the end, he lifted his top hat to them all. "A merry Christmas to each of you." His voice echoed in the polished foyer.

"A merry Christmas to you, Mr. Drake! And Miss Drake!" rang their voices.

"They'll have such a grand time. I hear Cook made cider and doughnuts," Anna said as they descended the front steps. Snow dusted her hair, and sleigh bells chimed as the driver called to the horses to remain steady.

William thanked the driver and helped Anna in. He joined her on the seat, careful not to jostle the presents he'd procured for his friends. The closest thing to Christmas cheer he could summon.

In his pocket rested a telegram he needed to discuss with Callum. News from New River that could change everything.

"William," came Anna's soft voice. "You are a mile away in your mind."

He offered a smile as the sleigh glided into motion. "Merry Christmas."

She scrunched her nose. "You've said that. Three times already now."

He chuckled. "Fair. How about you pick the topic?"

With scarcely a breath, Anna unboxed stories of her year at school. Of the girls she roomed with, her least favorite instructors, and how Aunt Catherine had even visited and taken her out to tea.

William listened, soaking in her humor and life as the sleigh glided down the lane beneath the first blinking stars. The gates were decorated with garland. His request for Anna's sake. Some semblance of beauty that they desperately needed this winter. His property spread for forty acres all around the nineteen-room house. All blanketed in snow but despite the three Christmas trees beneath his roof, and the celebratory breakfast they'd share with their aunt tomorrow, the home felt empty. Another reason he intended to spend Christmas Eve somewhere else to help escape his own mind.

Anna filled the mile ride with joy, and soon, the driver angled the sleigh up to the Brydolfs' estate.

"Shall we?" William climbed out and, taking Anna's arm, led her up the grand entrance and into the Brydolfs' home. Servants buzzed in the foyer, carrying trays and gifts alike. Anna dashed toward the tree with its electric lights. Just as William made to follow, a berry-red dress caught his eye.

Caroline Brydolf descended the stairs. "William." Her regal voice floated from above. "Such a pleasure you could make it." She smiled.

He removed his coat and hat. "Caroline."

With a lithe figure and a delicate face, Caroline Brydolf had a knack for turning heads. As usual, it seemed his head alone that she wished to turn. Her gloved hand trailed down the polished banister and the neckline of her gown capped delicate shoulders. Her hair, a wintery blonde, was swept up in fashionable frills, displaying her slender neck.

Between their two fortunes, they could conquer the world, and yet he saw no joy in such a future.

Not wanting to be left alone with her, William looked around for Callum.

The man entered from the adjacent room. "William! Just in time. Dinner is ready." He wore a simple shirt and waistcoat.

William lowered his attention to his tuxedo. "I seem to be overdressed."

"Nonsense. I can head back upstairs and change."

"No need." William offered his hat and coat to a maid.

"Shall we?" At his side, Caroline slid her slender hand through William's arm. "We've a few other guests." She led the way toward the dining rom. "Some of Callum's old friends from university are here along with a neighbor or two, but you're seated by me."

William gave a brief nod.

"Do make sure to sit with Anna," Caroline instructed Callum, who didn't seem to hear. "I believe my brother is taken with your sister," Caroline whispered.

"I'm not so sure—"

"A marriage that would suit everyone, I think." Her voice was smug as Callum knelt and showed sixteen-year-old Anna how the newest ornaments glinted in the electric strand of lights.

"You may find yourself surprised, then," William said.

Caroline ignored him.

The dining room opened up before them and William pulled out a chair for Caroline. As the chair legs glided against the polished floor, he was struck by what it would be like to pull out a chair for Lizbeth. What it would be like to introduce her to the room and for her company to be what carried him through the evening and beyond. William cleared his throat at a painful tightening, scarcely hearing Caroline speak beside him.

"Will you be racing your horse at the new track this spring?" She reached for a glass of wine as a footman unfolded her napkin. "I hear Belmont Park is scheduled to open soon. They say it's the finest track New York has ever seen. Perhaps the nation."

"In May." William overturned his own glass so it wouldn't be filled. "I've been in discussion over the prospect. And her name is Lady Light."

Caroline averted her eyes at the reminder of a name she knew perfectly well. She simply didn't care for animals. "I don't know how your aunt approved such a nonsensical name." The electric chandelier lent Caroline's face a healthy glow as she turned William's crystal glass back over and snapped her fingers for the footman to return with the bottle. "So Lady Light will run, then?"

"She will." William offered space for another footman to place a bowl of steaming soup in front of him.

"Then Callum will have to secure a box!"

"No need, I've already secured one. You're both invited, of course." William dipped his spoon into the soup, preferring to keep his gaze there rather than on the woman beside him. "Lady Light has been invited to practice on the track at her earliest convenience. As a preview of sorts. I believe the landscapers are still sorting out the pitch of the ground."

"No doubt the added practice will improve her odds."

"I doubt it." He was anxious if she'd clear the preliminary. Since horse racing was illegal in Vermont, he stabled Lady Light on his estate but she travelled by rail for any races including the upcoming opening in New York.

"It will be one of the finest tracks this nation has ever seen. Do you know how many guests it holds?" she asked.

"Forty thousand." While he wasn't as interested in rubbing elbows with the upper class as Caroline, he wouldn't miss the opening for the simple experience of seeing the facility. Few thoroughbreds were qualified for the elite circuit. Still, a full calendar felt empty without deeper purpose. Something William tried to ignore day in and day out lately.

Ever since he'd spilled his soul to Lizbeth and she'd refused him. Rightfully so. He'd no more demonstrated that she could rest in his assurances than in those of any other man she'd known for a month's time. More courses arrived—roasted meats, sauteed vegetables, and buttery dinner rolls. William wondered what she would be feasting on this night. Likely stewed apples with cream from their farm, or roasted chestnuts from the woods. Perhaps pies would be on the menu, seasoned with cinnamon. When dessert was served, William dipped his fork into a chocolate ganache decorated with gold leaf, longing instead for a sense of home. Whatever that meant.

"The ladies are retiring to the parlor," he finally heard Callum say over the hum of memories and lost hopes. "Port's being served in the study. Figured I'd let you know since you're a mile away."

William rose and followed his friend from the nearly empty dining hall.

Wood crackled and popped in the study hearth. After ensuring that all the other men were preoccupied, William pulled the telegram from his vest pocket. "This arrived two days ago. A *Merry Christmas* from Mr. Jorgensen."

Callum opened the paper.

"The final offer has come in on the New River Coal Company." William spoke calmly yet felt anything but. "I don't know all the details but apparently it's the highest yet. The buyer intends to take all the other farms as well."

"What do you plan to do?"

"Get a hurry on. I've sped up the pace of my own proceedings. I have an electrician coming the day after tomorrow. I have a lot to sort out."

"An electrician? The day after Christmas?"

"Running out of time. I need an electrician to help me decide if I can truly lead New River into a viable future." William quietly described his second trip down into the mine before he'd left New River the following day. He was yet to know when he might make his third. Did he still need to? "I better understand the other levels now and have made progress on viable solutions to improve the mine."

One of Callum's university friends crossed the room. "Are you thinking of adding electricity to a *coal mine*? Unheard of!"

"Not quite." William set aside his glass of port, still not tasting any. "I have power running to the offices of my Chess Creek mine as of last year."

"But beneath the ground is an entirely different story."

"True. And still, the Pacific Coast Company at Black Diamond and Coal Creek are near to completion with installing electricity in their tunnels."

"Whatever for?" The young man polished off his cup in a single swig.

"To transport cars underground. It's the way of the future.

Electricity has more purpose than lighting homes such as our own. Or offices. It can reach the masses. Even beyond the cities."

The man scoffed. "Not likely. How do you know all of this?"

With all the businesses he owned? "It's my job to know these things." William noticed more men claiming chairs around them, so he veiled the details. "I've hired a geologist who's familiar with the region to supply some maps. All with the owner's approval of course."

Callum gave him a look that indicated he knew just the man—Bennet.

"And what will you do with these maps?" one of the university men countered.

Driven by a purpose he couldn't describe, William claimed his own seat. "If I can grasp what the possibility will be to run electricity through the mine, I'll know its viability for the future." He folded the telegram into his vest pocket.

"You say that easily," Callum said.

William gave him a look. From what they both knew of their time in New River, the decision to return to a place that had tested and changed them was far from easy.

"I represent some clients in electricity. For factories," Callum added. "Would you like me to seek their advice?"

"Please. I can send you a summary of the proposal, along with a list of concerns." The more opinions he gathered, the better.

"Consider it done. But do you think you'll have enough time?"

"That's my hope. The current owner plans to retire by summer so I'll return to New River soon," he explained. Then? Hopefully . . . place his own bid. He wouldn't do it before. No matter how tempting it became to rush this process. The reason he sat upon a fortune was because of savvy business dealings. He couldn't let matters of the heart cloud his thinking. No matter how much he missed Lizbeth.

Caroline entered in a huff. "Why have none of you come along to play cards?"

"Miss Brydolf." William pointed to the main hall in hopes of distracting her. "You'll find a package under the tree with your name on it. Wrapped in crimson paper. I hope you find the contents agreeable."

She smiled. "How kind of you."

William moved nearer to an open window, a needed shock to his senses. Leaning against the wall, he folded his arms. As for these business dealings, he needed to buy a little more time and proceed with as much grace and dignity as he could muster. Not to win Lizbeth—he didn't hold any hope for that. He no longer imagined a future with her, but he meant to deal honorably in any matter that concerned her. He would not be the cause for her discomfort ever again.

With a pang in his chest, William watched as Anna sat beside the Christmas tree and found a package with her name on it.

Callum stepped nearer. "Caroline is pleased with whatever you gave her."

"Satin gloves. I didn't select them, but they were the best that Bloomingdale's had to offer." He'd had them shipped in special.

Callum chuckled and William was grateful for this friend who knew him and his efforts at socializing better than anyone in the world.

"And you? What do you place under the tree for a young lady?"

"Paper and stamps."

"For Anna?"

"For Jayne." So intent was Callum's gaze that William couldn't look away. "That's what was in the package you delivered for me. Though I doubt it made it under the tree."

Smart man. "And have you received any word?"

"Not a single letter. I've inquired about the mail every day. And so far, there's been nothing."

"Have you thought of writing yourself?"

"I've written several times but still no response."

From her end of the room, Caroline laughed as she opened another present. She, the main force who desired a future between Callum and Anna and even between herself and William. Somehow, someway, a merging of the households of Drake and Brydolf. William turned his attention back to his friend. "Perhaps there's more to it."

"Perhaps." Callum ran a hand over the back of his neck. "I've thought of returning to New River countless times."

"Have you?" William tried to keep his tone inquisitive but in truth, he shared the longing. He was yet to tell his friend of his failed attempt at impressing Lizbeth with a suggestion of marriage. He'd keep that to himself. "And what would you say?"

"That's what I'm still working out. It's hard to hope, when . . . when . . ." Callum shook his head. "Do you think there's still a chance?"

"It all depends."

"On?"

"On what you're willing to do." William cast a look past his friend's shoulder and lowered his voice. "Listen. I have my own pursuits that I need to tend to, and I believe you know what those are. As for you . . ." Moistening his lips, William regretted what he needed to imply about Callum's own sister, but it had to be said. Even if he wouldn't have such happiness, it was still possible for Callum and Jayne. "You need to see the world as it truly is. Own your actions. Own the consequences."

Callum's eyes searched for understanding.

"Try writing Jayne one more time and when you do . . ."

William lifted his gaze to Caroline. "Make sure that no one, and I mean no one, has a chance to tamper with the mail."

Understanding dawned on Callum's face as he glanced his sister's way.

"You have a genuine chance at happiness, my friend. Make sure nothing stands in the way of that."

24

February 1905

"Next stop Stroudsburg, Pennsylvania!" The conductor ambled down the aisle between coach seats.

The train chugged as it slowed. In her seat, Lizbeth nestled the borrowed copy of *Jane Eyre* into her carpetbag. Just beneath that lay the embroidery piece she'd worked on through all the journey. It was nearly finished now. If she stayed focused, she would have it completed in a day or two. Just in time to try and sell it in Stroudsburg. As for the verse, she was still working to unearth its guidance—much like her journey to be the friend that Hattie deserved. To be a young woman who walked with grace and kindness amid these twists and turns of life. What did it mean to embrace the truths of each stitch? That the night was indeed behind her—filled with doubt, regret, and things that she could not go back and change. Instead, the day was at hand along with new opportunities and brand-new hopes.

The window shade rocked as the train stopped. Lizbeth braced a hand against the seat back in front of her. Already, she had seen more of the world out these windows than she could have imagined. Rolling hills, dense forests, colorful cities, and wide-open skies. Now she searched only for sight of Mr. and Mrs. Jorgensen, who had retreated to the dining car to pay the tab for their midday meal along with Lizbeth's own. They'd advised her to meet them near the exit, so she rose and lugged her carpetbag down the aisleway.

With each step between seated passengers, she still felt like a stranger to herself in such new clothing. Jayne had sewn her a skirt from the tablecloth she'd cut up for fabric before Christmas. Striped colors of wheat and sky hinted at the coming spring atop her petticoats, which Ma had washed and starched like new. In place of an apron, Lizbeth's sash brushed the seat backs as she passed by, made from ivory lace that she'd scrounged from the rag bag. The lace had borne a nasty hole, but Maryanne had darned it to near newness with creamy thread. To her best blouse, Lizbeth had embroidered flowers with dainty scallops on the collar. The same flowers in the sampler she was stitching. Both kept her hands and heart busy on snowy nights. All leading her to this very moment.

When she bumped into a man's arm as he braced a suitcase over his head, Lizbeth righted the wooden comb Ma had lent her. Her once-stylish knot felt a mite crooked, but she could remedy that once her hands were free. Even her younger sisters had joined in to create her ensemble. Kit put a stout polish to Lizbeth's boots, Maryanne had ironed all her things with care, and Lacey had knitted up a simple drawstring pouch out of deep red yarn to hold the coins Pa had given her along with two handkerchiefs. It graced Lizbeth's wrist now as she disembarked with other passengers.

Here she was, out in the great big world, a girl from coal country dressed up in lace.

Lizbeth eased down the train car's steps, spotting Mr. Jorgensen waiting on the platform near the telegrapher's office. He waved and she aimed that way.

"Soon as my husband gets all his messages sent, we'll hail a carriage." Mrs. Jorgensen straightened her hat beneath the afternoon sun. "My, what nine hours aboard a train can do to oneself."

"It's been ever so lovely."

Mrs. Jorgensen glimpsed Lizbeth's carpetbag. "Are you all right carryin' that?"

Lizbeth didn't want to admit that she owned very little. "I'm just fine, thank you." She followed Mrs. Jorgensen through the crowd as the sights and sounds of Stroudsburg enfolded them into its beating heart.

"I see our driver," Mrs. Jorgensen called over the bobbing heads.

Lizbeth followed her to a waiting carriage and climbed aboard, marveling at the glossy wood and sleek mares.

Behind them, Mr. Jorgensen helped the driver load the Jorgensens' trunks along with Lizbeth's humble suitcase, which Pa had dug from the attic and dusted off. Her carpetbag, she kept in her lap. At sight of the familiar items from home, Lizbeth sat, feeling grounded even as excitement brimmed inside her.

Mrs. Jorgensen patted her hand. "It's such a joy to have you with us. I know Hattie'll be just beside herself to see you again."

"Thank you. I'm eager to see her as well."

"As am I!" Mrs. Jorgensen braced her hat again as the wagon lurched into motion.

Lizbeth held on tight, watching the road as the driver sent the horses clip-clopping into motion. Lingering traces of snow dusted the hedge line, but the lane was dry. With every turn through town, she kept watch for any sight of the parsonage where Hattie and Reverend Coburn lived. Cool, crisp air filled her lungs.

"Such a lovely little town," Mrs. Jorgensen mused as the carriage swept past shops, quaint houses, and stables.

"It is. I can see why Hattie's spoken so highly of it in her letters."

"Oh." Mr. Jorgensen patted his coat pocket. "That reminds me." He pulled out a telegram and read it.

Perhaps this was the chance to broach the subject of another person they all knew. "Along with Hattie's letters, we've expected word from Mr. Brydolf," Lizbeth braved. "Who visited us not too long ago."

"Oh?" Mrs. Jorgensen said.

"He gave Jayne some writing stationery so as to keep in touch."

Mr. Jorgensen's attention stayed on his telegram.

"How thoughtful," his wife answered in his stead. "Your ma hinted that he'd taken a shine to your sister. Which I daresay we could all see for ourselves." Mrs. Jorgensen's smile was genuine as she touched her high lace collar. "Has he said any more about it? Or was he too busy being persuaded by his glum friend, Mr. Drake?"

"Now, Martha." Mr. Jorgensen looked up from his reading. "Drake's a fine man."

A small ache met Lizbeth's heart at mention of William. "It's hard to say just yet, but we hope to hear more soon. Are you well acquainted with Callum Brydolf?"

Mr. Jorgensen folded the telegram into his vest as shadows from roadside trees wove shade over the moving carriage. "A fine, fine fellow. We had the two boys over for supper a time or two. While Drake's usually reserved, his friend always lightened the mood considerably."

"He had us all laughin' with his stories," Mrs. Jorgensen chimed in. "Those were good evenings."

"Do you still have the pleasure of hearing from him?" Lizbeth asked. Hopefully that wasn't too forward a question. "Mr. Brydolf, that is."

"Afraid not." Mr. Jorgensen consulted his pocket watch. "Most of my dealings have been with Drake. In fact, he's the reason I needed to send those telegrams back there."

Lizbeth felt a little pang flicker through her again.

"They seemed awfully urgent." Mrs. Jorgensen's voice lowered.

"They were."

All at once, Mrs. Jorgensen clutched the side of the carriage door. "There it is!" She pointed to the end of the lane.

Lizbeth tipped up her chin, catching sight of a stone cottage tucked among the trees. "It looks just as Hattie described."

In a flutter of birds from the lawn, Hattie stepped out in the sunlight and waved. Reverend Coburn joined her, matching the posture of the stone fountain beside him.

Lizbeth waved alongside the Jorgensens, all discomfort dashed at sight of her friend. She had long since decided that it mattered none that Reverend Coburn had asked her to marry him, and for her to have declined. He now had his rightful future and she'd grown glad for him and Hattie. That peace warmed Lizbeth as the carriage pulled up to the gate braced by the bare branches of a sleeping rosebush.

Lizbeth made space for the others to climb down first. They embraced their daughter in turn and Lizbeth hung back to allow for their teary reunion. Reverend Coburn hedged in with handshakes, and soon, Lizbeth was out of the carriage and being pulled into a hug by Hattie. The comforting sense of home somehow wrapped around her.

"Oh, Lizzy. It's so good to see you!"

"I'm glad as all get-out to be here." She shook Reverend Coburn's hand when he extended it, a further assurance that they could lay all discomfort by the roadside. Her dearest friend had found contentment, even if it was with the man who still had a knack for being clumsy in his speech as he showed them through the garden, pointing out the various plants. Lizbeth smiled, recalling her goal to see others in a new light.

Hattie gently tried to hurry them along as the reverend announced all the varieties of herbs along the path. She winked in Lizbeth's direction, and soon they were all indoors and being shown upstairs to their rooms.

"This one has a nice view of town." Hattie pushed open a narrow door. "Take some time to settle in and unpack. Then come down when you're ready. The fellas are plannin' an evening stroll, so I thought us ladies might have some tea." She squeezed Lizbeth's hand before slipping out.

As Lizbeth unpacked, she soaked in the views along with each detail of the day, meaning to recount it all to Jayne and her sisters once home. Lizbeth tucked the small satchel with her sampler and embroidery thread neatly on the nightstand and withdrew the hoop and linen. She smoothed her fingers over strands of delicate blue thread that now read:

The night is far spent,
the day is at hand:
let us therefore cast off the works of darkness,
and let us put on . . .

The verse gave her hope and yet her heart still weighed as a branch beneath a load of snow. Was it because she had yet to find the guidance that these beautiful words held? They implied that light was at hand, if she simply turned her mind and heart in that direction. The peace in humility and the healing of new beginnings.

A thawing that came with redemption. But it had to begin with her surrender, and more importantly, a sacrifice of pride . . . and the seeking of forgiveness. If that was the need, how did she accomplish such a thing? Her heart circled back to her nightly prayers, which seemed the right place to begin. And from there?

She touched the letters *cast off.*

It meant action. That something needed to change. More importantly, something needed to go. For the last few weeks, she'd been feeling the effects of where her pride had led her. That by assuming she knew all that the world needed and required of her, she'd made bold assumptions that weren't always right.

Lizbeth fingered the embroidery needle. If the opposite of pride was humility, was that the cause for the sleeplessness she'd been experiencing of late?

The actions of others had slowly been humbling her. Hattie's courage to face the unknown with dignity. Jayne's and Pa's generosity for her to come here. All along with simply seeing that the world was so much bigger than she. Setting aside her pride was one thing, but there was more work to do.

The seeds of that humility rooted more and more inside her. A rather tender reckoning. Perhaps Jayne wasn't the only one who had reason to pen a letter of the heart. Perhaps Lizbeth had a letter to write all her own. An apology even. Since, like Jayne, any sentiments of the heart could no longer be said in person. She longed to ease the hurt she had so clearly inflicted upon a man who had simply extended his hand to her in an open field. One who she now knew was laboring, quietly and humbly, to help save her family's farm.

Shame riddled her. Not because she'd refused his hand. But because she'd been unkind. She'd shown the very failings she'd accused him of. If there was a way to somehow remedy that . . . to explain her regrets . . . then perhaps it was time to try.

25

"Where do we stand?" William asked. Just past the stables, he turned toward Lady Light's trainer to better gauge the man's response. Behind them, workers loaded straw and hay into a wagon heading for the depot.

"With the skies this clear?" The gray-haired Scotsman looked up from a list that held tallies for sacks of oats, corn, and barley. "She's set to leave tomorrow for conditioning."

"Good. She'll be glad for the sunnier weather."

"Aye, and she'll have enough time to get into shape before the season starts."

"Indeed." William watched as his jockey guided Lady Light in a gentle exercise. The track on his estate curved around at eight furlongs and was where the thoroughbred had spent nearly all of her autumn preparing until the snows flew. "I'm just sorry I won't be able to accompany her to training this year." William patted his vest pocket, which had spent its last raspberry drop. From now on, Lady Light would only eat what the trainers allowed. A pristine diet curated for performance.

"She'll be in good hands." The trainer pulled on a plaid cap with weathered hands. "And ye won't miss the races." He smiled beneath bushy eyebrows.

"Still, I'm questioning my usefulness just now."

"Ye've prepared her and that's what counts. But we'll need 'er colors to have the silks made up for the jockey. Have ye decided?"

"I've asked my sister for help so that Lady Light looks her best." He was all thumbs when it came to colors and tastes. Better to leave that sort of thing to someone who had an eye for style. "If you can give me a few more days, I'll get a swatch sent your way."

"Aye, that'd do fine. And if all else fails, we'll default to last year's colors."

"Let's hope not."

The trainer chuckled and William smiled. The orange-and-red combination that his aunt had selected had been dreadful. Besides . . . it was time he was granted full ownership of the mare who—by heart and dedication—was his own. Still, it was not his name on the ownership papers. It was his aunt's. She'd allowed him to take over the care of Lady Light from the start, since the horse was bred for a life in the spotlight and since Aunt Catherine no longer had the interest nor the energy to navigate the world of professional horse racing.

Since it was William who had walked alongside the broodmare the many months of the pregnancy, and he who sat up with the new mother and foal the night of the birth, Aunt Catherine had given him leave to raise the mare and see her properly trained. Since then, it had been he who had warmed towels, shoveled stalls, and named the very creature who had won a piece of his heart in the three years that followed. Even so, every race Lady Light ran was under his aunt's name. Buying the horse outright wasn't a question. While he had the funds, his aunt didn't need money. She needed his commitment and so long as she kept ownership of Lady Light, she had a prime piece of William in the bargain.

A situation that was growing increasingly uncomfortable.

The trainer tucked his ledger beneath his arm. "While we might not get a victory at Belmont Park, we'll ensure Lady Light enters the arena in all her glory."

"Agreed." William shook the trainer's hand. "I have a copy of the itinerary, and please be in touch as needed. Once I wrap up some business in Chess Creek, I'll return here, then it's on to New River, but I intend to be in New York before May."

The trainer doffed his cap. "Excellent. And your aunt has requested a copy of the itinerary as well. Shall I forward one along?"

"I'm afraid not."

Bushy brows reached the cap's bill in surprise.

"It's time. If she has any qualms with that, please have her be in touch with me."

"Of course." The trainer's smirk lent William courage to finally stand up to his aunt. "Safe travels, sir. We have everything in hand."

William retreated toward the house and forced himself not to glance back. Besides Anna and Aunt Catherine, Lady Light was the closest kin he had. Soon she would be whisked north and he in the opposite direction. This time, with engineers and electricians in tow.

In the house, William aimed down the corridor to his office where his final preparations sat waiting. Based on the estimates the electricians had recently made, it could cost him a fortune to equip the coal mine with electricity, but it had to be the way of the future. It would save on costs in the long run and make procuring coal more efficient for the company as a whole. The change would increase safety and eliminate child labor. All crucial to any business he oversaw. It would also reduce if not eliminate the need to force livestock beneath the earth. Something he knew mattered to

Lizbeth, and he was beginning to better understand the freedom it could give to the lowly animals.

But executing the vision remained complex, which was why he needed to get boots on the ground again. And those boots needed to be his own.

He just didn't know what he would do if he crossed paths with Lizbeth.

He'd behave as a gentleman. He would be a neighbor to her and not ask for more. Easier said than done, but his quest in New River was quickly becoming less and less about his own future and more about hers.

William stacked papers. Lists, sums, and tallies. All that he needed to make this plan work. While Callum had scrutinized the details of the sale and drawn up the offer for Mr. Jorgensen, William worked with the operators of his Chess Creek mine to craft a plan on what this endeavor would mean for the miners themselves. With change came confusion, which brought the risk of chaos. Avoid the first, and he could eliminate the latter. That's why he needed to give the miners of New River a sure vision of what their futures would look like with the addition of electricity. A change that he intended would bring good, yet with any shift in infrastructure, some change was ill-received, and fairly so.

He meant not to disrupt the community of New River, so he would tread carefully. His job was to ensure a smooth and peaceful transition. One that he could hold his head high about, and that the miners could too. That's if he managed to solve the riddle himself. One piece of the puzzle at a time. That's what he kept telling himself. A puzzle he had less than thirty days left to solve.

Time was of the essence.

William slipped his pocketbook inside his vest then slid his shoulder holster on, not bothering to fasten it.

"It's half past noon, sir," his butler said from the doorway.

"Thank you." William checked his pocket watch. "And the Pemberley?"

"She's coupled in place for your travels to Pennsylvania this evening."

"Excellent." At the ring of the telephone, the butler retreated.

William donned a wool coat and started for the front doors and the carriage awaiting him just outside. Behind him, two footmen lugged the first trunk across marble flooring.

The butler returned. "It's a call for you, sir."

"Can you take a message?"

"The operator said it was urgent."

"All right." William entered the alcove where the butler's telephone resided. He raised the earpiece and gripped the handle of the mouthpiece. "This is Drake."

"Mr. Drake. I have a caller for you from Pennsylvania. A Mr. Jorgensen. Shall I put him through?"

Why was Jorgensen in Pennsylvania? "Please."

The line clicked as the operator connected them.

"Mr. Jorgensen?" William held the earpiece nearer.

"Mr. Drake. Good man. I'm calling to—" The line buzzed with static.

"Could you repeat that sir?"

"I'm calling to let you know that I'm in Stroudsburg."

Scarcely thirty miles from his Chess Creek mine. "I'm heading that way myself. How can I be of service?"

Jorgensen's static-ridden voice continued to break through. "Yes, I've been in touch with the operator at the Chess Creek mine as you advised me to and he mentioned you're en route as well, which is why I'm telephoning."

William spoke as clearly as possible. "My train leaves within the hour. How long will you be there?"

"Just over a week."

"Excellent." If Jorgensen was travelling with his family, William would need to socialize, but he was learning that it wasn't so terrible. And he'd have a chance to present his offer—and vision—in person to the man who would make the final decision.

Not that the details mattered much beyond dollars and cents, but he meant to win Jorgensen's favor with more than money. Give the man the assurance that the company he'd spent a lifetime building would remain in good hands. As would the families.

"I'll be staying near the depot." William resisted the urge to check his pocket watch even as his butler tapped him on the shoulder. "Send me a telegram with your location and we'll arrange a meeting if that suits you." He needed to leave. Now.

"Most definitely." Mr. Jorgensen said more, but the connection crackled again. All William could hear was something about his daughter and some other detail. Perhaps where the man was staying? He'd heard that Hattie Jorgensen had recently been married but when the butler tapped again, William didn't have time to find out.

"See you in Pennsylvania," William said. He handed the earpiece to his butler. "You'll make sure he understands?" William rushed toward the doorway even as the driver called out to the horses to steady.

"Absolutely. And safe travels, sir!"

26

Lizbeth pushed the bedroom curtains aside. Sunday morning light spilled in and she wondered if that was cause for the strange sensation that had woken her with a quickening of her chest. She'd heard a train's long low whistle just now, along with the piercing dawn, waking once again to thought of William. She didn't know what the day might hold, but she meant to keep her mind and heart open to it. Perhaps the Sunday service would hold the growing clarity that she craved.

She turned and reached into her carpetbag when a knock sounded at the door.

"Lizzy?" Hattie called. "It's me. I have tea and toast for you, along with a message."

Still in her nightgown, Lizbeth peeked around the door. "Why good mornin'."

Her friend smiled. "For you." She passed over a wooden tray where cinnamon and butter melted atop thick toasted bread. "Eat this. We usually have a quick breakfast since my husband likes to get to church early." She winked. "And Pa said that he's got to tend to a little business after church so you and I can fix a quiet luncheon."

"Of course. I can lend you a hand."

Hattie smiled again. "I'll leave you to get ready. See you downstairs."

After dressing quickly, Lizbeth checked her appearance in the narrow mirror. Her best white blouse was neatly pressed and tucked into the waistband of her striped skirt. She had tied her lace sash in a bow and wound a ribbon around her braid, as fancy as she'd felt when boarding the train just three days before. Lizbeth took another bite of the sweet toast along with a sip of creamy tea.

She heard a clock chime eight times as she slipped downstairs.

Reverend Coburn was already at the door, placing a hat on. "We mustn't be late. Do come along. Come along all."

"Church is just across the way," Hattie explained as Lizbeth joined the parade in the doorway.

Lizbeth draped a shawl around her shoulders and followed the others out into the crisp morning and the wondrous sights of Stroudsburg. Brick buildings stood closer together than kerchiefs pinned to a line. Wagons and carriages rattled by and the children who played along picket fences were scrubbed clean, all dressed for Sunday service. Trees, planted in neat order, stood bare of leaves, reaching toward a clear sky. Lizbeth soaked it all in as she walked down the brick path.

Hattie walked arm in arm with Reverend Coburn, looking the picture of a new bride. Her coloring was more vibrant and she'd begun wearing her hair in the latest fashions, much like the Gibson Girls Lizbeth had spotted in the copy of *McCall's* magazine that Mrs. Jorgensen had bought for the train ride. Lizbeth didn't know if the changes in Hattie were due to her new position as a minister's wife or simply the warmth of wedded bliss.

To her surprise, Hattie fell back a few steps to link arms with Lizbeth. "I thought we might walk a spell."

Lizbeth squeezed her friend's arm. "Always. You seem happy. I'm so glad for you, my friend."

Hattie gave a soft sigh. "I believe I am, mostly."

"Mostly?"

"Oh, we get on well enough. But in a sensible sort of way."

Lizbeth nodded. In truth, she hadn't seen a touch between the new couple's hands, or a lingering gaze of any kind. Reverend Coburn sought his wife's opinion on matters of the cottage, from the food they served to the way he trimmed the garden, and Hattie took pains to admire his handiwork while showcasing her own. But was that the end of their contented bliss?

"At times there's a peculiar sort of strain, but I imagine that will change in time," Hattie admitted.

"Love blossoms gently sometimes."

"That it does." Hattie squeezed her arm. "I suppose that's it. My husband and I are *slowly* learning to understand one another. It's a bit clumsy at times, but most new things are."

Lizbeth gave what she hoped was an understanding smile. "If I were in a new marriage, I imagine I'd have a fair bit to sort out too."

"It isn't always easy. But we work at bein' considerate. And I believe more will grow in time."

"That's a good way to think of it."

Lizbeth pondered Hattie's words as she trailed her now up the narrow churchyard path. She hoped for a marriage one day that was rooted in admiration and tenderness. If not, then the poets of old had it all wrong and Lizbeth knew nothing of what to expect if affection ever came knocking. Had she grown too idealistic? Would time quiet such longings within her?

Perhaps it wasn't about heart-pounding awareness but about what Hattie had with Reverend Coburn—polite sensibilities. But Lizbeth had a memory of something akin to the quickening of heart that she longed for. She just wasn't ready to admit who the man had been.

At the church door, Hattie led them inside and down the aisle where she showed the Jorgensens and Lizbeth to a front pew. Lizbeth sat, still pondering the ways of a husband and wife. Hattie folded her hands in her lap as she watched her husband take his place at the pulpit. There, Reverend Coburn coughed and cleared his throat.

Lizbeth watched the exchange, yearning for a man who took a bright interest in what she had to offer, just as she would do for him. Yearning for sincere fervency and even passion with a future husband. It was why she had refused Reverend Coburn. As for William, she *had* felt a spark. She'd simply been distrusting, and in truth, rather blind. Lizbeth pondered the different encounters. William had demonstrated not only his sincerity, but his depth of character several times now. It was William who had lent her his own copy of *Jane Eyre*. William who had wanted to know what in this life brought her joy. With Reverend Coburn it seemed about the convenience and necessity of marriage.

Lizbeth blew out a slow breath, hoping to ease the ache in her chest. Those days were behind her and the novel with its soul-stirring love story was ready to be returned.

When a man entered the aisle beside her, she was about to move aside when she caught a glimpse of a familiar face. A familiar stance. All beneath a wool flatcap.

"Mr. Drake!"

Someone shushed her and Lizbeth's cheeks heated for more reasons than one. William looked at her in earnest, his surprise as evident as her own. A mutual shock that had them both frozen in place. His handsome face was cleanly shaven, eyes bright in the morning light. In the silence that followed a person behind them coughed. A baby whined. With William the only person left standing in the entire church, he indicated a need for the space beside her, sitting as soon as she inched over though there was scarcely room for them both.

"William, please," he said in a low tenor. The first words he'd said to her since he confessed his affection for her. His desires. As real as ever, seated beside her now, smelling of evergreen with his coat sleeve brushing her arm.

Lizbeth swallowed hard, and at the pulpit, Reverend Coburn called the congregation to attention. William removed his flatcap and set it in his lap. He wedged a briefcase beneath their seat. The space between them only narrowed as they rose for the first hymn. Lizbeth fumbled with the hymnal, dropping it with a clatter. Several people glanced their way. From where he stood above them all, Reverend Coburn arched a bewildered brow. Hattie looked at her in surprise. Lizbeth pinched her eyes shut a moment and before even a note could be sung, she sent up a prayer for rescue.

A prayer that was gently answered when William retrieved the hymnal and balanced it open between them so that she might find the page.

"Thank you," she whispered.

Although he stood a fair deal taller than she, he held the book low enough that she could read the stanzas with ease. Here she'd been pondering the difference between passions and polite affection and now this man who had offered her his heart, his being, and his future stood beside her. The man who had once taken great pains to express his love for her, who had asked her to share a life with him, and who she had quarreled with instead.

Lizbeth fought to keep her breath steady. With him silent beside her, she braved a glance up to his face. His focus rose straight ahead. Lizbeth searched for the words to the hymn's chorus but they blurred on the page. It seemed the English language was failing them both. Her hands shook at her sides. William shifted his stance.

"That must be what Pa's business was about today," Hattie whispered from her other side. "I didn't know it'd be Mr. Drake or I'd have warned you. I'm so sorry."

"Please don't be."

The congregation sang on until at last, Reverend Coburn bid everyone be seated. Lizbeth twined her nervous fingers together and was nearly about to sit on them when William reached into his vest pocket.

He pulled out a small Bible and offered it to her. "Sometimes it's nice to hold something during a long service," he said softly.

"I'm worried I may drop this one too." Just like the hymnal and his beautiful novel.

He gave a small smile. "Hasn't even crossed my mind."

Their fingers brushed as she took it. Bowing her head, Lizbeth searched the tiny book for the Psalms, finding the place. Leaning back, William folded his hands in his lap and kept his focus on Reverend Coburn.

Never had Lizbeth tried to sit so still. Never had she been so aware of a person beside her. His hair was cropped short again. Neat as ever. His whole demeanor from his crisp collar to his tailored suit bespoke composure except his feet, which he shifted nervously every few minutes. The nearness of him frayed her every thought, and it was a sweet relief when a faint breeze trickled in through the open window and across their pew.

She took a deep breath, as did he. As Reverend Coburn preached on, Lizbeth suddenly heard only William's words from that day in the meadow.

Never have I encountered a woman who has so enriched my world as you. Who has so made me long to enrich the world of another.

Lizbeth's gaze lifted to William's face once more. He was looking at her now. His gaze was steady, pensive, and full of regret. His eyes lifted back to the pulpit as Reverend Coburn led the congregation in a benediction of thanksgiving. Of reverence . . . and of peace.

At sermon's end, William was as eager to rise as he was to linger. The same kind of torment of his mind the last two months, but now, the subject of his heart was seated beside him. As people rose and exited the building, he tarried. What to say? Lizbeth handed the Bible back to him. He accepted it, this token he'd received from his late mother, and one he always carried on a Sunday, no matter where life took him. A piece of home. Now he'd had the honor of sharing that piece of home with Lizbeth.

He leaned just near enough to the woman beside him to be heard. "Thank you for letting me share the seat beside you." He pocketed the Bible, and excused himself to speak with Mr. Jorgensen. No sense lingering near her any longer than needed. He had no wish to make her feel uncomfortable. Not ever again.

He'd come here to speak frankly with Mr. Jorgensen and yet here he was, still unsteady after the shock of seeing Lizbeth. His heart still thrummed to have claimed the seat beside her. To have enjoyed her company if only for the stretch of a single morning. He longed to find a way to tarry with her longer, but there would be time enough for that. Perhaps he'd even be brave enough to seek a private audience with her. Say the few things he'd needed to get off his chest.

First, to clear his head and speak to Jorgensen. The man must have stepped out while William was speaking to Lizbeth. William carved his way through the crowd to the cool of noon, searching.

"Mr. Drake!" Mr. and Mrs. Jorgensen strode up to him, arm in arm. "A pleasure to see you, my good man." Jorgensen tipped the brim of his top hat. "You came in earlier than I'd anticipated. Very glad to have you!"

"I have business at the Chess Creek mine tomorrow, not far from here, so I figured it was the best day to travel to Stroudsburg. The train arrived early this morning and since I can't check into the hotel until this afternoon, I decided to join the service." It beat sitting alone on a bench at the depot. "I'll be here just one night."

"Good, very good. I hope you'll join us for luncheon."

A dozen desires and worries worked through his mind and William recalled the advice he'd given his best friend on Christmas Eve.

Own your actions. Own the consequences.

That guidance remained no less true for him.

"Of course. Thank you."

He could spend an afternoon making small talk then still carve out the chance to speak with Jorgensen of business. As for Lizbeth, by grace, this could be his chance to smooth things over between them. If that went well, then perhaps he and she could even find a way to part as friends.

27

William ducked beneath the doorway of the cottage, which was as white walled and welcoming as the church itself.

"Please make yourself at home, Mr. Drake." Surrounded by her humble home, Hattie pulled off a bonnet and touched her hair. "Lizbeth and I'll put on some tea. Soup's been simmerin' and I'll put some biscuits in the oven."

"It sounds perfect." He pulled off his cap.

Mr. Jorgensen waved him over to a pair of wingback chairs near the hearth. "Come sit. Warm yourself by the fire. Let's hear of your findings and hope it's moral to speak of business on a Sunday."

William claimed the chair opposite him while Lizbeth followed the other ladies into the kitchen. Through the front window, he saw Reverend Coburn detaining a few parishioners in the churchyard in what appeared to be a one-sided conversation.

This was his chance.

William slid his briefcase to the floor near his high-laced boots and unclasped the straps. "I've been doing some research and have a few final questions for you." He retrieved a folded map and splayed it on the small table beside them. "I've been examining this ventilation tunnel here, some hundred yards beyond the main shaft of the one-hundred level. The tunnel runs to the outside, just behind the hoist house, correct?"

Jorgensen studied the drawings. "Correct. It's an old slant tunnel that hasn't been used in years."

"Which would leave both space and access here for an electric generator."

Jorgensen's forehead wrinkled in surprise. "Electricity?"

"Yes, sir."

"Impossible." Jorgensen examined the tunnel again with a slow shake of his head. "It's unfathomable."

"It would seem that way, but it's being done elsewhere." William slid a newspaper article over that described the very miracle in another mine. "I believe electricity is the key to not only keeping New River afloat, but to improving the town and living conditions entirely. Additionally, it would allow me to contract out further work to the surrounding farms and cultivate income for local farmers." He would need timber, water, and new employees. Work for farmers such as Bennet and the like.

"How so?"

William offered a rare smile. "That would be for me to coordinate."

Mr. Jorgensen chuckled. "Fair. Keepin' your cards close to your chest. That's the way of business. And what of Bennet?"

Braced by his forearm, William leaned forward and kept his voice low. "I've been trying to think of a way that Bennet's land could be put to good use in a way that might satisfy everyone involved. It's good land and could benefit the mine in a way that doesn't have to hinder the Bennets' future, but could actually secure it."

Jorgensen's brows rose.

"It's possible there could be ways for him to summon up the final funds needed to pay the taxes."

In a rush, Lizbeth stepped from the kitchen carrying a stack of plates. Her eyes drifted to William. Had she heard?

He longed to watch her, but instead, waited for her retreat before continuing in a softer voice to Jorgensen. "If you can verify that these findings are correct, I'm prepared to make an offer." William handed over a list of inquiries that he'd written up. One by one, they detailed all that would be required to bring electricity into the region. From road conditions and accessibility to labor skills and availability and even the population of the town as it was now. Each detail mattered.

Mr. Jorgensen examined the list. "These inquiries will take me some time to compute."

"Of course." William snapped his briefcase closed.

"The deadline is approaching quickly. Only a month off."

"I understand, sir. I'll be ready." He nodded again to the paperwork. "If you could oversee that end of the bargain, I'll have an offer on your desk by the end of the month. If you can get me these findings, I'll have cash in hand."

"Don't you want to know what the other offers are?"

"I don't need to." His offer would be higher. More importantly, his vision broader. No—crucial. The more confident he was now, the more likely Jorgensen would delay.

And he desperately needed him to stall. If the other coal barons were willing to lay down money without a plan, then they had the advantage of speed. But he meant to have the advantage of intent. Not for himself, but for those who were reliant upon this sale going well.

"I mean to ensure the welfare of the town and its people with these developments," William continued. "I mean to keep New

River a place on the map. To give it a future." This was more than business to him. "I believe electricity could do this but I need to be certain."

"Electricity." Jorgensen examined the list again. "It's unprecedented."

"That's how I do things, sir."

"So I see." He ran a weathered hand over his mustache. "All right then. I'll see that I have all of these answers for you by the end of the month." With Jorgensen intending to retire in the summer, he could only hope this was enough time for everything to fall into place. "How should I get them to you? I'll be back in New River by then where there's no phone service."

Right. "I'll be in touch."

"And if not?"

"Then please consider our dealings peacefully nulled by then and proceed with one of the current offers in good conscience."

Surprise deepened the lines of the mine owner's forehead. "Then we have a deal." The man held out a hand and William shook it.

"Thank you, sir."

Seeing Reverend Coburn passing through the cottage gate, William straightened.

"Perhaps tuck that aside." Jorgensen thumbed toward William's briefcase. "No sense shocking the poor minister." He pocketed the list as the women emerged from the kitchen with tea and fixings. In the commotion, William slipped a copy of his travel itinerary from his briefcase along with a fountain pen. He uncapped the pen and turned the paper over, using the table's edge to scrawl a note. He'd managed the first burden he needed to address and only a few lines beyond before Mrs. Coburn beckoned them to the table.

"Thank you." William added one final request, signed his name in haste, and pocketed the note. He rose and joined everyone at the table near a nine-paned window.

"Please have a seat," Mrs. Coburn bid him.

Lizbeth returned with a basket of bread and a crock of butter.

"May I help in any way?" William asked as Mrs. Jorgensen emerged with a tray of sweets. He'd never carried a tray in his life but was eager to start now.

Lizbeth looked surprised. "We just need the pot of soup." She set her own offerings down. "It's on the stove."

"I can help with that." He followed her into the adjoining kitchen to where a pot of soup sat simmering.

While he'd spent little time near a stove, it didn't take his college degree to warn him about hot handles. William touched them gingerly then searched for a solution.

Lizbeth moved to his side and nabbed two thick cloths. "These should do the trick."

William dropped his gaze to her face and saw the spark of amusement in her eyes. "Thank you." He thought of the note in his pocket. Should he give it to her now?

His hands were already filled so he lifted the pot instead and followed her to the table where he placed it in the center. With Mrs. Jorgensen at his right, William pulled out the chair for her and the woman sat, thanking him. William took his own seat and had to labor not to notice Lizbeth, who sat directly across from him.

Reverend Coburn prayed a blessing, then Hattie dipped a wide spoon, filling each bowl with broth and vegetables. Small talk ensued. Of the sermon. Of their journey by train. Time to address Lizbeth directly. She was busy speaking with her friend, so William waited for a brief lull. It settled as she reached for the butter.

William cleared his throat. "Have you enjoyed reading *Jane Eyre*, Miss Bennet?"

She looked surprised as she lifted the small lid and dipped a knife. "Lizbeth, please."

A sweet relief. "Lizbeth."

"I've enjoyed it so much. I nearly finished it on the journey here. Just a few pages left."

He nodded. "I admit to having never read it before, but I'm inspired to now."

The surprise he saw only increased. As for the rest of the table? They were stone silent. Even Reverend Coburn's constant mutterings had ceased. Everyone stared at them.

William needed to somehow get her alone. "Might I . . . might I check the publication date when you have a moment?"

"Of course. I can fetch it when we're done."

He nodded his thanks and turned his attention back to his food, relieved when Mrs. Jorgensen started in on how fine the weather was, and there he sat, his moment with Lizbeth ahead, all the while having absolutely no idea what he was going to do with the publication date of *Jane Eyre*.

William waited in the upstairs hallway just outside of Lizbeth's room where a small alcove offered a reading bench and a view of the churchyard across the way. Downstairs, Mr. Jorgensen had drifted off, the ladies were occupying themselves with tea, and Reverend Coburn was reading the first lines of a sermon aloud. As for William, he stood there, hat in hand, clinging tighter to the wool the moment Lizbeth appeared.

"Please." She waved toward the cushioned window seat in the alcove. Lizbeth moved an embroidery hoop with dangling thread aside. "We can sit."

"Of course." He felt her nearness as he did and kept his focus on his hands, only to grow more distracted by her own, which now clutched his novel.

A scrap of cloth, the same colors as her skirt, marked what must have been her page. She offered the novel over and William cracked the cover, more engaged by her presence than anything else.

She leaned nearer and read from the title page. "Written in 1847."

He let out a little chuckle as the ruse continued. "Indeed."

She looked at him brightly. "And now we both know."

"I'm sure we'll never forget." He gave her a small smile, which she returned.

When he tried to offer the book back, Lizbeth pressed it forward. "You oughta take this with you now. That way you'll have it back."

"But you only have a few pages left."

"Yes, but—"

He held the novel over. "Please. You're going to need to find out how the story ends."

Lizbeth took it gently. "How it ends," she repeated softly. Her eyes lifted to his again. "And when I finish?"

His heart was pounding faster now. Did she know that he'd thought of little but her in the months since they last spoke? Since the day his heart had wrecked upon a rocky shore? Only to be rebuilt again. Newer, stronger. And more able to see what it was that she needed from him. Patience and sincerity. He'd meant to give her both the first time, but instead had produced only confusion and dismay. "My address should be inside." He'd just added it with a sleight of hand.

Her brow furrowed.

"Better yet, you can hold on to the book until I return to New River."

"You'll be comin' back?" She was clutching the sampler now.

As though holding on to the familiar made it easier to make sense of the new.

William shifted his shoes, nearly bumping her own. "I have business with Mr. Jorgensen. In two weeks' time."

Lizbeth gently fingered a delicate thread. "About the mine."

"Yes." And on that subject he owed her an explanation. "What West said . . . I want to assure you that your father's land is in no danger from me. If you'll give me the chance, I can make sure both you and your father know that without a shadow of a doubt."

She drew in a slow breath. How he wished to know what she was thinking.

"I just need a little bit of time." He braced his hand to the seat between them. Not so different from the church pew. Especially with them nearly as close.

"West wasn't honest," she said.

"No, he wasn't. He was misinformed, at the very least."

"I was too quick to believe him. I see him differently now." She touched his sleeve. "For that I apologize. I'm so very sorry, William."

He couldn't help but look at her face now. "No need to be."

"I am all the same, if you'll forgive me for what I said." Her eyes searched his own. "I've regretted it since."

Dawn broke inside him but he had to fight it back lest he rise and reach for her. "Of course. If you'll forgive me in return."

"I don't know what there is to forgive. You spoke honestly when West didn't. You had conviction, when I was instead blinded."

He shook his head, longing to stem her worries. And quite frankly, overwhelmed with the grace of this moment. It was all that he could have hoped for and more. "May I ask what's changed? Concerning Westgard?"

A speckled bird landed on the windowsill behind them. Peering back over her shoulder, she admired it. "I realized that I'd taken the word of someone I scarcely knew who used charm to mask other traits. He still writes now and again to Lacey, which worries me as, more than once, I saw her slip a few pennies into an envelope before mailing it back."

William didn't like the sound of it. "You do right to mind the situation. I regret summoning the man to New River in the first place."

"I will."

"And if there's any way I can be of service to your family, please let me know."

Her eyes widened.

"Business takes me a few counties over from here next. I travel again by rail in the morning."

"Aboard the Pemberley?"

He smiled again. A habit around this woman. "No. I travelled coach believe it or not."

"And lived to tell the tale?"

He chuckled. "As have you. I'm glad you've enjoyed your own travels."

"I have." She acknowledged the alcove with its watercolor paintings and floral curtains. "These are memories I won't soon forget."

He hoped not. His gaze landed on the unfinished embroidery she held. "Is this one of them?"

"Yes." She tilted the wooden hoop to the light. "I'm going to show it to a shop owner tomorrow. I only need to finish a few more stitches in one of the words."

"You're going to sell it?"

Her nod was delayed as though she regretted her disclosure. "A small way to help Pa with the farm. There's a shop across the street from the depot that I'm going to check in at."

A pang hit his chest. Made worse knowing that he could prevent the effort she was going through by a simple snap of his billfold, and yet at the same time, he wasn't at liberty to. Not if it cost her pa his pride and appeared as though he were trying to buy her hand. He could never do that. He longed for her still, but only through sincerity and hard work.

Hard work he was ready for.

Taking the sampler gently, he read, *"The night is far spent, the day is at hand: let us therefore cast off the works of darkness, and let us put on the armour of—"* His gaze, downcast, searched the threads and the theology laced within them.

Linen still in his grip, he smoothed his thumb against the delicate fibers. Did it show? The effect these words had on him? The effect that this woman had on him? The blessed sight of her tiny stitches and the hours, days, and likely months she would have spent with this in her care. He longed to touch the ornate lines but not at risk of marring her handiwork.

He imagined Lady Light. He imagined the stern face of Aunt Catherine looking down upon him. And he was ready for something to change. The ornate loops and curls of the letters in hand struck another pang to his heart. Such time. Such dedication. "This is beautiful."

A pink tinge brightened her cheeks and he fingered the loose threads at the back of the linen. "Are these to be discarded?"

"Yes, I still need to trim them away."

He admired the soft gold and robin's-egg blue. Summer in a whisper, if the colors could talk. The same shades as the skirt she wore, all warm and bright. "Might I have a few strands?"

She arched an eyebrow.

"You've inspired me about something. For my racehorse."

From a cloth bag at her feet, she retrieved a small set of shears. William held the embroidery in its hoop steady while she snipped two loose strands. The tension of their fingertips on the cloth brought balance. A near touching that heated his arms, his shoulders.

"Thank you." He tucked both threads into his vest pocket. Not wanting to overstay his time with her, he rose. "For your train ride home . . . the best way to enjoy coach is with a cherry cola, if I might recommend one. You won't regret it." He needed to step away. Needed to leave so he didn't imagine he'd have more times like this with her. Though, heaven help him, he didn't want to go. "It's been a pleasure seeing you again."

The slant of her face followed the way his height filled the alcove. "And you also."

He tapped the novel in her hands. "I hope you enjoy the ending, Lizbeth."

"And when the time comes, you as well, William."

Her demeanor was softening with him, and her eyes, once guarded, were clear as day now. Did she, by any chance, return his feelings from the autumn? His feelings from every hour since? There would only be one way to find out, but he had to proceed in order. One thing at a time. He would not rush his desires as he had last time. The cost had been too great, and this young lady was too precious to him.

He smiled at her for what he hoped wouldn't be the final time. "I believe I shall."

28

A brass bell clanged as Lizbeth tugged on the shop door, but the door didn't budge. Locked? Leaning toward the window, she peeked inside. The parcel wrapped under her arm was too important for her to simply turn away. At the sight of a worker within the store, she tapped lightly on the glass.

The man angled her way, black apron and moving broom stating his purpose. "We're closed today." His voice came muffled through the glass.

The man went to turn away, but Lizbeth knocked this time. She didn't wish to startle him but needed this moment. This chance.

Shoulders slumped, the man shook his head in irritation. Lizbeth stepped back, relieved when he turned a key in the lock. "I'm sorry, miss. You'll have to come back on Saturday. We're only open during the week for appointments."

"Please, sir. I haven't come to shop. I have an item for you to consider. For purchase. It's a sampler that I stitched. I see you have others hanging."

"They're some of the finest pieces in the nation." He began to ease the door closed. "But if you must, try again on Saturday."

Her foot caught the edge of the door before it could click closed. "Please, sir. My train leaves before then. I've come a long way. All the way from Virginia."

The man consulted a pocket watch.

"I'll only take a few moments of your time."

Sighing, he sized up the paper package she clutched in her arms. "Five minutes."

The door creaked on its hinges as he braced it open for her. Heart stuttering, Lizbeth slipped into the shop where ornate samplers hung on the walls, some looking a century old. With Hattie and the Jorgensens expecting her for an afternoon drive through the countryside, she had mere minutes to spare before they had intended to leave by carriage. Lizbeth swallowed hard. A beautiful mirror graced the nearest tabletop along with pocket watches for sale, lacy fans and silk top hats.

The man slung open a curtain, bringing in more light. He leaned the broom against the wall and repeated, "Five minutes."

She steeled all her courage as she set the bundle on the counter and tugged at the twine. "This is stitched on a piece of antique linen." In truth, she'd found it at the bottom of a trunk once belonging to her grandmother.

"Hmm." The man adjusted his spectacles. "Where did you get this from?"

"I—I made it. Honestly."

His brows pinched together.

"I stitched it myself over the last year. The motifs are inspired by the woods where I live and the threads are all colors from my family's farm. I've hand dyed the threads myself. The blush color comes from rose petals that grow just outside our churchyard." The same roses that once snagged poor Reverend Coburn's coat.

It was her story, splayed here on the counter, and she was blessed to get to share it. Blessed to get to live it—trials and all. Lizbeth unfolded the paper further and watched as the shop owner carefully unfurled what lay within. Her sampler shone delicately in the electric lanterns overhead.

"Silks?" he asked.

"Wool." It would mean a lesser value, but wool thread was all she could come by.

"Hmm."

The man liked that sound.

Holding the piece up to the light, he examined her handiwork. His face was drawn and stony. "How did you come by this deep violet?" he asked.

"Blackberries, sir. From beside our creek."

"And the verse?"

"From the book of Romans." She brushed a strand of hair from her cheek. "It's seemed fitting lately."

He turned the piece over, scrutinizing the back. All the knots and trimmings that weren't meant to be viewed. He flipped it over again. "Did you have a price in mind? I do have clients at times looking for unusual designs but usually such pieces are passed down through the generations." He looked at her over the spectacles on his nose. "It's why we mostly sell antique pieces. But this aged linen is, as you mentioned, quite something." He pulled off his spectacles and for the first time since coming here, she sensed a softening. "Are you certain you don't want to hold on to this?"

Dearly, she did, but it wasn't an option. "I would prefer to sell it, sir. It would be better for my family."

Leaning one arm on the edge of the counter, the man studied her sampler again, even measuring it with a length of tape. He wrote down the dimensions and finally jotted down a sum that she couldn't see. He slid the slip of paper her way. "This is my offer."

$6.00

Not as much as she had hoped for. The sampler had taken her months to finish. How could this make a dent in the debt her pa owed for the farm? How could it make any kind of real difference? Lizbeth touched the sampler again, recalling the way William had snipped and kept two of the threads. Could she not do the same? A way to keep it with her . . . while stepping forward into the future that awaited her and her family.

She could do this.

"I'll take the six dollars, sir. Along with a new piece of linen. And might I borrow a pair of scissors?"

His eyebrows shot up.

"That is the best I can do in return," she explained. And she would stitch and work her way into the future for her family. One thread at a time. It wouldn't be enough to help Pa save the farm, not in the near future, but it was one more way she could give it all she had. "The scissors are so I can snip a few threads to keep and remember."

"And a second piece of linen?"

"So that I can make another sampler for you and your shop. I can dye threads in all sorts of colors from the woods and garden. That might help them stand out to your customers. Help it be unique. If you're agreed, I'll gladly mail the next piece to your shop here. Three months' time?"

It would be slow progress . . . but steady.

With a sigh, the shop owner opened a cashbox and withdrew the six dollars. He slid the bills over. "Linen is in the cabinet in the far corner. You may select your piece and I'll cut you a portion to size." With a fresh scrap of paper, he scribbled the shop's address and gave it to her. "I'm not sure why I'm doing this, but we have a deal."

Chest filling with air, Lizbeth pocketed the money. Another small step forward. "I'll see it done. Thank you, sir." She reached out a hand and he shook it.

"And here are those scissors."

Carefully, she trimmed away two threads from the back and tucked them into her skirt pocket.

At the cabinet, Lizbeth chose the prettiest piece of linen she could find. This one a square of dove gray. So pale and soft, she could nearly imagine more of Bennet Hollow stitched upon it. Perhaps the roses that grew wild down by the river. The cheery golds and reds of Ma's chickens, or even the ebony plumes of smoke that lifted on the horizon—the same shade as when the Pemberley had journeyed into town. A sight she longed to see once more.

Heart both full and aching at once, Lizbeth turned for the door. "Thank you, sir. I appreciate this more than I can say."

"Did you sign the piece?"

She halted. "No, sir. I didn't know if I should."

The first smile. A small one. "Please do. That way if the first sells, I can alert the buyer that there will be more in the future. We'll also need a name for it. I'll create a small placard to hang beside the frame on the wall."

Her chest lifted at the notion. "I didn't bring a needle and thread."

The man opened a wooden box. "Just here."

With his help, Lizbeth selected a glinting needle and piece of bright white thread. With Hattie and the Jorgensen's needing her to return for their afternoon drive into the countryside, her fingers moved as fast as they could against the bottom right corner. Finally, she finished and held the cherished cloth over.

Lizbeth Bennet, 1905. As was customary with samplers.

"And the name of the piece?"

She thought a moment, looking one last time at the swirling vines and flowers—all colors of home. "Mark it down as *The Heart of Bennet Hollow*, if you would."

"Excellent. I'll be seeing you again, Miss Bennet. A good day to you."

"Thank you, sir." Lizbeth left the shop and as soon as she was on the front steps, she silently bid farewell to the sampler that felt a part of her all these months. All these regrets and hopes and prayers. It would soon belong to another, but this was the path she needed to walk and finally—*finally*—she could do it with a lighter heart.

She started down the road, aiming for the Coburns. Within minutes, she found Hattie and the Jorgensens out in front of the cottage, loading a picnic basket and several blankets into the back of a carriage. Mr. Coburn stood speaking to the driver, making sure that the man had a clear understanding of the day's itinerary.

"Lizzy!" Hattie waved. "Just in time! It's going to be chilly today, but we'll be snug in the carriage, and I've packed us some supper and hot tea."

"That sounds splendid. I'm sorry I'm late." Lizbeth embraced her friend and kissed Hattie's cheek. "Is there time for me to grab my things?"

"Of course."

"I'll be quick!"

Lizbeth hurried up the stone walk and to her second-floor room where she grabbed her shawl. William's novel sat on the nightstand and she fetched that as well. The perfect way to pass an afternoon on a peaceful drive and finish the final pages. As she opened the book to ensure that her page was still marked, a sheet of paper tumbled free.

The single page hit the floor and fluttered open. Handwriting that she didn't recognize caught the light. Lizbeth reached for it, just spotting the signature at the bottom. Her heart nearly stilled.

William Drake.

Horses nickered outside and as she stepped toward the door, she couldn't look away from the letter. Hoping she had a few more moments to spare, Lizbeth skimmed back to the top and read.

Dear Lizbeth,

Please don't be alarmed by the haste of this note, only know that I hope to get it into your hand sometime today. I won't repeat the sentiments which were so off-putting to you when we spoke at your father's farm, and I believe we can both lay that meeting behind us. From this day forward, please think of me only as a friend and advocate.

And now, I hope to explain to you the situation surrounding your father's land and Mr. Westgard's implications sometime while we're together today, but just as importantly, and perhaps even more urgent, is addressing the sorrow that I believe has been suffered by both your sister Jayne and my friend Callum.

From our first coming to New River, it was obvious that they formed a connection, and yet, to what degree? And to what outcome? As a friend, I attempted to guide Callum to be cautious, but in that, was mistaken. I since have seen the error of my understanding of their hopes for one another. For that I must apologize. If she were to write him, please give her the address written here. I'll ensure her letter's delivery to Callum myself. I understand that would take faith in my character, and for that, I can only pray to have provided the beginnings of such. As for the future, I wish them both well and pray for a renewed acquaintance between them. I add their happiness to the service I'm available to be called upon for.

Along with yours.

There's more to say, but for now, I'm out of time. May God bless you.

William Drake

Hattie called out to her.

Folding the letter, Lizbeth retreated down the stairs as new waves of understanding broke free of the clouds. In the months of William's absence, she'd begun seeing that she'd been wrong about him. As for sitting beside him in the alcove? How peaceful she'd felt beside the quiet coal baron. If she were honest . . . a sense of yearning had blossomed for his calming, steady presence. His intelligent conversation and gentle ways. The care he took with her, then and now. Perhaps always, if he were to ask once more. A request she would never expect of him.

Back outside, Lizbeth greeted her companions and climbed into the carriage. Hattie tucked a blanket over their laps. Reverend Coburn's excited chatter blurred as Lizbeth safely hid William's letter into the book again. Despite the beauty of the day, she saw only him in her mind's eye. The way he'd stood in a church aisleway this Sunday past, his gaze earnest as he claimed the seat beside her. Sitting beside her in an alcove near her room. His soft smile as he'd spoken to her of life, of optimism. The way he'd once reached for her hand. Asked for her.

Last of all was the memory of him standing in the field back home. His flatcap in his anxious grip as he explained the way he saw her. Cared for her. Sentiments she'd realized ran deeper than even his silence had since his coming to New River.

A pursuit from his heart to her own.

One he was asking her to forget all about. To lay behind them. That instead, they might be *friends*. He no doubt going his separate way and she going hers.

The horses clopped into motion and Lizbeth steadied herself with a hand to the side of the carriage. She glanced over her shoulder, toward the train depot where William mentioned he would depart today, wondering if she was moving farther from her future or toward it.

spring

29

March 1905

Jayne Bennet of Bennet Hollow
New River, Virginia

Dear Jayne,

I received your letter this morning and was so pleased to open it. I sat there at breakfast and read each word. Twice, to be honest. I'm relieved to hear that you're doing well and enjoying this milder weather. It's still quite crisp in Vermont, but it will pass soon.

Just yesterday, the coachmen brought out my carriage for the first time in months. Not that I mind travelling by sleigh. The bells are festive and bring cheer to the colder days. Have you ever travelled by sleigh? I think it may be one of life's joys. But here I am, blathering on.

Please tell me more about the spring garden you wrote of. How is it faring?

You inspired me to take a walk through my own gardens and while there's not much to be had, the ideals you described have me looking forward to summer.

I hope you receive this letter safe and well—and that you are the same.

William Drake, as you recall, delivered your letter to me. It has been the first I've received and from what I gather, you had not received the three letters I mailed you over the winter. I apologize for such confusion. It seems something went awry with the post coming and going to my home and that's my missight entirely. The world is a little clearer now, and hearing your voice in it once more is the clearest sound of all. If you would enjoy writing again, yours will be the first I read.

Warmly,
Callum Brydolf

Mr. C. Brydolf
C/O Mr. W. Drake
127 Ridgeview Lane
Shelburne, Vermont

Dear Callum,

I too enjoyed getting your letter. It was also the first I've seen and I'm grateful to have received it. It came as a surprise today while I was in town and I'm rather glad as I got to be the first to read it. A rarity in the Bennet home.

It's been some time since I've travelled by sled. I was a girl and Pa used to pull my sisters and I on a wooden sled not made to hold all of us five girls at once. We'd bundle up in our mittens and coats, and it was how he got us out of the house in midwinter and out from under Ma's feet. Likely, those rides were a mite bumpier than your own, and one or two of us would usually fall off, but they are fond memories. We would always return to cups of hot tea and a roaring fire that felt as comforting as Ma draping a blanket around us.

As your letter was posted a week ago, I'm curious if the weather has brightened further for you. In anticipation of sunnier days, I've included some seeds—rosemary and yarrow. I've added a few notes on starting them indoors until the ground is more welcoming.

Please do tell me if you have any luck with them. I'm not very good at saving seeds. This has been my first attempt. So, it's an experiment for us both. I sewed up the paper packets myself so we will see if they arrive unspilled. I do hope so.

Thank you again for your letter. I've addressed this one to Mr. Drake's estate once more.

Most sincerely,
Jayne

Jayne Bennet of Bennet Hollow
New River, Virginia

Dear Jayne,

First to herald in good news—the packets arrived in perfect condition. You've a fine hand with a needle. I've planted the seeds you sent and started them indoors as you advised. I've never had a knack for gardening so I'll be honest that I asked my gardener for assistance. We spent the afternoon in the potting shed where I used two small pots (per your recommendation) which were unfortunately cracked (per my clumsiness) and with just the right amount of soil, I got the seeds settled into place. They're on the sunniest side of the greenhouse where I do believe they'll soon outshine even the heritage roses. I keep a close eye on the sleeping seeds, visiting each day though I sense it isn't making them grow any quicker. Please send any further advice you have for this humble gardener.

The weather is indeed brightening. I can almost imagine how Vermont will be in the summer. Some of my favorite delights are the blueberries that grow wild and the honey that comes from the back acreage of this estate. I rather wish I could call it a farm, as you have known, but perhaps one day it will get there. I'll be thinking of a way to share its offerings with you when the time comes. Perhaps a package in the mail or some other clever way to deliver blueberries and honey. And maybe a little more.

Be on the lookout.

And please do tell me how this next letter arrives to you. I'm rather curious about the excitement that the mail brings to the Bennet household and much enjoy the pictures your descriptions create in my mind. Already, I've smiled with memory of your sledding days without having ever been there.

Warmly,
Callum

30

"I *hate* radishes," Lacey whined.

"Well"—Jayne wedged a trowel into the earth—"you don't have to eat them."

Lacey tugged at a carrot that had wintered in place, only to fall back onto a mound of dirt. "Besides, it's not even warm yet."

"You just sow your row the way I've asked and stop your fussin', li'l missy," Ma called from the laundry line.

Nearby, Kit and Maryanne lifted a damp sheet to dry in the sunshine.

"Radishes don't mind cooler weather." Lizbeth reached for a paper bag with seeds. "Then we'll be done and can reap the rewards this summer."

Lacey flicked a messy braid off her shoulder. "Speak for yourself. I don't know that I'll be here by then."

Jayne's trowel stilled against the damp earth. "What are you talkin' about?"

"None of your nevermind." Lacey peeked in Ma's direction as she ambled farther down the line and out of earshot.

"I agree. What do you mean by that?" Lizbeth sat back on her legs, not minding the dirt on her work skirt.

Lacey jabbed at the spring soil with a trowel bent by her own doing. She struck a pebble and tossed it aside. "Well, it might have somethin' to do with my fine fella, West."

"Mr. Westgard?"

"Ugh. It sounds so formal when you say it like that."

As was right. They scarcely knew him. "I don't think he's all you imagine him to be."

"I agree." Jayne dug through the basket of the rattling seed packets and squinted at a handwritten label. "You'd do well to end this correspondence between you two."

"Nonsense. I'd never dream of doin' such a thing." Lacey's own hands, thrown up in argument, were much too clean considering the chore before them. "And he's plenty able. He'd provide for me good and well, you'd see."

Lizbeth shook her head. "Please don't do anything foolish. You don't know enough about him."

"Maybe you just want him for yourself."

"Not in the least."

Lacey aimed her chin toward the sky. "Then you won't mind if I take him off the market."

"Do Ma and Pa know you're talkin' this way?" Jayne angled to where Ma was finishing up.

Kit carried the empty basket into the house as Maryanne pinned the final sheet into place, all of them flapping briskly in the breeze.

The only response Lacey gave was to throw her hands up in the air again. "Can I be done now? I've got readin' to finish for school."

Lizbeth sprinkled a smattering of radish seeds into a furrow. "Finish your row and you can be off."

Lacey did, sulking all the while and lumping too many seeds together before discarding her tools for Jayne and Lizbeth to gather when they, too, were finished. Over the garden gate, as Lizbeth shared her worries with Ma, she was countered that Mr. Westgard was a fine man. Handsome and capable with a good position as a miner in Pennsylvania. He could offer Lacey a decent future. "When Lacey's of age in a year or two, he'd make a good match for her," Ma explained.

"I'm not so sure. I fear they'd be the ruin of one another." Lacey was much too childish, and the man she was sweet on, questionable in return.

Ma waved away the concern. "Well, there's time enough to worry about that. Lacey ain't goin' away from us just yet."

"I hope you're right." Lizbeth watched as Ma shuffled off to cluck at one of the barn cats for swatting at her clean sheets and wished that rogue suitors might be as easy to shoo away.

A luster lived in the evening, one akin to optimism as Lizbeth stood upstairs in their bedroom, tying a rag into Jayne's hair. "These curls should set up real nice come mornin'."

Jayne touched her rag-covered head, then raised Mrs. Jorgensen's used magazine that she'd given to Lizbeth along with Mr. Jorgensen's unwanted newspapers. There on the cover of *McCall's* stood a woman in high fashion, her hair done up in the latest style. "I wonder how they managed these folds in the front."

"I suppose we'll just have to practice." Lizbeth tied the last rag at the nape of Jayne's neck.

"Don't wind it too tight. It says here the curls are just for body and'll be brushed out in the mornin'."

"Too late."

Using the magazine, which held everything from new dress patterns to an advertisement for Heinz Tomato Soup, Jayne swatted at Lizbeth's arm.

"You best be careful with that, now. May be the last one we ever see." Lizbeth bent to better inspect her handiwork. "Though I saw in the back that if you become a subscriber, they'll send you nine doilies in the mail."

Jayne laughed. "At fifty cents a year, I better get the job down at the mine office to afford it." Her smile in the mirror was hopeful as she gently smoothed the cover of the magazine. "Thank you for the help. I'm sure I'm goin' to too much bother. It's only for an afternoon. But I mean to present myself as neatly as possible tomorrow. This is a good opportunity. Eighty-five cents a payroll. Just to do sums."

"I'm already proud of you." Lizbeth adjusted a rag.

"I'll be glad for the work. Just think how quickly that could add up and I could give all of it to Pa. Do you think Mr. Jorgensen'll hire me? I didn't get as high of grades as Hattie but came in third on the state exams our last year of schooling, right behind her."

"I think you have a better shot than anyone. And he'll need someone until the mine sale goes through. There's a good chance the future owner would keep you as well, just like the miners." Lizbeth tucked the unused rags back into their lidded basket.

"Exactly. It's one of the reasons I want to try and get the position now," Jayne said. "And as for you—I hear you have more stitching to do. I'm so proud of you, Lizzy, for what you did for Pa. All of us."

Lizbeth glanced to the new piece of linen now draped over a chair that already held the first row of alphabet letters. "Lots of stitching to do, which I don't mind. And I've been thinking I might help Pa fix up the pasture fence. I haven't done that sort of thing yet and it's time I learn. I wonder if there's a way to make a living carin' for mules."

There was a smile in Jayne's voice as she crawled beneath the quilt of her bottom bunk. "If anyone can find a way, it'd be you."

Lizbeth climbed the ladder to the top bunk and settled in. Jayne blew out the lantern. In the silence of the room, she sensed Jayne just as awake.

"Jayne?"

"Yes?"

"Will you tell Callum about your interview in your next letter?"

"I will," Jayne answered in the dark.

Sitting up, Lizbeth fumbled for the matchbook. She found it, struck a flame, and lowered the glow to the stub of a candle on the windowsill beside her, then peered over the edge of her top bunk. The soft spark flickered across the room. "What do you think'll happen if he asks you to marry him?"

Jayne pushed aside one of her rag curls to squint sleepily up at Lizbeth. "Do you reckon he's thinkin' about that already?"

"Oh, I believe he was thinkin' of that the first night he met you."

Jayne smiled. "I hope so, but we've only written a few letters back and forth."

"Well, I suspect there'll be many more."

Jayne smiled again. "It's so good to hear his voice. Even in a letter. I can imagine him. His heart and his kindness. It's a gift like no other. I want to cherish it for as long as I can. I'm so thankful to his friend, Mr. Drake, for helpin' us as he has. Lizzy, he's really not as bad as you once described." Jayne tucked her pillow back beneath her head.

Not yet brave enough to admit how wrong she'd been about him, Lizbeth reached for the candle and blew it out. Along with the scent of smoke came her sister's soft words in the dark.

"But . . ." Jayne sighed. "Maybe I don't know as much about love as I thought I did. I'm glad we get to figure it out together. Makes the road a mite less lonely."

31

The Vermont air was clear and bright as William descended the carriage steps and tossed a wave to his driver. "Thank you, sir!"

"Safe travels to you, Mr. Drake!"

With sure steps, William aimed for the crowded depot of Shelburne. Farther away from his estate just a mile back up the road. Ahead, the Pemberley stood coupled into position at the end of the southbound train. The location would afford an unguarded view of every mile the train wound into the Appalachian hills, half a dozen states away. And he was *so* close to a solution for the New River mine. The main hurdle left to resolve was how he would generate electricity in a town so remote. He was getting closer, but the clock ticked endlessly in his mind, and Jorgensen would need an offer on his desk soon.

Time was of the essence.

As he wove through the crowd, William patted his coat pocket where he kept the itinerary for this trip, including meetings with several hand-selected engineers and electricians in just as many cities. Somewhere in the midst of those, he would try and intercept

Lady Light to ensure that she was well settled into her new training routine. His Aunt Catherine had telephoned, announcing she'd meet them as well and was still arranging the specific location. As William remained in touch with the trainer and jockey, he'd confirmed that the new silks were being commissioned by a tailor. He needed the jockey's uniform to be finished before the opening at the Belmont races in May.

Everything was in motion. All of it needing his attention.

First, the rails would guide him back to New River.

Walking the length of the fifty-eight-foot Pullman car, William confirmed that she was in tip-top shape. All looked ready for his departure in a few hours' time. Cook had finalized the menu and laid up enough supplies for the first leg of the journey, but he meant to correct the travelling numbers. While he'd expected Callum to venture with him again, the man was out of state. So the passenger number for this voyage across the miles was *one*.

At the clatter of a wagon approaching, William moved out of the way, just missing a puddle. Horses clomped down the street, pulling a loaded cart. Hay spilled from a pile on top, floating to the road. Nearby, one of his maintenance men balanced on a ladder. The man looked as old as time with a few strands of white hair peeking out from beneath a tattered cap. A wrinkled hand rose to unscrew a lightbulb from an exterior sconce with fingers that struggled.

William persisted down the length of the car where he braced a hand to the edge of the man's ladder. "Everything looks in good order. Thank you."

The old-timer squinted down. "Be that Mr. Drake?" His voice was as gravelly as the soil between the tracks.

"It is, sir. How are you today?"

"Oh, fine. Fine, sir. Another day above ground so I can't complain." The man carefully loosened the bulb with wrinkled fingers. When he finished, William reached up to take it.

"Why thank you, son."

From *sir* to *son*. He liked this man and always had.

"If you don't mind handin' up the new one. It'll be there in the tool chest." The hand that pointed that way tremored.

William knelt and pulled a boxed bulb from the metal chest with care. Just last year, he'd paid several thousand dollars for the Pemberley's gas lamps to be converted to electric lighting.

"Do these burn out often?" he asked.

"Oh, not all that often. Just now and again when the filament gives out."

William noted the four coils meant to brighten and glow. The cogs in his mind spun, but he couldn't assemble the order yet. Still, the constant grinding reminded him that three coal barons had made offers on the New River mine now. And none of them would have the town's best interest in mind. Nor the surrounding farmland's. He needed to find a way to secure all of it. Which had one substantial idea rolling around in his mind—*electricity*. If only he could make this idea work. "May I ask you something?"

"Anything."

William heeded the way the new bulb was screwed into place. "What is the secret?"

"To how the bulb works?"

"I mean electricity in general. What makes it a success?"

"Well . . ." The man's legs shook as he descended. William braced the ladder again. "I suppose it be a few things. It makes folks awful happy. The flip of a switch and they can see their suppers. Their loved ones' faces good and bright. It also brings convenience as well as consistency."

That was all true. He'd witnessed it himself.

"Though there's somethin' romantic about candlelight. If with the right company." The man—probably married for fifty years now—smiled.

Well said. "And beyond that?"

"Well, I don't quite know what you're gettin' at, son." Worn work boots finally reached the ground.

William folded the ladder and laid it aside. "Can you spare a moment?" Since the maintenance man knew every detail about this home on rails, William led the way to his office at the back. "I'd like to know what you think of something."

With light from the observation dome filtering down, William dug through the papers on his desk that smelled of lemon and beeswax thanks to his housemaids giving his office a once-over.

William offered over a set of drawings. "These are an exact rendering of a coal mine. The various tunnels, exits. This is where I'd like to place electricity and exactly where several engineers have said it's a fool's errand."

"Mmm." The man leaned nearer and studied the drawings.

"Please, sit." William pulled out a chair.

There was that dry chuckle again. "We both know I'm not allowed to sit in your company."

"Please." William pulled up a second chair and sat.

The man's joints creaked as he lowered himself. "Well, then." With knobby hands, he lifted the nearest drawing closer. His milky-white eyes roved each sketch.

William inched his chair nearer. "I've reached out to a number of engineers and so far each has advised against attempting to install electricity in a coal mine. But it's currently being done by another company. I tried to stress that but the professionals I've spoken to are unwavering."

"What will you do then?"

"Find one that believes it's possible. I travel this week in hopes of doing just that." And he was running out of time. "The concern doesn't seem to be about power itself so much as it is with *generating* that power."

"Exactly."

"I still don't see the solution."

The man examined the drawings again. "Fascinating. Just fascinating."

With muted footsteps and a swish of her gray dress, Cook entered the office. Wood clattered against the metal hearth as she lowered an armload of sharp-scented pine. William nodded his thanks when she promised to fix up a pot of coffee for his guest. William meant to help with these final preparations, but first . . .

"The question is, can it be done?" he asked. "I'm heading to a very remote town. Scant resources. It would mean starting from the ground up. Introducing technology that has never been present there before. Which circles me back to the question if this is madness."

The man chuckled. "A fair question, but one you haven't asked yet. And your reason for this?"

William matched the man's amusement. "Let's say I'm strongly motivated." It was in his power to help the town of New River and he would do so, but he couldn't proceed without a clear plan. Especially if his aunt chose to disown him and remove his inheritance. Should that happen, he would need all of his businesses to be as profitable as possible to maintain his estate, which was not only his and Anna's home, but their servants' as well. No, Aunt Catherine didn't know he longed for a girl from coal country—and had even sought her hand—but there was a good chance the woman would find out, as he meant to ask that girl again.

Humbly. Softly. Just once more . . .

"The mine's for sale," William explained, trying to steady his focus. "One buyer or another is going to walk away with its future in their hands. Should it be me, I want to ensure I do the best job I can."

A tattered cap came off and thin white hair caught the brightness of day from the overhead dome. "Basically, it all depends."

"On what?"

"On your generator." His eyes searched William's, driving home the crucial detail. "Size'll matter as will power source. Water—steam or current. Coal? Somethin' else entirely? The world is changing awfully fast, Mr. Drake. When I was a lad, I couldn't fathom a lightbulb. And now replacing them is my job."

William pondered that. The air chilling in the car, he rose and piled several chunks of wood in the small fireplace. "What do you suggest?"

"You want advice from a crusty old laborer like me?"

Yes. He needed wisdom from a man who understood what the passing of time resulted in. This man had what the engineers lacked. Time across the eras. Perseverance.

"Well, if the goal is electricity, then I say you should go straight to the top."

"Thomas Edison?" William crumpled up a sheet of old newspaper.

That produced a louder laugh. "Nah, son. You don't need to reinvent the lightbulb. Just the generator."

The generator. William watched as the laborer skimmed the drawings again.

"To Pullman." The man admired the ceiling, then the rest of the car's interior. "Pullman himself oversaw the making of the generator for this very mansion on the tracks. You mentioned this mine being remote and yet you get electricity any day of the year—no matter how distant between towns aboard these rails. You've got light, even refrigeration. You want for nothing. If anyone is the genius of what's capable in the middle of nowhere, it's Pullman. The creator of these cars. You need to think like *him.* Forget all the commentary about that town being remote. It doesn't matter one drop."

William struck a match and lowered it to the paper, considering that. He didn't want to tell this man that George Pullman had died a few years back. "The Pullman company," he mused aloud, shaking out the match. Smoke curled. The tiny flames that had caught grew and sparked as the newspaper blackened. "Not because they invent sleeping cars . . ."

"But because they make power. This entire car is a moving generator. Every time the wheels beneath you turn, they produce energy. It's a perfect design."

William straightened. "Right, but when the car is parked for days on end, the porter has to change out the battery. Probably why none of my engineers have mentioned such a possibility."

"'Cause they're seeing it all too close." The man illustrated that by moving the paper near his face. "A narrow view makes everything go dark." He raised the paper to the window. "When you're tryin' to solve a riddle, you gotta take a step back." He gave a scraggly-toothed smile. "You gotta hold an idea up to the light. That's what makes just about anything clear."

"Wise words." William returned to the desk. "Can I ask you where the generator is located?"

A wrinkled thumb angled toward the carpeted floor. "Just below this beauty. Between her axles. The generator draws power from the wheels whenever the axles are in motion. And if you can find a source in this town of yours that can do the same, that just might be the ticket."

Wheels. Axles. He made mental note of that.

Rising fully now, William moved his chair aside. All New River had currently was a small battery at the depot to power a telegraph machine. He knew of waterpower, but would that be enough to fuel an entire mine? "Can you show me?"

"Well, son, my crawlin'-under-train days are over."

All the more reason for a promotion. They had a little time left before this train departed. William called down the hallway to Cook, asking her to serve their guest his coffee outside. Then he pulled off his jacket and loosened his tie. "How about I strike you a deal. I'll do the crawling, if you do the talking."

32

"Do you reckon Jayne got the job?" Kit leaned so near to the window that her nose bumped the glass.

Lizbeth set her stitching aside. "I sure hope so. Do you see her yet?"

"Not a thing." Kit squinted. "Wait! There!"

Moving to the open door, Lizbeth spotted Jayne on the lane. Pa walked beside her. Kit darted outside first, running up the dirt path. Lizbeth followed. Kit circled Jayne, asking questions that couldn't be heard.

"Don't say anything good until I get there!" Lizbeth called.

Jayne waved overhead. "I got the job!"

Grabbing up her skirts, Lizbeth broke into a run. "Tell us everything."

Jayne clasped her hands when she reached her. "Mr. Jorgensen gave me the position! Put me to work right away, askin' me to balance several time cards from the week before."

"Only took her twelve minutes," Pa added. "Least that's all I had to wait."

"Mr. Jorgensen seemed relieved." Jayne's eyes danced and Kit clapped as she bounced up and down. "I'm to return tomorrow, then every Thursday. So, it shouldn't take me away from the farm for more than a day or so each week. I promise, Pa."

He chuckled. "No need to make *me* any promises."

"I'll go tell Ma!" Kit raced back toward the house.

Pa slowed his steps, muttering about a downed fence post. "I left my toolbox there to try and fix it earlier. I'll only be a few minutes, girls." His heavy boots took him toward the pasture.

Turning, Lizbeth looped her arm around Jayne's to start for home.

But Jayne didn't budge. "Lizzy, there's somethin' more."

Lizbeth swung to a halt as Jayne withdrew a letter from her apron pocket that read *Callum Brydolf, Shelburne, Vermont.* Jayne peeked toward the house where Kit disappeared inside.

After opening the envelope gently, Lizbeth read. She gasped. "Jayne! He asks if he can come visit you."

"I know! I can hardly believe it!" Jayne's blonde curls flounced around her shoulders as she shook her head and she looked like a bride, standing here beneath a glorious sky.

"Well then, let's get you home so you write him back!" Laughing, she looped her hand through Jayne's elbow again, giving a tug this time. "Sneak up to our room and take all the time you need. I'll go see if Pa needs a hand to give you some time alone."

Jayne's cheeks tinted pink. "Thank you."

Lizbeth kissed her cheek. "Off you go! And I want a full account of what you write back when I come upstairs tonight. So don't seal the envelope!"

Jayne laughed. "I promise!" Jayne's feet flitted down the lane. It was the closest she'd come to running in a long time.

Turning, Lizbeth followed after Pa. He stood at the edge of the pasture fence, trying to lift a board back into place. Reaching him, she lifted the other side.

"Mind the splinters." He eased his own end back into place and Lizbeth followed suit. Pa's bushy eyebrows tilted toward the house. "I do believe your sister has a beau."

Lizbeth smiled. "I hope so."

Pa dug through his pocket. "Picked up a handful of nails just now in town." At his feet sat his toolbox where he'd been working that very morning. "Good thing I spotted the fall-down. We wouldn't want Sassafras to get loose."

Her laugh huffed out from the exertion. "Pa, Sassafras wouldn't want to go anywhere if she can help it. Nor Eugene. He's a homebody, make no mistake."

Pa's chuckle was as deep as the rich, damp earth around them. "Those mules don't have much aim for an adventure, do they? They know where their meals come from and like to stay close." Using a hammer, he placed the first shiny nail against the wood. The crack of the first blow rang out through the hollow, echoing off the distant hills. "'Bout that." Pa retrieved another nail and seemed to study it more than anything else. "I spoke to Mr. Jorgensen today."

"About Jayne?"

"No. Eugene."

Still bracing the rail, she felt a splinter scrape her skin. "Eugene?"

"He's made an offer for him." Pa stated it matter-of-factly as though he were making a grocery list and she simply on her way to town. "They've lost some mine stock this month and it'll be some time until he can get the animals replaced. In the meantime, it's slowing production down on their quota. He knows you've kept these two mules over the years and he asked if we'd accept his price."

"His price?" Lizbeth worked at the tiny splinter that had found its way into her palm. "Pa, no. They'd send him down in the hoist cage. He'd be smashed into it. Terrified. He *can't* work in the mine."

"It's not easy on the animals, but they make it through. Once below, they're with their kin again." He handed her a nail.

Lizbeth took it, her mind on anything but the chore. "That's no kind of life. You can't consider it, Pa." Even if Eugene endured the trip down, he would never exit again. He wouldn't see Sassafras. This meadow. Or her. "We just can't."

"I know how you care for those two, so I'm reluctant to mention it. But you're growin' up now, and you oughta know how these things work. Eugene has some good years left in him and Jorgensen would pay a fair price. Offered forty-five dollars. You'd likely be able to bargain up to fifty."

The sum hit her square in the chest. Forty-five dollars?

"We don't depend on Eugene the way we need Sassafras." Pa's gray mustache tilted down in a frown. "Seein' as the animal's been yours all these years, I don't feel right selling him off without talking to you about it."

Lizbeth touched the edge of the fence. Nearby, Eugene's one lopsided ear tilted toward her as it always did. "Are you saying it could cover the rest of the debt?"

"It would come close." Pa's eyes were soft. "Think on it for a few days. I hate to suggest this, but it's important we face the facts of the matter." When she didn't respond, he offered over the hammer. "Now, let's talk more on it later. How about for now, we get this rail finished before it gets dark."

Blowing out a sigh, Lizbeth took the hammer. She tapped the silvery head, then hit firmer, just nicking the edge of the nail. It sank farther in.

"That's fine work. Right fine." Pa inspected the shiny speck that was more crooked than flush before handing her several more nails. "Might as well finish the job."

Lizbeth raised the hammer but lowered it back to her side. "What if I can't do it, Pa?"

"Doin' rather well so far."

"I mean . . ." She tossed a hand toward the field. "What if I can't lead another mule to the mine? I want to help—in all the ways that I can—but *this*?" Again?

Pa scraped at a patch of dirt with his boot. "I understand the weight of it, my girl. Believe me, I do." He took the hammer and held it in place before beckoning for her to accept the handle again. His own worries showed on his weathered face.

A gust of air stirred her hair as Lizbeth took hold of the roughened hammer handle again.

"How about we take it one moment at a time together?" Pa said. "We'll keep looking for other ways, but we can do so knowin' the facts."

"Yes, sir."

He squeezed her shoulder. "All will work out, Lizzy girl. And I'm proud of all the ways you've helped. We'll solve this. One way or another. I promise you, we will."

33

"You haven't touched your coffee, Mr. Drake." Cook filled the other cups around the table.

"I will. Thank you." He glanced around at the engineers and electricians surrounding the rectangular table. Men who he'd taken on board in various cities, all in an effort to have this final meeting. He'd pay their return fares within a day or two.

Cook set down a tray of almond bread and the men thanked her. They would be aboard until dawn tomorrow, giving William a few more hours to cement a workable plan, so the food was appreciated.

"So far, we're six hours into this escapade and making absolutely no progress," one of the engineers grumbled as he served himself a slice of cake.

Another man scratched a thick crop of dark hair and turned an unlit cigar in his fingers. "I just think it would be more economical to install a cable system and steam engine," the man stated. "Forget this notion of electricity. A mine is too intricate and complicated. Too vast. And in the case of New River, so far removed from any other city, that you would have to build everything from the ground up. It seems a fool's errand."

The other engineers seconded that with a round of grumbles. Again.

The first continued. "Install another cable lift or two. Power it with steam. Not electricity."

"Hear! Hear!" one of the others said, loosening a striped necktie. He pointed to the map of the mine. "You can install the boiler here, above ground, then run steel cable down to the main haulage ways. The pit ponies would still haul their carts to the main sections and the ore would be taken out from there by steam. Let that be advancement enough."

"I do understand the logic," William responded. "But I want to do away with the labor of the pit ponies." For all the reasons he'd already explained.

"You mean to run electricity the entire way? All of it?" one of them asked. "In a coal mine? It's nonsensical. Electricity is not for the masses. It's for those who can afford it."

William adjusted his chair. "Maybe it shouldn't be that way." But it would be until men like him—who could afford it—helped to pave the way to ordinary folk who would only ever be able to dream of such a world. "Think of the electric engines that have rolled out of Baltimore," William explained. "That was over ten years ago. Maybe this isn't as unprecedented as everyone is making it out to be."

"Yes, but that was in an advancing city," the man with the cigar countered. "Not a coal town that will soon fade off the map and be forgotten about. A place no one has ever heard of or cares to hear of. If what you've said is true, then these other investors see that. They know that New River is a temporary investment. A way to make a quick income and be done with it."

"And the people?"

"They'll figure it out. Folks in towns like these always do."

William shook his head.

"I agree." The fourth and final engineer rose and tapped a stout finger to the center of the map of New River. "Forget this nonsense about the pit ponies. Move the stables here, so that you free up this whole area to be updated. Treat this entire level like a slope mine instead of a shaft mine. You have a vent here—looks like an old slope tunnel that comes down from the surface. Can it be expanded?"

There was something to that. "But what of the lower levels?"

"It may be wisest to start at the top and work your way down. It would buy you time at least. How many years could this operation have left. Ten, maybe twenty? Is the investment worth it?"

"What about the boys?"

"Boys in a coal town are used to hard work."

"But if they were educated—they could advance even further in life. Become teachers, doctors. Even businessmen."

"I understand the fight, but is it a fight you can win?"

One would hope so. "And what about the livestock?" William asked.

The man slammed a hand to the table. "Forget the blasted ponies!"

Breathing in deep, William leaned back in his chair. The tension broke as Cook brought in a tray of sandwiches. "Nothing like a little nourishment to break up a long day." She didn't look too pleased about the rising tension, so William gave her a muted smile.

He could handle this. These men spoke numbers and predictions and while he valued such conversation, he couldn't help imagining New River the way Lizbeth saw it. A place that held purpose and possibility. Real people with real needs and aspirations.

"What has caused you to think this is your burden to bear?" a man asked.

Before William could answer, the train began to slow. He pushed away from the table. "We're to the next stop. Take a few minutes.

Have a smoke and we'll board again soon." He checked that he had a few coins in his pocket. "I need to make a quick phone call. I'm also expecting two more guests, so we'll have fresh ideas at supper tonight." As for lodging, the Pemberley had enough bunks for all.

Amid their grumbles over his *bizarre* ideas, William escaped to the exit, opening the door and descending the steps before the train was even to a standstill. He crossed the wooden platform to the stationmaster's window. This was one of the few stations he knew had a telephone. As he walked, he kept an eye out for Callum and one more engineer. They were supposed to be here at the station, but he didn't see his friend anywhere.

William slid a coin across the counter and the stationmaster placed the tall black telephone in front of him. William raised the earpiece and when the operator spoke, he placed the call.

"You're connected now, Mr. Drake."

"Thank you."

All at once, Lady Light's trainer was on the line, his Scottish brogue so thick amid the static that William ducked into his shoulder to try and block out the noise of the crowded depot. With little time, he cut straight to it. "Hello? This is William. I'm going to be delayed a little further in getting there. How is she faring?"

"Lady Light is good and well, sir. However, we've had a visit from your aunt who revised her training schedule."

"She did?"

"Yes, sir."

William listened as the trainer described the updated eating and training regime. William pinched the bridge of his nose. He'd already taken care that his aunt had been excluded from Lady Light's itinerary in an effort to try and take responsibility for the thoroughbred and now this? "I see."

"I'm sorry, sir."

There was nothing he could do about it now. Not without being there in person. "It's not your fault. Proceed as best you can and I'll sort things out with my aunt." It was hard to say when but he'd have to pay her a visit once all this other business was wrapped up if not sooner.

Steering clear of a porter laden with suitcases, William ducked further beneath the eaves of the stationmaster's window. "Please be in touch if anything else changes."

"I will, sir."

Good man. The whistle blew again. After hanging up, William checked his pocket watch—3:19 in the afternoon. The train was scheduled to leave at 3:26. Only seven minutes. He scanned one end of the depot to the other. Where on earth was Callum?

Passengers climbed aboard as staff loaded luggage. Porters pushed empty carts away. He and Callum had arranged to meet here along with one more engineer who had studied electricity, and judging by the heated crowd William had left on board, he needed someone—anyone—on his side. He checked his pocket watch again. 3:20.

Where were they?

Steam hissed. "All aboard!" the conductor called. "Next stop Charleston!"

William turned away, stirring open his wool coat. Confounded time. Why was it stacked against him? Was there something he wasn't seeing? Some detail he was missing? William turned again, searching.

3:22.

Closing his eyes and not caring what passersby might think of him, he breathed in deeply. It seemed trivial to ask for guidance, as though he were seeking only his own good. But this plan was for the benefit of others. If only there was a way to catch a break right now.

"All aboard!"

William sought wisdom anyway. Eyes squeezing tight. He may have looked like a madman standing on an empty depot platform while his $30,000 Pullman car was about to churn down the tracks without him. But so be it. He whispered a heartfelt plea. Nigh unto surrender. At the end of the letter he wrote to Lizbeth, he'd penned, *may God bless you*. He'd meant it and ached for such blessing himself. Not in wealth or riches, but in guidance. He pulled his hat off and tried to fill his chest with peace that everything would work out as it was meant to, even when he couldn't see the way. He was only human, so he wasn't meant to see beyond this moment. Never easy. Yet one more thing he asked about in the space between here and heaven. Overwhelmed by the call he felt upon him, mixed with his own inability to set it into motion, William breathed in—then out.

In doing so, he released the outcome into greater hands.

Finally, letting it all go. Just like the way he'd lowered his aunt's portrait from the wall and stored it away. It was time. The spot sat bare now, but he had something new to hang in its place.

Slowly, William opened his eyes.

Ahead, the engine belched steam as it prepared to leave Richmond with or without him.

William aimed toward the rear car and hustled up the steps, the sound of his shoes against metal final. This was it. Flushed, he pulled off his coat, entered his office, and tossed the coat on the chair beside his desk. Murmurs from the other engineers sounded from the dining room.

3:26.

The whistle blew its final farewell. Pulling out his desk chair, William sat and pocketed his watch again.

The train eased into motion.

"Wait!" The call was distant. Too distant.

Slowly William straightened.

"Over here!" The shout sounded nearer now.

Rising, William moved to the window. In the distance, he saw a man racing through the congested depot. William ducked lower to see better. Callum. Suitcase in hand, the man ran like the devil chased his heels. William rushed through the doorway and onto the balcony. Behind Callum jogged a man in a suit who had to be the engineer. The man's gray hat flew off. He skidded to a halt as though to retrieve it but when the train edged further forward, the man abandoned his hat.

William's suspender dug into his shoulder as he waved an arm overhead. The train chugged along at a crawl, but it was moving all the same and gaining momentum. He hurried down to the bottom step. With Callum nearing, William gripped one hand around the sun-warmed railing and extended his other. He crouched, bracing for impact. Callum's feet pounded faster. A chance he would make it, but the trailing engineer was slowing. The poor man huffed as he jogged. As an engineer for General Electric and one of the men who'd helped design the Baltimore Belt Line, he probably hadn't run since he was a boy.

With Callum nearing, William reached further out. His friend's hand bumped his own, finally locking on. William pulled with all his might and Callum stumbled onto the steps beside him. Laughing, William patted him on the back and pushed him farther up onto thc balcony. Leaning forward, he called out to the engineer. "Almost there!"

The man's round face was flushed. His skin glistened as he sped up.

"Just a bit further!" William gauged the end of the platform. They were about to run out of wood. Only a dozen feet left, at best.

"Almost there!" he shouted again, not quite believing it, but the man needed his own dose of faith just now.

Thud, thud, thud.

The engineer's shoes pounded against the platform in rhythm with the rolling stock cars. His fingertips grazed William's and William reached further out, latching onto the man's arm. He gripped it, braced himself, and pulled. The engineer crashed into him and a second pair of hands reached around, bracing them both firmly. Callum. William moved back, pulling the panting engineer higher onto the balcony. The man gasped for air as he fell to his knees.

Callum patted the poor soul on the back and tilted an ear to whatever the man muttered.

"Is he all right?" William panted.

Callum chuckled. "He'll be just fine. Only mentioned that he's not getting paid enough for this."

Laughing, William rose and patted the newcomer on the back too. "Then I'll make sure that he is. And that he receives a new hat."

34

Leaning over the simmering iron pot, Lizbeth dipped a wooden spoon and stirred. Maryanne watched from beside her. The dark green liquid swirled around the long strands of embroidery thread she was steeping. Steam wafted into her face, dampening her cheeks and lashes. She lifted the spoon. Liquid trickled with the same fervency as the rain pattering outside the kitchen window. The wool strands—once a soft white—were now a delicate green from the carrot tops simmering alongside them. Lizbeth lowered the spoon. "Another hour yet, I think."

"Such pretty colors." Maryanne touched a skein of earthy pink now cooling on a nearby tray, colored from the beets they'd grown in the garden over the winter. She touched another shade. "And the blue might be my favorite."

"Nettle. Though I had to take care."

"It's terribly pretty. Do you know what flowers you're gonna stitch this time?"

"Not yet, but I thought I'd decide once I know all the threads."

Maryanne smiled and peeked inside the pot once more.

At a clatter of coins, Lizbeth glanced over her shoulder to where Pa and Ma sat at the table.

"To think of what we've gathered in another month's time." Ma shook her head. "Is it enough yet?"

Pa finished his arithmetic with a stubby pencil. "Not quite."

"Did you get the sixteen cents I made at the farmstand this week?" Maryanne asked.

Pa nodded. "It's in the total. Thank you, dear girl."

"I reckon we'll make just as much next week." Maryanne moved to her piano bench and sat. "By and by, we might win out yet."

Pa's smile was sad. Lizbeth watched the exchange and fresh to her mind was the conversation they'd shared about Eugene the day before. She blew out a slow breath and when Ma rose to check a bowl of resting dough, she swiped at her hands. It was time.

The clock on the mantle neared three. The only sound to be heard in all the house apart from the rain still dripping off eaves. Maryanne sat ever so still at her piano bench, studying a piece of music. The lined paper was etched with ink blots and curls that spoke of new creation.

Kit lay curled up on the window seat, a new kitten in her apron folds as she solemnly watched the road where Lacey had walked to town earlier that day. "If only she'd return." Kit nibbled the tip of her thumb. "She's been gone for *hours* now. Why bother bringin' muffins to her school friends on a day like this?" Kit put her chin on her raised knees and the kitten yawned. "Too dreary a day. And can't her friends do their own bakin'?"

"Oh, leave the girl be." Ma pressed a tin cutter into a round of dough. Her plump hands stilled as she studied an old recipe from the box. "How's your letter comin' along, Jayne?"

From the corner of the room, Jayne looked up and blushed. She said nothing but instead, the gentle scratching of her pen continued across the page, the only sound to be heard. It seemed the entire house held its breath for what might come.

Pa rose and retreated to his reading chair beside the fire. There, he lit his pipe. Finally braving the moment, Lizbeth crossed the room and pushed the cushioned footstool nearer and sat.

He lowered the burnt match to the hearth, looking weary and worn. "What's on your mind, Lizzy?"

"It's about Eugene."

"I figured as much."

"And something William might be able to help us with."

"How so?"

Smoothing her skirt, Lizbeth sat on the footstool. "When I was in Pennsylvania, I overhead William and Mr. Jorgensen speaking of the mine—and our land. Of a possible connection between the two."

Pa nodded pensively.

"And I'd nearly forgotten about it until last night after you mentioned Mr. Jorgensen wanting to purchase Eugene. It reminded me that maybe there could be another way entirely. A way of building up this farm instead of slowly taking it apart. That's if I understood William correctly. But I'll need to find out." It hadn't sounded like William was sure what direction to take, so that's where she could come in.

"I see."

"If you'll let me, I'd like to try one last thing." She gulped. It meant swallowing her pride once and for all, but she was learning to do that and by William's kindness, he was making it easier. A way they could both lay regrets of the past aside together.

"If you're sure." The words held unspoken questions, as did his widened eyes.

"I am." She'd turned down the chance to join William in this life, and while she regretted it, perhaps she could still pursue the chance to work with him and his quest to better New River . . . and most of all, help this farm once and for all. It began with the mules in the mine and if what William had said were true, that he meant to find homes for the mine mules one day, could they not begin that process now? Maybe William would be willing to pay up front for them to start building more stalls and troughs. It was a risk—a long shot since William might not even be the future owner. But worth it for Eugene. And for her. When Lizbeth explained all that, Pa nodded somberly.

Pa's eyes shone as he smiled again. "Alright, Lizzy. But we best be quick about it."

"Of course." Lizbeth squeezed Pa's hand. She still had one of the coins Pa had given her from her travels. "I think I'll try to reach him by telegram. That would be the fastest—" She startled when the front door clattered open.

A soaking wet Lacey rushed in. "Mercy, if I've ever seen rain like this. I'm soaked down to my socks." A crisp wind tumbled in with her. Chilly and forceful.

Ma hurried to push the door closed. "Come and hang your things by the fire. Jayne, fetch your sister a dry towel?"

Jayne stood and Lacey pulled a piece of paper from her apron pocket.

"Mail came for you, Pa. I promised the postmaster I'd see it delivered." She held over several envelopes that were splattered in raindrops. "And one for you, Lizzy. From Hattie." The look that Lacey flashed in turning away was one of worry. Even guilt. All set within eyes that were rosy and puffy as though she'd been crying.

Jayne pressed a dry towel into Lacey's glistening hands, and the girl bounded into a speech about how hungry she was.

"By and by," Ma declared. "It'll be quicker if you make yourself useful. Fetch me the cornmeal and tell me about your afternoon."

Lizbeth started for the stairs to fetch her satchel when a ruckus rose from the corner.

Kit's voice countered Lacey's. "You gotta tell Ma!"

"Hush up!" Lacey shot back.

"Now, now, girls!" Ma cried over them both as she struggled to light the lantern. "What is this about?"

Kit crossed her arms. "Tell them what you just admitted," she demanded.

Lacey glared at her. A piece of paper crinkled in her curling fingers. When Kit reached for the paper, Lacey dodged away.

"Lizbeth, is Eugene in the pasture?" Kit's voice was teary now.

Lizbeth rose and moved to the window, where the rain had stopped. "Of course he is." Though evening was setting in, she could just see well enough to spot Sassafras in the distant meadow. Lizbeth searched for him, seeing nothing but the bend of grass in the breeze. She spun. "Lacey, where is Eugene?"

Lacey's cheeks burned even redder. "He's gone, all right?" Her next words bit at Kit. "And you weren't supposed to say a thing!"

"What have you done?" Ma demanded.

Lizbeth stepped around the table to where her sisters huddled together over what she now saw was a sales slip. But it didn't help. Not with understanding the words that came from Lacey's mouth. The confession.

"Last I saw, West had him." Lacey's eyes flashed. "He's been sold to a mine."

35

Lizbeth snatched the paper from her youngest sister's hand.

"West promised it was foolproof!" Lacey wailed. "He said it'd buy us a future together. And now I can't find him anywhere and this was hiding where we'd promised to meet one another." She swiped at her red cheeks.

Sick, Lizbeth read the bill of sale from a mine she'd never heard of.

Age: 15. Height: Fourteen hands. Name: Eugene. Purchase Price: $45. Paid to Owners: Lacey Bennet and Mr. Westgard.

She stepped back. "What mine did you sell him to? Is he here in New River?"

"I—I don't know. I can't remember the name of it but we met some man down near the train yard. West said he heard that mules were bein' sent to Kentucky and that Eugene could go too. Y'all were plannin' on selling him anyway so I didn't think you'd be too sad about it."

A prickly heat crept over Lizbeth's body, intensified when Pa's voice rose over Lacey's tears. "And now no one has seen hide nor hair of this man since he put you up to this. That so?"

Lacey scrubbed a palm against her damp cheek. "Yes, sir."

Lizbeth sank into a chair.

"When did you last see them?" Pa's gaze all but pierced Lacey.

Chin trembling, Lacey shook her head. "Maybe an hour ago? West took him down to watch for the four o'clock train. Mr. Jorgensen had said that mules were in transit and that he was buying several himself."

Pa's gaze narrowed. "And do you know where he is at this exact moment?"

"Mr. Jorgensen's in his office," Lacey stammered.

"I mean the mule." Pa's voice barely concealed his anger.

Lacey's chin trembled again. "No, sir. Just that West has him and plans to get him onto the northbound this evenin'."

"Can we still find him?" Lizbeth's voice shook.

Pa reached for his coat. "We'll head over there now."

Lizbeth rose for her sweater.

Pa slid into his coat, turning up the worn collar against his beard. "I'll go hitch up the wagon." He pointed a thick finger at Lacey. "And you. We're gonna have a long talk when I get back. Where's the money from the sale? We'll need it to try and get that mule back."

"I don't have it," Lacey wailed. "West has it all. He has it!"

"Confounded child." Pa trailed behind Lizbeth, tugging on his coat. "We'll have to look for West as well."

"Something the matter?" Callum asked.

William lowered the itinerary that he'd been staring at for ten minutes now. "At the last depot, I noticed the train coupled to several new stock cars. Carrying mules."

"Mules?"

"Heading the same direction we are."

"What do you suppose that means? Beyond the obvious, that is."

William shifted in his seat, the pistol in his shoulder holster brushing the padded upholstery. Across the dining room, the only remaining engineer sat reading a newspaper. The others had disembarked at the last several stops, one at a time. Yet the engineer Callum had scouted out remained. Finally, William had one on his side. Now to just arrive in New River . . . "It means that I'm not confident the mining industry is ready for the kind of change we're thinking of."

"It might not be, but is this the time to panic?"

"No." William shook his head. "I'm not panicking."

"Just worrying."

"We've been told a few dozen times that this plan is far-fetched. Yes, I truly believe it's the way of the future. But is it the way of the *distant* future?"

"But you said it was being done in another mine. You even have proof."

William rubbed his jaw with a tired hand. "But it doesn't mean people are ready for that kind of change. Not Jorgensen or even New River."

"But Jorgensen won't be the owner. Not much longer."

"Fair. But he's the one who will make the decision." What would happen if someone else became the owner of the New River mine? What would that mean for the Bennet family and their farm? Lizbeth's future . . . her livelihood? When William voiced that concern, Callum chucked him on the shoulder.

"You'll cross that bridge when you come to it. Not sooner, my friend." He flashed a cheery grin that missed its landing. "Which has never been your way. You like to be one step ahead at all times."

"That I do." A strength, yes, but sometimes a weakness.

"Worry won't get you anywhere. What do you intend to *do*?"

"Right." Rising, William moved to the center of the room to show Callum what the maintenance man had taught him. Of how the battery was charged by the simple movement of the train's axles. Its wheels.

The squeal of brakes broke the silence.

At the window, Callum nudged the curtain aside. "Is it just me or are we going slower?"

"Maybe we're approaching a grade." Not possible, though. He knew where they were and this section of track never gave cause to slow.

The train lurched. Cups rattled. William braced a hand to the wall.

"Oh!" The portly engineer slunk down in his seat. His glasses fell off, landing on his padded chest. He struggled to slide the earpieces back into place. "I don't believe that was supposed to happen."

William fought for balance. "We shouldn't be slowing. Not yet." He had spent his adult life travelling these rails and knew the routes by heart. How many hours lived between one depot and the next. There was no reason for this train to slow.

The train lurched again. Brakes squealed louder.

"What in tarnation?" The engineer fumbled his spectacles again.

Not liking what this could imply, William unclasped the holster against his rib cage.

"Is it a robbery?" the engineer cried.

"I highly doubt it." William snapped the holster across his chest. He would be prepared nonetheless. "You're welcome to put your billfold in the safe if you'd like." Before he could even walk that way, there came a pounding on the door.

The engineer dabbed at his glistening forehead with his handkerchief.

"I'll keep an eye on the back end." Callum started that way.

William strode the opposite direction, past the kitchen and servants' berths.

There, the porter clung to the wall like a strip of peeling paper. "What should I do, sir?"

Seeing Cook standing wide-eyed in the kitchen, William summoned her out. "Both of you can go to my stateroom." It was farthest from either entrance. "Lock the door for good measure."

"I'm not leaving you, sir." Cook's chin squared toward whoever their intruder was.

The pounding came again.

William approached the door. "Is this the conductor?" He unholstered his pistol and braced it between both hands.

The pounding came again. "It's the carriage driver. For your aunt, Mrs. Catherine de Bourgh. She's here waiting."

"Oh, move aside!" Aunt Catherine's voice stabbed through the painted slab.

William lowered the gun.

The woman's gravelly voice clawed at him. "Open this door right now, William, or so help me, I'll put a stop to more than just this train."

36

William holstered his gun. The moment he unlatched the door, his aunt appeared dressed in silks and taffeta and brimming with perfume. Her silver hair was piled high and the gold comb holding it in place held sparkling jewels.

"Aunt."

"William." She brushed past him, barely acknowledging the servants, or the engineer in the dining room.

Instead, she turned to him in a rustle of skirts. "We need to speak. We don't have much time and this conversation has cost me a fortune."

Moving to the window, William shoved the curtains aside. Lights from her summer estate glowed in the distance like the eyes of a jack-o'-lantern through the evening haze. He'd scarcely given their location much thought with it so early in the year when the house usually sat empty. Clearly his aunt had other plans.

He let the curtains conceal the sight. "You paid the conductor to stop the train here?"

Callum returned, looking shocked as well. When his face held questions, William shook his head.

"This way, aunt." After running a hand over his forehead, William led the way down the hallway to his office. His nerves frayed for more reason than one as his ears pricked for any sound of a coming train. These were lives she was toying with and here this train sat—asleep on the rails, just waiting for a disaster. "We'll speak here." He braced the door open and shoved it closed after her.

She spoke without turning. "I've had some unsettling news."

He worked to keep his voice even. "Have you?" While he'd always been one to keep his cards close to his chest, this woman who had helped raise him spoke her every thought and whim.

"Regarding your time in that coal town you're so fond of."

"Would you like to sit?"

Her voice stretched like an iron track between them. "We haven't the time and you know it." Marching forward, she stepped close enough that he might have felt like a child again had he not stood a good head taller than her now.

William straightened his shoulders.

"Your lovely friend, Miss Caroline Brydolf, has written to me of a place called *Bennet Hollow*." The name snapped off her tongue. "And the local girls living there. The daughters of a *coal miner*."

William's jaw tensed. "He's a geologist, actually."

"Do you have anything to say for yourself?"

"It depends on what it is that you're asking."

Her gray-blue eyes sparked. "Do you intend to engage yourself to one of these young ladies? To the daughter of a lowly backwoodsman with barely a degree to his name?"

"He graduated top of his class. Or so I've heard."

"William!" Swiping her thick skirts aside, she stepped nearer, perfume cloying the air between them. "Tell me here and now that it is not so."

"To answer your question directly, aunt, no engagement has been made."

"And you promise it will stay that way?"

"No, ma'am."

She scoffed, an aged scrape against his confidence. Her skin paled further beneath her rouged cheeks. "The nerve!" The fire in her eyes brightened. "Your grandfather and I did not build this empire, this family and its wealth, for you to throw it away on some girl from the garden shed!"

"Let me assure you that I have no intention of doing such."

She lifted her chin and her thin lips pursed.

"But I do intend to speak again to the young woman who I believe you're referring to. A Lizbeth Bennet."

With a huff she waved the name aside. "Be sure that no such thing occurs."

"That I will not promise you. I do apologize for upsetting you but I must proceed as I see fit."

Her eyes narrowed. "And do you have any idea what it will cost you?" Gold earrings caught the glow of lights overhead.

"I'm beginning to sense the answer, ma'am."

She stormed across the carpet, stopping just in front of the bookshelf. Overhead, the glass dome grayed under the evening sky.

"Think of Lady Light," she demanded.

"I have."

"And you're willing to forfeit her entirely?"

"I've been hoping it wouldn't come to that. If you'd let me take over ownership, I can pay her worth."

How uncanny that like Mr. Bennet, William stood in a similar situation. A promise made on a handshake and nothing more. "However, if you decide to confiscate her, I ask that you do so after the Belmont races." At a sting in his throat, William swallowed. Few things were his soft spots, but his sister and Lady Light were two of them. As was Lizbeth now, which was why he couldn't stand down. No matter how much it hurt. "She has worked hard to get there."

"I'll be the decider of that."

Rubbing his thumb and forefinger together, William steeled his nerves. "Is there anything else you wish to speak of?"

She stared at him for several heartbeats and despite the fact that her anger was palpable, he knew he had won. For himself at least. His future and where it needed to take him.

"This will not be the end of it." She moved to brush past him, but he stopped her.

"As for me . . ."

She halted.

"I need you to know that I'm on your side."

Another scoff.

"I'm on the side of this family. Our fortune. And all that you and my parents have done to build it up for generations. I mean only to carry on that legacy. To see it through to a good future."

The powdery lines around her eyes tightened, but vulnerability tiptoed across the steely gaze.

"In order to do that, I must marry for love." Whenever that might be. "I must also make the business decisions that I can stand behind with a clear conscience. I don't ask you to agree with that, but it must be said all the same." He took her cold, wrinkled hand in both of his. "I hope to earn your faith again one day."

Blinking away a glossy look, she turned aside and without another sound, left the room.

William waited, standing there as murmurs filtered through the dining room. The far door opened and then closed. In the distance, a horse and carriage clomped into motion.

The train whistle blew.

With a kindled resolve, William returned to the dining room and stopped in front of the fireplace. There he pulled his aunt's portrait from behind a padded chair. Flipping the frame over, he broke the seal on the matting and hefted out the oil painting. He gave the painting the dignity of a quick roll up before leaning the canvas in the corner. From the mantel, he pulled down a paper-wrapped parcel and split it open. A delicate sampler unfurled, one he'd purchased before it even reached the shop's wall. One of berries and brambles and hand-dyed threads. A piece he'd worked hard to procure and that spoke more joy into his soul than any portrait of the old woman ever could. This piece of art was stitched with care, and wise words whittled their way into the very core of his being as he laid it across the open frame.

The night is far spent,
the day is at hand:
let us therefore cast off the works of darkness,
and let us put on the armour of light.

37

Once she and Pa reached the hoist barn, once the door clattered open, Lizbeth squeezed through the doorway and inside. So close was the press of miners within, so strong the scent of grease and sweat, that she could scarcely tell which man she followed through the echoing building until she heard Pa's voice among them.

"This way, Lizzy. Hopper cars are over here." Pa reached a foreman at the other end. "We need to get through to the track. It's urgent."

The man thumbed over his shoulder to another set of doors. "That way. Mind the cargo. And best hurry." He consulted a dented timepiece. "Train's leaving as soon as possible to make up time. We got a wire that it was unexpectedly delayed and the train has finally pulled in. The line is running thirty minutes late. So we need to make up time." He shook his head.

Pressing her way through the crushing crowd of miners, Lizbeth squeezed past the second open doorway and back to the world outside. She ducked around men carrying sacks of animal feed. Just below, the train stretched long and lean beneath a coming sunset.

It inched forward as coal spilled, pound by pound, from the New River hopper into a series of open hopper cars.

A man balancing a clipboard stopped her on the outer deck. "Can I help you, miss?"

She halted on the top step of the rear coal yard where dust swirled and pouring coal clattered. "We're looking for a certain mule," she called over the ruckus. "Mr. Jorgensen's already given us permission."

"Then take those stairs there." The man pointed with a craggy hand. "Stock cars are just beyond."

"And have you seen a man named Westgard by any chance?"

"No miss. Not lately."

Her feet pounded down the stairs which zig-zagged past another doorway—this one leading into a tunnel where carts came and went. A man guarding the doorway into the earth below raised the flame on his lantern. The tunnel within brightened. Just beyond, a low ceiling was carved from earth. Rough-hewn stalls narrowly separated mules. Several blinked longingly in her direction. A rat scurried the length of the floor, disappearing into shadow. Lizbeth coughed at the ripe smell, William's fears now in focus at what she would see in the underground stables. All intensified with an ache to help. To find Eugene. Such a quest required help, so she was all the more grateful for Pa's constant presence right behind.

New River spoke to William the moment he disembarked. He longed to go and find Lizbeth first, but with the train delayed, time was of the essence. He needed to catch Jorgensen before the man locked up for the evening.

A clatter came from the Pemberley where railway workers uncoupled her from the rest of the train, per protocol. It was with the same haste that William aimed for the coal company office, which sat against the hillside that spewed black smoke from two pipelines. Steeling himself beside the door, he knocked quickly.

A shuffle sounded within, and Jorgensen opened the door.

William pulled off his cap. "Good evening, sir. I have your offer," he blurted in a rush.

Forehead creasing, Jorgensen pulled a napkin from his shirt collar. "Mr. Drake. I hadn't expected you."

William shook his head. "For that I apologize. The train was . . . *delayed* unexpectedly, and I didn't get a chance to wire you." There was no way to explain his aunt's appearance, so he didn't try. "To make up the time, the conductor halted all opportunities to disembark save the few moments it takes to switch passengers. I was unable to send or receive any telegrams the last twenty miles."

"Well, perfect timing, I'd say. I was just considering the final offers." When Jorgensen waved him over to the desk, William took a seat. Jorgensen tossed his napkin aside. "I had feared you were out of the running."

"No, sir. Not at all." William pulled an envelope from his vest pocket. "And if you'll allow me, I have my official offer. Here." He slid the envelope across the crowded desk.

The mine owner flicked open the envelope and he glimpsed the number written inside. A flush rose up his neck. "I—I understand you've given this a lot of thought."

"I have, sir. And I'm ready to make the deposit if you wish to accept the offer. I have cash."

"Cash?"

"Yes, sir." It was the cleanest way to go about it. William adjusted the knot of his tie.

Jorgensen scanned the distant wall as if trying to compute what this meant. "Well, here's the problem . . . It's the same amount as the last offer that came in. Just before yours."

"I see."

"I received a message just yesterday that the offer was increased by a thousand dollars." Jorgensen slid over a telegram. "You can read it here. To prove I'm not bluffing."

After reading the telegram, William ran a thumb over his mouth. He had no more funds liquidated. Not unless he sold some of his property or holdings. Not unless he made changes amid his other businesses or . . .

Lady Light flashed through his mind.

Her silken coat as she stood in the sunshine, greeting him. One of the most valuable possessions in his care but he didn't own her. He couldn't sell the horse even if he wanted to and even that would break him.

Had he reached the point of failure? In all these months . . . it had come down to this.

His mind bounced from Lady Light to his carriages. He had a collection of guns he could part with. Then there was the silver. Rubbing fingertips against his forehead, William spoke without looking up. "I'll see what I can do, but I need an hour or two to make some phone calls. Would you allow me that?"

"Well—"

"If I might send a few urgent telegrams—"

"Er—it's just that, Mr. Drake—"

"I won't take any more time than—"

"She's yours, sir."

William slowly lifted his head. "I'm sorry?"

"The mine here in New River. She's yours."

His brow lifted. "I don't understand."

Jorgensen gave a slight chuckle. "I've been speaking to my wife the last few days, and what with her opinions, and my own understanding of you, my own years spent here . . ." His expression went wistful. "She and I both agreed that the mine should be sold to you."

"And the difference in price?"

"Allow us to remain on as shareholders. At, say, two percent?"

The sun awoke in William's spirit. He reached over and extended a hand. "Consider it done."

"We'll have paperwork drawn up, of course."

"Of course. I have my lawyer, Mr. Brydolf, here with me. But I have a hunch he's down at Bennet Hollow, where I'm due myself."

"Good, good. Tomorrow morning it is. Bright and early. Bring your man here at nine and we'll settle all the paperwork."

"Excellent." After shaking the owner's hand again, William rose. "I'll go and let him know."

"Of course. Though, if he's gone to speak with Bennet, the man's not at home. He's here, down at the coal yard."

"This close to nightfall?" William's steps led him to the door.

"Headed that way not long ago. There was a mix-up over a mule. His daughter's there with them. They're tryin' to find their animal before it's loaded onto a stock car. Lucky for them, the train's been delayed."

In the distance, the whistle blew.

"May still be too late."

"Is there anything you can do?" William's hand fumbled for the door latch.

"Afraid not. He was sold to a different mine. Somewhere in Kentucky. But there might be time to help if you can catch them."

38

Reaching the train as it crawled beneath the spilling hopper, Lizbeth ran the length of it to the nearest stock car. Before she even reached the door, she spied a padlock fastened into place. She hurried to the second stock car and reached up for the door latch. It didn't budge.

Lowering her hand, she rose onto her tiptoes but could only see barred metal. With the train still inching forward, she was forced to step back from the ever-moving stock car. "Pa, I don't know which one he's on!"

He lumbered her way and cupped his hands to the side of his mouth. "Hello? Anyone here?" he hollered over the rattle of dumping coal.

The whistle blew.

"Pa, the train's leaving."

"Can I help you folks?" A worker hurried toward them with a ring of keys at his belt.

"We're looking for a mule that was brought here by mistake." Lizbeth nearly tripped over a railroad tie. "He may already be on one of these cars." She patted a hand to the side of the stock car but it was moving, inch by agonizing inch, and once the final hopper was filled to the brim with coal, the train—and Eugene—would be gone.

The man shook his head. "Sorry, miss. All set to head off. I saw a man load a mule onto this car just a few minutes ago but the train's pulling out any moment. I can't stop it now."

"Do you know where the man is?"

"Already on board. He worked for a mine out in Kentucky. There's a heap of passenger cars but you can try and find him."

"Do you have any way to open this door? The mule wasn't supposed to be sold."

The man grimaced beneath a wiry black beard. "No, ma'am." He touched the brim of his hat. "If you still have the cash, you might be able to board and make arrangements at the next depot." He shrugged. "All I can offer ya."

Lizbeth's heart slowed along with her steps, spirit now as empty as her pockets. She looked to Pa whose face was as drawn as she felt. Neither of them had the money for Eugene. It was gone, along with West, to who knew where.

All around, miners flipped on lanterns with the darkening light of evening. Some pushed wheelbarrows into the mouth of the nearby tunnel. Others lugged sacks of materials into carts. Lantern light slanted this way and that as they worked. Overhead, a star winked at her. To her right, the massive hopper cars brimmed with coal now and stood ready for distant lands.

She had to do something. Could she be brave and face the unknown? This time with dignity instead of doubt? "Pa. If we can get on board, we might be able to get someone to help us release Eugene at the next depot." Even as she said it, the idea sounded mad. She had no money to offer and people didn't give away livestock for free.

Slowly, Pa shook his head. "I don't know how we'd—"

"Lizbeth!" A familiar voice pierced the air. Reached her heart. "Mr. Bennet!"

She turned to see William.

He strode their way as he pulled off his coat. A gun holster spanned his shoulders, and his white shirt caught the light of a dozen bouncing lanterns from miners.

"How can I help?" he hollered over the noise of clattering coal. Within steps, he was at her side.

"I'd say this lady needs a train ticket." The man with the beard tugged off his hat. "And some cash at the other end."

Slowly Lizbeth shook her head. There was no way she could pay William back.

But he was already opening his billfold. "Which way?" he asked.

All at once, the noise settled as the last nugget of coal clattered into place and the hopper operator held the signal.

William touched her elbow. "I'd like to come with you."

Overwhelmed, she turned. "I—I don't have a plan." Maybe William had been right, all those months ago. Maybe she had no part in trying to help. What difference could she make?

The whistle blew again.

"We can come up with one together?" William asked, his tone so different than it had been the day he'd refused her idea in the mine office. "I can buy us some time, and we'll figure out the next step. But—"

"We'll need to get on that train."

"The pair of you better hurry," the man said.

Lizbeth started toward the passenger car. They'd have to move quickly if Pa was to clamber aboard with his struggling steps. "Pa, I think we'll be able to make it!" she called.

"Lizzy." Pa's somber voice brought her back to reality.

"Pa. Somehow we need to—"

"I know what we need to do, Lizzy girl. And so do you." His voice was resolute even as his steps started to slow. "And you need to go on ahead. You and William."

"But—" Her gaze swung to William, who nodded his willingness.

Pa surveyed the distance to the passenger car even as he stumbled several more steps. Limp intensifying. "One of us needs to stay behind to wire the next station."

Lizbeth's chin trembling, she nodded.

"And you'll stay with her?" Pa asked William.

"Absolutely, sir."

Pa finally caught up with them. Gravel clattered under his steps. "You two better git, then. I'll go over to the depot and get a wire through to the next station. Let them know what's happening and buy some time."

William flagged down the nearest porter. Steam hissed. Lizbeth nearly stumbled again, torn between her past and her future and what she needed to do. The massive wheels of the train continued to churn forward, leaving without her if she didn't hurry. It was now or never.

Pa pulled Lizbeth close, his voice low. "I'll send that wire and do all I can from here. We'll find him."

She nodded, fighting tears. "And the money?"

"We'll have to sort that out later." His voice lowered for her ears alone even as he helped her forward, along with the train that was slowly gaining speed. "He's a good man and he'll look after you." Pa brushed the side of Lizbeth's cheek with his thumb. "I wouldn't be able to part with you, my Lizzy . . . to any man less worthy."

Nodding, she squeezed his hand then pulled away to catch up with William. Her hand gripped his own as he braced her to climb up the moving train steps. A feat Pa would have never managed.

Struggling, she found her footing and William climbed up, right behind.

"Where do I go?" she asked over the noise.

His voice reached her ear. "To the right. We'll get seats and I'll secure our passage."

With wind pulling at her hair, she ducked into the nearest car. William followed close behind. Inside, she worked her way down the center aisle. The train was crowded but finally she came to an empty seat. Lizbeth sat and William joined her on the plush velvet.

Outside, the air was darkening. A distant sunset burned pink as the train reached open land. She wanted to strain to catch sight of the stock car, but had to rest in the assurance that Eugene was here on this train, as was she, and they would be together again soon.

Passengers cast them curious glances. Lizbeth smoothed her hair and then her skirt front. She was still dressed from her chores with blackberry sauce on her apron and a spool of thread in her pocket.

"Tickets, sir?" A man in a black cap halted in the aisleway.

William pulled his billfold from his vest. "This is en route to D.C., correct?"

"Yes, sir."

William calculated that. "We'll disembark before then, but I'll pay for the full passage to be safe."

"I thought the mules were heading to Kentucky," Lizbeth said.

"Train's gotta go north, miss, before it can go west," the porter explained.

Lizbeth watched as William retrieved several dollars. She hadn't expected the passage to be so much. "Thank you," she whispered as he handed over the money.

William nodded gently.

The porter tipped his cap. "Very good, sir."

William angled his pocket watch to the overhead lighting and spoke to Lizbeth. "Once this train hits D.C., some of the cars will head down to Charlottesville and on to Kentucky. Others will continue to Baltimore. We'll try and intercept Eugene before then. It'll be a few hours of waiting until we get to a stop long enough to do anything."

"When will that be?"

"Hopefully Alexandria, if I recall correctly. That break at that depot is usually around forty minutes. In the meantime, can I get you something to eat or anything else?"

Lizbeth shook her head. She didn't want to owe him any more than she already did. This kind man who was going well out of his way to help her. A man who had done so much more than she'd ever realized before. "I—I have nothing with me."

"Well, I wouldn't exactly say that. You had a fair dose of courage back there. You're the first woman in my acquaintance who has boarded a moving train."

She'd hardly noticed.

When he offered his coat for warmth, Lizbeth draped it across her lap. "And now here we are."

A small furrow tugged at his brow when he glanced at her.

She went on, "I was actually about to send you a telegram before all of this happened."

"You were?"

"I wanted to thank you for the letter you gave me. The one you tucked into the book. I've thought on it ever since." She couldn't quite look at him now. "And there's so much I've needed to say." Her heart was beating faster now. "But . . ."

"Sometimes it's easier to put it into writing than to say it out loud?"

She nodded. How did he understand her so well?

"Well, then if I had my briefcase with me, I'd slide you a piece of paper and a pen."

She smiled. "No need. I—I was going to ask about our farm." She finally looked at him and there was an assurance in his expression that helped her say more. "I overheard you talking about electricity with Mr. Jorgensen—that day that we were at the Coburns'."

"I was wondering if you might have caught that."

"I did. And also what you said about the farm and finding a use for it." She drew in a steadying breath. "If it's true, I thought we might be able to help stable some of the mine mules who need extra care. I'd like to offer Bennet Hollow. And I could do all the work. As a business arrangement." She felt strange saying such along with the implication that she was coming to him for money twice in the same day. "I would mean to earn every penny."

His gaze, as soft as ever now, filtered over her face.

"I know it's a long shot and you're not even certain if you're going to be the owner of the mine. But if you are . . ."

William shifted his feet when a woman stuffed a carpetbag under the seat. "May I confide in you a secret? Well, two."

"Of course."

"First, you're sitting here with the new owner of the New River Coal Company."

She had to stifle a gasp.

"And second . . ." His sideways glance was tentative. Humble. "That owner has a lot of work to do and he's realized it can't be done alone."

Did he see the hope she felt? "You need my help?"

With a corner of his coat still on his lap, William brushed the collar with his thumb. "You have a lot to offer, Lizbeth, and I was wrong to make you feel otherwise."

Her chest tightened.

"I was wrong to not give you the opportunities you were asking for to help with the mules of the mine. You're as capable as anyone else with new ideas. For that, I owe you an apology. You have a special grace and care that those animals deserve. That New River needs."

She searched his gaze and the sincerity there. A sincerity she no longer doubted and hadn't for some time now.

"Along the lines of what you overheard that day, I've been researching a way to bring electricity to the mine," he explained. "To New River itself. Electric lighting and even electric carts. All by underground rail. No more need for mules to pull carts along the tunnels. Along with that, the mine stock would need the home you're referring to."

Was she hearing him correctly? It seemed too good to be true, but sitting with him now, she knew beyond any shock or doubts that this was a man of integrity and if he saw a way to make this possible, she trusted him.

He nodded soberly. "I'd pay for their stabling with the intent of selling them back to nearby farmers so they could live out the rest of their days. They'd become an integral part of the community again. This time, above ground. I have other ideas for more changes—with schools and for the boys of New River."

Her lap was beginning to warm beneath the offering of his coat and her heart even more so with each word that landed.

"You know this place as well as anyone else and I want your advice."

Tears stinging, she swallowed hard. "I'd be—I'd be honored."

The side of his mouth lifted in a smile. "When we return to New River, we can sort out a plan. For now, I'm grateful for us to be on the same side."

She gave him a small smile as she tried to hold on to the possibility that this could work out somehow, someway. "To be honest . . . I think we've been on the same side for quite some time."

39

William was used to the rumble of a train. Used to the stop and start at depots. He was accustomed to the hiss of brakes and the long, mournful whistle across a distant, star-studded countryside. What he *wasn't* used to was having a young woman asleep on his shoulder. Nor the warmth that brought to him body and soul.

William glanced to Lizbeth, who was still asleep. A tear stained her cheek and he longed to smooth the trail away. In her restlessness, he'd draped his coat over her. Pulled up snug now—her own doing. Though he had no such covering, he was far from cold. He needed to sit up but didn't want to disturb her. Quite frankly, for a good long while.

This was one of the few times she'd ever been away from home and she had little to turn to, save her own grit and what he might offer. He didn't blame her for feeling unsettled in the night. To his relief, the cheek to his shoulder said that it wasn't because of him.

William leaned his head against the padded rest. The world outside the window was entirely dark. A landscape he needn't see to gauge their location. He knew these routes and rails by heart.

Knew how long it took between depots for all the years he'd spent travelling between them. Though not often from a coach seat, so he took stock of the other sleeping passengers. No one else seemed concerned about a near arrival, so William leaned back into the velvet seat and closed his eyes.

Time sped on, warm and slow, and with the occasional sigh that reached him even in slumber. Whether his or hers he wasn't sure until a soft shaking at his shoulders woke him again. He opened his eyes to the sight of Lizbeth perched on the edge of the seat beside him. Rubbing at his face, William sat forward.

"I'm so sorry," she whispered. "But I need to use the lavatory, and . . ." At a little tug on the edge of her dress, he realized he was sitting on it.

So, she'd trapped him and he'd done the same in return. "Of course." William shifted so she could free herself. "I'll leave my coat here to save our seats and go see what I can find to eat in the dining car. We'll be to our destination soon and I don't know when we'll have another chance." He wanted to ensure that she was fed. "Would you mind meeting me there?"

"Certainly."

"Do you drink coffee?"

She shook her head but the gratitude in her eyes shone in the dimmed sconce lighting. "But thank you." Gently, her hand touched his arm. "Thank you for all this and more." She swiped her palm against her cheek as though feeling the sensation of dried tears.

A thumping in his chest made him feel as alive as ever. "Of course." They weren't out of the woods yet, so he rose to make space for her to exit, then started down the length of the car. Out the doors and into the night air, he crossed onto the jostling platform of the next car and repeated the rhythm until he finally reached the dining car in the center of the train. There he deposited a bill onto the counter in exchange for a tray of anything the cook could drum up for him.

"Thank you." Tray in hand, William turned for a dining table, as Lizbeth passed through the doorway, rubbing both hands up her sleeves in the chilly night air. She chose a table between them and he sat across from her and their steaming breakfast.

"I just saw that it's four in the morning." Her eyes were wide.

He slid the tray forward to distract her from the fact that it was deep into the night. "Take your pick."

With an inhale, she surveyed the offerings. "I didn't realize how hungry I was until now."

"Me neither. Please. Don't be shy." He angled the tray closer to her. "Looks like we have breakfast potatoes, bacon. Some kind of cherry pie and oats. Coffee for me and I hope you like orange juice." He doubted she'd ever had it before.

"Thank you." Her fork broke into the corner of the pie first.

He went for the bacon, gaining only a few bites and a swig of coffee before it was time to rise again. William pushed away from the seat. "I'll leave you to eat. I want to go find someone in charge so I can inquire further about the stock car. Just to make sure we can find the man who has the keys."

"Of course. Can I help you?"

She could. How he wanted her to know that. But he'd rather her take this chance to eat before the long day ahead. "Please enjoy all you can and if you wouldn't mind, keep an eye out for Westgard. If we see him aboard, I want to try and get your pa's money back."

"Of course. What can I save you?"

"I wouldn't mind that second slice of bacon and a few bites of pie."

"Consider it done."

His chest warmed and he forced himself to step away, hardly daring to imagine that this could be his future—sharing each dawn with her—if he could only ask her once more if she might want the same.

"He said he'd meet us near the stock car?" Lizbeth asked as she squeezed down the aisle, past passengers and luggage alike. Her feet and heart carried her to Eugene. If only she could get there.

"That's what he promised." William stayed close behind her.

As her shoes touched the platform in the chilly dawn air, she hurried toward the stock cars that took up the rear of the train. With a gasp, Lizbeth stretched onto the pads of her shoes to try and see above the growing crowd. Passengers spilled from the train, others boarding in search of a seat and new vistas.

"Do you see him yet?" William asked. "The man?"

"Not yet." Ducking through the crowd, Lizbeth worked her way forward, feeling as though she were wading through a vast sea of people amid the coming sunrise. William touched the small of her back, a reassuring presence.

Since she was a girl, she had believed that in order to truly help her family, love had to come second. It was the very voice she reckoned with the day she had helped Pa lead the mules to the mine. And ever since, she'd kept her heart on careful guard, believing that anything more than duty was a distant dream. But more and more, she was learning that wasn't so. That instead, her heart could guide her, not disarm her. Pa had acted with courage when he needed to do what was best for his family and the farm—and now she could, too. Each of them had their own path to carve out. With the help of those around her, she was finally finding her way.

It was a path she might have missed had she held people like William at arm's length, choosing instead to put too much stock in falsehoods. Be that pride or prejudice, she was learning to observe a person's actions much more than their words. Now it would be William who helped her bring this hope to completion—that there could be a home for her mules. And that Bennet Hollow would be saved in the process. A home for her sisters and herself for many years to come.

There was no time to think more on it when the rattle of keys caught her attention near the second stock car.

"Hello?" she called over the tall structure.

"Over here!" a man called back from the other side. "Are you the ones lookin' for the one-eared mule?"

"Yes!" She glanced back to William. "He's opening the door on the other side." Hiking up the edge of her dress, she clambered over the coupling that bridged two cars together, just feeling William's hand at her elbow as she climbed onto the other side of the track.

He slid across after her.

"Hello?" There on the other side of the car, she blinked into the blinding light of sunrise. She held up a hand, just barely making out the shape of a man with a jangling ring of keys. Then his lined face. Last of all, a friendly smile. "I hear we've got a stowaway that doesn't belong."

"Yes, sir." It was all she could do to stand still as the man fiddled with the lock.

He tried a key. Then switched to another one. Lizbeth shifted her feet. William checked his watch.

"If we could somehow help—" William began.

Click. The lock opened. With a shimmy of the metal padlock, the man tugged it free. He pushed on the edge of the massive door, inching it open. Lizbeth gripped the edge to climb in.

"Miss!" the man called.

She scrambled up, aided by William's hands at her waist. She brushed straw from her palms and hurried past each stall, glimpsing dozens of mules confined to pens. William followed right behind. Finally, she reached the end. There was no Eugene.

Lizbeth worked her way back out. "He's not here."

"There's two more cars but we only have so much time."

Lizbeth was about to hop down when William reached up and took her waist. She paused before letting him help her down and the gesture made her head a little light. Back on the platform, she searched the slats of the car, seeing hooves of every shade of brown. There was no telling which belonged to Eugene. Then she saw a mule duck his head. He blinked at her and the one missing ear said it was Eugene. The damp muzzle that bumped her palm through the slats said he'd been awaiting his ticket home. "This one!"

The man hustled her way and fiddled with the lock. William waited impatiently until the latch finally clicked free. Lizbeth was inside before she could think and once again, she dashed down the length of the car. Tethered to a post, the final mule tossed his head in her direction.

"Eugene!"

Her throat tightened as she wrapped both arms around his thick neck. She pressed her face closer and squeezed tight. He snorted in satisfaction and she blinked back the sting in her eyes. Somewhere in the distance, rail yard workers shouted out commands followed by the crash of boxes and cargo. The fur on Eugene's back prickled and she smoothed her hand there.

"We'll get you out of here." As she untethered his line, she ached for the mules that would be left behind.

Lizbeth tugged Eugene's lead rope back down the aisleway. Just below, William slipped a fold of bills to the car owner. The price of Eugene's freedom. Two men slammed a ramp into place and she led her friend down the length of it to the platform below. Eugene tossed his head as though he were a fine racehorse.

William angled his shoulders to block Lizbeth from the rising sun. "I've made plans for us to travel home again on the two o'clock train."

"Thank you. More than I can say." Lizbeth thought of the bills William had passed to the car owner. As for West, she doubted they'd ever see him or the money again. "I—I want to repay you somehow. Some way."

"Say nothing more of it. I'm just sorry we can't take the others."

"Maybe we'll find a way one day."

He smiled as he peered down at her. "I say we try. Now how about we head on home?"

Home. "Please."

Eugene's hooves clopped down the brick pavement toward a waiting train. This one leading back the way they'd come. Lizbeth could scarcely remember what town they were in. All she knew was that Eugene was at her side once again and thanks to William's care and kindness, her oldest friend was finding his way back home. As was she.

40

"I'm hopin' this won't be too hot." Ma carried a bowl of sudsy water out onto the farmhouse stoop. "To think that the pair of you spent this whole day in a stock car comin' home."

"That was my idea," Lizbeth confessed from her perch.

Ma offered the bowl to William, who sat on the edge of the raised herb bed, boots squared and back straight, but still covered in so much dust and bits of straw that he'd declined Ma's invitation to please come in and rest himself.

His leather shoulder holster and pistol sat discarded beside him. "I didn't mind." He accepted the bowl in dirty hands. "Thank you, ma'am." His eyes lifted nearly to Lizbeth in the graying light of day, before lowering again.

She understood. How to even begin?

With simple things. With clean, hot water and two rags. Easier than other matters needing to be discussed and unraveled. Lizbeth swiped her hands on the sides of her skirt, but it was as covered in hay and soot as the rest of her.

Ma handed her a second bowl. "For you, Lizzy." She smiled. "I've got fresh bread with a pot of beans simmerin' along with some stewed berries that Lizzy canned this summer. I'll have it all served up real soon, so don't you two take too long."

"Well, if it's anything like her hand pies . . ." William said.

Ma beamed.

"Thank you, Ma." The bowl of water was warm to the touch as Lizbeth balanced it on her lap.

The wet rag soothed her fingertips as she wrung it out. Much easier to focus on this than on the man beside her who was busy doing the same.

Beyond them, a low New River sunset spoke the sweetness that she didn't know how to. William rubbed the rag up one of his forearms. Water dripped, in gray rivulets like the earth during a storm. He scrubbed again, this time finding his skin. As he turned his wrist, wiping away the day's work, his gaze found hers.

She swallowed a rising strain. There was so much to say. Such longing within her that words weren't to be found. He looked just as conflicted as he swiped at his neck with the rag, dampening his shirt collar and capturing all of Lizbeth's attention again. He studied the soiled cloth as though it, too, were easier to try and make sense of.

Uncertain, Lizbeth rose so quickly that water sloshed over the side of the bowl, dampening her apron. "I'll just go and see how Eugene is faring. I saw some marks on his neck from the tether."

William nodded as she peeled away from the stoop, as desperate to flee as she was to stay. Striding off, she tried to appear sure, despite her collapsing confidence.

A little time in the field would cool her senses.

Haze stretched in the distance as she started for the pasture, and the sky bloomed pink. At the fence line, Lizbeth pushed the bowl beneath it before climbing over. Eugene roamed in his favorite clover patch, brown coat shuddering as two birds flew too close to his tail. He swished them away, here with this new taste of freedom. Lizbeth found her feet again, not minding the lengthy walk to reach him.

"Thatta boy." She smoothed her hand along the side of his neck, swiping at the lingering traces of his travels. Water trickled as she rinsed the rag. At the sound of footsteps, she turned to see William approaching.

Her hands stilled.

Tall, dried grasses rose nearly to her knees, but he traversed the field with ease, as though he too had stood in pastures all his life.

At the fence, he climbed over and as he walked, all his focus was upon her. William crammed his hands into his pants' pockets. Here she stood, nearly in the same spot where they'd last spoken together on this farm. She'd been angered by his actions. No, by her misconceptions. Her lack of clarity and really, her prejudice against him.

To her shame.

Since the night they'd first met in the hoist barn, surrounded by fiddle music and spiced cider, she'd assumed him arrogant and reclusive. Now she knew him differently. He was quiet, yes, but when he spoke—when he *acted*—profound purpose lived within him. He stated half of what other men did which only deepened his intention. Had she only recognized that sooner.

A soft breeze stirred her hair, chilling her damp fingers as she twisted the rag again. Lizbeth pressed it to Eugene's neck once more as William neared. He joined her in the middle of the field where the farmhouse stood far in the distance.

"I hope it's all right that no one can see us here," he said.

Us. The word soft and making it impossible for her to turn away.

Something about him had altered her. It was different from the type of affection she'd always thought would be a bubbly feeling in her middle. How different this was. It was the sight of him in her mind more often than not. It was her recalling the few words they'd shared as small treasures to be stored away. It was a respect for him as a person, and a longing for him as a friend and a man. For as long as possible.

She now knew she loved him.

The bowl in her hands trembled. Silence filled the space between them along with the ripple of birdsong. She watched as William considered first the house, then her again. Needing to busy herself, Lizbeth worked around to Eugene's other side.

"How is he faring?" William asked without following.

"He looks quite well." She patted Eugene's shoulder with the rag, brushing away more dust and debris. She must look a fright herself yet William observed her as though she were anything but. "I owe you so much gratitude. We all do."

"Please don't think twice about it."

Her heart thumped harder and he stared at the ground as though having an arguing match with it.

"Pa and I can come up with a way to pay you back."

"It's not necessary." He reached out and brushed a hand to Eugene's burly side. "In fact, there's something I need to tell you."

She lifted her eyes, just seeing him over the ridgeline of the mule between them.

"Do you remember when we were in Stroudsburg and you showed me the sampler you were making? You were going to try and sell it to the shop across from the depot."

"Yes. I managed to."

"Right." William dug through his pocket. "Well, it's—it's been purchased. A little higher than the asking price which, after a few words with the shop owner, increased your commission."

Gingerly, she came around again to see him better.

"And because of that, I have a slip here from the shop owner, with an advance on your next piece."

"An advance? That's—that's not possible."

William unfolded the envelope. "I wanted to give you this sooner, but I decided to wait until now. I didn't want to risk you trying to use this for Eugene, when I think it may be better suited for your pa."

Tears burned her eyes and she accepted his offering. After glimpsing the check inside, she gasped. "I don't understand. This is enough . . ." Her chest burned. She didn't know hope could feel like this.

He looked at her as though longing to swipe her tears away. "For the farm's debt? Hopefully, the rest of it."

Chin trembling, she nodded. "But how?"

"Because your next piece has already been acquired."

"Acquired? By who?"

"By me."

She blinked up at him. "And the first?"

"That's in my possession as well. I thought to make a gift of it. In parting. A mark of friendship and continued peace. If you'd allow that?"

"We truly are friends now." Wonder filled her voice.

"If possible. At the very least, that is."

Hope stirred again inside her. "And at the most?"

William glanced away from her. At the softening sky. To the bowl of filthy water she'd set at her feet. Finally to her hands, which she clasped in front of her, the rag forgotten. He was crushing his own cloth still. Part of her wanted to liberate it from such a grip, but she was too overcome to know what he meant to say.

"We spoke here some months past." His voice was soft but sure.

"Yes."

"And I hope I don't act out of turn when I say this." Another step toward her. As sure as the others had been. "But I must state that I have thought of none but you. Even still." His focus on her face was earnest. "If you would consider, once more, if you would accept my hand."

This man was offering himself once more . . . to her?

"Your hand?" Lizbeth touched fingertips to her mouth as emotions threatened to spill. She squeezed her eyes tight, then wiped the tears away. There were many reasons she intended to forgive Lacey, one being that she herself was being forgiven in this very moment. Perhaps long ago.

Warmth flooded her as Lizbeth looked up at William again. His own manner was hopeful. "I—I want to understand you," she whispered. "After the way I treated you."

"Right." Then, "More plainly," he muttered to himself. "Perhaps this . . ." William stepped closer and reached for her hand, taking it securely in his just as he had when he'd guided her onto the train the evening before. "I offer you both my heart, which is already yours, and my love, if you will have it."

It was a gallop now, the beating in her chest. His thumb grazed the back of her knuckles. Warm and right. A tender caress and one that she sensed was only the beginning.

"And I ask if you will do me the honor of becoming my wife, Lizbeth Bennet."

If it was a quiet love she was accepting from William Drake, one of whispered sentiments, soft touches, and stolen glances, then it would be all the more satisfying. One she yearned for from him and no other.

He lowered his face so that their foreheads nearly touched. Such tenderness in his eyes. Such peace. A look she wanted to know all her life. "Would you—would you be agreed to this? To me asking your pa for your hand?" he asked.

Wind stirred the short locks of his hair as he straightened again. The same breeze twirled her own. She scarcely thought of him as a wealthy coal baron, nor herself as a poor girl from coal country in a straw-speckled apron. She only thought of him as her own.

"In marriage," he added as though unsure if he'd been quite clear enough.

Lizbeth held tighter to the hands wrapped around her own. "I—I would like that very much." Her place was beside him, now and in the years to come.

His shoulders rose, eyes alight. He lifted their entwined fingers to his chest, which was beating as hard as hers. William smiled.

"Lizzy! Mr. Drake!" Ma called from the house. "Supper's on!"

Lizbeth let out a little laugh.

But William's eyes were unwavering. "I'll go now and speak to your pa, then."

Her smile matched his. "And I'll go with you. At least as far as I'm able."

He took her hand again with a freedom that sent a rush of warm chills through her. As they walked back toward the house, his fingers grazed hers in the tenderest of ways. Delicate touches that held more meaning than she had ever thought was possible between her and a man. A soft sweetness and a mere taste of all that was to come. What was once a distant hope was now right and filling her in ways she'd never imagined. This was a hand—solid and warm—that she needed to hold and would now have the joy of doing so all her days.

He glanced at her, and she at him. Many times, as they shared smiles and even a blush or two. Suddenly, they both stopped, her stammering, "I forgot the bowl!" and him sliding a hand to the side of her hair, asking, "Might I kiss you now?"

All to the music of the door bursting open and Lacey running into the yard, followed by Ma and Jayne in pursuit.

"Oh, Lizzy! I'm so terribly sorry!" Lacey cried.

William lowered his hand but stayed just as near.

"I was terribly wrong to have done what I did, and Ma and Pa have already lit into me but you can, too, if you'd like to." Lacey clutched her apron theatrically. "If you'll forgive me, I promise I'll make amends. I just promise. They're makin' me do extra chores to earn back the money for Eugene so that I can pay everyone back. Oh, Lizzy, it'll take years! And West, don't you worry one bit about him. It'll all work out and he'll come back around and Pa'll like him just as much as he likes Callum and maybe even your—" She peered up at William as though forgetting his name.

"William Drake" came his stern reply.

Lacey prattled on. Ma tried to shush her, and Jayne covered a teary smile as Callum stood behind her, resting a hand to her shoulder.

A ring now glinted on Jayne's finger.

Kit and Maryanne peeked around the doorjamb as though to see if they were to witness another engagement in the span of a single day. Amidst all of it, Lizbeth smiled and, taking William's hand in her own, followed her family back into the warm house, feeling the graze of William's kiss to the top of her head. Lizbeth's eyes fluttered closed as she savored what was just the beginning. She squeezed his hand tighter and he squeezed back, for finally, the man beside her was William in her heart and for all her future. Just her William.

41

May 1905

"Afternoon, Mr. Drake. Can I help you?" Cook balanced a bowl of white frosting in the crook of her arm. Behind her, the stove was covered in bubbling pots and two trays of fresh baked bread for the start to his and Lizbeth's honeymoon travels.

"Yes, thank you." He tugged at the cuffs of his crisp starched shirt. "I'm looking for my wife."

Cook's cheeks were as rosy as her hair. "She was just in here helping me make the frosting. We thought we'd make a smaller version of your wedding cake to bring on the trip. Seein' as the pair of ya didn't hardly get a taste. We were just pullin' the cakes out to cool when she was summoned for a telephone call."

"A call?"

"Yes, sir. She hurried out just a moment ago. Try the butler's room."

"Of course." William retreated from the kitchen and with maids and a footman watching, he strode the length of the downstairs servants' corridor toward the butler's quarters. A daily habit for him to venture down here in search of his bride. Ever since they'd exchanged vows at the church, he suspected that he would spend the rest of his days finding his wife in the unlikeliest places and he rather liked it. Yesterday she'd been in the greenhouse, talking to the gardener as they planted hydrangeas near a footpath, and this morning, she'd been up to her elbows in cakes and frosting.

With the butler's door open, he heard Lizbeth as he neared.

"Are you still there, Pa?" came her sweet voice.

William entered and relief flooded her face. She waved him nearer then lowered the mouthpiece with its dangling black wire. "It's Pa. He's callin' from the new telephone you had installed at the mine office, but when I answered, we got disconnected."

"Can I help you try again?"

"Please." She held over the phone. "I was helpin' Cook make a cake. The same one from our wedding since we didn't get any."

He smiled at the second reminder in as many minutes of that blessed day. Her family had been in attendance, along with his friends and relatives. All save Aunt Catherine, who had sent a card instead. Now a band of gold glinted on Lizbeth's slender finger, next to a princess cut emerald. The jewel matched the dark green of her new dress as she peered up at him, and her finger was the same one resting on the lever that ended her telephone call.

"I think I may have figured it out." He kissed her forehead and accepted the telephone. "Hello, Operator? I'd like to place a call."

"Go ahead, sir."

William's focus stayed on Lizbeth's face. "To New River, Virginia."

"Hold please."

While he waited, he offered the handset and receiver back to Lizbeth.

"Oh!" Her eyes widened. "It's connected now."

Leaning nearer, William listened. Her pa's voice came through the line. "Lizzy girl?"

Her eyes watered. "Hello, Pa. It's so good to hear your voice."

"And yours, sweet girl. I'm callin' from William's office."

"He's here with me."

"Tell him I said hello. And that I've got good news."

Rising onto her tiptoes, Lizbeth ensured the earpiece was balanced between them. "We're listening."

"It's about the mules, and the farm."

"Yes?"

"The workers finished the last corral just days ago. It's somethin' else, Lizzy, all bright and new and as wide as the whole meadow. Not a splinter or sliver in sight."

Her gaze found William's and he saw her heart shining there.

"And yesterday, you'll never guess what I saw."

At the pause, William felt Lizbeth holding her breath.

Bennet's voice came through the line, patient and earthy. "I was standin' there, puttin' my tools away with the workers, and when I looked up I saw a mule in the distance, comin' toward the farm."

William watched his wife's face as her father's story unfolded there.

"And then I saw that it wasn't just one. It was near a dozen."

Her lips parted and she squeezed a hand to her chest. At the worry that she was going to accidentally end the call again, William offered to hold the telephone while she balanced the receiver.

"All bein' led by a few of the mule drivers from the mine just minutes before. The first pit ponies of many, I suspect. They were a sight, Lizzy girl. All lit by a settin' sun. You'd have been amazed by it. Some practically pranced right into the meadow. Some bucked. Others sniffed the wind. It was as though they couldn't believe they'd finally made it home, right there in Bennet

Hollow. I'm thinkin' I might have a new sign made up. What do you think?"

Chin trembling, Lizbeth swiped at her eyes. She was gripping the front of her apron now. The very apron she'd brought along from her beloved farm.

William kissed the top of her hair, which was warm and sweet.

"They all came from the one-hundred level," Mr. Bennet continued. "Where production's been the slowest. We figured those ones would be the best to start with. The first ones to let loose back into the open and the first place to put in the electricity for electric carts. You did that, my girl. You and William."

Her eyes glistened as she nodded.

"Your Eugene would have made you mighty proud. He trotted all around greeting each one. I think he may have recognized a few of his brothers or sisters."

William squeezed Lizbeth's hand again. It was trembling now.

"And William?" Mr. Bennet said.

He cleared his throat. "Yes, sir."

"The funds you sent to cover the corrals and feed supply. It more than covered the materials. And the pasture there. It's a thing of beauty."

It always had been. Overwhelmed, William nodded. "Very good, sir. It was my honor and I can't thank you enough for all the work you and the men have done to get the farm ready like that."

"Of course." Bennet's own voice quieted, and William sensed a knot of emotion on the other end. From a man who had just given two of his daughters in marriage. "I can't thank you enough, son."

"It's my pleasure, sir." Reaching over, William squeezed Lizbeth's hand.

How had God blessed them so? This richly? In the lives they

not only had the privilege to lead, but now to share each and every day. The blessings came in ways William had never imagined. All the years he'd spent walking the halls of this estate, longing for it to speak of home and now, it was a home unlike any other.

"You two have safe travels," Mr. Bennet said at last. "Enjoy the races and we'll see you after your trip."

Lizbeth thanked her pa and William stepped back to give his wife a few more minutes to say goodbye. Taking the chance, he retreated to the kitchen to confirm with Cook that all would be ready for their evening departure aboard the Pemberley.

"Yes, sir. I'll be heading over soon with the last of the supplies to light the oven and make sure there's a nice supper awaiting you and Mrs. Drake upon boarding. Several maids are there now, giving the master suite a once-over and to add touches they thought a young lady might appreciate. Fresh flowers and the like."

He could hug the woman. "You're a wonder."

From the butler's room, William heard Lizbeth hang up the receiver. Her footsteps were soft, the rustle of her taffeta skirt softer still as she joined him. "I hope I haven't made us late."

"Not in the least."

"Should we finish packing?"

"Let's."

She led the way up the stairs that took them from the servants' hall to the living quarters. "I wonder if it'd be possible to add a stop in New River to our travels," she mused. "Only for a day." The look she gave him was tentative. Especially since he'd arranged a bridal month for them that would begin at the Belmont races in New York, landing the Pemberley just steps from the track for the Long Island Rail Road. There, they'd have the joy of meeting up with Jayne and Callum for an entire day. After the race, William and Lizbeth would journey onward to the New Jersey shore where a stay at Brighton House promised views of the ocean and an easy walk to the beach.

William touched the small of her back. "I think that's a marvelous idea. How about we take a look at the itinerary tonight once we board and see what changes we can make." Since they would be travelling the US and Canada by rail for a month's time, there should be a way to stop in Virginia before heading out west.

"But you've told me that train itineraries can't easily be adjusted. Nor with a train car in tow."

"What if I tell you that I'm learning to change my ways?" He winked. "And if necessary, we can always leave the Pemberley behind and try our hands at coach."

She laughed softly, here in this hallway that had needed that sound for so very long.

Lizbeth felt the crack of a pistol as she raised a set of binoculars toward the starting gate. With a gasp, Jayne did the same. Their elegant sleeves brushed together in the warmth of the day. Callum stood proudly at Jayne's other side here in William's private owner's box. The air brimmed with the aromas of popcorn, lemonade, and horses as in a thunder of hooves, twelve thoroughbreds barreled down the track. The crowd filling the grandstand roared so loudly, Lizbeth felt it straight through her chest.

She gripped William's hand with all her might. "They're so fast!" she cried.

The crowd's cheers shook even the platform beneath them. Flags of bright colors waved in the breeze and men waved hats and newspapers overhead in excitement while women clutched gloved hands together, or lifted opera glasses to peer through.

Heart pounding, Lizbeth peeled her gaze away from the track just long enough to see William whisk his hat off and toss it on the seat beside him.

His focus stayed fixed on Lady Light. "Come on, girl."

Each brightly colored jockey balanced in the stirrups, hunched over as they rode for gold and glory. Jerseys in oranges, reds, blues, and purples brightened the afternoon as the horses thundered along another furlong. Lady Light and her jockey—both done up in the colors from Lizbeth's sampler threads—kept pace with them in a smooth silhouette of strength and beauty. Lizbeth passed the binoculars to William then gripped the handrail so tightly, she nearly toppled a bag of popcorn that belonged to the stranger in front of her.

She cheered, hardly able to contain her excitement, and as the furlongs wound down, she watched her husband's face grow more and more amazed as both horses and riders barreled toward the finish line. A horse named Blandy crossed first, immediately crowned the winner with a wreath of flowers. Lizbeth leaned forward, watching in awe as photographers captured the moment with the pop of camera bulbs, while newspaper reporters scribbled every embellishment they could think of about the spectacle.

After sweeping his top hat off, Callum offered up a toast. "To fifth place! Your best yet, if I'm not mistaken."

William tipped his own glossy hat. "It certainly is. Maybe it has something to do with the new training style my aunt implemented."

At his humble words, Lizbeth looped her elbow through his, still amazed that his aunt, Mrs. Catherine de Bourgh, had signed Lady Light over to him as a wedding gift. The card she'd sent for the wedding had explained the transfer and her best wishes for him and Lizbeth. While Lizbeth didn't know the full history there, something about the card had given William cause to read it twice. It was also the first of the thank-you notes that he'd penned.

"She was a wonder, Lizzy!" Jayne's blue eyes were bright and the same color as the hat she wore with its ribbon and feathers.

"Will you be expected at the owner's club?" Callum asked.

William reached for his hat again. "Possibly, but I'd rather head down to the paddock. What do you all think?"

"Please," Lizbeth answered and the others nodded their agreement.

Already, spectators and owners alike spilled from the stands to glimpse the horses being led to the paddock.

When William took hold of Lizbeth's gloved hand, she savored the touch that was both steady and comforting. A reminder that they were together and a warmth—a gift—like no other.

"Will we be able to see Lady Light as well?" Lizbeth asked.

"We will indeed." William wove them carefully to the steps and down to the turf level. Women fluttered fans, describing the majesty they'd just witnessed, and men toasted pints of beers for bets well placed. Overhead, a crisp May sky was the day's crowning glory.

Walking arm in arm, Lizbeth and Jayne chatted away until they finally reached the paddock where racehorses were being unsaddled.

"I see her." William pointed toward the tall chestnut mare. The horse's head lifted at sight of them and her ebony mane caught a rise in the breeze.

Hurrying forward, Lizbeth reached the mare first and smoothed a gloved hand up the thoroughbred's glistening neck. "Well done, sweet girl."

William gave a loving pat all his own, looking proud. "I need to go check on the jockey in a few minutes as well. If you and Jayne want to enjoy the sights here, I won't be long."

"Of course."

"Callum, would you like to join me?"

"Certainly."

Jayne patted Callum's cheek with her gloved hand and he captured that hand with a smile before starting off with William.

"Isn't it a wonder, Lizzy? To be standin' here right now?" Jayne said, holding her hat secure against the lifting breeze. Her beautiful blue dress with its high lace collar fluttered.

"It makes me so glad to see you this happy. And oh! I spoke to Pa recently."

"Tell me!"

Lizbeth rested her hands on the railing that outlined the paddock and recounted her conversation of Bennet Hollow. The glory of it and of all that had come to pass. A glory and goodness that shone in Jayne's own eyes for these turns of events. The newness of this life that they'd been blessed with. Not only to be standing here in New York with their husbands, but in knowing that their family back home was enjoying the comforts of life and the security of hope in so many precious ways.

"And what of Lacey?" Jayne asked at the end of the story.

Lizbeth scrunched her nose. "Oh, Pa assured me she's been on manure duty. He said she hasn't stopped complaining since."

Jayne laughed. "Well, I'd say that sounds good and fair!"

"I agree!" Lizbeth squeezed Jayne's arm. "I most definitely agree."

As dusk settled and the track grounds quieted, William stood at the Long Island train terminal, just yards from the grandstand. He watched his bride comb Lady Light for her journey home.

"That's a good girl," she whispered. "And I have someone for you to meet. His name is Eugene. He's just got one ear so he might not hear you comin', but I think he'd be glad to make a new friend. I hear he's gotten good at that lately." Lizbeth brushed the comb the length of the mare's neck again. "You did a rather good job of that yourself today."

Lady Light flicked her head in agreement.

Laughing, Lizbeth topped off the horse's bin of oats and stepped to the edge of the stock car.

William watched her, overcome. "What a sight you are, m'lady. With straw in your hair and oats on your dress."

Several passersby took stock of this woman in their midst at the most prestigious racetrack in the nation, and William's chest lifted, more proud of her than he could ever describe.

Lizbeth made a show of gently brushing the luxurious fabric of her skirt. "I do try, good sir."

He grinned. "Now, how about some supper that Cook promised us?"

"Please." Bending, she placed her hand on his shoulders and he helped her down. Her brown hair, which had been pinned back into place, now tumbled down to her back. A perfect sight.

In the distance, the train whistle blew.

"That's our cue." William led her up the steps to the rear balcony of their own car, then followed her inside.

They discarded their hats in their stateroom, washed their hands—laughing all the while as they kept bumping into one another. A danger that he minded not one bit.

"I see we're bound to dance after all," he said.

"Oh, you dance now, do you?" she winked.

"Clearly." He swept her a bow.

"Perfect!"

And the evening was.

As he sat there at their shared dining table, her hand in his as they ate, having the company of Lizbeth—his bride—made his life and heart expand in ways he was only beginning to understand.

Never, in all the miles, would they want for anything to talk of.

"Tell me your favorite part of the day," he began, wanting more of her voice, of her.

With a breath, she dove in, describing everything from the crowds to the beautiful horses, to time spent with Jayne and Callum.

He soaked in every detail, musing on the adventures yet to come. Laughter and smiles were nearly as plentiful as the stars out the window. A joyous sound for their ears alone as the Pemberley rattled down the tracks—this piece of home that now sheltered them together. With a heart and smiling eyes that captivated his own, Lizbeth was more real to him than any person he'd ever known, and for the first time in his life, he finally had the words to say as much and the grace to show her. All beneath the shadow of the sampler she'd stitched and he'd been honored to obtain. A tender reminder that the night was far spent, and a new day was at hand.

A Note from the Author

I'll never forget the weeks and months I sat up late at night, sometimes with two different copies of *Pride and Prejudice* in my lap, and read by the glow of the book light my husband gifted me for Christmas. One copy of the novel was for its crisp, easy-to-read print, and the other copy was for highlighting purposes. As a working and homeschooling mom, those nights were for study, and by the warm glow of that book light, I read until sleep took me. I do believe I dreamed of Longbourn and Netherfield, and now, both novel copies are nestled on my shelf where they'll be cherished always.

Every margin of that marked copy was filled with notes on Mr. Bingley and the reactions of Mrs. Bennet to his every move. Squiggly little hearts marked the romantic moments and special symbols even reminded me of which characters were in which scene. It was a quest—through Austen's world—and I was honored to be on this journey alongside her. Though armed with a pink highlighter instead of a feathered quill, I felt a part of Jane and her purpose. I saw into her story, as so many have before me, and I was awed by what I found.

To take those words—every precious line—and to try and craft them into a new adaption was as sobering as it was thrilling. How thankful I am to my editor, Sarah, for reminding me that writing such a retelling can be harder even than writing a regular novel as I have done many times before. So much of my time was spent in striving to get each detail and nuance of Austen's original correct that I sometimes floundered in my storytelling abilities unlike I ever had. Stumbling and bumbling at times, I finally worked my way through, and with the help of my talented editors, and endless inspiration from the classic, *The Heart of Bennet Hollow* came to be. I was a newbie in ways, but if Austen was my mentor, a newbie I was glad to be.

It reminds me how beautifully Jane Austen sprinkled romance and laughter into the unlikeliest of places. I've come away from this first novel completely inspired. Inspired to see the world through a more grace-filled lens and to be inspired by the ways that hope is healing and that humor can often be filled with so much heart.

I pray that the book you hold in your hands gives you one more reason to fall in love with Jane's stories and gives you an all-new spark of faith. All because of her characters. Her world. And most of all, the purpose that shines behind them. To shed light and hope into a world where it was so desperately needed. Tales of redemption that speak into our modern lives today with lessons of grace, humility, and courage that gently reflect the God who first shared these gifts with us.

Acknowledgments

It's always a joyful task to sit down at one's keyboard and try to find the words to thank all the people who helped make a novel come to be. This story of gratitude begins with my mother, who first taught me a love of Jane Austen—the books, films, and audio productions. Mom's love of all things Austen has warmed my heart and life for years, giving me all the more reasons to love the books too. From there, the gratitude continues on to my father, who never ceases to make us giggle with his impressions of *Pride and Prejudice,* which are quite delightful from a retired mailman with a Texas accent. Thank you both for many wonderful movie nights, endless heart-hugs, and so much more.

To my agent, Cynthia Ruchti, for first looking at this series idea in one-sheet form at a writer's conference in California. Thank you for taking a chance on me as an author and for believing in this series in all the ways that you have.

To the wonderful people at Tyndale House Publishers who then took hold of this series and began to give it life. To Elizabeth Jackson and Sarah Rische for your editing expertise, kind guidance, and generous enthusiasm. You both have made these pages what they are today, and you've helped to grow me as a writer along the way.

To my students and fellow staff at The Author Conservatory for teaching me more and more about the craft of writing—and the love of storytelling—each and every day. To my family and friends for always asking me when my next book is coming out, and being some of the first in line to grab a copy. You all bless me more than I can say.

To my husband who endlessly supports me, my children who daily inspire me, and to the God above who walks beside me—thank you.

Discussion Questions

1. While my goal in writing *The Heart of Bennet Hollow* was to keep to the spirit and overall storyline of Jane Austen's beloved classic, it was also important that I give my characters challenges that are true to their time and place. For example, William Drake wrestles with whether to buy the New River Coal Company and how to do right by the local families who depend on the mine. What did you think of his decisions? Should William have been more honest with Lizbeth about what might happen to the Bennet land once the mine was purchased?

2. Meanwhile, Lizbeth struggles with knowing what her life's purpose should be. How do you see her trying to find her place in the world? How do her goals and focus change once she learns about the threat to her family's farm?

3. Though each of my characters has an Austen counterpart, each also has a unique personality, from Aunt Catherine to Kit and Lacey, to Jayne with her quiet grace and

Lizbeth with her spark. Which person from the cast do you most relate to? What qualities of theirs do you see reflected in yourself? Any characters that you would aspire to learn from or be more like?

4. If you've read *Pride and Prejudice*, which characters are your favorites? What did you think about the ways they were represented in *The Heart of Bennet Hollow*? Which characters felt the most obvious from the original classic and why? Which were a little harder to find?

5. When Lizbeth and her sisters visit the Pemberley, the vast difference in Lizbeth's and William's worlds becomes apparent. But they also find a surprising bond in their love of books. If you were Lizbeth, how do you imagine you would respond in the face of such differences? How might you have tried to find common ground? And what if you were William, with family expectations to consider as well?

6. Throughout the novel, as Lizbeth stitches on her sampler, she learns patience and dedication even when it's difficult. She also takes inspiration from the message she's stitching: *The night is far spent, the day is at hand: let us therefore cast off the works of darkness, and let us put on the armour of light.* What do those words come to mean to her? What do you think it means to "put on the armour of light"?

7. While writing this story, I had the pleasure of hinting at some beloved lines—both from Jane Austen's novel and from cherished film adaptions. What lines or moments stood out to you as familiar? Any favorite ways that *Pride and Prejudice* shone through in *The Heart of Bennet Hollow*?

8. And speaking of film adaptions, you know I have to ask: If you're a *Pride and Prejudice* fan, which adaption is your favorite and why? Are you team #ColinFirth or team #KeiraKnightley? And if you were casting a film version of *The Heart of Bennet Hollow,* who would you choose to play Lizbeth and William? Stop by my social media and let me know!

About the Author

Christy and Carol Award–winning author **Joanne Bischof DeWitt** writes romantic fiction that tugs at the reader's heartstrings. Her historical romance *The Lady and the Lionheart* received an extraordinary 5 Star TOP PICK! from *Romantic Times Book Reviews* and was the very first independently published novel to win a Christy Award. It has also recently taken to the stage.

As a longtime Jane Austen fan, Joanne is often making popcorn with her mom so they can rewatch their favorite adaptions, and as a new wife, she celebrates God's own redemptive love stories. Joanne thanks the Lord daily for bringing along her very own hero who's a perfect balance between Colonel Brandon and Mr. Darcy. Together, they're a blended family and the grateful parents of six teens and young adults, making them huge advocates for conversations, laughter, and large dinner tables. You can find her at joannebischofdewitt.com.

CONNECT WITH JOANNE ONLINE AT

joannebischofdewitt.com

OR FOLLOW HER ON

joannebischof

joannebischofdewitt

Joanne_Bischof

JoanneBischof

CP2060